Hot Flashes & Homocide

Copyright © 2025 by Patti Petrone Miller
All rights reserved.

No part of this publication may be reproduced, stored in a retrieval system, or transmitted in any form or by any means—electronic, mechanical, photocopying, recording, or otherwise—without the prior written permission of the author, except in the case of brief quotations embodied in reviews, articles, or scholarly analysis.

This is a work of fiction. Names, characters, places, and incidents are either the product of the author's imagination or used fictitiously. Any resemblance to actual persons, living or dead, events, or locales is entirely coincidental.

Publisher: AP Miller Productions
ISBN: 9798281519717
Cover Design by: Pixel Squirrel

Printed in the United States of America

For more information, visit:
https://pattipetronemillerexecutiveproducer.wordpress.com/

First Edition: April 2025

Patti Petrone Miller

HOT FLASHES & HOMICIDE

Social Media Links
htttps://www.facebook.com/pattipetronemiller/
https://www.facebook.com/pattipetronemillerexecutiveproducer/
https://www.facebook.com/halloweenismyfavoriteholiday/
https://www.pinterest.com/pattipetmiller/
htps://www.threads.net/@pattipetronemiller
Website and Blog
https://pattipetronemillerexecutiveproducer.wordpress.com/2024/09/22/a-comprehensive-guide-to-crystals-history-magic-and-tinctures/

Praise For Author "Patti Petrone Miller's books hit different from your typical feel-good stories. Sure, Hallmark's got their formula down pat, but Miller brings something fresh to the table - authentic characters that actually feel like people you know, dealing with real-life stuff while still keeping things wonderfully uplifting.
I honestly get the same warm fuzzies reading her books as I do curling up with hot cocoa for a Hallmark marathon, but without all the predictable plot points we've seen a million times. She's nailed that sweet spot between heartwarming and genuine that's super hard to find these days. If you're looking for stories that'll leave you smiling but don't make you roll your eyes at how perfect everything is, Miller's your girl. She's got that special touch that makes you feel like you're hanging out with friends rather than just reading about characters. Move over, Hallmark - there's a new queen of wholesome in town!"

Authors Book List

Accidental Vows
A Very Merry Krampus Christmas
A Devil's Bargain
The Devilf of London
Sin Takes A Holiday
Barking Up The Wrong Bakery, Thankgiving
Barking Up The Wrong Bakery, Christmas
Best Served Dead
Bewitching Charms
Christmas at Hollybrook Inn
Christmas on Peppermit Lane
Cabinet of Curiosities
Krampus
Hex and the City
Love in Stitches
Pies and Perps
Spectres and Souffles
Mamma Mia It's Murder
Once Upon A Christmas
The Fatman
The Frosted Felony
The Purr-fect Suspect
The Boogeyman
The Gingerdead Men
Vikings Enchantress
Welcome to Scarecrow Hollow
The Pendleton Witches
Christmas In Pine Haven
Love in the Stacks
Once Upon A Christmas
Frosted Felony
Truth or Dare
Before the Fire
Heart of the Beast
Savage Bloodline
The Secret Ingredient, Mad Batter Bakery Mysteries Prequel
Drive By Pies, Mad Batter Bakery Mysteries book 1
Venom in Vanilla, The Sundae of Secrets Series
A Scoop of Murder
Blood Moon Justice

Patti Petrone Miller

HOT FLASHES & HOMICIDE
By Patti Petrone Miller

Patti Petrone Miller

Chapter One

A Body and a Barnacle

Daisy Picklesworth believed firmly in three things: a proper cup of tea required exactly two minutes of steeping—no more, no less; a good book was worth sacrificing sleep for; and dead bodies shouldn't turn up on one's private beach before breakfast. Especially not during the Conch Key Annual Seafood Jamboree.

"Well, butter my biscuit and call me Sally," Daisy muttered, tightening the belt on her turquoise caftan as the morning breeze off the Gulf of Mexico ruffled her impressive silver bouffant. She squinted at the unexpected arrival that had washed up approximately twenty feet from The Barnacle's back porch steps.

The corpse in question—bloated, sun-reddened, and definitely past its prime—was dressed in what had once been an expensive cream linen suit, now soaked with seawater and decorated with strands of seaweed that gave the unfortunate gentleman the appearance of wearing a particularly unappetizing corsage.

Daisy adjusted her cat-eye reading glasses, which dangled from a beaded chain around her neck, and took two cautious steps closer. The morning sun was climbing steadily over the horizon, casting a deceptively cheerful glow across the crime scene. A flock of seagulls circled overhead, their raucous cries adding a macabre soundtrack to the grim tableau.

"Not before I've had my coffee," she grumbled, glancing back at the mint-green Victorian beach house she shared with her three best friends. "And definitely not in Gucci loafers."

The dead man's feet were indeed clad in what appeared to be genuine alligator-skin loafers, their leather darkened by seawater but still unmistakably expensive. This detail struck Daisy as particularly odd, given that she'd attended enough beach funerals over the years to know that no sensible person wore fine Italian footwear to the shore.

A loud gasp from behind made Daisy turn, nearly losing her balance in the soft sand.

"Sweet mother of Methuselah!" came the dramatic exclamation, delivered in a voice that could carry to the back row of a Broadway theater without amplification.

Barbara "Babs" Zuckerkorn stood frozen at the bottom of the porch steps, one heavily ringed hand clutching the doorframe while the other pressed against her ample bosom. She wore a leopard-print silk robe that billowed around her like an exotic tent, her flame-red hair (which owed its vibrant hue to monthly appointments with Giuseppe at Curl Up and Dye) was secured in large velcro rollers, and her face was covered in a green mask that gave her the appearance of a surprised extraterrestrial.

"Is that—?" Babs began, taking a tentative step forward.

"A dead man on our private beach? Yes indeed," Daisy confirmed, her Mississippi drawl thickening as it always did in times of stress. "And judgin' by the smell, he's been marinatin' for a spell."

Babs clutched at her throat, the numerous gold bracelets on her wrist clanking like wind chimes in a hurricane. "My word! And just when I was about to try that new French toast recipe. There goes my appetite." Despite her words, she moved closer, her natural curiosity overcoming her initial shock. "Who is it? Can you tell?"

Daisy shook her head. "Face is too bloated. But those shoes..." She pointed with the tip of her walking cane, which she carried more for dramatic effect than actual need. "Those are Brock Hamfist's alligator loafers if I've ever seen 'em."

"The Bulldozer?" Babs gasped, referring to the real estate magnate's well-earned nickname. "Are you sure?"

"About as sure as I am that you've been secretly smoking cigarettes behind the gardenia bushes again," Daisy replied dryly.

Babs had the grace to look momentarily abashed before returning to the matter at hand. "We should call Morty."

"Already on it." Daisy pulled a cell phone from one of the many hidden pockets in her caftan—a feature she insisted upon when ordering her extensive collection from her favorite online store, Dramatic Drapes for Distinguished Dames. She punched in the number she knew by heart but would never admit to having memorized. "And put some clothes on,

Babs. Last time you greeted the police in that getup, Officer Butterworth walked into a palm tree."

Babs sniffed indignantly. "That boy needs to learn focus. Besides, women my age are invisible to young men."

"Not when they're wearing animal prints and enough perfume to asphyxiate a manatee," Daisy muttered as she waited for the call to connect.

As if on cue, the back door of The Barnacle slammed open again, and Rita Calabaza emerged, wooden spoon in hand, dressed in a sensible cotton housedress covered by an apron that proclaimed "Kiss the Cook (At Your Own Risk)." Her salt-and-pepper hair was pulled back in a no-nonsense bun, and she wore practical slip-on shoes that Daisy privately referred to as "surrender to the aging process footwear."

"What's all the commotion? The fritatta is getting cold, and—" Rita stopped short, her gaze landing on the corpse. She crossed herself rapidly. "¡Dios mío! Is that a body?"

"No, Rita, it's a new type of seaweed designed to look exactly like a dead real estate developer," Daisy replied, rolling her eyes. "Yes, it's a body. And I'm fairly certain it's Brock Hamfist."

Rita's eyes widened as she moved to stand beside her friends, her wooden spoon now held like a weapon. "The man who wants to build that horrible resort? The one who called my award-winning key lime pie 'pedestrian' at last year's bake-off?"

"The very same," Daisy confirmed.

"Hmph," Rita snorted, looking suspiciously unmoved by the man's demise. "I'm not saying he deserved to drown, but perhaps the sea has better taste than the Conch Key Bake-Off judges."

The sound of delicate footsteps on the wooden porch announced the arrival of the fourth resident of The Barnacle. Mabel "Mae" Noodleman peered out from behind her oversized spectacles, a fluffy pink cardigan wrapped around her slight frame despite the already climbing temperature. Her silver-gray hair was styled in a perfect bob, and she clutched a mug of tea in hands adorned with a collection of knitted wristbands she'd made herself during her "fiber arts phase" last winter.

"Good morning, everyone. I thought I heard voices and—oh my!" Mae's hand flew to her mouth as she spotted the body. "Is that person... sleeping?"

"Only in the permanent sense, honey," Babs said, patting Mae's shoulder. "It's Brock Hamfist, and he's kicked the proverbial bucket."

"Oh dear," Mae murmured, looking genuinely distressed. "Should I... should I check if there's anything I can do? I was a nurse for forty-two years, you know."

"Unless you've discovered how to resurrect the dead, I think he's beyond medical help," Daisy said, finally connecting with someone on her phone. "Morty? It's Daisy Picklesworth." She paused, listening. "No, I'm not calling about the noise ordinance this time. We've got something considerably more interesting on our beach... Yes, more interesting than Mrs. Huffington's midnight saxophone practice... It's a dead body, Morty. And unless I'm sorely mistaken, it's your old fishing buddy, Brock Hamfist."

The squawking from the other end of the line was loud enough for all four women to hear.

"Yes, I'm absolutely sure it's a dead body. I've been to enough funerals to recognize the condition," Daisy continued, her tone dripping with sarcasm. "No, we haven't touched anything... Well, of course I looked at his shoes, Morty, they're Gucci alligator loafers in a town where most men consider flip-flops formal attire... No, that's not tampering with evidence, that's basic fashion observation... Just get over here, would you?"

She hung up with a huff. "He'll be here in ten minutes. Says to secure the scene and not let anyone near the body."

"Secure the scene?" Rita echoed, looking around at the open beach. "What does he expect us to do? Form a human chain around the corpse?"

"I have crime scene tape in my crafting supplies," Mae offered helpfully. "From my murder mystery dinner party phase."

The other three women stared at her.

"What?" Mae blinked innocently. "I like to be prepared."

"Of course you do, sweetie," Babs said, patting her arm. "Why don't you go get it while I put on something more appropriate for receiving law enforcement?"

"By 'appropriate,' do you mean something that doesn't cause cardiac events in men over sixty?" Daisy asked dryly.

"I was thinking my blue sundress," Babs sniffed. "The one with the strategic support."

"That'll be a first," Rita muttered.

As her friends dispersed to their various tasks, Daisy remained by the body, her keen eyes scanning the scene with more attention to detail than she'd ever admit to. Something wasn't adding up, and it wasn't just the unexpected arrival of a dead developer on their private beach.

For one thing, Brock Hamfist was notorious for his pathological fear of water—a peculiar phobia for a man determined to build a beachfront resort. He refused to set foot in any body of water bigger than his marble soaking tub and was known to break out in hives at the mere mention of swimming. Yet here he was, having apparently drowned.

For another, while his face was too bloated for easy identification, Daisy was certain about those shoes. Brock had commissioned them specially from an Italian designer and never missed an opportunity to mention their cost—a detail that had made Daisy dislike him instantly, as she firmly believed that discussing money was only slightly less vulgar than serving red wine with fish.

But most importantly, there was something about the positioning of the body that struck her as odd. If he'd drowned and washed up with the tide, he should have been face down. Yet Brock lay on his back, arms spread wide as if embracing the sky, his waterlogged watch (which Daisy recognized as the limited-edition timepiece he'd boasted about at the last town council meeting) still secured to his wrist.

"This isn't right," she murmured to herself, carefully circling the body without disturbing the sand around it. "Something here is fishier than Rita's experimental anchovy soufflé."

A flash of color caught her eye—something small and iridescent nestled in the sand near Brock's right hand. Squinting, Daisy leaned closer without touching it. It appeared to be a tiny charm in the shape of a jellyfish, its tentacles rendered in delicate silver filigree tipped with what looked like small gemstones. The morning sun caught the facets, sending prisms of light dancing across the sand.

The sound of a siren in the distance made Daisy straighten up. She memorized the charm's exact location before quickly scanning the rest of the scene. There were no obvious footprints other than her own and her friends', the overnight tide having washed the sand smooth. No signs of a struggle, no convenient murder weapon half-buried nearby—not that Daisy had expected a smoking gun, but crime novels had given her rather theatrical expectations of murder scenes.

The siren grew louder, and soon the distinctive sound of Chief Mortimer "Morty" Crabbitz's ancient cruiser—which wheezed and backfired like an emphysemic dragon—could be heard pulling into the shell-lined driveway of The Barnacle.

Mae reappeared, somewhat winded from her trip up and down the stairs, clutching not only crime scene tape but also a collection of plastic evidence markers she'd fashioned from ping pong balls and Popsicle sticks.

"I found them!" she announced triumphantly, her face flushed with excitement. "And I brought my investigation notebook too." She held up a floral-patterned journal with "CLUES" written across the front in glitter pen.

"Mae, honey, this isn't one of your murder mystery dinner parties," Daisy began gently.

"I know that," Mae replied, looking slightly wounded. "But proper documentation is essential for any investigation. That's what my nephew Tyler says, and he watches all those crime shows."

Rita returned with a thermos of coffee and a basket of muffins. At Daisy's questioning look, she shrugged defensively. "What? You know how Morty gets when his blood sugar is low. Besides, it's rude not to offer refreshments to guests, even if they're here for a dead body."

Babs was the last to rejoin them, having transformed herself with impressive speed. Her hair was now styled in voluminous waves, her makeup applied with precision that suggested years of practice, and she wore the aforementioned blue sundress, which managed to be both tasteful and attention-grabbing—a balance Babs had perfected over decades of dressing to be noticed.

"How do I look?" she asked, striking a pose that seemed out of place given the circumstances.

"Like you're auditioning for 'CSI: Retirement Community,'" Daisy replied.

Babs looked pleased. "Perfect. I want Morty to regret divorcing his third wife. It keeps him humble."

The police cruiser door slammed, and heavy footsteps crunched on the shell path that led around the side of the house to the beach. Chief

Crabbitz appeared, his perpetually sunburned face clashing violently with his white hair and mustache. He wore the standard Conch Key Police Department uniform—khaki shorts, a light blue polo shirt with the department logo, and a wide-brimmed hat that did little to protect his chronically reddened nose. Despite being seventy-two, he moved with the purposeful stride of a man half his age, though the effect was somewhat undermined by the antacid tablet he was openly chewing.

"Ladies," he greeted them, his voice gruff. "This better not be another false alarm like the 'suspicious prowler' that turned out to be Mrs. Finkelstein's escaped ferret."

"Good morning to you too, Morty," Daisy replied coolly. "I see you're as charming as ever before your second cup of coffee."

Morty's retort died on his lips as his gaze landed on the body. "Well, I'll be damned."

"Language, Chief," Mae admonished gently, though no one paid her any mind.

"Is that who I think it is?" Morty asked, approaching the corpse with the caution of a man who'd seen enough floating bodies in his thirty years on the force to know they were rarely pleasant experiences.

"If you think it's Brock 'The Bulldozer' Hamfist, then yes," Daisy confirmed, falling into step beside him. "Though you might want to check dental records to be absolutely sure. His face isn't exactly in yearbook condition."

Morty pulled a pair of latex gloves from his pocket and snapped them on with practiced ease. He knelt beside the body, his knees popping loudly in protest. "Any of you touch him?"

"Of course not," Rita said, sounding offended. "We watch crime shows. We know about contaminating evidence."

"Though Mae did consider checking for a pulse," Babs added helpfully.

"Just out of professional habit," Mae clarified, looking embarrassed. "But then I remembered that lividity is a much more reliable indicator of death than pulse absence in apparent drowning victims, and I could clearly observe fixed lividity along the posterior surface, indicating —"

"Thank you, Nurse Noodleman," Morty interrupted, looking slightly queasy. "I'll take it from here."

He examined the body with methodical thoroughness, occasionally grunting or murmuring to himself. The four women watched in silence, each making mental notes for their inevitable discussion later. Finally, Morty straightened up, wincing slightly and pressing a hand to his lower back.

"Well?" Daisy prompted.

"Well what?"

"What's your professional assessment, Chief?" she pressed. "Accidental drowning or something more sinister?"

Morty gave her a look that suggested she was overstepping, but years of dealing with Daisy Picklesworth had taught him the futility of trying to keep her out of police business. "Hard to say without an autopsy. Could be drowning, could be something else. The body's been in the water for hours, possibly overnight."

"During the Seafood Jamboree," Babs noted. "When the whole town was at the harbor."

"Including Brock," Rita added. "I saw him arguing with Gladys Pickle by the crab cake judging table around seven last night."

Morty's eyes narrowed. "You saw him at the festival?"

"We all did," Mae confirmed. "He was wearing that same suit, actually. I remember thinking it was impractical for a seafood festival. Tartar sauce stains are nearly impossible to remove from linen."

"But he wasn't wearing those shoes," Daisy said firmly. "He had on white deck shoes. I specifically noticed because they were the only sensible thing about his outfit."

Morty glanced down at the victim's feet. "You're sure about that?"

"Morty, I spent forty years teaching fashion history at Emory. I notice footwear the way you notice fishing conditions. He was wearing canvas deck shoes at the festival, not alligator loafers."

This seemed to interest the chief. He pulled out a small notebook —standard issue, not floral or embellished with glitter—and made a note. "Anyone see him leave the festival?"

The women exchanged glances, each mentally reviewing their memories of the previous evening.

"I left early," Mae admitted. "Around eight. The crowd was getting a bit much for me."

"I stayed until closing," Rita said. "But I was busy arguing with Lou about the proper way to steam clams. That man wouldn't know authentic cuisine if it slapped him with a wet fish."

"I was judging the Miss Seafood Pageant until nine," Babs offered. "And then I had a nightcap with Eugene from the bait shop." At the others' raised eyebrows, she added defensively, "It was purely professional. He's designing a fishing lure inspired by my statement earrings."

"And you, Daisy?" Morty turned to her.

"I was at the library fundraiser booth until they closed down at ten," she replied. "Then I came straight home and finished my mystery novel with a glass of sherry on the porch." She nodded toward the wicker furniture visible on The Barnacle's back deck.

"So none of you saw Hamfist after the initial sighting around seven?" Morty clarified.

"No," Daisy answered for the group. "But Morty, don't you think it's odd that a man with hydrophobia ended up drowned?"

"With what?"

"Fear of water," Mae explained. "Brock was famously terrified of the ocean. He wouldn't even wade in the shallows during the Blessing of the Fleet last year."

Morty frowned, adding another note. "And you think that's suspicious?"

"About as suspicious as finding a vegan in a steakhouse," Daisy said dryly.

"I'll take it under advisement," Morty replied, though his tone suggested he already was. He glanced down at the body again, then at the water line. "Tide was high around midnight, then receded. Body could have washed up anytime after that."

"There's something else," Daisy said, lowering her voice conspiratorially. "Look there, by his right hand."

Morty followed her gaze to the small jellyfish charm glinting in the sand. "What is that?"

"Some kind of jewelry piece. A charm, I think. And look at the marks on his face and hands."

The chief leaned closer, examining the reddened welts visible on the victim's bloated skin. "Could be jellyfish stings. We've had a bloom of moon jellies this week."

"Maybe," Daisy allowed, though her tone suggested she wasn't convinced. "But don't you think it's quite a coincidence to find a jellyfish charm right next to supposedly jellyfish-stung victim?"

Morty straightened, a familiar expression of exasperation crossing his features. "Daisy, are you playing detective again?"

"I'm merely making an observation, Chief Crabbitz," she replied primly. "As a concerned citizen."

Before Morty could respond, the sound of another vehicle pulling up interrupted them. A moment later, Officer Peanut Butterworth came jogging around the side of the house, his athletic build and boyish good looks making him seem out of place in tiny Conch Key, like a television cop who'd wandered onto the wrong set.

"Chief, dispatch said—whoa." He stopped short at the sight of the body, his hand automatically moving to the service weapon on his hip before he registered that the threat, if there had been one, was long past. "Is that Brock Hamfist?"

"That's what we're figuring," Morty confirmed. "Radio Doc Patel and tell him we need him here ASAP. Then get the scene secured properly." He cast a pointed look at Mae's homemade crime scene tape, which she was still clutching hopefully.

"On it, Chief." Peanut pulled out his radio and stepped away to make the call, but not before offering a respectful nod to the assembled women. "Morning, ladies."

"Good morning, Officer Butterworth," Mae replied with a warm smile. "I made blueberry muffins if you'd like one later."

"Thanks, Miss Noodleman," he answered with genuine appreciation. "Maybe after we get things squared away here."

As Peanut walked back toward the cruiser to retrieve proper police tape, Morty turned to the women with his best official expression. "I'm going to need statements from all of you about your movements last night and when you discovered the body. And I'd appreciate it if you'd refrain from discussing this with anyone until we've had a chance to notify next of kin and determine cause of death."

"Of course, Morty," Daisy agreed, a little too readily for the chief's comfort. "We wouldn't dream of speculating about whether Hamfist was murdered and who might have wanted him dead."

Morty's already ruddy complexion darkened. "I didn't say anything about murder."

"Didn't you?" Daisy's eyes widened with faux innocence. "My mistake. Must be all those mystery novels affecting my thought process."

The chief looked like he wanted to say something more but was interrupted by a commotion from the direction of the street. A sleek red convertible had pulled up behind the police cruiser, and a woman was now making her way toward them, navigating the shell path in stiletto heels with surprising agility.

"Oh lord," Babs muttered. "It's Candi Bubbleshine."

The woman approaching them looked like she'd been designed by a committee with conflicting ideas about subtle taste. Her platinum blonde hair was piled high in a style that defied both gravity and current fashion trends, her makeup applied with a generosity that suggested she bought cosmetics in bulk, and her outfit—a form-fitting pink ensemble adorned with an improbable number of sequins—sparkled blindingly in the morning sun. Despite being well into her fifties, she moved with the confidence of someone who considered age to be nothing more than an administrative detail.

"What's happened? I was driving by and saw the police car," Candi called out as she approached, her voice carrying the slight nasal quality of someone who'd spent significant time in New Jersey despite claiming to be a Florida native. "Is everything—OH MY GOD!"

Her scream upon spotting the body was theatrical enough to make Babs—no stranger to dramatic reactions herself—roll her eyes.

"Is that Brockie?" Candi wailed, taking a step toward the corpse before Morty blocked her path.

"Ma'am, this is an active investigation scene. I need you to step back."

"But that's my Brockie! My poor baby!" Candi attempted to push past him, her numerous bangle bracelets jangling with the effort. "What happened to him? Is he hurt?"

"He's dead, Candi," Daisy stated flatly. "And unless the afterlife includes a significant wardrobe upgrade, he's going to be buried in that unfortunate suit."

Candi's painted mouth opened in a perfect O of shock before her knees buckled. Officer Butterworth, returning with the proper police tape, dropped everything to catch her before she hit the sand.

"Nice save, Peanut," Babs commented appreciatively. "Those reflexes come in handy for more than just directing traffic at the elementary school."

"Ms. Bubbleshine, I think you should sit down," Peanut suggested gently, guiding the distraught woman toward the porch steps.

"How long were you and Mr. Hamfist involved?" Morty asked, following them.

"Eight glorious months," Candi sniffled, producing a lace handkerchief from somewhere within her outfit. "We were soul mates. He was going to leave his wife for me."

"Ex-wife," Rita corrected. "They divorced three years ago."

Candi shot her a venomous look. "Well, he was going to make an honest woman of me, anyway. We had plans." She gestured vaguely toward the water. "His resort was going to have a special cabaret lounge just for my performances. 'Candi's Sugar Shack,' he called it."

Daisy and Rita exchanged glances that spoke volumes about their opinion of this proposed establishment.

"When did you last see Mr. Hamfist?" Morty continued, pulling out his notebook again.

"Last night at the festival," Candi replied, dabbing at her eyes carefully to avoid smudging her mascara. "Around nine. He said he had a business meeting and that he'd call me later, but he never did." Her bottom lip trembled dramatically. "And now he never will!"

This prompted a fresh wave of tears. Mae, ever compassionate, sat down beside her and patted her sequined shoulder. "There, there. Would you like a muffin? Carbohydrates can be very comforting in times of grief."

"I'm watching my figure," Candi replied automatically, then paused. "What kind of muffins?"

"Blueberry with a streusel topping."

"Well... maybe a small one."

As Mae led the still-sniffling Candi toward the house, accompanied by Officer Butterworth who seemed torn between duty and the promise of baked goods, Morty turned to the remaining women.

"I need to secure the scene and wait for Doc Patel. I'll take your statements once he's examined the body."

"We'll be right inside, Morty," Daisy assured him. "Not discussing potential murder suspects or anything like that."

The chief gave her a warning look. "Daisy, I mean it. No amateur detective work. Let the professionals handle this."

"Absolutely," she agreed solemnly. "Though I do wonder who Brock's business meeting was with last night, don't you? And why he changed his shoes."

Morty's expression suggested he was calculating the days until his retirement. "Inside. All of you."

"Come on, Daisy," Rita said, taking her friend's arm. "The fritatta is getting cold, and we can't solve crimes on empty stomachs."

"We're not solving anything," Morty called after them as they made their way back to the house. "This isn't one of your mystery novels!"

Daisy merely waved without turning around. Once they were out of earshot, she leaned closer to Rita and Babs. "Did either of you notice the jellyfish charm in the sand? Or the fact that those welts don't actually look like jellyfish stings up close?"

"What do they look like?" Babs asked, curiosity piqued.

"I'm not certain yet," Daisy admitted. "But I intend to find out. And I'm also very interested in who Brock had that business meeting with."

"Daisy Picklesworth, are you suggesting what I think you're suggesting?" Rita asked, though her tone indicated she already knew the answer.

"I'm suggesting that a man with hydrophobia doesn't accidentally drown," Daisy replied firmly. "And I'm suggesting that someone in Conch Key knows exactly how Brock Hamfist ended up dead on our beach."

Babs clapped her hands together, eyes sparkling with excitement. "Ooh, this is just like that mystery novel you lent me! The one where the victim appears to have drowned but actually was—"

"Shh!" Daisy hushed her, glancing back at Morty, who was now crouched beside the body again. "Let's discuss this inside. Over breakfast."

"And mimosas?" Babs suggested hopefully. "Murder investigations call for champagne, don't they?"

"It's not even nine in the morning," Rita pointed out.

"It's five o'clock somewhere," Babs countered. "Besides, I can feel a hot flash coming on. Champagne has medicinal purposes."

As they climbed the porch steps, Daisy cast one last look at the scene behind them—the body on the beach, Morty kneeling beside it, and the small glint of the jellyfish charm catching the morning sun. Something wasn't right about Brock Hamfist's death, and if there was one thing Daisy Picklesworth couldn't abide, it was an unsolved puzzle.

"Ladies," she said as they entered the kitchen where Mae was serving muffins to a still-sniffling Candi, "I believe we have a mystery on our hands."

"And a dead developer on our beach," Rita added pragmatically. "Which means we'll need to delay the garden club meeting scheduled for this afternoon."

"Death waits for no gardener," Babs agreed solemnly, heading straight for the refrigerator and the bottle of champagne she'd been saving for a special occasion. "Now, who wants mimosas while we compile our suspect list?"

Outside, the tide was beginning to rise again, gradually erasing the footprints around the body. But as Daisy knew all too well from her mystery novels, not all traces were so easily washed away. And she had a feeling that the secrets surrounding Brock Hamfist's death would prove far more persistent than mere footprints in the sand.

What she didn't know—couldn't know yet—was just how dangerous those secrets would turn out to be.

Chapter Two

Muffins and Motives

"I still don't see why we need to make a suspect list," Rita Calabaza said, vigorously whisking orange juice into the champagne Babs had poured. "Morty specifically told us not to get involved."

The kitchen of The Barnacle was a testament to the eclectic tastes of its four inhabitants. Vintage floral wallpaper provided a backdrop for Rita's collection of international cooking implements, hanging alongside Babs' framed playbills. The large pine table at the center—rescued from a going-out-of-business sale at Conch Key's only antique store—was surrounded by mismatched chairs, each one chosen by its owner. Daisy's was a high-backed wicker throne upholstered in turquoise fabric; Babs' was a plush pink velvet number that had once graced a Las Vegas showgirl's dressing room; Rita's was a sensible oak captain's chair reinforced to withstand her energetic cooking demonstrations; and Mae's was a delicate painted rocker adorned with needlepoint cushions she'd made herself.

"Since when have we ever done what Morty told us to do?" Daisy replied, settling into her wicker throne and accepting a mimosa from Babs. The morning sunlight streamed through the large bay windows, casting a warm glow over the breakfast spread that Rita had prepared before the unexpected arrival of their deceased visitor.

"Besides," Babs added, carefully pouring a small amount of champagne into a flute for Candi, who had moved from sniffling to quiet hiccupping, "we're the ones who found the body. That practically makes us involved by default."

Mae nodded in agreement as she bustled around the kitchen, adding a plate of bacon to the already impressive breakfast array. "And as the person closest to the victim, Candi might have valuable insights." She patted the sequined woman's shoulder sympathetically. "If you feel up to talking about it, of course."

Candi dabbed at her eyes with a monogrammed handkerchief, somehow managing to avoid disturbing her elaborate makeup. "I suppose Brockie would want me to help." She took a delicate sip of her mimosa. "He always said I was the most observant person he knew."

"Did he now?" Daisy murmured, exchanging a skeptical glance with Rita. "How fascinating."

Outside, they could hear the increased activity as more police vehicles arrived. Officer Butterworth had reluctantly returned to his duties after accepting a muffin "for the road," and through the kitchen window, they could see Doc Patel's distinctive vintage Volkswagen Beetle pulling up behind the police cruiser.

"They're going to take him away soon," Candi said, her voice wavering. "My poor Brockie."

"Yes, dead bodies typically don't make good lawn ornaments," Daisy observed dryly, earning herself a reproachful look from Mae.

"Daisy, please. Show some sensitivity."

"My apologies," Daisy said, not sounding particularly apologetic. "The discovery of a corpse before my morning tea tends to sharpen my tongue."

"Everything sharpens your tongue, dear," Babs replied. "It's one of your more consistent qualities."

The kitchen door swung open, and Chief Crabbitz entered, removing his hat and looking uncomfortably warm in his uniform despite the early hour. His perpetually sunburned face had taken on the deeper hue it acquired when he was stressed, making him resemble an agitated lobster in khaki shorts.

"Ladies," he greeted them, nodding to each in turn before his gaze landed on Candi. "Ms. Bubbleshine, I'll need to ask you some more questions once the medical examiner has finished his preliminary examination."

"Of course, Chief," Candi replied with a sniff. "Anything to help find out what happened to my darling Brockie."

Morty's expression suggested he was struggling not to roll his eyes, a restraint that Daisy noted with mild admiration. "In the meantime," he continued, "I need statements from each of you about when and how you discovered the body."

"I made fresh coffee," Mae offered, already reaching for a mug. "And there's plenty of breakfast if you're hungry."

The chief's resolve visibly weakened at the mention of food. He glanced at the spread on the table—fluffy frittata, blueberry muffins still warm from the oven, crispy bacon, and fresh fruit arranged in an artistic pattern that only Rita could achieve—and sighed in defeat.

"Maybe just a quick cup of coffee," he conceded, accepting the mug Mae handed him. "And perhaps one of those muffins. For energy."

"Sit down, Morty," Rita instructed, pulling out the chair across from her. "You look like you're about to pass out from hunger, and I refuse to have another body to deal with today."

The chief complied, dropping heavily into the chair and taking a grateful sip of coffee. "Doc Patel's looking at the body now," he informed them. "Preliminary cause of death appears to be drowning, but we won't know for sure until the autopsy."

"Those marks on his face and hands didn't look like typical drowning indicators to me," Daisy observed casually, buttering a piece of toast with exaggerated focus.

Morty gave her a sharp look. "And when did you become a medical examiner, Professor Picklesworth?"

"I haven't," Daisy replied serenely. "But I have read extensively about forensic pathology. Did you know that jellyfish stings leave very distinctive marks? Usually multiple parallel lines where the tentacles make contact."

"Is that so?" Morty's tone was carefully neutral, but Daisy could tell he was listening.

"Indeed. And the marks on Mr. Hamfist's face looked more like... well, I'm not sure what, exactly, but not jellyfish stings."

"There have been a lot of jellyfish in the bay lately," Mae commented, passing a plate of frittata to Morty. "I nearly stepped on one during my morning walk yesterday."

"The moon jellyfish mating season," Babs interjected with authority. "They always bloom this time of year. Something about the water temperature." At the surprised looks from the others, she shrugged.

"What? I dated a marine biologist once. Number four—or was it five? Anyway, he was very educational."

"Brockie hated jellyfish," Candi volunteered, her painted lips turning down in a pout. "He hated anything in the water, really. Wouldn't even go in the shallow end of a pool. He had a special lounge chair built for his deck so he could sunbathe without getting wet."

Daisy filed this information away, her suspicions about the incongruity of Hamfist's supposed drowning growing stronger. "Yet he supposedly drowned," she mused. "How very odd."

"People with aquaphobia drown all the time," Morty countered. "In fact, they're often at higher risk because they panic in water."

"But why would he be in the water at all?" Rita asked, voicing exactly what Daisy had been thinking. "Especially at night, in his expensive suit?"

"That's what we're trying to determine," Morty replied, taking a large bite of muffin and chewing thoughtfully. After swallowing, he turned to Daisy. "Now, tell me exactly how you discovered the body."

For the next twenty minutes, each woman provided her statement about that morning's events, with Daisy carefully recounting her observations without mentioning her suspicions about murder. Candi had little to add, having arrived after the body was discovered, but she did confirm that she'd last seen Hamfist at the festival around nine p.m.

"He said he had an important meeting that could change everything," she recalled, twisting her handkerchief. "He seemed excited, not worried."

"Did he say who the meeting was with?" Morty asked.

Candi shook her head, causing her elaborate hairstyle to wobble precariously. "No, just that it was about the resort project. He'd been having trouble getting the final approval from the town council." She leaned forward conspiratorially. "That awful Gladys Pickle and her turtle-loving friends have been blocking it for months. Brockie was furious."

"Gladys is passionate about environmental conservation," Mae said diplomatically. "Her turtle sanctuary does wonderful work."

"Well, that 'wonderful work' was costing my Brockie millions," Candi sniffed.

The back door opened again, and Officer Butterworth appeared, looking solemn. "Chief, Doc Patel's ready for you. And the, uh, removal service is here for the body."

Morty nodded, rising from his chair and setting down his empty coffee mug. "Thank you all for your cooperation. I'd appreciate it if you'd stay available for further questions. And please, no amateur detective work." This last comment was directed pointedly at Daisy, who met his gaze with an expression of perfect innocence.

"Why, Morty, whatever do you mean?" she asked, placing a hand over her heart. "We're just four retired ladies having breakfast."

"And one grieving girlfriend," Candi added with a theatrical sniff.

The chief looked unconvinced but merely put his hat back on and followed Butterworth out to the beach. As soon as the door closed behind them, Daisy leaned forward, lowering her voice.

"Now, about that suspect list..."

"Daisy!" Rita exclaimed. "He just told us not to get involved."

"No, he told us not to do any amateur detective work," Daisy corrected. "Making a list is simply organizing our thoughts. Besides, don't you find it suspicious that a man terrified of water supposedly drowned? And in his expensive suit, no less?"

"It is rather odd," Mae admitted, collecting the empty plates and stacking them neatly. "And there's the matter of his shoes. If he was wearing deck shoes at the festival, as you said, why was he found in loafers?"

"Precisely!" Daisy exclaimed triumphantly. "Someone changed his shoes. And there's the jellyfish charm I spotted near his hand—a piece of evidence that Morty would have missed if I hadn't pointed it out."

"You think he was murdered?" Candi gasped, her eyes widening dramatically. "My poor Brockie!"

"It's too early to jump to conclusions," Daisy cautioned, though her tone suggested she'd already leaped to several. "But if he was meeting someone about the resort project last night, that person may have been the last to see him alive."

"The resort project has caused quite a stir in town," Rita observed, beginning to wash the dishes. "Brock had his share of enemies."

"Starting with Gladys Pickle and her Conservation Crusaders," Babs said, rising to help with the cleanup. "They've been fighting the development for months."

"Gladys wouldn't hurt a fly, let alone a person," Mae protested. "She dedicated her life to saving animals after her husband died."

"People have killed for less noble reasons than protecting endangered species," Daisy pointed out. "And Gladys did threaten to 'stop Hamfist by any means necessary' at the last town council meeting."

"She meant legally," Mae insisted, but her voice carried a hint of uncertainty.

"Then there's Ziggy Hamfist," Rita added, scrubbing a pan with unnecessary vigor. "Brock's son hasn't exactly been subtle about wanting his inheritance."

"Ziggy's in town?" Daisy asked, surprised. "I thought he was living in Australia or some such place."

"He showed up yesterday," Candi confirmed, reapplying her lipstick using a compact mirror. "Caused quite a scene at Brockie's office. I heard them shouting at each other about money."

Daisy made a mental note to follow up on this information. "And let's not forget Councilwoman Moneypenny," she continued. "She's been suspiciously enthusiastic about the resort project, especially for someone who campaigned on preserving Conch Key's 'small-town charm.'"

"She just bought that ridiculous gold-plated golf cart," Babs recalled. "Must have cost a fortune on a councilwoman's salary."

"And Captain Crustybutt refused to sell his beachfront property to Brock, even though it's the perfect location for the resort's main entrance," Rita added.

"The captain has turned down offers from every developer for the past thirty years," Mae pointed out. "He's hardly going to start committing murder now."

"We're merely compiling possibilities," Daisy said soothingly. "Not making accusations."

"Well, if you're making a list, you should include that awful Lou from the Fishy Business restaurant," Candi declared. "He and Brockie had a terrible argument last week about the chowder contest. Lou accused him of bribing the judges."

Rita's eyes narrowed dangerously. "Lou wouldn't know a good chowder if it slapped him in the face with a halibut. He uses canned clams." She pronounced this last part as if describing a particularly heinous crime.

"Perhaps we should write all this down," Mae suggested, ever practical. She disappeared briefly and returned with her floral investigation notebook and a set of colorful gel pens. "For organizational purposes only, of course."

"Of course," Daisy agreed, hiding a smile. "Now, does anyone know if the town council approved the final permits for the resort? Brock said he had a meeting that could 'change everything'—that sounds like a significant development."

"The vote was scheduled for next week," Candi replied, surprising everyone with her knowledge of local government procedures. At their looks, she bristled slightly. "What? I pay attention to things that affect me. The resort was going to include my own performance venue."

"Yes, the, ah, Sugar Shack," Daisy recalled, struggling to keep her tone neutral. "How... imaginative."

"I still don't understand why someone would change his shoes," Rita mused, drying her hands on a dish towel embroidered with dancing spatulas. "What possible reason could there be for that?"

"Perhaps to make it look like he went into the water voluntarily?" Mae suggested. "Deck shoes would be more appropriate for boating or walking on the dock, while loafers suggest he was dressed for a meeting."

Daisy gave Mae an appreciative nod. "Excellent thinking, Mae. Someone could have been trying to create a specific narrative about his movements last night."

"Or maybe he really did change his own shoes for a meeting," Babs pointed out reasonably. "Men can be surprisingly vain about footwear. My third husband had different shoes for every occasion, including 'meeting the ex-wife's lawyer.'"

"Brockie was particular about his appearance," Candi confirmed. "He always said presentation was ninety percent of success."

Through the kitchen window, they could see the medical examiner's assistants carefully loading a body bag onto a stretcher. Candi let out a small sob at the sight, and Mae immediately put a comforting arm around her shoulders.

"Perhaps we should move to the living room," she suggested gently. "Away from the window."

The living room of The Barnacle was a comfortable clash of four distinct personalities. Daisy's literary influence was evident in the floor-to-ceiling bookshelves lining one wall, organized by genre and then alphabetically by author. Babs' theatrical flair manifested in dramatic artwork and a collection of ornate mirrors strategically placed to maximize the light. Rita's practical nature could be seen in the sturdy, comfortable furniture, while Mae's gentle touch appeared in handcrafted quilts draped over the couches and potted plants that somehow thrived despite the salty air.

As they settled into their usual spots—Daisy in the wingback chair by the window, Babs on the chaise lounge, Rita in the oversized armchair with the best view of the kitchen door, and Mae on the floral loveseat—Candi hovered uncertainly before choosing a spot beside Mae, perhaps drawn by the woman's nurturing presence.

"Before I forget," Daisy said, turning to Candi, "did Brock wear any jewelry? A bracelet or perhaps a charm?"

Candi looked surprised by the question. "Not really. Just his Rolex watch—he never took it off—and his college class ring. Why do you ask?"

"I noticed a small charm in the sand near his hand," Daisy explained. "A jellyfish design, quite delicate, with what looked like tiny gemstones on the tentacles."

Candi frowned, clearly puzzled. "That wasn't his. Brockie hated jewelry on men. He even refused to consider a wedding band for when we..." Her voice trailed off, and her bottom lip trembled again.

"Interesting," Daisy murmured, filing this information away. "Very interesting indeed."

"Perhaps it belonged to whoever he met with last night," Mae suggested, already jotting notes in her book with a purple gel pen.

"Or it could have simply washed up with the tide," Rita pointed out pragmatically. "The beach is always depositing odd things. Last month I found half of a porcelain doll's face—gave me nightmares for a week."

"True, but the timing seems rather coincidental," Daisy countered. "And coincidences make me suspicious."

"Everything makes you suspicious," Babs said affectionately. "You once conducted a three-day investigation because someone ate the last piece of your key lime pie."

"And I discovered it was you," Daisy reminded her. "Mystery solved."

"The pie was calling my name," Babs defended herself. "It was practically entrapment."

A knock at the front door interrupted their banter. Mae rose to answer it, returning moments later with Gladys Pickle in tow. Despite the already climbing temperature, Gladys was dressed in her trademark outfit: khaki pants, a button-up shirt with multiple pockets, and a wide-brimmed hat adorned with buttons proclaiming various environmental causes. Her silver hair was pulled back in a no-nonsense braid, and she carried a clipboard that seemed permanently attached to her left hand.

"Ladies," she greeted them, her keen eyes taking in the gathered group before landing on Candi with obvious surprise. "Ms. Bubbleshine. I didn't expect to see you here."

"I came when I heard about Brockie," Candi replied, lifting her chin defiantly. "Not that it's any of your business."

"My condolences," Gladys said stiffly, before turning to the others. "I apologize for dropping by unannounced, but I heard about what happened from Peanut—Officer Butterworth—when he was redirecting traffic past my turtle sanctuary."

"News travels fast in Conch Key," Rita observed, rising to her feet. "Can I get you some coffee, Gladys? Or perhaps a muffin?"

"Coffee would be wonderful, thank you," Gladys accepted, taking the seat Rita had vacated. "Is it true? Hamfist drowned?"

"That appears to be the working theory," Daisy replied carefully, watching Gladys's face for any reaction. "Though the medical examiner hasn't confirmed it yet."

"How terrible," Gladys said, though her tone lacked genuine sorrow. "Especially given his fear of water."

"You knew about his aquaphobia?" Daisy asked, leaning forward slightly.

"Everyone knew," Gladys shrugged. "He made a scene at every waterfront event. Remember the Blessing of the Fleet last year? He refused to even step on the dock for the ceremony."

Rita returned with a mug of coffee, which Gladys accepted gratefully. "I heard you had quite the confrontation with him at the festival last night," Rita remarked casually. "Something about the crab cake contest?"

Gladys's cheeks colored slightly. "He accused me of influencing the judges against his restaurant's entry. Which was absurd. The Bulldozer Grill's crab cakes tasted like seasoned rubber. They lost on their own lack of merit."

"You were seen waving a serving fork at him rather aggressively," Babs noted, reapplying her lipstick without using a mirror—a skill she'd perfected during her years in theater. "Some might interpret that as threatening."

"I was making a point about sustainable seafood harvesting," Gladys defended herself, setting her coffee down with enough force to slosh some over the rim. "And if I'd wanted to harm Brock Hamfist, I certainly wouldn't have done it in front of the entire town."

"A fair point," Daisy acknowledged. "Though I'm curious about what happened to his resort project. The final vote was next week, correct?"

Gladys nodded, her expression grim. "Yes, and it was going to be close. I've spent months gathering evidence about the environmental impact the development would have on the turtle nesting grounds, but Hamfist had deep pockets. He'd been wooing certain council members with promises of economic growth and increased tourism."

"By 'certain council members,' you mean Meredith Moneypenny?" Mae asked innocently.

"Among others," Gladys confirmed. "Though lately, there had been rumors that the project might be facing unexpected obstacles."

This caught Daisy's attention immediately. "What kind of obstacles?"

"Financial ones, primarily," Gladys explained, warming to her subject. "Word around town was that his investors were getting nervous about the delays and the mounting opposition. The Conservation Crusaders have been very effective in our public awareness campaign."

"You mean those posters showing bulldozers running over baby turtles?" Babs asked. "Subtle."

"Effective," Gladys corrected primly. "We've gathered over two thousand signatures opposing the development."

"Did you speak to Brock after your argument at the crab cake contest?" Daisy inquired, steering the conversation back to the previous night's events.

"No," Gladys replied firmly. "I said my piece and then went to help judge the sandcastle competition. I didn't see him again after that."

"And where were you around midnight?" Daisy asked, her tone conversational.

Gladys's eyes narrowed. "Are you interrogating me, Daisy Picklesworth?"

"Merely making conversation," Daisy replied smoothly. "As one does when a body washes up on one's beach."

"I was at home, reviewing environmental impact reports until nearly one in the morning. Alone, if that's your next question." Gladys took a sip of her coffee, her gaze challenging over the rim of the mug. "And before you ask, yes, I wanted Hamfist's resort project stopped, but not at the cost of a human life. Contrary to what some people think, environmentalists don't value turtle lives over human ones."

"No one's suggesting that," Mae soothed, though Candi's expression clearly indicated she might be doing exactly that.

"Did you know Brock's son is in town?" Daisy asked, changing tack. "Apparently they had quite the argument yesterday."

Gladys looked genuinely surprised. "Ziggy's here? Last I heard, he was living on some commune in New Zealand, making hemp sculptures or some such nonsense."

"Hemp necklaces," Candi corrected sourly. "He tried to give me one last time he visited. Looked like something the cat coughed up."

"And you say they argued?" Gladys asked, her interest clearly piqued. "About what?"

"Money, according to Candi," Daisy replied. "Though the specifics remain unclear."

"Brockie refused to keep funding Ziggy's 'alternative lifestyle choices,'" Candi elaborated, making air quotes. "Said it was time his thirty-five-year-old son got a real job instead of, as he put it, 'braiding plant fibers and chasing spiritual enlightenment on Daddy's dime.'"

"How did Ziggy take that news?" Rita asked, rejoining the group after cleaning up the breakfast dishes.

"Not well," Candi admitted. "There was shouting, something got thrown—a paperweight, I think—and Ziggy stormed out yelling that Brockie would regret cutting him off."

"That sounds potentially significant," Daisy remarked, exchanging glances with her friends. "Did Brock seem concerned about the threat?"

Candi waved a bejeweled hand dismissively. "Brockie said Ziggy was all talk. 'That boy couldn't follow through on ordering a pizza, let alone a threat,' is what he said."

"Still, a financial motive combined with a recent heated argument..." Daisy let the implication hang in the air.

"Are you ladies playing detective again?" Gladys asked, looking from one to another with a mixture of amusement and concern. "Because I distinctly heard Chief Crabbitz telling you to leave the investigation to the professionals."

"We're simply discussing the situation," Daisy replied primly. "As concerned citizens."

"With a murder suspect list," Candi added helpfully, pointing to Mae's notebook where "SUSPECTS" was written in glittery purple ink at the top of a page.

"It's a 'persons of interest' list," Mae corrected hastily, closing the notebook. "For organizational purposes."

Gladys sighed, setting down her empty coffee mug. "Well, if you're making a list, you might want to add Councilwoman Moneypenny. That woman's sudden support for the resort project never made sense, given her campaign promises. And her new golf cart isn't the only unexplained luxury she's acquired lately."

"You think she was taking bribes from Brock?" Daisy asked, intrigued.

"I have no evidence," Gladys replied carefully. "But her voting record took a suspicious turn right around the time she began renovating her house with imported Italian marble."

"Fascinating," Daisy murmured. "And the council vote was next week, you said?"

"Yes, and—" Gladys stopped short as the front door opened again, this time admitting a harried-looking Rita Morty, trailed by Officer Butterworth.

"Ladies," Morty began, then spotted Gladys. "Ms. Pickle. I didn't expect to find you here."

"I came to check on my friends after hearing about the incident," Gladys explained smoothly. "And to inquire if the Garden Club meeting is still on for this afternoon."

"I'm afraid we'll need to reschedule," Mae told her apologetically. "Under the circumstances."

Morty looked around the room, his expression making it clear he suspected they weren't just discussing garden club business. "The medical examiner's preliminary findings indicate drowning as the cause of death," he informed them. "But there are some... unusual aspects to the case that warrant further investigation."

"Such as?" Daisy prompted when he hesitated.

Morty gave her a look that suggested he knew exactly what she was doing. "Such as details that I'm not at liberty to discuss at this time," he replied firmly. "Ms. Bubbleshine, if you're feeling up to it, I'd like to ask you a few more questions down at the station."

Candi nodded, gathering her purse. "Of course, Chief. Anything to help discover what happened to my poor Brockie."

"And Ms. Pickle, I understand you had an altercation with Mr. Hamfist at the festival last night," Morty continued, turning to Gladys. "I'll need to take your statement as well."

"I'd hardly call it an altercation," Gladys protested. "A heated discussion about judging standards in the crab cake contest, nothing more."

"Nevertheless, I'd appreciate your cooperation," Morty insisted. "You can follow us to the station in your own vehicle."

Gladys sighed but nodded agreement. "Very well. Though I should check on the turtle sanctuary first. My volunteers were expecting me an hour ago."

"I can call them for you," Mae offered helpfully. "Tell them you've been delayed."

"Thank you, Mae," Gladys said, rising to her feet. "The number's on the website."

As the trio prepared to leave, Daisy called out, "Oh, Morty, one quick question—did you find anything unusual near Brock's right hand? A small jellyfish charm, perhaps?"

The chief paused at the door, his expression confirming Daisy's suspicion before he even spoke. "As a matter of fact, yes. The crime scene techs collected it as evidence. How did you know about that?"

"I noticed it when I first discovered the body," Daisy replied innocently. "It seemed out of place."

"It's been logged as potential evidence," Morty told her, his tone making it clear he wasn't going to elaborate. "And I'd appreciate it if you ladies would refrain from discussing case details with anyone."

"Of course, Morty," Daisy assured him with a smile that didn't quite reach her eyes. "We wouldn't dream of interfering with your investigation."

The chief looked skeptical but merely nodded before escorting Candi and Gladys out. As soon as the door closed behind them, Daisy turned to her friends, her expression triumphant.

"Did you hear that? 'Unusual aspects' that warrant further investigation. He suspects foul play!"

"That doesn't necessarily mean murder," Rita cautioned. "It could be any number of things."

"Like what?" Babs challenged. "A man who's terrified of water just happens to drown while wearing expensive loafers that aren't the shoes he had on earlier? And with mysterious marks that don't look like typical drowning indicators? Come on, Rita, even you can't be that skeptical."

"I'm just saying we shouldn't jump to conclusions," Rita defended herself. "And even if it is murder, it's not our job to solve it."

"Maybe not our job," Daisy agreed. "But certainly our civic duty to assist the investigation with our unique perspectives and local knowledge."

"In other words, you want to snoop," Rita translated flatly.

"I prefer the term 'conduct informal inquiries,'" Daisy corrected with dignity. "And you have to admit, we have advantages that Morty doesn't."

"Like what?" Rita asked, folding her arms across her chest.

"For one thing, people talk to us," Mae pointed out, reopening her notebook. "No one sees four older ladies as threatening."

"For another, we're already involved by virtue of finding the body on our property," Daisy added. "And we have connections throughout town that even Morty can't match."

"Plus, I can flirt information out of half the male population over fifty," Babs contributed with a wink. "A skill the Conch Key Police Department sorely lacks."

Rita's resistance was visibly weakening. "And I suppose my regular customers do tend to gossip quite freely at The Salty Mermaid," she admitted reluctantly. "Especially after a glass or two of my sangria."

"Exactly!" Daisy exclaimed. "Between the four of us, we can gather information from practically every corner of Conch Key without raising suspicion."

"Unlike Morty, who can't order a coffee without everyone knowing he's investigating something," Babs added.

"So it's settled," Daisy declared, rising to her feet with purpose. "We begin our inquiries immediately. Rita, you open The Salty Mermaid as usual and keep your ears open for any gossip about last night's festival. Babs, you were scheduled to help with the set decoration for the community theater's production of 'South Pacific' today, correct?"

"Yes, and half the town volunteers there," Babs confirmed, already planning which of her most flattering outfits would be appropriate for interrogating unsuspecting set builders.

"Perfect. Mae, didn't you have your weekly visit to the senior center today?"

Mae nodded. "I lead the gentle yoga class at eleven and then stay for lunch. It's pot roast day," she added with a small smile. "Very popular."

"Excellent. The seniors see everything in this town and love to talk about it. And I," Daisy continued, "have a meeting with my book club at the library, where Meredith Moneypenny happens to be the guest speaker today."

"The councilwoman?" Rita asked, impressed despite herself. "What's she speaking about?"

"'Fiscal Responsibility in Small Town Governance,'" Daisy replied with a smirk. "Which should be fascinating given her recent spending habits."

"And what about Ziggy Hamfist?" Mae asked, making notes in her book. "Shouldn't we try to locate him as well?"

"According to Candi, he's staying at the Conch Key Cabanas," Daisy recalled. "Perhaps we could pay him a condolence visit later today."

"A condolence visit with interrogation on the side," Rita muttered, though she was clearly warming to the plan. "Morty's going to have a conniption when he finds out what we're doing."

"*If* he finds out," Daisy corrected. "And by then, we'll hopefully have some useful information to share. Now, let's get ready. We each have our assignments."

As the women dispersed to prepare for their respective missions, Daisy paused by the front window, looking out at the beach where Brock Hamfist's body had lain just an hour earlier. The crime scene tape still fluttered in the sea breeze, a jarring contrast to the picturesque setting.

Something about this case bothered her beyond the obvious incongruities. The jellyfish charm, the changed shoes, the mysterious meeting that could "change everything"—all pieces of a puzzle that didn't quite fit together yet. But Daisy Picklesworth had never met a puzzle she couldn't solve, and she wasn't about to start now.

What she didn't realize was just how dangerous this particular puzzle would prove to be—and how close to home the danger would strike.

Chapter Three

Snooping at The Salty Mermaid

The Salty Mermaid Café occupied prime waterfront real estate along Conch Key's main harbor, a testament to Rita Calabaza's business acumen rather than the astronomical rents that had driven most local establishments inland. She'd purchased the building twenty years ago when waterfront property in the sleepy town could still be had for a reasonable price—before developers like Brock Hamfist had arrived with their luxury resort dreams and inflated valuations.

At ten o'clock sharp, Rita unlocked the café's front door, flipping the hand-painted "CLOSED" sign to "OPEN" with the practiced flick of someone who had performed the same action thousands of times. Morning sunlight streamed through the large windows, illuminating the café's cheerful interior with its nautical decor that somehow managed to avoid the kitschy tourist-trap aesthetic that plagued many of Conch Key's eateries.

Hand-carved mermaids with the faces of famous women throughout history—Rita's personal touch—served as the café's signature design element, watching over patrons from their perches on exposed ceiling beams. Tables crafted from reclaimed boat wood gleamed with the patina of countless meals and conversations, while bright blue chairs added a pop of color against whitewashed walls decorated with local artists' seascapes and the occasional prize catch mounted by a regular customer.

"Good morning, Ms. Calabaza!" called a cheerful voice from the kitchen. Lupe Mendoza, Rita's assistant manager and culinary protégé, was already hard at work, her round face flushed from the heat of the ovens. At twenty-eight, Lupe represented everything Rita loved about the younger generation—hardworking, respectful of tradition but not afraid to innovate, and completely immune to the lure of chain restaurants and their microwaved mediocrity.

"Morning, Lupe," Rita replied, tying her signature apron around her waist—royal blue with "The Queen of Cuisine" embroidered across the front, a Christmas gift from Mae three years ago. "Sorry I'm late. We had a bit of excitement at The Barnacle this morning."

"I heard!" Lupe exclaimed, eyes wide. "Is it true Brock Hamfist washed up on your beach? Dead as a doorknob?"

Rita sighed, mentally calculating how many times she'd need to recount the morning's events before the day was through. News traveled at supersonic speed in Conch Key, usually gaining embellishments with each retelling.

"It's true," she confirmed, washing her hands at the sink. "Though I'd say he was more dead as a developer than a doorknob. Any coffee made yet?"

"Just finished brewing," Lupe replied, gesturing to the industrial coffee maker that Rita considered the café's most important appliance. "Sourdough's in the oven, key lime pies are cooling, and I've prepped the vegetables for the lunch specials." She hesitated, clearly bursting with questions. "Did you... I mean, were you the one who found him?"

"Daisy found him first," Rita explained, pouring herself a much-needed cup of coffee. "I was the third on the scene, after Babs. Poor Mae nearly fainted, though she recovered quickly enough to start taking notes."

"Notes?" Lupe raised an eyebrow. "Are you ladies investigating again?"

Rita gave her a warning look. "We're simply being observant citizens. And you didn't hear anything about notes from me."

Lupe grinned, making a locking motion across her lips. "My mother didn't raise a gossip. Though speaking of gossip, Lou from Fishy Business was in here at dawn trying to sweet-talk our bread recipe out of Miguel." She nodded toward the young baker who was shaping dough in the back corner. "Said something about how he'd need to 'upgrade his menu now that he'd be getting all the Bulldozer Grill's business.'"

Rita narrowed her eyes. "Did he, now? Seems he's wasting no time capitalizing on Brock's death."

"That's what I thought," Lupe agreed. "Especially since I'm pretty sure I saw him arguing with Mr. Hamfist at the festival last night. By the chowder booth."

This caught Rita's attention immediately. "Really? What time was this?"

Lupe thought for a moment. "Must have been around nine-thirty? After the crab cake judging but before the fireworks. They looked pretty heated—Lou was poking Mr. Hamfist in the chest with a ladle."

Rita filed this information away to share with Daisy later. "Interesting. Did you happen to hear what they were arguing about?"

"Something about the restaurant, I think. Lou was saying 'You won't get away with this' or something dramatic like that." Lupe shrugged. "I didn't stick around. Lou gets red-faced when he's angry, and I was worried the ladle might start flying."

The bell above the door jingled, announcing the first customers of the day—a group of regulars Rita affectionately referred to as "The Morning Manatees," four retired fishermen who had been starting their day at The Salty Mermaid for so long that Rita kept their preferred mugs on a special shelf.

"Gentlemen," she greeted them warmly. "The usual?"

"Morning, Rita," called Herbert Finnegan, the unofficial leader of the group, his weathered face creased into a smile beneath his ever-present captain's hat. "Heard you had quite the surprise delivery this morning. Hamfist washed up deader than last year's catch, they're saying."

"News travels fast," Rita observed dryly, gesturing for them to take their regular table by the window. "Though I'd appreciate it if you didn't discuss a dead man quite so casually in my establishment. It's bad for digestion."

"Sorry, sorry," Herbert apologized without sounding particularly remorseful. "But you gotta admit, it's the most excitement we've had around here since that pelican got stuck in the church bell tower during Easter service."

The others chuckled as they settled into their chairs, the familiar sound of their good-natured ribbing providing a comforting backdrop of normalcy after the morning's macabre discovery.

"Coffee's coming right up," Rita promised, turning to prepare their usual order—black coffee for Herbert and Roy, cream and sugar for Dennis, and a strange concoction involving three sugars and a splash of half-and-half for Wally, which Rita maintained would eventually give him diabetes but fixed for him anyway. As she arranged their preferred breakfast pastries on a serving tray, she kept her ears open, knowing that the Manatees were better than the local newspaper for current events.

"...saw him at the docks after the festival," Dennis was saying in a low voice. "Arguing with that hippie son of his. What's his name? Ziggy?"

"That boy's a disgrace," Roy declared, adjusting his hearing aid. "Forty years old and still living off his daddy's money. My grandson's half his age and already running his own business."

"Thirty-five," Wally corrected. "And from what I hear, Daddy dearest had just cut off the money tap. Told him to get a real job or forget about his inheritance."

Rita nearly dropped the sugar bowl. This aligned with what Candi had mentioned earlier. Setting the coffee pot and mugs on a tray, she approached their table, moving with deliberate casualness.

"Here we are, gentlemen," she announced, distributing the mugs. "Almond croissants for Herbert and Roy, cinnamon roll for Dennis, and a slice of orange cardamom bread for Wally." She poured their coffee with practiced precision. "Now, what's this about Brock cutting off his son?"

The men exchanged glances, seemingly deciding whether sharing the gossip was worth potentially incurring Rita's disapproval. Herbert finally shrugged.

"Town's small, Rita. Voices carry on the water. Especially angry ones. Hamfist and his boy were going at it something fierce down by slip fourteen last night, sometime after the fireworks. The kid was shouting about his 'rights' and his 'inheritance,' and Brock was telling him to grow up and get a job."

"That doesn't sound like a peaceful father-son chat," Rita observed, refilling Herbert's mug.

"Wasn't," Roy confirmed, dunking his croissant in his coffee despite Rita's disapproving look. "Ended with the kid shouting something like 'You'll be sorry' before storming off toward town."

"And Brock?" Rita prompted. "Where did he go after that?"

Dennis shrugged. "Can't say for sure. I left to catch the shuttle back to Lighthouse Point. But he was heading toward the marina office last I saw."

Rita nodded thoughtfully. The marina office closed at ten, according to the posted hours, but she knew the harbormaster, Eugene Finch, often worked late during festival weekends. Perhaps he had seen Brock later in the evening.

"I heard Ziggy's staying at the Conch Key Cabanas," Wally volunteered, clearly enjoying being the center of attention. "Showed up two days ago without a reservation, flashing cash around like he's some big shot. Judy at the front desk says he's been charging everything to room service—champagne, fancy meals, you name it."

"Spending the inheritance before it's even his," Herbert snorted. "Some people's kids, I swear."

"Speaking of the resort," Dennis said, lowering his voice, "I heard Hamfist had a meeting with someone from the town council last night. Very hush-hush. Something about changing the plans."

This piqued Rita's interest. "Changing the plans how? And which council member?"

Dennis shrugged. "Don't know the details. My nephew works security at Town Hall, said he saw Hamfist and Councilwoman Moneypenny going into her office around ten. Said they looked mighty serious."

Rita mentally added this to her growing list of information to share with Daisy. The Town Hall being open that late during the festival wasn't unusual—many official functions took place there during town celebrations—but a private meeting between Brock and Meredith Moneypenny was certainly intriguing.

"Interesting," she murmured. "Very interesting."

The door chimed again, and Rita looked up to see Eugene Finch himself entering the café. Speak of the devil, she thought, noting his uncommon appearance this early in the day. The harbormaster was a creature of habit, typically taking his lunch at The Salty Mermaid at precisely 12:30, never earlier or later. His arrival at barely 10:15 was unprecedented.

"Morning, Eugene," she called. "You're early today."

Eugene—a barrel-chested man with the permanent tan of someone who spent most of his life outdoors—nodded distractedly as he approached the counter. "Morning, Rita. Just needed some coffee to go. Been up since before dawn dealing with police questions."

"About Brock Hamfist?" Rita asked, already reaching for a to-go cup.

"What else?" Eugene sighed heavily. "Last person to see him alive, apparently. Besides the killer, I suppose." He rubbed a hand over his face, looking exhausted. "Chief Crabbitz has been grilling me for hours."

Rita nearly dropped the coffee pot. "The last person? When did you see him?"

"Around ten-thirty last night," Eugene replied. "He came by the marina office asking about boat rentals, of all things. Me, I thought it was a joke at first—man's afraid of water, everyone knows that. But he seemed dead serious. Wanted something small and easy to handle."

"Did you rent him a boat?" Rita asked, trying to keep her tone casual as she filled his cup.

"Course not," Eugene scoffed. "Marina was closed by then anyway. I was just finishing up paperwork. Told him to come back during regular hours, and he got all huffy about it being 'urgent business.' I reminded him that the last time he was on a boat, during that charity fishing tournament two years ago, he threw up over the side for three hours straight and had to be towed back to shore."

"How did he take that reminder?" Rita asked, securing a lid on the coffee cup.

"Not well," Eugene admitted. "Called me some names I won't repeat in mixed company, then stormed off toward the public dock. That's the last I saw of him." He accepted the coffee with a grateful nod. "Cream and three sugars?"

"Just how you like it," Rita confirmed. "The public dock, you say? Not the private slips?"

"Definitely the public dock," Eugene said, dropping a few bills on the counter. "Which is odd, since that's just for day visitors, fishing charters, and water taxis. No private boats moored there."

"Very odd," Rita agreed, making change. "Especially for a man who hates the water."

Eugene shrugged. "People do strange things when they're angry. And Hamfist was definitely worked up about something." He pocketed his change. "Thanks for the coffee, Rita. Doubt I'll make it for lunch today—still have to deal with the festival clean-up and the police want to search the marina again."

As Eugene left, Rita's mind was racing. Brock Hamfist, a man famously terrified of water, had been looking for a boat the night he drowned. Had he found one despite Eugene's refusal? And if so, who had he gone out with? The public dock hosted water taxis to neighboring islands, fishing charters, and sightseeing boats—all of which would have stopped operating by that hour unless specially chartered.

Rita was so deep in thought that she nearly missed the arrival of her next customer. The bell's cheerful jingle drew her attention to the door, where Councilwoman Meredith Moneypenny stood adjusting her designer sunglasses with manicured fingers. Even for a casual café visit, Meredith was impeccably dressed in white linen pants and a coral silk blouse that probably cost more than Rita's monthly utilities. Her honey-blonde hair was styled in a sleek bob that somehow never moved despite the sea breeze, and her makeup was flawless—all part of the polished image she had cultivated since winning her council seat three years ago.

"Good morning, Rita," Meredith greeted her with the practiced warmth of a career politician. "Ghastly business about poor Brock, isn't it? The whole town's simply beside itself."

"Good morning, Councilwoman," Rita replied, gesturing to an empty table. "Yes, it's been quite the shock. Coffee?"

"Please," Meredith said, settling into a chair with the grace of someone who had taken deportment lessons. "And perhaps one of your famous blueberry scones? I have a council emergency meeting at eleven, and I doubt I'll have time for a proper lunch."

Rita nodded, signaling to Lupe to prepare the order. "An emergency meeting about Brock's death, I presume?"

"Partially," Meredith confirmed, removing her sunglasses to reveal expertly applied eye makeup. "But also to discuss the status of the resort project. There are investors and contracts to consider, not to mention the economic impact on the town."

"I imagine his death puts the whole project in jeopardy," Rita observed, placing a napkin and silverware before the councilwoman. "Unless there's a contingency plan."

Something flickered across Meredith's perfectly composed face—so quickly that Rita might have missed it if she hadn't been watching carefully. "Yes, well, these large development projects always have complicated legal structures. I'm sure Brock's business partners will sort it out eventually."

Lupe appeared with a coffee mug and a freshly warmed scone on a blue plate decorated with hand-painted mermaids. "Here you are, Councilwoman. Cream or sugar?"

"Just a splash of almond milk if you have it," Meredith replied with the air of someone accustomed to having her specific preferences accommodated.

As Lupe returned to the kitchen, Rita decided to take a chance. "I understand you met with Brock last night at Town Hall," she said casually. "After the festival."

Meredith's coffee cup paused halfway to her lips. "News certainly travels quickly in this town," she remarked, a slight edge to her voice.

"Small towns," Rita said with a shrug. "Was it about the resort project?"

Meredith set down her cup with deliberate precision. "It was a routine meeting about town business, nothing more. Though I suppose there's no harm in mentioning it was related to the final permit approvals for the resort. Everything was in order for the council vote next week." She took a small bite of her scone. "Delicious as always, Rita."

"Thank you," Rita acknowledged the compliment with a nod. "It must be quite a shock, working closely with someone on a project of this magnitude and then having them die so suddenly."

"Devastating," Meredith agreed, though her tone suggested more inconvenience than devastation. "Particularly given the timing. We were so close to finalizing everything."

"What happens to the project now?" Rita asked. "Does it die with Brock, or is someone else waiting in the wings to take over?"

Meredith's perfectly shaped eyebrows rose slightly. "That's a rather direct question, Rita."

"I've never been one to waste time dancing around a topic," Rita replied unapologetically. "And given that the resort would dramatically reshape our town, I think it's a fair question for a business owner like myself."

"The project's future will be determined by legal and financial considerations," Meredith answered smoothly. "Brock's company has several partners and investors. I believe his business attorney, Harold Jenkins, will be addressing the council at our meeting today." She glanced at her diamond-encrusted watch. "Speaking of which, I should finish up. The mayor insists on punctuality."

Rita nodded, recognizing the deflection but deciding not to push further—at least not yet. "Of course. Would you like a coffee to go?"

"That would be lovely," Meredith replied, reaching for her designer handbag. As she opened it to retrieve her wallet, Rita caught a glimpse of something glittering inside—a charm bracelet with what appeared to be several ocean-themed charms dangling from it.

"That's a beautiful bracelet," Rita commented, nodding toward the bag. "I noticed it sparkling. Is it new?"

Meredith quickly snapped her purse shut, a fleeting expression of alarm crossing her face before her political smile returned. "Just a little something I picked up on my last trip to Miami. Now, about that coffee?"

As Rita prepared the to-go cup, her mind was racing. The glimpse had been brief, but she was almost certain one of the charms on Meredith's bracelet had been in the shape of a jellyfish—quite similar to the one Daisy had described finding near Brock's body.

"Here you are," she said, handing over the coffee. "Good luck with your meeting."

"Thank you, Rita," Meredith replied, placing a crisp twenty-dollar bill on the table. "Keep the change. And please, give my condolences to your friends for the unpleasantness of this morning's discovery."

As the councilwoman departed in a cloud of expensive perfume, Rita remained by the table, her suspicions growing. First the secretive meeting with Brock the night before his death, then the evasiveness about the resort's future, and now a bracelet that potentially connected her to the crime scene? Meredith Moneypenny had just moved several spots higher on Rita's mental suspect list.

The morning continued at a steady pace, with the café filling up as locals and visitors alike sought both breakfast and the latest information about the town's unexpected tragedy. Rita moved efficiently between tables, simultaneously serving food and collecting gossip, carefully noting anything that might be relevant to Brock's death.

By eleven-thirty, she had amassed quite a collection of potentially useful tidbits:

> Captain "Barnacle" Bob Crustybutt had reportedly received a "final offer" from Brock for his prime beachfront property the day before the festival—an offer that was apparently high enough to make even the notoriously stubborn captain consider selling.

Ziggy Hamfist had been seen entering the Bulldozer Grill—his father's restaurant—shortly after his argument with Brock, where he'd apparently helped himself to several expensive bottles from the wine cellar before the manager could stop him.

Gladys Pickle had been overheard telling her Conservation Crusaders that she had "big news" that would "change everything" about their fight against the resort project, planned for announcement at their meeting scheduled for the day after the festival.

Candi Bubbleshine's claim to be Brock's steady girlfriend was being disputed by at least two other women in town who believed themselves to hold that title—including, most surprisingly, Fleur DuBois, the reclusive French artist who owned the gallery next to Town Hall.

Just as Rita was contemplating taking a quick break to call Daisy with these updates, the bell above the door jangled again, and a collective hush fell over the café. Rita looked up to see Ziggy Hamfist himself standing in the doorway, looking decidedly uncomfortable under the sudden scrutiny of every patron.

Despite sharing his father's substantial height and broad shoulders, Ziggy couldn't have been more different from Brock in appearance and demeanor. Where Brock had been meticulously groomed and dressed, favoring expensive suits and a military-precise haircut, Ziggy wore tattered hemp pants, a faded t-shirt emblazoned with "Save the Whales, Shoot the Whalers" in peeling letters, and his dark hair in tangled dreadlocks that reached halfway down his back. Multiple beaded necklaces adorned his neck, and his feet were clad in sandals that appeared to be constructed from recycled tires.

"Uh, hey," he mumbled, raising a hand in an awkward wave. "Heard this place has good food."

Rita approached him, professional smile firmly in place despite her internal curiosity. "Welcome to The Salty Mermaid. Just one today?"

"Yeah," Ziggy replied, shifting uncomfortably as he noticed the stares from the other customers. "Maybe somewhere quiet? If that's cool."

Rita nodded, leading him to a small table in the corner partially screened by a large potted palm—her designated spot for patrons seeking a bit of privacy. "Our lunch specials are on the board," she told him, gesturing to the chalkboard menu. "Today's soup is roasted red pepper bisque, and the catch of the day is mahi-mahi with mango salsa."

"Got anything vegetarian?" Ziggy asked, slouching into the chair. "I don't eat, like, anything with a face."

"The roasted vegetable panini is quite popular," Rita suggested. "Or I could have the kitchen prepare a quinoa bowl with seasonal vegetables and avocado."

"That sounds dope," Ziggy nodded. "The quinoa thing. And maybe an herbal tea? Something calming?"

"Chamomile with lavender," Rita recommended. "Good for stress."

Ziggy gave her a grateful look. "Perfect. Thanks, uh..."

"Rita," she supplied. "Rita Calabaza. I own the place."

Recognition dawned in his bloodshot eyes. "Oh, right. You're one of the old ladies who found my dad."

Rita bristled slightly at the "old ladies" designation but maintained her professional demeanor. "Yes, that was quite a shock this morning. I'm very sorry for your loss."

Ziggy's expression was difficult to read—a mixture of grief, anger, and something else that Rita couldn't quite identify. "Yeah, well... it's complicated," he muttered. "Dad and I weren't exactly tight, you know?"

"So I've heard," Rita replied neutrally. "Still, losing a parent is never easy."

Ziggy shrugged, picking at a loose thread on his shirt. "Guess not. The cops have been grilling me all morning, like I had something to do with it."

"Standard procedure, I'm sure," Rita said, though she was mentally cataloging his every word and reaction. "They have to talk to family members first."

"Yeah, but they seemed extra interested in our argument last night," Ziggy continued, apparently not noticing Rita's sudden heightened attention. "Like, yeah, we fought. We always fought. Doesn't mean I wanted the old man dead."

"Of course not," Rita soothed. "What were you arguing about, if you don't mind my asking?"

Ziggy hesitated, then sighed. "Same old stuff. He wanted me to 'grow up,' get a 'real job,' stop 'wasting my potential.' I wanted him to stop destroying the environment with his tacky resorts and actually listen to me for once." He ran a hand through his dreadlocks. "Then he dropped the bomb that he was cutting me off financially unless I came to work for his company. Like, actually put on a suit and help him destroy pristine coastlines for profit."

"That must have been upsetting," Rita observed.

"Yeah, it sucked," Ziggy admitted. "But not kill-him upset. More like get-drunk-and-steal-his-wine upset, which, yeah, I did." He looked momentarily abashed. "Not my proudest moment."

Rita nodded sympathetically while mentally adding this confession to her notes for Daisy. "I'll put your order in right away," she promised. "The tea will be out in just a moment."

As she turned to head back to the kitchen, Ziggy called after her, "Hey, is it true he washed up on your beach? Like, right behind your house?"

Rita paused. "Yes, that's true."

"Weird," Ziggy remarked, shaking his head. "Dad hated the water. Wouldn't go near it if he could help it. Used to joke that he built beach resorts for people braver than him."

"That's what makes his drowning so... unexpected," Rita agreed carefully.

Ziggy's brow furrowed. "Yeah. Super weird." He leaned forward suddenly. "The cops aren't saying much, but... was there anything strange? About how they found him?"

Rita hesitated, weighing how much to share. "I'm not sure what you mean."

"Like, was he wearing his watch?" Ziggy asked. "His fancy Rolex? He never took that thing off. Said it was his first big purchase when he made his first million."

"I believe he was still wearing it," Rita confirmed, remembering the waterlogged timepiece on Brock's wrist. "Why do you ask?"

Ziggy sat back, looking troubled. "Just checking something. Dad always said if he ever got mugged, they'd have to cut his arm off to get that watch. It was like... his thing, you know? So if he still had it on, probably wasn't a robbery."

"I wouldn't think robbery would be a likely motive in Conch Key," Rita noted. "We hardly have any crime here."

"Yeah, well, not the obvious kind maybe," Ziggy muttered. "But Dad always said the worst thieves wear suits and carry briefcases. Should have listened to his own advice."

Before Rita could inquire further about this cryptic statement, the kitchen door swung open and Lupe emerged with a steaming mug of tea. "Here you go," Rita told Ziggy, accepting the mug from Lupe. "Your food will be ready shortly."

Leaving him to his tea and thoughts, Rita returned to the kitchen, where Lupe was already preparing the quinoa bowl. "So that's the son?" her assistant asked in a low voice. "Doesn't look much like his father."

"Takes after his mother, I imagine," Rita replied, glancing through the service window to where Ziggy sat slumped at his table, staring morosely into his tea. "Keep an eye on him, will you? I need to make a quick phone call."

Slipping into her small office at the back of the kitchen, Rita pulled out her cell phone and dialed Daisy's number. After three rings, her friend's distinctive Southern drawl came through.

"Daisy Picklesworth speaking."

"It's Rita," she said without preamble. "You'll never guess who just walked into my café."

"Unless it's Brock Hamfist's ghost ordering the catch of the day, I imagine I'll need more hints," Daisy replied dryly.

"His son, Ziggy," Rita informed her. "Looking like he just stepped off a Grateful Dead tour bus and ordered possibly the first quinoa bowl in Conch Key history."

"How fascinating," Daisy murmured, her interest clearly piqued. "And has young Mr. Hamfist had anything interesting to say about his father's untimely demise?"

"He confirmed their argument last night," Rita reported. "Brock was cutting him off financially unless he joined the family business. He also admitted to stealing wine from his father's restaurant afterward but denies any involvement in his death."

"As most murderers tend to do," Daisy observed.

"There's more," Rita continued, lowering her voice though the office door was closed. "Eugene Finch was in earlier. Says Brock came to the marina office around ten-thirty last night asking to rent a boat."

There was a pause on the other end. "Our aquaphobic victim wanted to rent a boat? How curious."

"Gets better," Rita promised. "Meredith Moneypenny stopped by too. Admitted to meeting with Brock at Town Hall after the festival, supposedly about permit approvals, but she was definitely being evasive. And Daisy—she has a charm bracelet. I only caught a glimpse, but I'm almost certain one of the charms was a jellyfish."

"Now that is interesting," Daisy said, and Rita could practically hear her friend's mind working. "Very interesting indeed. Did she seem nervous when you noticed it?"

"Snapped her purse shut faster than Babs at an all-you-can-eat buffet," Rita confirmed. "And changed the subject immediately."

"Excellent observation, Rita," Daisy commended her. "My book club meeting with the councilwoman has been postponed due to the emergency council session, but this gives me something specific to look for when it's rescheduled."

"How's your investigation going?" Rita asked.

"Quite productive," Daisy replied with satisfaction. "I've learned that our dear departed developer was seen arguing with not only Gladys Pickle and his son last night, but also with Harold Jenkins—his business attorney—near the bandstand around nine-forty-five. According to Mrs. Finkelstein, who was manning the Friends of the Library booth, they were having a 'heated discussion about paperwork' that ended with Jenkins saying something to the effect of 'You can't do this' and Brock responding that 'It's already done.'"

"What do you suppose that means?" Rita wondered.

"I'm not entirely sure yet," Daisy admitted. "But apparently Jenkins left the festival immediately afterward, looking, in Mrs. Finkelstein's words, 'like someone had just told him his stock portfolio had crashed.'"

"Curiouser and curiouser," Rita murmured. "Oh, and The Morning Manatees mentioned that Captain Crustybutt received a 'final offer' from Brock for his beachfront property the day before the festival—supposedly high enough to make even him consider selling."

"That piece of land is the lynchpin for the entire resort project," Daisy noted. "Without it, they'd have to significantly alter the design or abandon it entirely."

"And according to town gossip, Gladys Pickle was planning to announce some 'big news' that would 'change everything' about the fight against the resort at today's Conservation Crusaders meeting," Rita added.

"The plot thickens like your famous gumbo," Daisy remarked. "I wonder if—"

A sudden commotion from the dining area interrupted their conversation—raised voices, followed by the distinctive sound of something shattering.

"I need to go," Rita said quickly. "Sounds like trouble out front. I'll call you back."

Hanging up without waiting for a response, Rita hurried from her office to find Ziggy Hamfist standing toe-to-toe with Lou Pescatore, owner of the competing Fishy Business restaurant. Lou—a short, stocky man with a perpetual scowl and a questionable approach to seafood preparation that Rita had been criticizing for years—was red-faced and pointing an accusatory finger at Ziggy, while the younger man stood with his fists clenched. Between them lay the shattered remains of what had been Ziggy's mug of tea.

"You've got some nerve showing your face around town after what you did!" Lou was shouting, his thick New Jersey accent becoming more pronounced in his anger. "Your father wasn't even cold yet, and you were helping yourself to his wine cellar!"

"Back off, man," Ziggy growled, his earlier slouch replaced by a tense, defensive posture. "You don't know anything about me or my dad."

"I know he was about to cut you off without a penny," Lou sneered. "And suddenly he's dead. Mighty convenient timing, wouldn't you say?"

The café had gone silent, every patron watching the confrontation with undisguised interest. Rita moved swiftly between the two men, her wooden spoon appearing in her hand as if by magic.

"That's quite enough," she declared firmly. "Lou Pescatore, you are causing a disturbance in my establishment. Either sit down and order something or leave immediately."

Lou glared at her. "You're serving this ungrateful punk after what he did? His father was a pillar of this community!"

"My father was a pillar of crap," Ziggy retorted. "And you were just mad because his restaurant was putting yours out of business with actual fresh seafood instead of whatever frozen garbage you serve."

Lou's face darkened further, and for a moment, Rita thought he might actually take a swing at Ziggy. Instead, he jabbed his finger toward the younger man's chest.

"Your father and I had our differences, but at least he understood business. He had respect. You? You're nothing but a leech. Everybody knows you needed his money."

"That's enough!" Rita stepped fully between them, wooden spoon raised like a weapon. "Lou, I won't tell you again. Out of my restaurant, now, or I'll call Chief Crabbitz myself."

Lou glared at her for a long moment before adjusting his stained chef's jacket with an attempt at dignity. "Fine. But don't say I didn't warn you about serving murderers." He turned to the rest of the patrons, several of whom were openly recording the confrontation on their phones. "You all saw him arguing with Brock last night! You all know he got cut off! Follow the money, that's what I say!"

"OUT!" Rita bellowed, brandishing her spoon with enough menace to finally send Lou backing toward the door.

"This isn't over," he muttered as he departed, the bell jangling discordantly with his forceful exit.

The café remained silent for several uncomfortable seconds before Rita turned to address her customers. "Show's over, folks. Please return to your meals. Lupe, bring Mr. Hamfist a fresh tea, on the house. And a broom for this mess, please."

As the normal buzz of conversation gradually resumed, Rita turned to Ziggy, who stood looking equal parts embarrassed and furious. "Are you all right?"

"Yeah. Sorry about the..." he gestured vaguely at the broken mug and spilled tea on the floor. "I'll pay for it."

"Don't worry about that," Rita assured him, guiding him back to his table. "Lou has always had more temper than sense. And he's been trying to sabotage my business for years, so consider anything he says highly suspect."

Ziggy slumped back into his chair, running his hands through his tangled dreadlocks. "People are gonna think I killed him, aren't they? Because of the money thing."

"People will speculate about all sorts of things," Rita replied diplomatically. "It's human nature, especially in small towns."

"It's just—" Ziggy began, then stopped as Lupe approached with a fresh mug of tea and his quinoa bowl. He waited until she had departed before continuing in a lower voice. "It's just that Dad and I fought all the time. It wasn't new. Yeah, he was cutting me off, but that wasn't new either. He'd done it before when I joined that pipeline protest in North Dakota." He shook his head. "He always came around eventually."

"I see," Rita said, sensing there was more to the story. "And you weren't concerned this time would be different?"

Ziggy hesitated, poking at his quinoa with a fork. "Actually, I think this time he might have meant it. He seemed... different. Said he was 'making changes' and that it was 'time to set things right.'" He frowned. "I thought he was just on one of his self-improvement kicks again. Last time it was CrossFit and protein shakes."

"Making changes?" Rita repeated, mentally filing away this interesting phrase. "Did he elaborate on what kind of changes?"

"Not really," Ziggy replied. "Just said he'd had a 'wake-up call' and was 'reassessing priorities.' Corporate buzzword bingo, basically. I didn't take it seriously." His expression grew troubled. "But now I wonder if he was really planning something major, you know? Something that got him killed."

Rita carefully kept her face neutral despite her internal excitement at this potential lead. "It's possible, I suppose. Did you mention this to Chief Crabbitz during your interview?"

"Yeah, for all the good it did," Ziggy muttered. "He seemed more interested in where I was after ten o'clock last night."

"And where were you?" Rita asked, unable to resist the direct question.

Ziggy's eyes narrowed slightly. "You sound like the cops. But whatever—I was at the Conch Key Cabanas, drinking the wine I took from Dad's restaurant and feeling sorry for myself. The night manager can vouch for me. I tried to get him to join my pity party around midnight, but he was too professional." He attempted a weak smile. "Probably for the best. I passed out shortly after that anyway."

"I see," Rita nodded. "Well, try to ignore Lou and his accusations. Grief makes people behave strangely sometimes."

"Lou didn't even like my dad," Ziggy pointed out. "They were competitors."

"True," Rita acknowledged. "But Brock's death affects the whole business community here. Change makes people nervous, especially unexpected change."

Ziggy took a small bite of his food, then looked up at Rita with surprising earnestness. "This is really good. Thanks for, you know, not throwing me out after that scene."

"You're welcome here anytime," Rita assured him, feeling a surprising pang of sympathy for the young man. Despite his disheveled appearance and apparent lack of ambition, there was something vulnerable about him that reminded Rita of her own son in his rebellious phase—before he'd straightened out, gotten married, and moved to Phoenix, where he now called her only on major holidays.

"I should get back to work," she added, gesturing to the other customers. "But please, enjoy your meal. And don't let Lou's outburst bother you."

As she moved away to check on her other patrons, Rita's mind was racing with the new information. Brock had been "making changes" and "reassessing priorities." He'd had a "wake-up call." He'd gone to the marina seeking to rent a boat despite his fear of water. And according to Eugene, he'd headed toward the public dock after being refused a rental.

The public dock, where water taxis and sightseeing boats departed... including the late-night glass-bottom boat that took tourists out to view the bioluminescent bay. The "Midnight Glow Tour," as it was advertised, departed at 11 PM every night during high season—which would have been right around the time Brock was seen heading in that direction.

Rita made a mental note to check with Bobby Glowacki, who operated the tour boat. If Brock had gone out on the glass-bottom boat, Bobby would know. And more importantly, he might know who else had been on board that night.

The lunch rush picked up, temporarily pushing thoughts of murder investigations to the back of Rita's mind as she focused on keeping her customers fed and happy. It wasn't until nearly two o'clock, during a brief lull, that she was able to step into her office again and call Daisy.

"It's Rita," she said when her friend answered. "Sorry about cutting you off earlier. Had a bit of a situation with Lou from Fishy Business confronting Ziggy in the middle of the café."

"How dramatic," Daisy remarked. "Did fisticuffs ensue?"

"Nearly," Rita confirmed. "I had to intervene with my wooden spoon. But the interesting part is what Ziggy told me afterward. He said

Brock had been talking about 'making changes' and 'reassessing priorities' after some kind of 'wake-up call.'"

"Indeed?" Daisy's interest was palpable even through the phone. "That aligns with what I've discovered. According to Harold Jenkins' secretary, who frequents my favorite bookshop, Brock had scheduled an urgent meeting with the entire legal team for this morning—which obviously he didn't live to attend."

"Did she know what it was about?" Rita asked.

"Unfortunately not," Daisy replied. "But she did mention that Brock had requested his entire file on the resort project be prepared for review, along with his personal will and estate documents."

"His will?" Rita repeated, surprised. "That seems ominous in retrospect."

"Indeed. As if he anticipated trouble," Daisy agreed. "I've also learned from my sources at the library that Brock had recently donated a substantial sum to Gladys Pickle's turtle sanctuary—anonymously."

"What?" Rita nearly dropped her phone. "But he was fighting her conservation efforts at every turn!"

"Apparently his public and private positions had diverged," Daisy observed. "Which makes me wonder what other changes he might have been contemplating."

"I think I might know a way to find out more," Rita said, explaining her theory about the glass-bottom boat. "I'll try to catch Bobby before his afternoon tour."

"Excellent thinking," Daisy praised her. "Meanwhile, I'm heading to the Bulldozer Grill to speak with the manager under the pretense of discussing catering for next month's library fundraiser. Babs is still at the community theater gathering intelligence, and Mae called to say she's learned something 'very interesting' at the senior center but wants to tell us in person."

"Shall we meet back at The Barnacle at, say, five o'clock?" Rita suggested. "I close early on Mondays anyway."

"Perfect," Daisy agreed. "I'll bring the wine, you bring the food?"

"As always," Rita confirmed. "See you then."

After hanging up, Rita checked the time. Bobby's afternoon Glow Tour preparation usually began around three, which gave her just enough time to walk to the public dock if she left now. After instructing Lupe to handle things in her absence, Rita removed her apron, tucked her wooden spoon into her large handbag (one never knew when it might come in handy), and headed out the back door.

The harbor was busy with the usual Monday afternoon activity—fishing charters returning with their catches, pleasure boats being refueled, and tourists wandering the boardwalk in search of souvenirs and cold drinks. Rita moved purposefully past the various attractions, nodding to familiar faces but not stopping to chat as she normally would. She had a mission.

Bobby Glowacki's glass-bottom boat, the "Glow Rider," was docked at the far end of the public pier—a sleek vessel with underwater lights and large viewing panels built into the hull. As Rita approached, she could see Bobby himself on deck, methodically cleaning the glass panels in preparation for the afternoon tour.

"Ahoy, Bobby!" she called, waving to catch his attention.

Bobby straightened up, pushing his captain's hat back on his head. At forty-five, he had the weathered tan of a lifelong boatman and the perpetually cheerful disposition of someone who genuinely loved his work. "Rita Calabaza! To what do I owe the pleasure? Don't often see you away from your café this time of day."

"Special circumstances," Rita replied, stepping carefully onto the boat's deck. "Mind if I come aboard for a quick chat?"

"Always welcome," Bobby assured her, setting aside his cleaning supplies. "Everything okay? Heard about the excitement at your place this morning. Body on the beach, they're saying."

"News travels fast," Rita observed, wondering how many times she would make that statement today. "Yes, it was quite the shock. Actually, that's what I wanted to talk to you about. Did you run your Midnight Glow Tour last night?"

"Sure did," Bobby confirmed. "Clear night, perfect conditions. The bay was putting on quite a show—best bioluminescence I've seen this season."

"And did Brock Hamfist happen to be one of your passengers?" Rita asked directly, watching Bobby's face closely.

The captain's cheerful expression faltered. "Well now, that's a specific question. Any particular reason you're asking?"

"Bobby," Rita said patiently, "the man was found drowned this morning. I'm trying to piece together his movements last night. Was he on your boat or not?"

Bobby sighed, glancing around as if to ensure they weren't being overheard. "Yeah, he was. Surprised me, too. Everyone knows Hamfist hated the water. But he paid for a ticket like anyone else, so I didn't ask questions."

"Was he alone?" Rita pressed.

"Nope," Bobby replied, lowering his voice. "Came with a woman. They sat at the back, kept to themselves. Seemed like they were having an intense conversation the whole time."

Rita's pulse quickened. "This woman—was it his girlfriend? Candi Bubbleshine? Blonde, lots of makeup, sequins?"

Bobby shook his head. "Definitely not. This lady was classy, you know? Understated. Dark hair, expensive clothes. No flashy jewelry or nothing like that."

"Could you identify her if you saw her again?" Rita asked.

"Maybe," Bobby said uncertainly. "It was dark, and I was focused on giving my tour spiel. Plus, I try not to stare at the customers, you know? Bad for business."

"Did they stay on the boat for the entire tour?" Rita continued, her mind racing through the possible identities of Brock's mysterious companion.

"That's the weird part," Bobby told her, leaning closer. "We do that slow circuit through the south bay, right? Takes about an hour. But when we were at the furthest point from shore, near Turtle Rock, they both got off."

"Got off?" Rita repeated, confused. "In the middle of the bay?"

"There was another boat," Bobby explained. "Small fishing skiff, no lights. Just appeared alongside us. The woman left first, then Hamfist followed—looking scared out of his mind, I might add. Nearly fell between the boats. I figured they'd chartered a private return or something."

"Did you recognize the other boat? Or whoever was piloting it?" Rita asked urgently.

Bobby shook his head. "Too dark to see clearly. But it had that distinctive engine sound—you know, the old Johnson outboards with the timing slightly off? Makes a sort of uneven putt-putt-putt noise."

Rita knew exactly the sound he meant—and she also knew only one person in Conch Key who still used that particular vintage of motor: Captain "Barnacle" Bob Crustybutt, the very man who had supposedly received a "final offer" from Brock for his beachfront property the day before.

"Bobby, has Chief Crabbitz questioned you about this yet?" she asked.

"Nope, not a peep from the police," Bobby replied. "But I figured it was just a matter of time, what with Hamfist turning up dead and all." He looked troubled. "You don't think I'm in any trouble, do you? I didn't know he was going to... you know..."

"I'm sure you're not in any trouble," Rita assured him. "But when the police do come asking, tell them exactly what you told me. It could be important."

Bobby nodded solemnly. "Will do. And, uh, Rita? I'd appreciate if you didn't mention I told you all this first. Don't want Morty thinking I'm gossiping about official police business."

"My lips are sealed," Rita promised, though her mind was already racing ahead to how she would share this information with Daisy and the others. "Thanks for your help, Bobby. I should let you get back to your preparations."

As she made her way back along the pier, Rita mentally reviewed what she had learned. Brock Hamfist, despite his fear of water, had taken the Midnight Glow Tour with an unidentified dark-haired woman. They had transferred to a small boat—likely Captain Crustybutt's—at the furthest point from shore. And sometime after that, Brock had ended up dead.

The pieces were starting to come together, but the picture they formed was still unclear. What had been so important that it drove Brock to overcome his aquaphobia? Who was the mystery woman? And what role, if any, did Captain Crustybutt play in the developer's demise?

As Rita approached The Salty Mermaid, her phone chimed with a text message. It was from Babs:

"MAJOR NEWS from theater. Moneypenny spotted with Fleur DuBois last night AFTER festival. Very cozy. Meet at Barnacle ASAP. Bringing costumes."

Rita frowned at the cryptic last line but quickened her pace. If Babs was bringing costumes, it could only mean one thing: tonight's investigation was going undercover.

Chapter Four

Costume Capers and Confessions

"You want us to do what?" Rita stared at Babs in disbelief, the half-empty wine glass frozen halfway to her lips.

The living room of The Barnacle was bathed in the golden glow of the late afternoon sun, casting long shadows across the eclectic collection of furniture that had come to define the shared space of the four friends. Outside, the waves lapped gently against the shore, a peaceful soundtrack that belied the excitement brewing within the mint-green Victorian's walls.

Sprawled across every available surface was an array of costumes and accessories that would have impressed a Broadway prop master—sequined gowns, feather boas, wigs in improbable colors, and various prosthetic additions that Daisy had been eyeing with increasing concern since Babs had dramatically unveiled them ten minutes prior.

"It's the perfect plan," Babs insisted, gesturing expansively and nearly knocking over a lamp in the process. Her flame-red hair was now partially hidden beneath a platinum blonde wig styled in a remarkably accurate recreation of Candi Bubbleshine's signature updo. "Tonight is the annual Conch Key Yacht Club fundraiser. Everyone who's anyone will be there, including at least half our suspect list."

"And you think we should infiltrate this event... in disguise?" Mae asked tentatively, picking up what appeared to be a false mustache with two fingers, as if it might bite her.

"Absolutely!" Babs beamed, clearly thrilled that someone was following her logic. "I have contacts at the yacht club from my brief but memorable marriage to husband number three—you remember, the one with the boat but no actual sailing ability? Anyway, they always need extra servers for these big events. We sign up as catering staff, we blend in, we eavesdrop, we solve the murder!" She spread her arms triumphantly, dislodging her wig slightly.

Daisy, who had been unusually quiet during Babs' enthusiastic presentation, finally set down her own wine glass with deliberate precision. "While I appreciate your initiative, Babs, I'm not sure how effective we would be as 'undercover agents' given that everyone in town knows exactly who we are."

"That's the beauty of it," Babs countered, reaching for a large makeup case. "With my theatrical expertise, no one will recognize us. I spent fifteen years designing costumes and makeup for Broadway productions. I once transformed a six-foot-four baritone into a convincing teenage girl for 'Little Women: The Musical.'"

"That explains so much about that production," Daisy murmured under her breath.

"Besides," Babs continued, blithely ignoring the comment, "people see what they expect to see. No one expects four retired ladies to be serving canapés at a fancy fundraiser, so no one will look closely enough to recognize us."

Rita, who had been gradually warming to the idea despite her initial skepticism, nodded thoughtfully. "There is some logic to that. And the guest list for this event would include Councilwoman Moneypenny, Harold Jenkins, and possibly Captain Crustybutt, if he's been invited as the potential seller of that prime beachfront property."

"Exactly!" Babs exclaimed. "Plus, I already confirmed that Candi Bubbleshine will be performing—apparently she was Brock's suggested entertainment for the evening, and they decided to keep her on the program as a sort of tribute." She rolled her eyes. "Though I suspect it has more to do with no one wanting to return the deposit."

"If Candi's performing, that means Ziggy might attend as well," Mae observed, always thinking of connections. "Despite their differences, he is Brock's son and would be expected at a tribute."

"And where there are wealthy donors, there's usually Gladys Pickle with her environmental pamphlets and petition clipboard," Daisy added, her resistance visibly weakening. "It would be an efficient way to observe multiple suspects interacting in a social setting."

"So you're in?" Babs asked eagerly, already reaching for her makeup brushes.

Daisy held up a warning hand. "I didn't say that. I merely acknowledged the potential intelligence-gathering advantages. There are significant logistical challenges to consider. For one thing, some of us..." she glanced meaningfully at Rita, "are not exactly unknown in local culinary circles. Rita caters half the events in town."

"Which is why she'll be our kitchen spy," Babs explained. "No disguise needed—she can legitimately volunteer to help the caterer, claiming she's bored with her evening off. You know how much the yacht club values your culinary expertise, Rita."

Rita couldn't help but feel a small glow of pride at this acknowledgment. "Marjorie does always ask for my advice on sauces," she admitted, referring to the yacht club's regular caterer. "And I have been curious about her new sous-chef. Rumor has it he trained in Paris."

"There you go!" Babs beamed. "Meanwhile, I'll transform into a convincing cocktail waitress named... Trixie." She struck a pose that suggested "Trixie" had a colorful past and questionable serving skills. "Mae will be our perfect shy busser, keeping to the background but hearing everything. And Daisy..." She turned to her friend with a gleam in her eye that made Daisy instinctively lean back in her chair. "Daisy will be our pièce de résistance."

"I beg your pardon?" Daisy's Southern drawl became more pronounced, as it always did when she was alarmed.

"You, my dear, will be Baroness Ekaterina Volkov, visiting Russian aristocrat and potential investor in Conch Key real estate," Babs announced grandly. "With your natural air of authority and the accent I know you can pull off from your starring role in the library's production of 'Anastasia' three years ago, you'll have all our suspects tripping over themselves to share their inside knowledge of the resort project."

"That is the most ridiculous—" Daisy began, but was interrupted by Mae's gentle interjection.

"Actually, it's rather brilliant," Mae said softly. "No one questions the rich, especially when they might be investing. And with Brock gone, everyone involved in the resort will be scrambling to find new backers."

Daisy's protests faltered as she considered this logic. "I suppose there is a certain strategic advantage to the position," she conceded reluctantly. "But I haven't acted in years, and I certainly don't have the wardrobe for a Russian baroness."

"Leave that to me," Babs assured her, pulling a garment bag from the pile. "Behold!"

With a flourish worthy of a magician, she unzipped the bag to reveal an evening gown in deep midnight blue, adorned with tasteful crystal embellishments that caught the light like stars. It was elegant, expensive-looking, and exactly Daisy's size.

"Where on earth did you get that?" Daisy asked, unable to hide her admiration for the garment.

"Community theater costume department," Babs explained. "From last year's production of 'The Importance of Being Earnest.' The director insisted on setting it in the 1920s, which made absolutely no sense for the script, but resulted in some spectacular costumes. This was for Lady Bracknell."

"It's beautiful," Mae sighed. "You would look stunning in it, Daisy."

Daisy approached the dress with the caution of someone who suspected a trap but was too enticed to resist. She touched the fabric reverently. "I do look exceptional in this shade of blue," she admitted.

"And with your silver hair styled in a sophisticated updo, plus some dramatic makeup and a few well-placed accessories..." Babs mimed placing a tiara on Daisy's head. "Baroness Ekaterina Volkov, at your service."

Daisy glanced at Rita and Mae, finding no support in their intrigued expressions. "This is utterly preposterous," she declared, though without much conviction. "But I suppose if we're committed to this ridiculous charade..."

"We are!" Babs confirmed enthusiastically.

"...then I shall do my part," Daisy concluded with as much dignity as she could muster. "Though I want it officially noted that I consider this plan only marginally less absurd than the time you convinced us to join that seniors' synchronized swimming class."

"Which, may I remind you, resulted in us winning the regional championship," Babs pointed out.

"And in you having a very public hot flash that caused you to emerge from the pool shouting about being 'boiled alive' in the middle of our final routine," Daisy countered dryly.

Mae giggled at the memory. "The judges did say our 'unique interpretation' of the music showed creativity."

"Water under the bridge," Babs waved dismissively. "Or over the hot flash, as the case may be. Now, let's focus on tonight's mission. Each of us needs to identify specific targets for intelligence gathering."

"I've been thinking about that," Rita said, setting down her empty wine glass and reaching for the notepad they'd been using to compile their suspect list. "Based on what we've learned so far, I suggest the following priorities: Meredith Moneypenny and her possible connection to the jellyfish charm; Captain Crustybutt and his boat's involvement in Brock's final hours; Harold Jenkins and the mysterious paperwork dispute; and Fleur DuBois, who apparently has a connection to both Brock and Meredith."

Daisy nodded approvingly. "Excellent analysis, Rita. I would add that we should be alert for any mention of changes Brock was planning to make to the resort project. Both Ziggy and the arguement overheard with Harold suggested he was altering course in some significant way."

"And we should watch for anyone wearing ocean-themed jewelry," Mae added thoughtfully. "Especially jellyfish charms."

"Precisely," Daisy agreed. "Babs, what time does this event begin?"

"Cocktails at seven, dinner at eight, dancing and Candi's performance to follow," Babs reported. "The catering staff is expected at six for final preparations."

Daisy checked her watch—a vintage Cartier that had been her mother's. "That gives us just under two hours to transform ourselves and perfect our cover stories." She turned to Babs with a resigned sigh. "Very well, Barbara. Work your theatrical magic."

Babs clapped her hands in delight. "Wonderful! Mae, darling, come with me to help arrange the wigs. Rita, there's a server's uniform in your size on the sofa—black slacks, white shirt, nothing complicated for you. And Daisy..." Her eyes gleamed with anticipation. "You and I have a baroness to create."

Precisely ninety minutes later, four transformed women gathered in the living room for final inspection. Rita, dressed in the simple black and white uniform of the catering staff, looked much like herself but with her hair tucked neatly under a service cap. Mae, similarly attired but with the addition of thick-framed glasses and a mousy brown wig styled in an unremarkable bob, seemed to have physically shrunk into her role as the unobtrusive busser.

Babs had undergone a more dramatic metamorphosis. Her usual vibrant persona had been channeled into "Trixie," a cocktail waitress with platinum blonde hair teased to impressive heights, dramatic cat-eye makeup, and a uniform altered to maximize her assets. She had somehow managed to add an extra inch to her already impressive height through strategic heel selection, and her normally extensive jewelry had been replaced with a single pair of oversized hoop earrings.

But it was Daisy who had undergone the most remarkable transformation. The elegant, sharp-tongued former professor had vanished, replaced by Baroness Ekaterina Volkov—a vision in midnight blue satin with a regal bearing that seemed to add inches to her stature. Her silver hair had been styled in a sophisticated twist adorned with a small, tasteful tiara. Dramatic makeup emphasized her cheekbones and eyes, while a string of what appeared to be genuine pearls (Mae's contribution) completed the ensemble.

"My word," Rita murmured, circling Daisy with undisguised admiration. "I wouldn't recognize you if I passed you on the street."

"The power of theatrical makeup," Babs declared proudly. "Contouring is everything. I added fifteen years to Mae and took ten off Daisy."

"I'm not sure whether to be flattered or offended," Mae commented mildly, adjusting her ill-fitting glasses.

"Be practical," Daisy suggested, her voice now carrying a subtle Russian accent that wasn't entirely convincing but would likely pass muster in a noisy social setting. "We need to coordinate our arrival. Rita and Mae should go first as legitimate staff. Babs will follow ten minutes later as a last-minute addition to the service team. I shall arrive fashionably late, as befits my station."

"I've arranged for Eugene Finch to escort you," Babs informed her. "He thinks he's doing a favor for an old theater friend by accompanying a wealthy potential investor who's new in town."

"Eugene?" Daisy raised an eyebrow. "The harbormaster?"

"He cleans up surprisingly well," Babs assured her. "And he's on our suspect adjacent list anyway, given his interaction with Brock last night. Plus, he knows absolutely everyone in town and can introduce you around without raising suspicion."

"Very well," Daisy conceded. "Though I anticipate spending most of the evening explaining why a Russian baroness would be interested in investing in a small Florida coastal town."

"You're considering a winter home and heard great things about Conch Key from your 'dear friend' the Countess of Wessex," Babs supplied promptly. "You're particularly interested in the wellness tourism sector and spa opportunities."

"You've really thought this through," Mae observed, impressed.

"I was stranded in a summer stock production of 'Witness for the Prosecution' for three months in the Catskills," Babs replied with a shrug. "Creating backstories for the characters became my coping mechanism."

"One final question," Rita said, retrieving her handbag. "How exactly are we meant to communicate with each other during this operation? We can hardly huddle together exchanging notes at a formal event."

"Already solved," Babs announced triumphantly, producing four small objects from her costume kit. "Earpieces! Left over from the community theater's disastrous production of 'Mission: Impossible – The Musical.'"

"I thought we agreed never to speak of that again," Daisy remarked, eyeing the devices skeptically. "The lead actor ended up hanging upside down from the catwalk for forty minutes."

"Which is precisely why we have spare communication equipment," Babs countered, distributing the earpieces. "They're quite discreet and operate on a simple frequency. Just tuck them into your ear, and we can all hear each other."

"Won't people notice us talking to ourselves?" Mae asked practically.

"In a noisy social event? Unlikely," Babs dismissed the concern. "Besides, servers are practically invisible to the wealthy. No offense, Rita."

"None taken," Rita assured her. "It's actually an advantage in this case."

"And as for Baroness Ekaterina," Babs continued, "she can simply excuse herself periodically to 'make an important call' if she needs to confer with us at length."

"This is either going to be brilliantly effective or spectacularly disastrous," Daisy observed, carefully inserting the earpiece. "I suspect the latter."

"Have faith, darling," Babs encouraged, checking her appearance one final time in the mirror. "We've pulled off more challenging feats. Remember the Great Garden Club Gladiola Heist of 2022?"

"How could I forget?" Daisy rolled her eyes. "Mae hid in that compost bin for three hours."

"And we caught the culprit," Mae reminded her, ever the optimist. "I'm sure tonight will be just as successful."

"Without the compost, one hopes," Rita added dryly. "Now, shall we depart? Marjorie will be expecting me soon, and I don't want to raise suspicions by being late."

With final adjustments to costumes and confirmation that their earpieces were functioning, the four friends prepared to embark on their undercover mission. Daisy, the last to leave, paused at the door for one final glance at her transformed reflection in the hallway mirror.

"Baroness Ekaterina Volkov," she murmured, testing the accent. "Let us see what secrets you can uncover."

The Conch Key Yacht Club occupied a prime position at the northern end of the harbor, its white clapboard exterior and deep blue trim embodying the nautical elegance that defined the establishment. Originally built in the 1920s as a private mansion for a shipping magnate, it had been converted to a club in the 1950s and had maintained its exclusivity ever since, though the membership requirements had gradually relaxed from "old money and older boats" to "new money and impressively large boats."

The annual fundraiser was the club's signature event, ostensibly raising money for maritime conservation but primarily serving as an opportunity for members to see and be seen in their finest attire. This year's theme, "Under the Sea," had resulted in decorations that transformed the grand ballroom into an underwater fantasy, with shimmering blue and green fabric draped from the ceiling, strategically placed spotlights creating a rippling water effect, and centerpieces featuring elaborate coral reef sculptures.

Rita arrived at the service entrance precisely at six o'clock, with Mae trailing behind. They were greeted by a harried-looking Marjorie

Wheatley, the club's regular caterer, whose usual impeccable appearance was showing signs of stress.

"Rita! Thank goodness you're here," Marjorie exclaimed, pulling her into the bustling kitchen. "Pierre is having a meltdown over the soufflés, and the ice sculptor delivered a mermaid that looks more like a manatee with identity issues."

"Deep breaths, Marjorie," Rita soothed, slipping easily into her role. "The soufflés will be fine. Tell Pierre to reduce the oven temperature by fifteen degrees and add an extra two minutes to the baking time. As for the ice sculpture, strategic placement under colored lighting can work wonders."

Marjorie nodded gratefully. "You're a lifesaver. And who's this?" she asked, noticing Mae hovering uncertainly in the doorway.

"This is my neighbor's niece, Mary," Rita improvised. "She's visiting from..." she hesitated momentarily.

"Iowa," Mae supplied in a voice so soft it was nearly inaudible. "I'm studying culinary arts and wanted to observe a professional operation." She pushed her fake glasses up her nose nervously.

"Well, we're short-staffed as usual, so you're welcome to help with bussing tables," Marjorie told her. "Check in with Stefan by the service bar for instructions." She turned back to Rita. "Now, about those crab puffs..."

As Rita immersed herself in kitchen crisis management, Mae slipped away to find Stefan. The service area was organized chaos, with staff in various stages of preparation arranging glassware, folding napkins, and reviewing table assignments. Mae located Stefan—a tall, severe-looking man with a clipboard and an air of perpetual disappointment—and introduced herself in her best 'invisible person' voice.

"Ah yes, the last-minute busser," Stefan sighed, as if her very existence was an inconvenience. "Your job is simple. Clear plates promptly but not obtrusively. Never reach across a guest. Never speak unless spoken to. And for the love of all that is holy, do not drop anything."

"Yes, sir," Mae replied meekly, secretly amused by how easily she had slipped into her role. Years of being underestimated had prepared her well for being overlooked.

"You'll be assigned to the east section, tables twelve through eighteen," Stefan continued, making a notation on his clipboard. "That includes the mayor's table and the Moneypenny party, so be extra vigilant."

Mae's pulse quickened at the mention of Councilwoman Moneypenny. "The Moneypenny party?" she asked innocently.

"Councilwoman Meredith Moneypenny," Stefan clarified with the air of someone explaining the obvious to a child. "She's hosting a table of VIPs, including Harold Jenkins, the attorney, and that French gallery owner, Fleur something-or-other. Important people, so don't embarrass us."

"I'll be very careful," Mae promised, mentally celebrating this stroke of luck. She would have direct access to at least two of their primary suspects all evening.

"See that you are," Stefan sniffed. "Now, familiarize yourself with the layout. Guests arrive in forty-five minutes."

As Mae dutifully began memorizing the table arrangements, her earpiece crackled to life.

"Testing, testing," came Babs' voice, slightly distorted by background noise. "Can anyone hear me?"

"Loud and clear," Rita murmured, presumably while measuring something in the kitchen. "Though I can't say much at the moment. Pierre is watching me like a hawk."

"I hear you too," Mae whispered, turning toward a corner to avoid being overheard. "I've been assigned to bus tables twelve through eighteen, including Meredith Moneypenny's."

"Excellent!" Babs exclaimed, causing Mae to wince at the volume. "I've just arrived and been designated as a cocktail server for the main floor. Did you know they're serving something called a 'Blue Lagoon Mystery' as tonight's signature drink? It comes with dry ice for a fog effect. Very dramatic."

"Try not to set anyone on fire," Rita advised dryly. "Daisy, are you connected?"

After a moment of silence, Daisy's voice came through, her Russian accent firmly in place even through the earpiece. "Da, I am here. Eugene is collecting me in fifteen minutes. He has promised to introduce me to several potential investment opportunities."

"Remember to ask about the resort project specifically," Babs coached. "And keep an eye out for anyone wearing ocean-themed jewelry."

"I am not new to investigations, Barbara," Daisy replied tartly. "Focus on your own assignment. And please try to maintain some level of decorum. 'Trixie' should not be doing body shots off the yacht club president."

"That was one time, and it was for charity," Babs protested. "Besides, he asked very nicely."

"Focus, everyone," Rita intervened. "The guests will be arriving soon. Report anything suspicious but keep communications brief. We don't want to attract attention."

With murmurs of agreement, they returned to their preparations. Mae, carefully arranging water glasses on a tray, glanced up as the kitchen doors swung open to admit a flurry of new arrivals—the additional serving staff for the evening. Among them was Babs, nearly unrecognizable in her Trixie persona, immediately commanding attention with her exaggerated platinum hairdo and confident strut.

"Hey there, kitchen crew!" she called out in a nasal voice entirely unlike her own. "Trixie's here to get this party started! Who's in charge of the booze?"

Stefan's pained expression suggested this wasn't the first time he'd encountered Trixie-type personalities. "Bar service is through there," he said stiffly, pointing toward a doorway. "Anton will assign your section."

"Fabulous!" Babs-as-Trixie exclaimed, sashaying past him with a wink. "Love the bow tie, honey. Very distinguished."

As she passed Mae, she gave an almost imperceptible nod of recognition before disappearing through the service door, already fully immersed in her character. Mae marveled at her friend's commitment to the role, mentally calculating how long it would be before Babs' theatrical instincts overwhelmed her investigative purpose.

"Three hours, tops," Rita murmured beside her, apparently following the same train of thought. "By then, she'll either have solved the case or started an impromptu cabaret."

"My money's on the cabaret," Mae replied with a small smile. "Though I have to admit, I'm rather enjoying this cloak-and-dagger business."

"Just remember to keep your eyes and ears open," Rita advised. "Particularly around Moneypenny's table. And if you get a chance to check for any jellyfish jewelry, even better."

Mae nodded, then quickly resumed her busser demeanor as Stefan approached with more instructions. The yacht club was beginning to come alive, with the first guests due to arrive at any moment. Somewhere out there, Daisy was transforming into a Russian baroness, preparing to infiltrate Conch Key's elite social circle. For better or worse, Operation Undercover was officially underway.

By seven-thirty, the Conch Key Yacht Club was in full swing. The ballroom glittered with the combined effect of the underwater-themed decorations and the assembled wealth of the town's elite, displayed in designer gowns, expensive watches, and jewelry that caught the light as guests mingled over cocktails.

Mae moved silently among the tables, clearing empty glasses and discarded napkins while keeping her ears tuned for any meaningful conversation. So far, she had overheard mostly typical party chatter—compliments on outfits, discussions of boat engine troubles, and mild gossip about absent club members. However, she had managed to confirm that Councilwoman Moneypenny was indeed wearing a charm bracelet partially concealed beneath the cuff of her elegant emerald silk blouse.

"Moneypenny accessory confirmed," she murmured into her earpiece as she passed near a large floral arrangement. "Can't see the charms clearly yet, but definitely a bracelet."

"Excellent observation," came Daisy's accented reply. "I have just arrived with Eugene. We are making our entrance now."

Mae glanced toward the main doors just in time to witness Daisy's arrival—a moment that could only be described as showstopping. Eugene Finch, almost unrecognizable in a well-tailored tuxedo with his usually wild hair tamed into submission, escorted Baroness Ekaterina Volkov with the proud bearing of a man who knows he has the most impressive date in the room.

And impressive she was. Daisy had fully inhabited her aristocratic persona, from her regal posture to the slight tilt of her chin that suggested she was accustomed to looking down at the world from a position of privilege. The midnight blue gown caught the light magnificently, and the small tiara in her upswept silver hair completed the image of old-world nobility.

A ripple of curiosity passed through the crowd as heads turned to observe the newcomer. Eugene, clearly enjoying his role, began making introductions to key club members, who responded with the slightly obsequious deference typically reserved for the very wealthy.

"Who is that with Eugene?" Mae overheard a woman nearby asking her companion.

"Some Russian baroness, apparently," the man replied in a lowered voice. "Felicity at the club office says she's worth millions from some family mining operation. Looking to invest in waterfront property."

"Well, with Brock gone, there's certainly opportunity," the woman observed. "I wonder if she knows about the resort project?"

Mae continued her methodical clearing of glasses, circling closer to catch more of the conversation.

"I imagine that's why Eugene brought her," the man said. "He's on the harbor commission, after all. Probably hoping to salvage the development now that Hamfist isn't around to shepherd it."

"Such a tragedy," the woman murmured unconvincingly. "Though between us, that resort would have been a monstrosity. Sixteen stories on our quaint little waterfront? It would have blocked everyone's view."

"Sixteen stories?" her companion echoed, surprised. "I thought the approved plan was for a maximum of eight."

"That was the original proposal," the woman confirmed, lowering her voice further. "But I heard from Meredith that Brock had secured a variance for a much larger structure. It was going to be announced after the final approval next week."

This was new information. Mae carefully memorized it as she moved away, not wanting to linger too obviously. Into her earpiece, she whispered, "Potential motive: Brock apparently doubled the resort's height with a secret variance. Would have blocked views and potentially angered waterfront property owners."

"Interesting," came Rita's soft reply. "The kitchen staff is buzzing about Harold Jenkins arriving with red-rimmed eyes. Apparently he's been emotional all day, telling people Brock's death is 'worse than they know.'"

"Jenkins is at table fourteen," Mae reported. "I'll pay special attention."

Meanwhile, across the room, Babs was in her element as Trixie the cocktail waitress, delivering blue specialty drinks with theatrical flair and extracting information with practiced ease.

"Another Blue Lagoon Mystery for you, handsome?" she cooed to an elderly gentleman who seemed equally captivated by the drink and her décolletage. "Careful with this one—it's got quite a kick. Just like me!" She punctuated this with a wink that made the man chuckle appreciatively.

"Don't mind if I do, darling," he replied, accepting the foggy blue concoction. "Been a day for strong drinks, what with poor Brock's passing."

"Oh, I heard about that," Babs-as-Trixie replied, wide-eyed with manufactured interest. "So sad. Were you friends with him?"

"Business associates," the man clarified, taking a substantial sip of his drink. "Captain Bob Crustybutt, at your service. Got the slip right next to his at the marina."

Babs nearly dropped her tray. Captain Crustybutt—one of their primary persons of interest—had practically fallen into her lap. "How fascinating," she gushed, quickly recovering. "I bet you know all the marina gossip. Did you see Mr. Hamfist last night, by any chance? I heard he was out on the water, which seems odd for someone afraid of swimming."

The captain's weathered face registered surprise. "Now how would a pretty little thing like you know about Brock's aquaphobia?"

Babs realized her mistake instantly. Trixie wouldn't have such specific knowledge of Brock. "Oh, one of the other girls mentioned it earlier," she improvised. "Said he was a big tipper because he was so nervous around water. Thought it was funny, him building beach resorts and all."

The captain seemed to accept this explanation, nodding sagely. "Ironic, ain't it? Man made millions off of oceanfront properties but couldn't stand to get his feet wet." He took another long drink. "And for the record, I did see him last night, though I ain't supposed to be talking about it. Police business and all that."

"Oh, I'm not one to gossip," Babs assured him with a smile that suggested exactly the opposite. "Just curious, is all. Must have been something important to get him out on the water, huh?"

Captain Crustybutt leaned closer, his breath smelling strongly of the blue cocktail. "Between you and me, sweetheart, I think he finally grew a conscience. Too little, too late, if you ask me."

"A conscience?" Babs prompted, mentally filing this information.

"About that monstrosity he was planning to build," the captain elaborated. "Sixteen stories of concrete and glass, blocking the sunset for half the town. Been fighting him on it for years, refusing to sell my land. Then yesterday, out of the blue, he comes to me with this crazy new offer."

"For your beachfront property?" Babs asked, trying to hide her excitement at this confirmation of their information.

"That's right. But here's the kicker—" The captain broke off as a commotion near the entrance caught his attention. "Well, I'll be damned. If it isn't Candi Bubbleshine herself, making an entrance."

Babs turned to see Candi sweeping into the room in a gown that appeared to be constructed primarily of sequins and wishful thinking. The dress—if it could be called that—resembled a mermaid's tail in shades of iridescent blue and green, with a bodice that defied both gravity and good taste. Her platinum blonde hair was piled impossibly high and adorned with starfish-shaped hair clips, while her makeup featured rhinestones artfully applied around her eyes like scales.

"Subtle as a hurricane," Babs murmured into her earpiece. "Candi has arrived dressed as what appears to be a Vegas interpretation of The Little Mermaid."

"Stay focused, Babs," came Daisy's accented reply. "I've made contact with Meredith Moneypenny. She's wearing the charm bracelet, and I can confirm one of the charms is indeed a jellyfish with gemstone tentacles. Attempting to get closer look."

Babs turned back to Captain Crustybutt, determined to pick up where they'd left off. "You were saying about Brock's offer for your property...?"

But the captain had been distracted by Candi's dramatic entrance and the subsequent ripple of reactions through the crowd. "Tell you what, sweetheart," he said, finishing his drink and handing her the empty glass. "Bring me another one of these concoctions, and I'll tell you the rest of that story. It's a doozy."

"You got it, Captain," Babs promised, adding a little extra sway to her walk as she headed for the bar. Into her earpiece, she reported,

"Captain Crustybutt has information about a 'crazy new offer' Brock made for his property yesterday. Getting him another drink to loosen his tongue further."

"Well done," Rita responded. "Be careful not to overdo the alcohol. We need him coherent."

"Please," Babs scoffed. "I was extracting secrets from tipsy theater donors when you were still perfecting your pie crust. Trust the process."

Across the room, Daisy was deep in conversation with Councilwoman Meredith Moneypenny, who had been eager to introduce herself to the mysterious baroness almost as soon as she'd arrived. Draped in an elegant emerald silk ensemble that complemented her honey-blonde bob, the councilwoman exuded the practiced charm of a career politician.

"Baroness Volkov, what a pleasure to welcome you to Conch Key," Meredith was saying, her smile not quite reaching her eyes. "Eugene mentioned you might be interested in investment opportunities in our little paradise."

"Da, this is so," Daisy replied, her Russian accent growing more convincing with every exchange. "I find your American coastal properties most... how you say... promising. Especially for exclusive wellness resorts."

Meredith's interest visibly intensified. "What a fascinating coincidence. Our town was just on the verge of approving a significant luxury resort development." She lowered her voice confidentially. "Unfortunately, the principal developer passed away unexpectedly, but the project itself remains viable. The right investor could step in quite seamlessly."

"Is tragedy," Daisy commiserated, noting how quickly Meredith had pivoted to business opportunities in the wake of Brock's death. "This developer, he was friend of yours, no?"

"A valued colleague," Meredith corrected smoothly. "Brock Hamfist and I worked closely on numerous community improvement initiatives." She touched her bracelet absently—a nervous tell that Daisy immediately registered.

"This is beautiful piece," Daisy remarked, gesturing to the bracelet. "May I see closer?"

Meredith hesitated fractionally before extending her wrist with a stiff smile. "Just a little something I picked up in Miami. I have a weakness for ocean-themed jewelry."

Daisy examined the bracelet with exaggerated interest, mentally cataloging the charms: a stylized wave, a seahorse, a sand dollar, a starfish, and—most importantly—a jellyfish crafted in silver with tiny gemstones at the ends of its tentacles. The craftsmanship was exquisite, and the jellyfish charm appeared identical to the description of the one found near Brock's body.

"Exquisite workmanship," Daisy commented. "Especially this little jellyfish. Is unusual choice, no? Many people fear such creatures."

"I find beauty in the dangerous," Meredith replied with a practiced laugh. "Much like in business. Speaking of which..." She deftly changed the subject. "If you're genuinely interested in the resort project, I'd be happy to arrange a meeting with our town attorney. The paperwork is quite advanced, and with the right investor, we could maintain our original timeline."

"So eager," Daisy observed, sipping her champagne. "One might think town is desperate for this development."

Meredith's smile tightened almost imperceptibly. "Not desperate, Baroness. Simply progressive. We understand the economic benefits of judicious growth."

"And personal benefits, perhaps?" Daisy suggested innocently. "I understand such projects often provide... how you say... advantages for those who facilitate them."

A flash of alarm crossed Meredith's features before she regained her composure. "I'm not sure what you're implying, but in Conch Key, we pride ourselves on transparent governance. My only interest is in the prosperity of our community."

"Of course," Daisy backpedaled gracefully. "Please, do not be offended. In my country, politics and business are more... entwined."

Before Meredith could respond, they were interrupted by Harold Jenkins, the attorney Mae had identified earlier. In his mid-sixties, with thinning gray hair and wire-rimmed glasses, he looked every inch the small-town lawyer—except for his reddened eyes and slightly disheveled appearance, uncharacteristic for a man known for his meticulous presentation.

"Councilwoman," he greeted Meredith with a curt nod before turning to Daisy. "I understand you're interested in real estate investment. Harold Jenkins, town attorney." He extended his hand with a slight tremor that didn't escape Daisy's notice.

"Baroness Ekaterina Volkov," Daisy replied, accepting his handshake. "A pleasure."

"Harold," Meredith interjected smoothly, "the Baroness was just expressing interest in the resort project. I mentioned you might be able to provide some insights on the current status."

Jenkins's expression tightened. "Yes, well, that situation has become considerably more complex since this morning." He turned to Daisy. "Forgive me, Baroness, but this may not be the best time to discuss investment opportunities. There are... complications that need to be resolved."

"Complications?" Meredith echoed, her tone sharpening. "What complications? The council emergency session this morning clarified that the project would proceed as planned, with Brock's partners assuming primary development responsibilities."

"That was before I received the amended paperwork," Jenkins replied in a lowered voice. "Meredith, we need to speak privately about this. It's not appropriate for a public venue."

"Nonsense," Meredith insisted, though Daisy noticed her knuckles whitening around her champagne flute. "The Baroness is a potential investor. Transparency is essential."

"Perhaps I should leave you to discuss business matters," Daisy suggested diplomatically.

"No, please stay," Meredith insisted, laying a hand on Daisy's arm. "Harold tends toward excessive caution. Whatever concerns he has can certainly be addressed in general terms."

Jenkins hesitated, clearly uncomfortable, before speaking in a careful, measured tone. "Very well. In general terms, it appears that Brock made significant alterations to the project proposal shortly before his death. Alterations that fundamentally change the nature and scope of the development." He directed a pointed look at Meredith. "Alterations that directly contradict the assurances made to certain council members."

Meredith's face drained of color. "That's impossible. The plans were finalized weeks ago."

"Nevertheless," Jenkins continued, "I have signed and notarized documents indicating otherwise. They were delivered to my office yesterday, with explicit instructions to present them at today's partnership meeting—which, of course, Brock did not live to attend."

"What kind of alterations?" Daisy inquired innocently.

Jenkins turned to her with a weary expression. "Rather than a sixteen-story luxury resort with premium shopping and a casino, the amended plans call for a modest eco-resort with a maximum height of four stories and a marine research facility dedicated to studying climate change impacts on coral reefs." He delivered this information with the gravity of someone announcing a terminal diagnosis.

"That's absurd!" Meredith exclaimed, her political composure cracking. "Brock would never—" She stopped herself abruptly, aware that she was attracting attention from nearby guests.

"As I said," Jenkins repeated quietly, "we should discuss this privately."

"Eco-resort sounds most interesting," Daisy commented, watching Meredith's reaction closely. "Very fashionable in Europe now. Wealthy travelers pay premium for sustainable luxury."

"It's financial suicide," Meredith snapped, before catching herself and softening her tone. "Forgive me, Baroness. This is unexpected news. The return on investment for an eco-resort would be significantly lower than our original projections."

"For investors, perhaps," Jenkins noted. "But not necessarily for the town. The amended plan includes substantial tax benefits and infrastructure improvements."

Meredith's expression hardened. "Harold, I need to see these alleged documents immediately. This sounds suspiciously like Gladys Pickle's influence."

"Actually," Jenkins corrected her, "Gladys was as surprised as anyone when I briefed the Conservation Crusaders this afternoon. She had no prior knowledge of Brock's change of heart."

"This is ridiculous," Meredith declared, emptying her champagne glass in a single unladylike gulp. "Brock and I spoke just two nights ago. He gave no indication of these changes."

"And yet, here we are," Jenkins replied with surprising firmness. "The documents are legally binding, Meredith. Brock's signature, with witnesses."

"We'll see about that," Meredith muttered, her carefully maintained facade crumbling further.

Into her concealed earpiece, Daisy murmured, "Significant development. Brock apparently altered the resort plans from luxury high-rise to eco-friendly low-rise. Meredith Moneypenny extremely agitated by this news."

Meanwhile, at the bar, Babs was delivering a fresh Blue Lagoon Mystery to Captain Crustybutt, who had settled onto a barstool with the air of a man prepared to tell sea stories until dawn.

"Here you go, Captain," she announced cheerfully. "Now, you were saying something about a crazy offer from Brock Hamfist?"

"Right you are, Trixie," the captain confirmed, accepting the drink with a nod of appreciation. "So there I was, sitting on my porch watching the sunset like I've done every evening for forty years, when up walks Brock Hamfist himself." He took a substantial sip of his cocktail. "Now, you gotta understand, this man has been trying to buy my land for five years. Offered me everything from cash to condos to a yacht. I always said no on principle. That little strip of beach has been in my family since my grandfather built the house in 1938."

"A man of principle," Babs commented approvingly. "Rare these days."

"Damn straight," the captain agreed, warming to her appreciation. "So I'm expecting another song and dance about how his resort can't properly function without my 'key parcel,' as he calls it. But instead, he sits down uninvited, looks me straight in the eye, and says, 'Bob, I've been an idiot. I want to buy your land not to build on it, but to preserve it.'"

"Preserve it?" Babs repeated, genuinely surprised.

"That's what I said!" the captain exclaimed, gesturing expansively. "Turns out, he wanted to create some kind of protected turtle nesting sanctuary as part of a completely redesigned eco-resort. Said he'd had a 'reckoning' after nearly drowning during a fishing trip last month. Something about seeing a sea turtle while he was underwater and having an epiphany about legacy and destruction."

"How fascinating," Babs remarked, filing away this new information. "So did you agree to sell?"

The captain chuckled. "Well now, that's the kicker. He wasn't offering me less money—in fact, he was offering more than before. But instead of giving me the boot, his deal included a lifetime residency right. I could stay in my house until I kicked the bucket, and then the property would become part of the sanctuary."

"Sounds almost too good to be true," Babs observed.

"That's exactly what I told him," the captain nodded. "Said I needed time to think it over, maybe have my lawyer review the offer. He seemed mighty anxious to get my answer, though. Said something about 'time being of the essence' and how 'certain parties wouldn't be happy' with his new direction."

"Did he say which parties?" Babs asked casually.

The captain leaned forward conspiratorially. "He didn't name names, but he did say, 'When you go against the money, you better watch your back.' Made me wonder what kind of hot water he'd gotten himself into."

"And did you give him an answer?" Babs prompted.

"Told him I'd sleep on it," the captain replied. "Was gonna call him this morning with my decision." His weathered face fell slightly. "Never got the chance."

"And what would your answer have been?" Babs asked softly.

The captain was silent for a moment, staring into his blue drink. "I was gonna say yes," he admitted finally. "First time in five years. Something about the look in his eyes—man seemed genuinely changed. Like he'd seen something that scared him straight." He shook his head slowly. "Shame he didn't live to see it through."

Babs patted his arm sympathetically. "Sounds like Mr. Hamfist was making some big changes."

"Biggest change was in here," the captain said, tapping his chest. "Man actually apologized to me. Said he was sorry for trying to bulldoze everyone to get his way. Never thought I'd hear those words from Brock 'The Bulldozer' Hamfist."

"Did he mention anyone else he needed to speak with about these changes?" Babs inquired.

"Mentioned something about meeting a business partner out at Turtle Rock later that night," the captain recalled. "Said it was the perfect place to 'seal the new direction,' whatever that meant."

Babs nearly dropped her serving tray. "Turtle Rock? In the bay?"

"That's right," the captain confirmed. "It's that big formation about half a mile offshore, part of the marine sanctuary. Popular spot for the glass-bottom boats because of all the fish that gather there."

"How interesting," Babs managed, her mind racing. Into her earpiece, she whispered, "Captain Crustybutt confirms Brock was planning to meet someone at Turtle Rock last night—the same place where Bobby Glowacki said Brock and an unidentified woman transferred to another boat."

"Ask if he took his boat out last night," came Rita's swift reply.

Babs turned back to the captain with her brightest Trixie smile. "Say, Captain, this is probably a silly question, but did you happen to take your boat out last night? I'm just trying to picture where this Turtle Rock is."

The captain's jovial expression faltered momentarily. "Now that's a peculiar question from a cocktail waitress," he remarked, studying her with suddenly sharper eyes.

Babs backpedaled quickly. "Oh, I'm just curious about everything! New to town, trying to learn all the local landmarks. The bartender was telling me there's great night fishing around here."

The captain seemed to accept this explanation, though his gaze remained somewhat suspicious. "As a matter of fact, I did take my skiff out last night. Had a bit of insomnia after Hamfist's visit, thought some night fishing might clear my head."

"Catch anything good?" Babs asked with manufactured enthusiasm.

"Nothing worth keeping," the captain replied cryptically. "Now, if you'll excuse me, I need to pay my respects to the widow."

"Widow?" Babs echoed, confused. "I thought Mr. Hamfist was divorced."

"Figure of speech," the captain amended, rising unsteadily from his barstool. "Meant his lady friend, the sequined one preparing to serenade us." He nodded toward the small stage where Candi Bubbleshine was conferring with the event's sound technician, her mermaid gown catching the light with every animated gesture.

"Of course," Babs nodded. "Can I get you another drink first?"

"Best quit while I'm ahead," the captain decided, patting his stomach. "Getting too old for multiple Mysteries in one evening."

As he ambled away, Babs murmured into her earpiece, "Captain Crustybutt admits to taking his boat out last night, supposedly for 'night fishing.' Claims to have caught 'nothing worth keeping.'"

"That puts him at the scene," Daisy's accented voice replied softly. "And potentially connects him to Brock's final hours."

"But it doesn't explain the mystery woman Bobby mentioned," Rita pointed out. "Or why Brock would be meeting anyone at Turtle Rock in the middle of the night."

Their speculation was interrupted by the tinkling of a glass, signaling a call for attention. The yacht club's president, Bertram Hollister, had taken the small stage, microphone in hand.

"Ladies and gentlemen, distinguished guests," he began, his voice carrying over the gradually quieting crowd. "Welcome to the Conch Key Yacht Club's annual fundraiser. As you know, this year's event takes on a bittersweet tone as we mourn the sudden loss of one of our community's most prominent businessmen, Brock Hamfist."

A murmur of acknowledgment passed through the assembly.

"Brock was to have been our guest of honor tonight, in recognition of his contributions to the club's marina expansion project," Hollister continued. "In his absence, we have decided to dedicate this evening to his memory and to proceed with the entertainment he personally selected for your enjoyment." He gestured toward the stage. "Please welcome the talented and beautiful Candi Bubbleshine, performing her signature cabaret act, 'Under the Sea: A Sequined Tribute.'"

Polite applause greeted Candi as she took the stage, blowing kisses to the audience with the practiced air of someone who had performed for far less appreciative crowds. As the lights dimmed and the first notes of a vaguely tropical melody filled the room, Mae took advantage of the distraction to circulate among the tables, clearing appetizer plates and eavesdropping with quiet efficiency.

She paused near Harold Jenkins' seat, where the attorney was engaged in intense whispered conversation with a young woman Mae recognized as his paralegal, Samantha.

"...absolutely certain the signatures are genuine?" Jenkins was asking, his voice barely audible over Candi's increasingly enthusiastic vocal performance.

"Verified by both witnesses and the notary," Samantha confirmed. "It's legitimate, Harold. He changed everything—the design, the purpose, the ownership structure. The new documents establish a non-profit trust to manage the property, with strict development limitations."

Jenkins ran a hand through his thinning hair. "Meredith's going to have a conniption. The kickbacks she was expecting from the casino licensing alone..."

"That's not our problem," Samantha replied firmly. "Our duty is to execute our client's wishes, regardless of who it disappoints."

"Yes, but our client was possibly murdered hours after making these changes," Jenkins hissed. "Don't you find that timing suspicious?"

Mae nearly dropped the glass she was pretending to collect. Into her earpiece, she whispered, "Jenkins suspects murder, potentially connected to Brock's project changes. Mentioned kickbacks to Meredith from casino licensing."

"Excellent intelligence," Daisy responded. "I've extricated myself from Meredith, who's gone to make a 'private phone call' after learning about the project changes. Looking distinctly unhappy."

On stage, Candi had launched into a remarkably aggressive rendition of a mermaid-themed song, complete with choreography that threatened the structural integrity of her gown. The audience watched with expressions ranging from fascination to horror as she belted out the chorus while attempting a shimmy that sent several sequins flying into the front row.

"Remind me never to complain about community theater again," Babs murmured into her earpiece as she circulated with a tray of champagne. "This makes our production of 'Cats' look like the Royal Ballet."

"Focus, Babs," Rita admonished. "I've just overheard something concerning in the kitchen. The chef mentioned seeing Meredith Moneypenny at the marina last night, 'dressed for business, not pleasure,' according to him."

"The marina?" Daisy repeated softly. "That potentially places her near Brock during his final hours."

"And potentially identifies her as the mystery woman Bobby mentioned," Babs added. "Dark hair, elegant clothes—fits his description."

"Ladies," Mae interjected urgently. "Ziggy Hamfist just arrived. And he appears to be intoxicated."

All four directed their attention to the entrance, where Brock's son had indeed appeared—swaying slightly and dressed in the same hemp clothing he'd worn at The Salty Mermaid earlier, now accessorized with what appeared to be a protest sign hastily converted into a placard reading "THE TRUTH ABOUT BROCK HAMFIST" in uneven lettering.

"Oh dear," Daisy murmured. "This has all the makings of a scene."

She wasn't wrong. Ziggy stumbled into the ballroom, looking around wildly until his gaze settled on Candi, still performing her enthusiastic number on stage. His face darkened as he raised his sign higher.

"Hey!" he shouted over the music. "Hey, everybody! Want to know the truth about my dad?"

The music faltered as Candi spotted him, her professional smile slipping momentarily before she signaled the band to continue playing. The assembled guests turned toward the disruption with expressions of collective disapproval.

"Young man," Bertram Hollister approached cautiously, "this is a private function. If you don't have an invitation—"

"Invitation?" Ziggy laughed bitterly. "I'm Brock Hamfist's son. That's my invitation." He raised his voice again. "Did you all know my dad had a complete change of heart about his precious resort? Decided to turn it into some kind of eco-friendly turtle paradise instead of a concrete monstrosity?"

A ripple of whispers passed through the crowd. Daisy noticed Meredith Moneypenny returning from her "phone call," her face pale with barely suppressed fury as she registered Ziggy's presence and announcement.

"Mr. Hamfist," Hollister tried again, "this is hardly the appropriate venue for—"

"It's the perfect venue!" Ziggy insisted, his words slightly slurred. "All of you fancy people were invested in my dad's big resort plans, right? Well, surprise! He changed his mind. Found a conscience. And I'm pretty sure that's what got him killed."

A collective gasp rose from the assembled guests. On stage, Candi had stopped singing, her heavily made-up eyes wide with shock.

"That's enough!" Meredith's authoritative voice cut through the murmurs as she strode forward. "Ziggy, you're clearly distraught and intoxicated. This isn't the time or place for wild accusations."

"Wild accusations?" Ziggy repeated incredulously. "He told me himself! The night before he died, he said he was 'making changes' and 'setting things right.' Said he'd had a wake-up call and wasn't going to be remembered as the guy who destroyed the coastline." He swayed slightly, pointing an accusatory finger at the councilwoman. "And I bet some people weren't too happy about that, were they, Meredith?"

At this direct confrontation, Meredith's political mask slipped entirely, revealing naked fury beneath. "How dare you!" she hissed. "Your father's death was a tragic accident. These conspiracy theories are disrespectful to his memory and potentially libelous."

"Accident?" Ziggy scoffed. "Dad was terrified of water. He wouldn't go near it unless he had a really good reason." He looked around the room wildly. "Who had the most to lose from his change of heart? Who stood to make a fortune from those casino kickbacks?"

Meredith's face went from flushed to ashen in an instant. "I don't know what you're talking about," she stammered, though her expression suggested otherwise.

From her position near the stage, Babs noticed something alarming—Candi Bubbleshine had abandoned her performance and was edging toward a side exit, her mermaid gown hampering her escape attempt. Making a split-second decision, Babs intercepted her, deliberately tripping and sending her tray of champagne glasses crashing to the floor directly in Candi's path.

"Oh my goodness!" Babs exclaimed in her exaggerated Trixie voice. "How clumsy of me! Let me help you, honey." She grabbed Candi's arm under the pretense of steadying her, effectively blocking her retreat.

"Let go," Candi hissed, her stage smile vanishing. "I need some air."

"Running off so soon?" Babs inquired innocently. "Just when things are getting interesting? That's not very professional of Conch Key's premier entertainer."

Candi's heavily mascaraed eyes narrowed suspiciously. "Do I know you? You look familiar."

Before Babs could respond, the confrontation between Ziggy and Meredith escalated.

"I want to know where you were last night, Councilwoman," Ziggy demanded loudly. "Were you out on the water with my dad? Were you one of the last people to see him alive?"

"This is outrageous," Meredith spluttered, looking around for support. "Someone call security!"

"I think that's an excellent suggestion," came a new voice from the entrance. Chief Mortimer Crabbitz stood in the doorway, resplendent in his dress uniform, his perpetually sunburned face contrasting sharply with the white of his collar. "In fact, I'd like to speak with several of you about your whereabouts last night."

A hush fell over the room as the chief's gaze swept deliberately from Meredith to Candi to Captain Crustybutt, who had been attempting to blend into the background near a large decorative coral arrangement.

"Ladies and gentlemen," Morty announced, his voice carrying in the sudden silence, "I apologize for interrupting your evening. However, new evidence has come to light regarding Brock Hamfist's death, and I need to ask a few individuals to accompany me to the station for questioning."

"What new evidence?" Meredith demanded, her composure fracturing further.

Morty fixed her with a steady look. "The medical examiner's final report indicates that Mr. Hamfist did not, in fact, die by accidental drowning." He paused for dramatic effect. "There were traces of a powerful sedative in his system, and the marks on his face and hands have been identified as consistent with contact burns from a specific type of stun gun."

The collective gasp from the crowd was almost theatrical in its intensity.

"In other words," Morty concluded grimly, "Brock Hamfist was murdered."

In the ensuing chaos—Candi's dramatic swoon, Meredith's stuttering protests, Captain Crustybutt's sudden interest in examining the ceiling, and Ziggy's vindicated exclamations—Mae caught Daisy's eye across the room. Baroness Ekaterina Volkov gave the slightest nod, the gesture barely perceptible but unmistakable in its meaning.

Their mission had officially transformed from gathering intelligence to identifying a killer. And based on the reactions they'd just witnessed, the list of suspects had narrowed considerably.

Into her earpiece, Daisy murmured, "Ladies, I believe it's time for phase two of our investigation."

What she didn't realize was that the killer had already identified a new threat—four meddling women who had seen and heard too much. And before the night was over, one of them would find herself in mortal danger.

Chapter Five

Dangerous Waters

The aftermath of Chief Crabbitz's murder announcement transformed the elegant yacht club fundraiser into a scene of barely controlled chaos. The once-dignified crowd now resembled a disturbed ant colony, breaking into clusters of frantic whispers and shocked exclamations while casting suspicious glances at their fellow attendees.

At the center of the storm stood Meredith Moneypenny, her political poise deserting her as she argued vehemently with Chief Crabbitz, her perfectly manicured hands gesturing with increasing agitation.

"This is absurd, Morty!" she hissed, her voice carrying despite her attempt at discretion. "You can't possibly think I had anything to do with Brock's death. We were partners in this development!"

"I don't recall accusing you of anything, Councilwoman," Morty replied evenly, though his sunburned complexion had deepened to an alarming shade of crimson. "But since you've brought it up, perhaps you wouldn't mind explaining where you were last night between ten and midnight?"

Meredith's mouth opened and closed several times before she found her voice. "I was... at home. Working on council business."

"Can anyone verify that?" Morty pressed.

"I live alone," Meredith snapped. "As you well know."

"Actually," a melodious French-accented voice interjected, "that is not entirely accurate, chérie."

All heads turned toward the source—a slender woman with an elegant silver bob and impeccable posture who had appeared beside Meredith. She was dressed in a simple but exquisitely tailored black gown that screamed Parisian design, with her only adornment being a striking pendant in the shape of a stylized wave.

"Fleur," Meredith said weakly. "I didn't see you arrive."

"Evidently," Fleur DuBois replied with a small, enigmatic smile. "Chief Crabbitz, I believe I can assist with Meredith's alibi. She was with me from nine o'clock until approximately eleven-thirty last night. At my gallery. We were... discussing art acquisitions."

The emphasis she placed on the last phrase made it clear to everyone within earshot that "art acquisitions" was a euphemism for something considerably more personal.

"I see," Morty said, making a notation in his small notebook. "And after eleven-thirty?"

"Meredith returned to her home," Fleur continued smoothly. "I received a text message from her at midnight confirming her safe arrival."

"You have proof of this text?" Morty asked.

"Mais oui," Fleur confirmed, retrieving an elegant smartphone from her clutch. "I keep all messages."

From her position near the dessert station, Mae observed this exchange with fascination, noticing how Meredith's complexion had shifted from paper-white to flaming red within seconds. Into her earpiece, she whispered, "Meredith has an alibi for part of the critical timeframe. Fleur DuBois confirms they were together until eleven-thirty."

"That still leaves thirty minutes unaccounted for," Daisy's accented voice responded softly. "Plenty of time for a quick boat trip, especially if she was already dressed for the occasion and had transportation arranged."

Across the room, Babs continued her strategic positioning near Candi Bubbleshine, who had recovered from her dramatic swoon and was now perched on a chair, fanning herself vigorously with a cocktail napkin.

"Good thing I caught you, hon," Babs cooed in her Trixie persona. "That fancy dress isn't made for fainting. You might have popped right out of it!"

Candi shot her a venomous look. "I need a drink. A real one, not that blue tourist trap in a glass."

"Coming right up," Babs promised brightly, though she had no intention of leaving Candi unattended. "Vodka martini, extra dirty?"

"How did you know?" Candi asked suspiciously.

"Lucky guess," Babs replied with a wink. "You look like a woman who appreciates things dirty." Raising her voice slightly, she called to a passing server, "Honey, be a doll and fetch a vodka martini for our star performer? She's had quite a shock, poor thing."

As the server hurried off, Babs settled into the chair beside Candi, assuming the pose of a sympathetic listener. "So awful about Mr. Hamfist being murdered! And you were so close to him. You must be devastated."

"Devastated," Candi echoed mechanically, her gaze fixed on Chief Crabbitz, who had now moved on to questioning Captain Crustybutt. "We were going to announce our engagement next week."

This was news to Babs, and based on the surprised murmur in her earpiece, to the others as well. "Engagement? How romantic! Did he propose on bended knee?"

"Not exactly," Candi admitted, momentarily distracted by the conversation. "It was more of an understanding. He said once the resort project was finalized, we'd make it official." Her heavily mascared eyes narrowed. "But now I'm hearing he was planning to change everything. That can't be right."

"Oh?" Babs feigned innocence. "What do you mean, sweetie?"

Candi leaned closer, her voice dropping to a conspiratorial whisper that carried the distinct scent of tequila. "Brockie wouldn't change the resort plans. Not after all our work. We were going to have a nightclub—The Sugar Shack—where I would perform exclusively." She gestured emphatically, nearly destabilizing her precarious bodice. "It was going to launch my career! No more small-town gigs and charity events. I'd have been a star."

"That sounds fabulous," Babs agreed, mentally adding career disappointment to Candi's potential motives. "When did you last see him, honey? Before... you know." She made a dramatic drowning gesture.

"At the festival," Candi replied automatically. "Around nine. He said he had a meeting and would call me later." Her carefully constructed façade cracked slightly. "But he never did."

"Did he say who the meeting was with?" Babs pressed gently.

Candi's expression darkened. "No. But I saw him talking to that French gallery snob afterward." She nodded toward Fleur. "They looked pretty intense."

Interesting, Babs thought. Fleur DuBois seemed to be popping up in multiple witness accounts. "And where did you go after the festival, sweetie?"

Candi's gaze sharpened with sudden suspicion. "Why do you care? Who are you, really? You don't look like any cocktail waitress I've ever seen."

Babs realized she'd pushed too far. Time for damage control. "Just making conversation, honey! Besides, I'm new in town—temporary staff for the event. Trying to learn all the local gossip." She patted Candi's sequined arm. "Here comes your martini!"

The arrival of the drink provided a welcome distraction, and Babs used the moment to murmur into her earpiece, "Candi claims she and Brock were planning to announce their engagement next week. She's upset about the resort changes, particularly the loss of her planned nightclub venue. Also says she saw Brock talking to Fleur after the festival, before his 'meeting.'"

"The plot thickens," came Rita's response from the kitchen. "I've just overheard something interesting from the catering staff. Apparently, Brock received a mysterious package at his office yesterday morning—delivered by special courier. His assistant said he locked himself in his office after opening it and canceled all appointments for the rest of the day."

"Could be connected to his sudden change of heart," Daisy suggested. "Perhaps evidence of something that prompted his reformation."

"Or blackmail," Mae added softly.

Meanwhile, at the opposite end of the ballroom, Chief Crabbitz had cornered Ziggy Hamfist, who had been attempting to make a discreet exit following his dramatic accusations.

"Not so fast, young man," Morty said, blocking Ziggy's path. "You seem to have some strong opinions about your father's death. Care to share the basis for these theories?"

Ziggy's previous bravado had deflated considerably, leaving him looking more like a confused young man than an angry protester. "It's just... it doesn't make sense, man. Dad was terrified of water. He wouldn't go out on a boat at night unless he had a really good reason."

"And what reason might that have been?" Morty pressed.

Ziggy ran a hand through his tangled dreadlocks. "I don't know, exactly. But he told me he was 'making changes' and 'setting things right.' Said he'd had some kind of wake-up call." He glanced around nervously. "Look, can we talk somewhere else? Everyone's staring."

"My office, first thing tomorrow morning," Morty agreed, scribbling something on a card and handing it to Ziggy. "Don't leave town."

As Ziggy nodded and shuffled toward the exit, Daisy made a swift decision. Maintaining her baroness persona, she glided elegantly across the room to intercept him, positioning herself as if examining a particularly interesting coral centerpiece.

"Young man," she called softly as he passed. "A moment, if you please."

Ziggy stopped, his bloodshot eyes regarding her warily. "Do I know you?"

"Baroness Ekaterina Volkov," Daisy introduced herself, extending a bejeweled hand. "I am... how you say... investor in sustainable development. Your father's new eco-resort concept interests me greatly."

"Eco-resort?" Ziggy repeated, his suspicion giving way to curiosity. "So it's true? Dad really was changing the plans?"

"Da, this is what I am told," Daisy confirmed, noting how Ziggy's demeanor had shifted from defensive to engaged. "Most fascinating transformation. Perhaps we could discuss further? I have great interest in preserving natural shorelines."

Ziggy's eyes lit up with unexpected enthusiasm. "Really? That's... that's actually what I've been trying to do for years. Dad always thought I was just being a hippie troublemaker, but there's solid science behind marine preservation."

"Perhaps," Daisy suggested, lowering her voice conspiratorially, "your father came to appreciate your... perspective? Before his unfortunate demise?"

"Maybe," Ziggy admitted, a flicker of emotion crossing his features. "We fought that night, but it was different somehow. He actually listened for once." He shook his head in bewilderment. "Said something about having seen 'the other side' and not wanting to leave a legacy of destruction. I thought he was being dramatic, you know? But now I'm wondering..."

"Wondering what, precisely?" Daisy prompted gently.

"If someone didn't want him changing his plans," Ziggy finished, his voice dropping to a whisper. "There's a lot of money at stake with that resort. And Dad had powerful partners."

"Partners such as...?" Daisy let the question hang delicately.

Ziggy glanced over his shoulder to where Meredith Moneypenny was still engaged in intense discussion with Chief Crabbitz and Fleur DuBois. "I probably shouldn't say more. But follow the money, right? That's what they say in the movies."

"Indeed," Daisy nodded sagely. "Money leaves trail. Like breadcrumbs."

"Exactly," Ziggy agreed. "Look, I should go before I get into more trouble. But if you're serious about sustainable development, maybe we could talk sometime?" He fumbled in his pocket and produced a crumpled business card that identified him as "Zigmund Hamfist, Environmental Consultant and Hemp Artisan."

"I shall treasure this," Daisy assured him, accepting the card with regal grace. "Do be careful, Mr. Hamfist. Truth can be... dangerous commodity."

Ziggy nodded solemnly before continuing his exit, looking somewhat steadier than when he had entered. Daisy watched him go, then murmured into her earpiece, "Ziggy confirms his father spoke of having seen 'the other side' and not wanting to leave a 'legacy of destruction.' Suggests following the money to identify who benefited from the original resort plan."

"The casino kickbacks Jenkins mentioned?" Mae suggested.

"Among other potential profits," Daisy agreed. "We need to—"

Her sentence was cut short by the sudden dimming of lights throughout the ballroom, followed by an announcement from Bertram Hollister, who had returned to the stage looking considerably more harried than during his earlier introduction.

"Ladies and gentlemen," he began, his voice strained with forced joviality, "in light of... recent developments, we will be concluding our formal program slightly earlier than planned. Chief Crabbitz has assured me there is no immediate cause for concern, but he has requested that several individuals remain for brief questioning." He consulted a note card. "The yacht club grounds remain open for your enjoyment, and the bar service will continue on the terrace. Meanwhile, please join me in thanking our generous sponsors for this evening's event."

A smattering of uncertain applause greeted this announcement as guests began moving toward the exits with barely concealed relief, many already engaged in animated discussions about the evening's unexpected drama.

"Time for phase two," Daisy murmured into her earpiece. "We need to track our primary suspects. Mae, stay with Meredith if possible. Babs, keep eyes on Candi. Rita, any sign of Jenkins in the kitchen area?"

"Negative," Rita replied. "But the staff is saying Captain Crustybutt slipped out through the service entrance. Apparently told the doorman he was feeling unwell and needed fresh air."

"Convenient," Daisy observed. "I'll attempt to locate him. Maintain communication and exercise extreme caution. If the murderer suspects we're investigating..."

She let the implication hang as she made her way toward the terrace, still fully inhabiting her baroness character even as she scanned the area for signs of the captain. The yacht club's expansive terrace overlooked the harbor, where boats of various sizes bobbed gently in their slips, their running lights creating a constellation of colors against the darkness of the water.

The night air carried the distinctive mixture of salt, sunscreen, and expensive perfume that defined Conch Key's social gatherings, with an underlying note of approaching rain. In the distance, heat lightning flickered across the horizon, briefly illuminating the silhouettes of palm trees against the navy-blue sky.

Daisy moved unhurriedly along the perimeter of the terrace, nodding regally to those guests who acknowledged her presence while maintaining a constant vigilance for Captain Crustybutt's distinctive weathered profile. She had nearly completed a full circuit when she noticed a solitary figure at the furthest corner, partially obscured by a large potted palm. The glow of a cigarette briefly illuminated the captain's face as he took a long drag, his gaze fixed on the water beyond the yacht club's docks.

With deliberate casualness, Daisy approached, pausing at the railing as if to admire the view. "Beautiful evening," she observed in her accented English. "Though perhaps storm is coming, da?"

The captain started slightly before composing himself. "Baroness," he acknowledged with a nod. "Didn't see you there. Yes, looks like we might get some weather rolling in. Barometric pressure's been dropping all day."

"You have sailor's eye," Daisy complimented him. "I admire those who understand sea's moods."

"Been on the water all my life," the captain replied, seeming to relax slightly. "You develop a sense for it after a while. Like having another set of senses tuned to the elements."

"Must be wonderful, such freedom," Daisy sighed wistfully. "In my country, many lakes, few oceans. I find sea... how you say... hypnotic? Especially at night."

The captain regarded her with newfound interest. "You like night sailing, Baroness?"

"Is magical experience," Daisy confirmed. "The stars, the bioluminescence in water... quite extraordinary."

"We have some impressive bioluminescence in our bay," the captain volunteered, warming to the subject. "Best viewed from Turtle Rock when the moon is new. Creates quite a light show on dark nights."

"Turtle Rock?" Daisy echoed innocently. "This sounds most intriguing. Is special place?"

"Local landmark," the captain explained, his weathered face animated now. "Big rock formation about half a mile offshore. Part of the marine sanctuary. Popular spot for the glass-bottom boat tours because of all the fish that gather there."

"I would very much enjoy seeing this phenomenon," Daisy remarked. "Perhaps you know someone who might arrange private tour? For suitable compensation, naturally."

The captain hesitated, his enthusiasm dimming noticeably. "Well, there's regular tours during season. Bobby Glowacki runs a glass-bottom boat that goes out nightly."

"But you also have boat, no?" Daisy pressed gently. "Perhaps more... intimate experience?"

"I do have a skiff," the captain admitted reluctantly. "But I don't generally take passengers. Insurance concerns and all that."

"Pity," Daisy sighed. "I had hoped to see this Turtle Rock tonight. Weather permitting, of course." She gestured toward the distant lightning. "Such places often have... how you say... legends attached? Stories of romance, perhaps? Or tragedy?"

The captain's expression closed like a porthole before a storm. "No particular stories that I know of," he said curtly. "Just a rock with a lot of fish."

"And yet," Daisy mused, watching him carefully, "I understand Mr. Hamfist was near this rock on night of his death. Quite coincidence, no?"

The change was immediate and alarming. The captain's weather-beaten face drained of color, and his hand trembled slightly as he dropped his cigarette, grinding it under his heel with unnecessary force.

"Who told you that?" he demanded, his jovial sailor persona evaporating entirely.

"Oh, conversations one overhears," Daisy replied airily, though she was mentally calculating the distance to the nearest group of guests. "Turtle Rock mentioned several times this evening. In connection with poor Mr. Hamfist's final hours."

The captain stepped closer, his voice dropping to a menacing rumble. "Listen here, Lady Whatever-you-call-yourself, I don't know who you really are or what game you're playing, but you'd best stay out of things that don't concern you."

"I assure you, Captain, I merely—"

"Don't," he cut her off sharply. "Don't pretend this is innocent curiosity. There are no Russian baronesses interested in Conch Key real estate. You're asking too many questions, and that's a dangerous hobby around here."

Daisy maintained her regal bearing despite the implied threat. "Are you threatening me, Captain Crustybutt?"

"Warning you," he corrected grimly. "Same warning I'd give anyone poking their nose where it doesn't belong. Accidents happen on the water all the time. Even to experienced sailors."

Without waiting for a response, he brushed past her and strode rapidly toward the steps leading down to the marina, his previously unsteady gait now remarkably sure-footed for a man who had consumed multiple Blue Lagoon Mysteries.

"Well," Daisy murmured to herself. "That was illuminating."

Into her earpiece, she whispered, "Captain Crustybutt just issued what I can only interpret as a thinly veiled threat. He became extremely agitated when I mentioned Turtle Rock in connection with Brock's death. He's heading toward the marina now—moving with surprising sobriety for someone who appeared quite intoxicated earlier."

"Should we alert Chief Crabbitz?" Mae's concerned voice came through.

"Not yet," Daisy decided. "We need more concrete evidence. His reaction is suspicious but not conclusive."

"I'm losing visual on Candi," Babs reported, her Trixie accent momentarily forgotten. "She slipped away while I was collecting empty glasses. Last seen heading toward the ladies' room, but that was ten minutes ago."

"I'll check," Mae volunteered. "I'm nearby and can claim to be tidying up."

"Be careful," Daisy cautioned. "If she's involved..."

"I know," Mae assured her. "I'll just peek in and report back."

As Mae signed off, Rita's voice came through the earpiece, sounding tense. "Something strange is happening in the kitchen. Meredith Moneypenny just came in through the service entrance and is having an intense whispered conversation with one of the bartenders—the young one with the tribal tattoo. They keep looking around like they're worried about being overheard."

"Can you get closer?" Daisy asked.

"Trying," Rita confirmed. "But they're—wait, they're moving. Heading toward the wine cellar stairs. Should I follow?"

Daisy hesitated. The wine cellar was notoriously labyrinthine, with limited exits and poor cellular reception. If Rita encountered trouble down there...

"Negative," she decided reluctantly. "Too risky without backup. Maintain position and alert us if they return. I'm coming to your location."

As Daisy made her way back into the ballroom, she noticed several staff members hurriedly clearing tables and removing decorations, their expressions suggesting they'd been instructed to wrap up the event as quickly as possible. The remaining guests had dwindled to small clusters of die-hards, primarily gathered around the remaining bar service on the terrace.

She was halfway to the kitchen when her earpiece crackled with Mae's voice, breathless with alarm. "Daisy! Candi's gone, but her purse is still here—dumped in the trash bin in the ladies' room. And there's something inside you need to see. A stun gun, exactly like the kind Morty described, and a bottle of prescription sedatives."

"Don't touch anything," Daisy instructed immediately. "We need to —"

"There's more," Mae interrupted, uncharacteristically urgent. "I just glimpsed Fleur DuBois heading down the path toward the private dock—with Candi. They looked like they were arguing, and Fleur was gripping Candi's arm rather forcefully."

Daisy's mind raced through the implications. "The private dock? Are you certain?"

"Positive," Mae confirmed. "It's the small one reserved for the club officers, on the east side of the property."

"Stay where you are," Daisy instructed. "I'll investigate." Into the general channel, she added, "Rita, maintain your position. Babs, we need eyes on the private dock. Approach with extreme caution—Fleur DuBois and Candi Bubbleshine are heading that way, possibly in conflict."

"On it," Babs responded instantly. "I can circle around through the garden. No one questions a cocktail waitress taking a cigarette break."

Daisy altered her course, moving swiftly but deliberately toward the eastern side of the yacht club. Her elegant evening gown wasn't designed for stealth operations, but the deepening darkness worked in her favor as she navigated the manicured grounds, staying close to the shadows of ornamental palms and tropical shrubs.

The private dock extended thirty yards into the protected harbor, accessible via a short path bordered by discreetly placed landscape lighting. As Daisy approached, she could make out two figures at the far end—one in a shimmering mermaid-shaped gown that could only be Candi, the other a slender silhouette in a simple black dress that had to be Fleur.

Their body language suggested confrontation rather than cooperation. Fleur stood rigidly, one hand extended palm outward in what appeared to be a cautionary gesture, while Candi's arms moved animatedly, her voice carrying across the water though the words themselves were indistinct.

Daisy paused, weighing her options. Direct intervention seemed unwise until she understood the nature of their conflict. Moving carefully along the perimeter of the dock's entry point, she positioned herself behind a large decorative anchor that served as the yacht club's marine-themed signpost.

From this vantage point, she could hear fragments of the increasingly heated exchange.

"—never meant for it to go this far," Candi was saying, her voice pitched higher than her usual affected purr. "It was just supposed to scare him into keeping the original plans!"

"You foolish woman," Fleur's accented voice replied coldly. "Did you truly believe he would change his mind after a minor electrical shock? The man was surprisingly resilient."

"You said the stun gun would just incapacitate him temporarily!" Candi protested. "Enough to make him reconsider canceling my venue. But then you kept using it, over and over, and with the sedatives—"

"Silence!" Fleur hissed. "Your amateur theatrics have already drawn too much attention. The evidence in your purse alone is enough to send you to prison for decades."

"My purse?" Candi echoed, confusion evident in her voice. "What are you talking about? You took the stun gun after... after it happened."

"And returned it to your possession this evening," Fleur informed her with chilling precision. "Along with the sedatives. Both items now conveniently discovered in the ladies' room trash, with your fingerprints prominently displayed. A clear case of a scorned girlfriend eliminating the man who was about to destroy her dreams of stardom."

A moment of stunned silence followed this pronouncement before Candi gasped in comprehension. "You're framing me! But we were in it together! You wanted the resort changed as much as I did—the original design would have blocked the view from your gallery!"

"A gallery I was planning to sell to developers once the casino was approved," Fleur corrected her. "The property value would have tripled with the resort in place. But your precious Brockie had a crisis of conscience and decided to replace profit with turtles." She made a sound of disgust. "Men are so predictably disappointing."

"So you killed him," Candi whispered, her voice hollow with shock. "You actually killed him."

"We killed him," Fleur corrected with terrifying calm. "A distinction the police will surely appreciate when I provide my tearful confession about how you manipulated me into helping dispose of the body after your crime of passion."

"No one will believe that!" Candi protested, though her voice wavered with uncertainty.

"They will when they find the texts you sent me—the ones detailing your plan to 'make Brock pay' for betraying your dreams," Fleur replied smoothly. "Technology is so convenient for establishing motive."

"What texts? I never—" Candi broke off as realization dawned. "You wouldn't."

"I already have," Fleur confirmed. "Your phone was remarkably easy to access while you were performing. So trusting, leaving it in your dressing room."

Daisy had heard enough. This confession, while damning, was useless without witnesses or recording. She needed to alert Morty immediately, but her phone was in her evening bag, which she'd left with Eugene for safekeeping.

The earpiece was her only option. "Attention," she whispered urgently. "Fleur DuBois has just confessed to killing Brock, with Candi as an unwitting accomplice. She's planning to frame Candi and is currently threatening her on the private dock. We need Chief Crabbitz immediately."

"On it," Rita's voice came back instantly. "He's still in the main ballroom. I'll get him."

"I have visual on the dock from the garden path," Babs added. "They're at the far end, no boat in sight. Wait—something's happening."

Daisy peered around the anchor to see Fleur advancing on Candi, who was backing dangerously close to the edge of the dock. The water lapped darkly below, occasionally illuminated by distant lightning that was drawing steadily closer.

"Such a tragedy," Fleur was saying, her voice carrying a theatrical note of regret. "The distraught girlfriend, overcome with guilt and remorse, takes her own life by drowning—just like the man she murdered. The symmetry will not be lost on the police."

"You're insane," Candi gasped, clutching at a mooring post to steady herself. "I can't even swim!"

"How perfect," Fleur purred. "Neither could Brock."

Daisy made a split-second decision. Intervention couldn't wait for Morty's arrival. Using her years of community theater experience, she projected her voice in her most authoritative baroness accent.

"That is quite enough, Madame DuBois!"

Both women froze, turning toward the sound. Daisy stepped out from behind the anchor, drawing herself up to her full height and channeling every ounce of aristocratic disdain she could muster.

"Step away from Ms. Bubbleshine immediately," she commanded, striding forward with deliberate confidence.

Fleur's surprise quickly gave way to calculation. "Baroness Volkov," she said smoothly. "I'm afraid you've misunderstood the situation. Candi is extremely distressed and I was merely preventing her from harming herself."

"What a fascinating interpretation of events," Daisy replied coldly. "Perhaps you could explain how intimidating someone to the edge of a dock constitutes preventing self-harm?"

Fleur's elegant features hardened. "You were eavesdropping. How vulgar."

"Less vulgar than murder, I should think," Daisy countered, continuing her steady approach. Behind Fleur, Candi had begun inching sideways, attempting to create distance between herself and the edge.

"You have no proof of anything," Fleur said dismissively. "Just the hysterical claims of a woman clearly unbalanced by grief."

"Perhaps," Daisy acknowledged, her eyes flicking momentarily to her right where a shadow was moving stealthily along the perimeter of the dock—Babs, approaching from the opposite direction. "But Chief Crabbitz will certainly find your confession interesting. As will your... how did you put it? Your 'tearful admission' about being manipulated by Candi."

Fleur's composure slipped further. "You understand nothing about this situation. Brock Hamfist was going to destroy years of careful planning with his ridiculous eco-conversion. Do you have any idea how much money was at stake? The casino consortium alone was prepared to pay millions for preferred vendor relationships."

"The kickbacks Councilwoman Moneypenny was expecting," Daisy surmised, taking another step forward. "You were partners in this venture."

"Meredith is an amateur," Fleur scoffed. "Concerned with her petty political aspirations and modest bribes. I was orchestrating a complete redevelopment of Conch Key's waterfront—one that would have made us all incredibly wealthy."

"Until Brock had his epiphany about turtles," Daisy supplied, noting with relief that Candi had managed to edge almost completely away from the drop-off. Just a few more moments of distraction...

"Turtles!" Fleur spat the word like a curse. "He throws away a fortune for reptiles! After months of negotiations and careful arrangements." Her elegant hand slipped into a concealed pocket of her dress. "You should have stayed out of this, Baroness. Or whatever you really are."

"Daisy, she's armed!" Babs' urgent whisper came through the earpiece. "I can see something metallic in her right hand!"

Before Daisy could react, Fleur lunged forward with startling speed, a small silver object clutched in her hand—the stun gun, Daisy realized with a jolt of alarm. She instinctively stepped backward, losing her balance on the uneven boards of the dock. As she stumbled, the stun gun arced through the air toward her chest, its electronic crackle audible even over the increasing wind.

"Not my friend, you French fraud!" came a fierce battle cry from behind Fleur.

In a blur of platinum wig and sequined cocktail uniform, Babs launched herself at Fleur with the determination of a linebacker. The full force of her charge sent both women tumbling sideways, the stun gun flying from Fleur's hand and skittering across the dock before disappearing into the dark water below.

"Rita! Mae! A little help would be nice!" Babs called out as she grappled with the surprisingly strong gallery owner. "This lady may be skinny but she fights dirty!"

Daisy scrambled to her feet, kicking off her elegant heels for better traction on the increasingly slippery dock. The first fat raindrops of the approaching storm had begun to fall, accompanied by more frequent flashes of lightning that briefly illuminated the bizarre tableau—Babs straddling Fleur, attempting to pin her arms while Candi stood frozen in shock, her mermaid costume glittering surreally with each lightning flash.

"Candi! Run and get help!" Daisy commanded, rushing forward to assist Babs.

The instruction seemed to break Candi's paralysis. She gathered her cumbersome gown and began an awkward half-run toward the shore, her progress hampered by her tight skirt and precarious heels.

Daisy reached Babs just as Fleur managed to get a hand free and deliver a stinging slap to Babs' face, nearly dislodging her platinum wig. "You meddling old fool!" Fleur hissed. "Do you have any idea who you're dealing with?"

"A murderer with awful taste in victim selection," Babs retorted, adjusting her grip. "Brock Hamfist? Really? Couldn't you have picked someone the town would actually miss?"

Despite the gravity of the situation, Daisy couldn't suppress a brief smile at Babs' irrepressible spirit. "Rita and Mae are coming," she assured her friend, kneeling to help restrain Fleur. "And Chief Crabbitz should be right behind them."

"If we survive that long," Babs grunted, narrowly avoiding another slap. "This woman fights like a cornered mink!"

"You have ruined everything!" Fleur snarled, bucking against their restraining hands. "Years of planning—millions in development contracts—all destroyed because of interfering old women!"

"I prefer the term 'seasoned investigators,'" Daisy corrected primly, using the sash from her gown to secure Fleur's wrists. "And really, murder over real estate? How tiresomely mercenary."

The rain was falling in earnest now, plastering Babs' wig to her head and turning Daisy's elegant updo into a bedraggled mess. Lightning flashed more frequently, followed by ominous rumbles of thunder that seemed to roll directly across the water toward them.

"We need to get off this dock," Daisy warned, eyeing the metal cleats and posts that suddenly seemed dangerously conductive. "Lightning and wet wooden docks make poor companions."

"Tell that to Madame Murderess," Babs replied, struggling to maintain her grip on the still-fighting gallery owner. "She's not exactly cooperating with our safety protocols."

As if in response to this observation, Fleur suddenly went limp, causing both women to momentarily loosen their hold in surprise. It was all the opening she needed. With a strength born of desperation, she twisted violently, breaking free from their grasp and scrambling to her feet in one fluid motion.

"You will not take this from me," she declared, her accent thickening with emotion. "I did not come to this backwater town and waste five years on provincial art collectors to leave empty-handed!"

Before either Daisy or Babs could react, Fleur darted toward the end of the dock where a small covered boat slip housed what appeared to be the yacht club's emergency craft—a sleek motorboat designed for quick harbor maneuvers.

"She's going for the boat!" Babs exclaimed, scrambling upright despite her sodden cocktail waitress outfit weighing her down considerably.

"Stop!" Daisy called, her baroness accent abandoned entirely in the urgency of the moment. "Fleur, you can't escape! The police already know everything!"

But the French woman paid no heed, leaping gracefully into the boat and immediately setting to work on the mooring lines. Her elegant fingers moved with the precision of someone who had spent considerable time on the water—not the fumbling of a desperate amateur.

"She knows what she's doing," Babs observed with grudging admiration. "Wouldn't have pegged gallery girl for a sailor."

"Babs, stay here and wait for reinforcements," Daisy instructed, already moving toward the boat slip. "I'm going to try to stall her."

"Like hell you are," Babs retorted, falling into step beside her. "We started this investigation together, we'll finish it together. Besides, I've been dying to try out my action-heroine moves since I played Amelia Earhart in the community theater!"

There was no time to argue. Fleur had already freed the bow line and was working on the stern, her movements swift and efficient despite the increasingly heavy rainfall. The boat rocked gently in its slip, ready for immediate departure once the final line was released.

"What's your plan?" Babs whispered as they approached. "Because mine involves a flying tackle, and I'm not sure my knees are up for it."

Before Daisy could respond, a new voice called from the shore end of the dock.

"Ladies! Get down!"

Both women instinctively ducked as Chief Mortimer Crabbitz appeared through the curtain of rain, his service weapon drawn and aimed steadily at the boat slip. Behind him, Rita and Mae huddled beneath a large umbrella, their expressions a mixture of concern and relief.

"Fleur DuBois," Morty called, his voice carrying over the storm with remarkable authority. "Step away from the boat. You're under arrest for the murder of Brock Hamfist."

For a brief moment, it seemed as if Fleur might comply. She straightened from her work on the stern line, raising her hands slightly. Then, with shocking suddenness, she reached into the boat's control console and produced a small flare gun—the type kept aboard for emergencies.

"Stay back!" she warned, pointing the flare gun toward the huddled group on the dock. "I will use this!"

"That's a flare gun, not a weapon," Morty pointed out, though he didn't lower his service pistol. "And you're outnumbered, Fleur. There's nowhere to go."

"There's always somewhere to go," Fleur replied, a strange calm settling over her features. "That's the advantage of having international connections. Unlike you provincial fools, I've always had a contingency plan."

With that, she fired the flare gun—not at the group, but toward the yacht club's main building. The fiery projectile arced through the rainy night, its red glare creating an eerie glow against the storm clouds before disappearing beyond the roofline.

Almost immediately, shouts of alarm rose from the direction of the club, followed by the distinctive wail of a fire alarm.

"Distraction technique," Daisy muttered, realization dawning. "Classic misdirection."

She was right. In the momentary confusion as heads turned toward the commotion, Fleur sliced through the final mooring line with a small knife that had appeared in her hand. The boat immediately began drifting from its slip, its engines rumbling to life with a push of a button on the console.

"Stop her!" Daisy cried, but it was too late. The boat was already moving, gathering speed as it cleared the protective cover of the slip.

What happened next occurred with such theatrical timing that Babs would later declare it worthy of a Broadway finale. As Fleur's stolen craft surged forward into the open harbor, a massive bolt of lightning split the sky directly overhead, momentarily turning night into blinding day. The accompanying thunderclap was instantaneous and deafening, felt as much as heard by everyone on the dock.

And in that brilliant flash, they all saw it—another boat, materializing out of the stormy darkness directly in the path of Fleur's escape vessel. A familiar, weather-beaten fishing skiff with a distinctive uneven putt-putt-putt engine sound.

Captain "Barnacle" Bob Crustybutt's boat.

The collision was inevitable. Despite Fleur's desperate attempt to swerve, the heavier yacht club craft plowed directly into the side of the smaller fishing boat with a sickening crunch of fiberglass and metal. The impact sent both vessels spinning, their occupants thrown violently by the sudden deceleration.

"Man overboard!" Mae cried, pointing toward a splash where Captain Crustybutt had apparently been ejected from his smaller craft.

Without hesitation, Morty holstered his weapon and sprinted toward the end of the dock, shrugging off his uniform jacket as he ran. With a practiced dive that belied his age and usual stiffness, he entered the churning water in pursuit of the floundering captain.

Meanwhile, the two boats had become entangled, their hulls grinding against each other as the wind pushed them inexorably toward the rock jetty that protected the harbor entrance. Fleur was visible in the yacht club boat's cockpit, apparently dazed but conscious, clutching the console for stability.

"We need to help them before they hit those rocks," Rita declared, appearing at Daisy and Babs' side with remarkable speed for someone who had been safely ashore moments before. "There's a rescue boat at the end of the main dock."

"You know how to operate it?" Daisy asked, already moving in that direction despite the increasing ferocity of the storm.

"I dated a Coast Guard captain for three months in my forties," Rita replied with grim determination. "Learned more about marine rescue than romance, but it might finally pay off."

The three women raced along the dock, their improbable costumes —baroness gown, cocktail waitress uniform, and catering attire—creating a surreal tableau against the dramatic backdrop of the storm. Mae remained on shore, frantically waving down additional help from the yacht club staff who had begun to emerge in response to the flare-induced fire alarm.

The rescue boat—a sturdy, orange-painted rigid inflatable with powerful outboard motors—was secured at the emergency response station at the end of the main dock. Rita moved with surprising confidence as she removed the cover and began the startup sequence.

"Babs, cast off the bow line when I tell you," she instructed. "Daisy, same with the stern. And both of you put on life jackets—they're under that bench."

As they scrambled to comply, another lightning bolt illuminated the harbor, revealing the perilous position of the entangled boats. They had drifted dangerously close to the jetty, waves pushing them inexorably toward the jagged rocks. In the distance, Morty could be seen struggling to keep Captain Crustybutt's head above water as he swam toward the nearest dock.

"Now!" Rita called, and Babs released the bow line while Daisy handled the stern. With a roar of powerful engines, the rescue boat shot forward into the turbulent harbor, Rita's hands steady on the controls despite the bucking motion caused by the increasingly rough water.

"Over there!" Daisy pointed toward the endangered vessels, now barely twenty yards from potential destruction on the rocks. "Fleur's moving!"

Indeed, the gallery owner had recovered enough to attempt a desperate measure. As they watched, she climbed onto the gunwale of the yacht club boat, apparently preparing to jump to the relative safety of the fishing skiff, which seemed less damaged and in slightly better position.

"She's going to miss," Babs predicted grimly. "The boats are moving too erratically."

Rita pushed the rescue boat to its maximum speed, expertly navigating the rough conditions. "We're not going to reach them before they hit the jetty," she warned. "Best we can do is be ready for recovery."

As if to confirm her assessment, a particularly large wave lifted both entangled vessels and slammed them directly into the first outcropping of the rock jetty. The horrible sound of fiberglass shattering and metal twisting carried clearly over the storm's fury. Fleur, caught mid-leap between the boats, was thrown violently into the water.

"There!" Daisy pointed to a splash of pale color among the dark waves—Fleur's designer gown, instantly identifiable even in the chaos.

Rita adjusted course immediately, bringing the rescue boat alongside the struggling woman with remarkable precision. Babs and Daisy leaned over the side, extending boat hooks toward the flailing gallery owner.

"Grab on!" Babs called. "Unless you'd prefer to drown in haute couture!"

Fleur, looking considerably less elegant with her perfect bob plastered to her skull and her expensive makeup creating raccoon circles around her eyes, reached desperately for the offered hooks. Between the three of them, they managed to haul her over the gunwale and onto the floor of the rescue boat, where she lay gasping and coughing.

"Now the captain's boat!" Daisy urged, pointing to the two wrecked vessels, which were being systematically pounded against the rocks by relentless waves. "There might be evidence aboard!"

"Evidence can be replaced; lives can't," Rita countered, already turning the rescue boat toward shore. "The harbormaster is launching additional craft. Our job is to get this murderer safely to custody."

As if to punctuate her statement, Fleur made a sudden lunge toward the side of the boat, apparently preferring the storm-tossed sea to capture. Babs, anticipating the move, caught her around the waist and wrestled her back to the deck with surprising strength.

"Not today, honey," she declared, sitting firmly on the struggling woman's midsection. "I've dealt with divas far more determined than you during my Broadway days. And most of them didn't have the excuse of being murderers."

Fleur ceased fighting, her expression transforming from desperate fury to calculated stillness. "You understand nothing," she said coldly. "I wasn't working alone."

"We know about Candi's involvement," Daisy replied, helping Rita navigate back toward the yacht club's main dock where several police officers could now be seen waiting. "Though it appears she was more of an unwitting accomplice than co-conspirator."

"Not Candi," Fleur scoffed. "That rhinestone-obsessed simpleton was merely a convenient tool. I'm referring to someone with actual influence."

A chill that had nothing to do with the storm ran down Daisy's spine. "Meredith Moneypenny."

Fleur's thin smile was confirmation enough. "The councilwoman has expensive tastes that her public servant salary cannot support. The casino licensing alone would have provided sufficient kickbacks to fund her lifestyle for years." She attempted to sit up, despite Babs' weight on her torso. "She knows things—things that will ensure I never face trial alone."

"Save it for your plea bargain," Babs advised, bouncing slightly to remind Fleur of her position. "Though somehow I doubt Meredith will be interested in sharing a prison cell, no matter how close your relationship was."

As they approached the dock, they could see that quite a crowd had gathered despite the ongoing storm. Chief Crabbitz, looking like a half-drowned retriever but very much alive, stood with a handcuffed Captain Crustybutt, who appeared similarly waterlogged but considerably less pleased with the situation. Mae was distributing towels to the soaked parties with her characteristic efficiency, while Eugene Finch directed the harbormaster's response to the wrecked boats.

And standing somewhat apart, her elegant emerald ensemble now protected by a yacht club umbrella, was Councilwoman Meredith Moneypenny, her expression an unreadable mask as she watched their approach.

"Speaking of your partner in crime," Daisy murmured, nodding toward the shore.

Fleur followed her gaze, and something passed between the two women—a look of such complex communication that Daisy, despite her years of studying human behavior, couldn't fully interpret it. Resignation? Warning? Conspiracy? Whatever it was, it lasted only a moment before Meredith turned abruptly and walked away, disappearing into the crowd of emergency responders and curious onlookers.

"Interesting," Daisy noted. "One might almost think she doesn't wish to be associated with you at this moment."

"Politics," Fleur replied bitterly. "Always the same, whether in Paris or this backwater. Everyone denies the alliance once it becomes inconvenient."

Further conversation was curtailed as they reached the dock, where Officer Peanut Butterworth waited with additional handcuffs and a rather unnecessary number of backup officers, all looking simultaneously excited and uncomfortable in the pouring rain.

"Ladies," Morty greeted them as they secured the rescue boat, his expression a mixture of exasperation and reluctant admiration. "I should have known you'd be in the middle of this chaos. Though I have to admit, your timing was impeccable."

"Just happened to be in the right place at the right time," Rita replied innocently, her sudden talent for boat handling apparently not requiring explanation.

"Mmmhmm," Morty hummed skeptically, watching as Butterworth escorted a now-subdued Fleur toward a waiting police vehicle. "And I suppose you 'just happened' to be discussing art investments with Baroness Volkov while dressed as a cater-waiter?"

"Cross-cultural exchange," Daisy suggested, struggling to maintain her dignity despite her sodden gown and ruined makeup. "The baroness was most interested in American service industry protocols."

"I see." Morty's gaze traveled from Daisy to Babs, whose platinum wig now resembled a drowned albino rodent atop her head, and finally to Rita, who met his skeptical look with practiced innocence. "And I suppose you just happened to overhear Fleur DuBois confessing to Brock Hamfist's murder while... what? Comparing canapé recipes?"

"Something like that," Babs confirmed cheerfully, adjusting her bedraggled wig. "Though technically, I believe the confession happened during the fruit tart course."

Morty rubbed his temple, where a vein had begun to throb visibly. "You realize I should arrest the lot of you for obstruction and interfering with a police investigation?"

"But you won't," Daisy observed calmly.

"And why is that, Professor Picklesworth?" Morty asked, though his tone suggested he already knew the answer.

"Because we just handed you not one but two suspects in a murder investigation," Daisy replied. "Complete with confession and physical evidence. The jellyfish charm found near Brock's body? It came from Meredith Moneypenny's bracelet—likely broken off during the struggle when they subdued him with the stun gun and sedatives before staging his 'accidental' drowning."

"Also," Rita added pragmatically, "we just saved a third suspect from drowning, despite his earlier threat to Daisy."

"Plus," Babs contributed, "we look absolutely ridiculous, and arresting three senior citizens who resemble drowned circus performers would generate paperwork that would haunt you until retirement."

A reluctant smile tugged at the corner of Morty's mouth. "There is that consideration," he admitted. "Though I still need official statements from all of you. Tomorrow morning, my office, nine sharp." He glanced at his waterlogged watch. "Make that ten. Some of us have a long night of processing ahead."

"We'll be there," Daisy promised. "With detailed accounts of everything we observed."

"I'm sure you will," Morty sighed. "And now, if you ladies will excuse me, I need to question Captain Crustybutt about his timely appearance in the middle of a storm-tossed harbor, directly in the path of a fleeing murder suspect." He shook his head in disbelief. "Some days I think Conch Key exists in an alternate reality where the laws of probability took a permanent vacation."

As Morty walked away, Mae approached with armfuls of oversized yacht club towels. "That was incredible!" she exclaimed, her usual reserve abandoned in the excitement of the moment. "You three were like something out of an action movie! The boat chase! The rescue! The—" She broke off, suddenly aware of her volume. "Sorry. I got carried away."

"Understandably so," Daisy assured her, gratefully accepting a towel. "It was rather cinematically convenient, wasn't it? Especially the captain's timely appearance."

"About that," Mae said, lowering her voice. "When I was distributing towels earlier, I overheard him telling Officer Butterworth that he was 'trying to make amends.' Said something about being paid to take Brock and Fleur out to Turtle Rock that night but not knowing their true intentions until it was too late."

"So he was the pilot of the mysterious boat Bobby Glowacki mentioned," Rita mused. "That explains his reaction when Daisy brought up Turtle Rock earlier."

"And his threat about 'accidents happening on the water,'" Daisy added. "He was speaking from very recent experience."

"The question remains," Babs said, attempting to wring out her wig with limited success, "why was Brock willingly meeting with Fleur and potentially Meredith on a boat at night, given his aquaphobia? Especially if he suspected they might oppose his plan to change the resort project?"

"Perhaps he didn't know who he was meeting," Rita suggested. "Or was misled about the purpose."

"Or blackmailed," Mae offered quietly. "Remember that mysterious package delivered to his office? The one that caused him to cancel all appointments?"

Daisy nodded thoughtfully. "This case still has unanswered questions. But for now..." She gestured to their bedraggled state. "I suggest we retire to The Barnacle for hot showers, dry clothes, and perhaps a medicinal brandy or two."

"Seconded," Babs declared, finally giving up on her wig and removing it entirely, revealing her natural ginger-gray hair flattened beneath. "Though I'm keeping Trixie's contact information for future reference. She was a hoot to inhabit."

"I doubt the yacht club will be extending cocktail waitress offers after tonight's excitement," Rita observed dryly. "Though they might need new service vessels, given the current state of their emergency craft."

As they made their way through the dispersing crowd toward the yacht club's main entrance, they passed Candi Bubbleshine, now wrapped in a foil emergency blanket that combined with her sequined mermaid gown to create an effect reminiscent of an exceptionally glamorous baked potato. She was giving a statement to a female officer, her hands gesturing dramatically despite her obvious distress.

"Poor thing," Mae murmured sympathetically. "She was misguided, but it seems she never intended murder."

"Unlike her sophisticated friend," Babs noted. "Funny how the elegant gallery owner turned out to be the truly dangerous one, while everyone was busy suspecting the obvious flashy girlfriend."

"People often underestimate those who don't draw attention to themselves," Daisy observed. "A mistake we ourselves should be careful not to make in the future."

They had nearly reached the parking area when a familiar voice called out from behind them.

"Ladies! A moment, please."

They turned to find Eugene Finch jogging toward them, his tuxedo as soaked as their own outfits but his expression considerably more cheerful than the circumstances might warrant.

"Baroness," he began, addressing Daisy before catching himself. "Or should I say, Professor Picklesworth? Remarkable performance tonight. All of you." He glanced around as if checking for eavesdroppers before continuing in a lower voice. "I believe these belong to you."

From inside his jacket, he produced Daisy's evening bag and the communication earpieces they had been using, now collected in a discreet pouch.

"I took the liberty of retrieving them before the police started collecting evidence," he explained, handing the items to a surprised Daisy. "Thought you might prefer to avoid explaining the high-tech communications system during tomorrow's statements."

"That's... unexpectedly thoughtful, Eugene," Daisy said, accepting the items with a bemused expression. "Though it raises the question of how long you've known about our investigation."

Eugene's weather-beaten face creased in a knowing smile. "Let's just say that very little happens on the Conch Key waterfront without the harbormaster being aware. Including four distinguished ladies conducting an unorthodox murder investigation while in dubious disguises."

"And you didn't think to mention this to Chief Crabbitz?" Rita asked, raising an eyebrow.

"Morty has his methods, I have mine," Eugene replied with a shrug. "Besides, I was curious to see how it would play out. You ladies have quite the reputation for solving local mysteries."

"Our reputation seems to be growing beyond our control," Daisy observed dryly.

"Like kudzu in August," Babs agreed. "Though considerably more enjoyable."

Eugene chuckled. "Well, I should get back to the harbor recovery efforts. Those boats aren't going to salvage themselves." He turned to go, then paused. "By the way, if you're ever interested in investing in legitimate waterfront property, Professor, I know of a lovely parcel that might soon be available. Captain Crustybutt's place will likely be on the market once his legal troubles are settled."

"I'll keep that in mind," Daisy replied, unable to suppress a smile at the thought of her baroness persona making a permanent investment in Conch Key real estate.

As Eugene walked away, the four friends shared a look of collective exhaustion and triumph.

"Home?" Mae suggested hopefully.

"Home," the others agreed in unison.

They made their way to Rita's sensible sedan, which waited in the yacht club parking lot like a beacon of normality amid the chaos of emergency vehicles and gathered onlookers. As they settled into the familiar comfort of its interior, Daisy couldn't help but reflect on the evening's extraordinary events.

"You know," she mused as Rita navigated carefully through the rain-slicked streets toward The Barnacle, "for a brief moment there, I found myself rather enjoying being Baroness Ekaterina Volkov."

"She did have a certain commanding presence," Mae agreed from the backseat.

"Not to mention excellent taste in midnight blue evening gowns," Babs added, still clutching her soggy platinum wig like a treasured pet.

"Perhaps we should consider alternate personas more often," Rita suggested, only half-joking. "They seem to provide a unique investigative advantage."

"Perhaps," Daisy allowed, watching the raindrops trace patterns on the car window. "Though I find our regular selves quite capable of extraordinary feats when properly motivated."

As The Barnacle came into view, its mint-green Victorian charm glowing welcomingly despite the stormy night, Daisy felt a profound sense of satisfaction settle over her. Another mystery solved, another killer brought to justice, another adventure shared with the three women who had become her closest friends and most trusted allies.

What she didn't yet realize was that their reputation as the "Seaside Sleuths" was about to expand well beyond the boundaries of Conch Key, bringing new mysteries, greater dangers, and even more outlandish adventures than they could possibly imagine. But those were concerns for another day.

For tonight, there would be hot showers, comfortable caftans, perhaps a late supper of whatever Rita could rescue from the refrigerator, and most definitely generous pours of brandy as they recounted their collective triumph over murderous developers and their elegantly lethal conspirators.

And if, in the midst of their celebration, Babs happened to experience another menopausal hot flash that sent her running for the porch in search of cooler air—well, that too was simply part of the rich tapestry of their golden years. Years that, contrary to society's expectations, were proving to be not a quiet fade into irrelevance, but rather a brilliant new chapter filled with purpose, excitement, and the incomparable joy of friendship.

After all, as Daisy would later observe while raising her brandy glass in a midnight toast: "Hot flashes may be inconvenient, but homicide is absolutely unacceptable. And fortunately, we excel at addressing both."

Chapter Six
The Morning After

Morning arrived at The Barnacle with the gentle persistence of Florida sunshine filtering through partially closed blinds and the considerably less gentle persistence of Daisy Picklesworth's alarm clock, which emitted a sound remarkably similar to an asthmatic goose being strangled.

"For the love of all that's holy, make it stop," groaned Babs from down the hallway, her voice muffled by what was presumably a pillow pulled over her head. "I feel like I've been hit by the entire Rockettes dance line."

The alarm continued its assault on tranquility for several more seconds before a solid thump followed by blessed silence indicated that Daisy had either successfully deactivated it or simply hurled it across the room. Given her mood this particular morning, either scenario seemed equally plausible.

Daisy emerged from her bedroom with the cautious movements of someone who suspected her joints might have been replaced with rusty hinges overnight. Her silver hair, normally styled into its impressive bouffant, resembled nothing so much as a distressed cockatoo's crest, and she had forgone her usual colorful caftan in favor of a plush bathrobe that had seen better decades.

"I believe," she announced to no one in particular as she shuffled toward the kitchen, "that I am experiencing what the youth refer to as 'feeling my age.' A sensation I find both inconvenient and deeply offensive."

The kitchen already showed signs of life. Rita, ever the early riser, had the coffee maker gurgling merrily and was methodically arranging ingredients for breakfast with the precision of a surgical nurse preparing for an operation. Unlike Daisy, she appeared remarkably fresh considering the previous night's aquatic adventures, her hair neatly combed and her practical housedress already accessorized with her cooking apron.

"Good morning, sunshine," she greeted Daisy with entirely too much cheer. "I thought pancakes might be appropriate for our post-crime-solving recovery. With blueberries," she added, as if this nutritional addition might somehow counterbalance the four hours of sleep they'd managed after returning from the yacht club debacle.

"Coffee first," Daisy mumbled, making a beeline for the largest mug in the cabinet—a souvenir from the Conch Key Shell Museum that declared its owner to be "Shell-ebratin' Life!" in aggressively cheerful typography. "Then possibly human conversation. Though I make no promises."

Rita wisely slid the coffee pot toward her friend without comment, focusing instead on whisking pancake batter with more vigor than strictly necessary. Years of friendship had taught her that Daisy required approximately 2.7 sips of caffeine before achieving minimal verbal civility.

The kitchen's pocket door slid open to admit Mae, who unlike her housemates showed no visible signs of their late-night excitement. Her silver-gray bob was perfectly in place, her pastel cardigan buttoned with mathematical precision, and her sensible slippers whispered softly across the tile floor as she entered.

"Good morning!" she chirped, her tone suggesting she'd already been awake for hours, possibly organizing something alphabetically. "I've collected our wet costumes from last night. The baroness gown needs professional cleaning, I'm afraid. Saltwater and fine fabrics do not mix well."

"Much like murder investigations and senior citizens, one might argue," Daisy observed dryly, now cradling her coffee mug like it contained the elixir of life itself. "And yet, here we are."

Mae smiled serenely as she retrieved her own mug—a delicate porcelain affair featuring hand-painted violets that she'd inherited from her grandmother. "I rather thought we acquitted ourselves admirably. Though perhaps next time we should consider water-resistant disguises."

"Next time?" Rita echoed, pausing her pancake preparations. "Mae Noodleman, are you developing a taste for danger in your golden years?"

Mae's cheeks colored slightly. "I simply found the experience rather... invigorating. Not the murder part, of course," she hastened to add. "But the puzzle-solving. The teamwork. The moment when all the pieces fit together."

"The high-speed boat chase in a lightning storm?" Daisy suggested, her lips quirking into the beginnings of a smile. "The hand-to-hand combat with a homicidal French art dealer?"

"Well, perhaps not those specific elements," Mae conceded. "Though you must admit, it made for an interesting evening."

"'Interesting' is not the adjective I would choose," came Babs' voice as she finally made her entrance, moving with the careful precision of someone intimately acquainted with the aftermath of strenuous physical exertion. She had opted for a silk kimono in a shade of turquoise that bordered on hallucinatory, and her flame-red hair was partially contained by a series of multicolored clips that suggested she had begun styling it before being distracted by something shiny. "Traumatic, perhaps. Or exhausting. Possibly revelatory, if we're considering my discovery that I can still perform a flying tackle at my age, albeit with consequences that make childbirth seem like a day at the spa."

"You did execute that maneuver with impressive commitment," Daisy acknowledged, raising her coffee mug in salute. "Particularly given the slippery dock conditions and your unfortunate footwear choices."

"Please," Babs waved dismissively as she made her way to the coffeepot. "I once performed the entire second act of 'Cats' with a dislocated shoulder. Broadway teaches you to commit to the moment, darling." She poured herself coffee, adding enough cream to render it nearly beige. "Besides, that French witch had it coming. The nerve of her, endangering my wig like that! Do you have any idea how difficult it is to find quality synthetic hair in that particular shade of 'Desperate Cocktail Waitress Blonde'?"

Rita snorted as she poured the first batch of pancakes onto the griddle. "I'm sure that was her primary consideration while attempting to escape murder charges. 'Oh dear, I mustn't damage Barbara Zuckerkorn's theatrical hairpiece while fleeing justice.'"

"Priorities, Rita," Babs replied with dignity. "We all have them. Mine happen to include proper respect for costume elements."

A knock at the front door interrupted their banter, causing all four women to exchange startled glances.

Hot Flashes & Homocide

"It's not even eight o'clock," Rita noted, glancing at the kitchen clock. "Who makes social calls at this hour?"

"Probably not social," Daisy surmised, setting down her coffee with reluctance. "Given our involvement in last night's excitement, I suspect we have an official visitor."

She was proven correct moments later when she opened the front door to find Chief Mortimer Crabbitz standing on their porch, looking only marginally less waterlogged than he had the previous evening. His uniform was fresh but his expression suggested he hadn't enjoyed much more sleep than they had.

"Morning, Daisy," he greeted her, removing his hat with one hand while balancing a box of pastries with the other. "Hope I'm not disturbing your breakfast."

"Not at all, Morty," she replied, stepping aside to let him enter. "We were just discussing the therapeutic properties of pancakes after nocturnal crime-solving adventures. Do come in."

Morty followed her into the kitchen, where he was greeted with varying degrees of enthusiasm by the other residents of The Barnacle. Mae immediately fetched an extra mug for coffee, while Rita transferred perfectly golden pancakes from griddle to serving plate with the timing of a Swiss watchmaker.

"Chief Crabbitz," she acknowledged him. "I assume this isn't a social call, despite the peace offering." She nodded toward the pastry box.

"Guilty as charged," Morty admitted, placing the box on the counter. "Consider it a small token of gratitude for your... assistance last night. Unofficial gratitude," he added hastily. "Nothing that would appear in any formal report or suggest that I endorsed civilian involvement in police matters."

"Heaven forbid," Daisy murmured, resuming her seat at the table. "We wouldn't want anyone thinking the Conch Key Police Department required assistance from four retired ladies to solve a murder case."

Morty's sunburned complexion darkened slightly. "Now, Daisy, that's not fair. We would have gotten there eventually. The medical examiner's findings about the stun gun marks and sedatives were already pointing us toward foul play."

"Of course they were," Daisy agreed soothingly. "And I'm sure you would have brilliantly deduced Fleur DuBois's involvement without us happening to overhear her literal confession of guilt while threatening a second victim."

Morty sighed, accepting the coffee Mae offered with a grateful nod. "Look, I didn't come here to argue jurisdiction or investigative procedures. I came because I have some follow-up questions about your statements from last night, and I figured you might be more... forthcoming in a less formal setting."

"How considerate," Babs observed, helping herself to a cheese danish from the pastry box. "And completely unrelated to the fact that our 'formal statements' last night consisted primarily of me alternating between wringing out my wig and demanding dry clothes while Daisy recited Russian literature in an accent that somehow migrated from Moscow to Mississippi."

"It was a stressful situation," Mae offered charitably. "I believe we all said things that might benefit from clarification in the clear light of day."

"Exactly," Morty agreed, looking relieved that someone understood. "And since you ladies seem to have gathered certain information through your... unconventional methods, I thought we might compare notes. Unofficially," he emphasized again.

"Quid pro quo, Clarice?" Daisy suggested, raising an eyebrow.

"I understood that reference!" Mae exclaimed, looking pleased with herself. "I watched that movie through my fingers, but I watched it."

Rita, who had been arranging pancakes onto plates with artistic precision, joined them at the table. "Eat while we talk," she instructed, placing generous servings before each person. "Food gets cold, but murder stays relevant."

"Words to live by," Babs agreed, reaching for the syrup. "Almost worthy of a needlepoint pillow. Mae, add it to your crafting queue."

Morty accepted his plate with obvious appreciation, watching in mild awe as Rita proceeded to distribute cutlery, napkins, and additional coffee with the efficiency of an experienced short-order cook. When everyone was settled, he pulled out his notebook and flipped to a fresh page.

"So," he began, between bites of what might have been the best blueberry pancakes he'd ever encountered, "let's start with the basics. How exactly did you ladies determine that Fleur DuBois was involved in Brock Hamfist's murder?"

The four exchanged glances, silently negotiating who would take the lead. By unspoken consensus, Daisy was elected spokesperson—a role she assumed with practiced ease, setting aside her coffee mug and straightening her posture in what her friends recognized as her "former professor explaining complicated concepts to freshman students" pose.

"It was a combination of factors," she began. "First, there was the jellyfish charm found near Brock's body—identical to one on Meredith Moneypenny's bracelet, which we observed during the fundraiser. This connected her to the scene, but the timing was problematic given her alibi with Fleur for part of the critical period."

"Then," Babs interjected, unable to contain herself, "there was Captain Crustybutt's revelation about Brock's complete change of heart regarding the resort project—transforming it from luxury high-rise to eco-friendly turtle sanctuary. A change that would have financially impacted several key players, including both Meredith and Fleur."

"Bobby Glowacki's testimony about seeing Brock and an unidentified woman transfer to another boat near Turtle Rock was particularly significant," Rita added, efficiently refilling coffee mugs without interrupting the narrative flow. "Especially once we confirmed the captain's involvement as the pilot of that second vessel."

"But most compelling," Mae contributed softly, "was the pattern of behavior. Fleur's gallery would have either lost its ocean view or gained tremendous value depending on which version of the resort was built. And when Candi mentioned seeing Brock and Fleur in deep conversation after the festival, just before his mysterious 'meeting'..."

"The pieces aligned," Daisy concluded. "Of course, we had no concrete evidence until we overheard Fleur's confession to Candi on the dock—a confession that conveniently included details about the murder method that matched your medical examiner's findings."

Morty listened to this summation with an expression that cycled through skepticism, reluctant admiration, and finally resignation. He made several notes before responding.

"That's... actually consistent with what we've pieced together from the physical evidence and subsequent interrogations," he admitted. "Though our timeline emerged somewhat less... dramatically."

"Understandable," Daisy nodded sympathetically. "Not everyone can have a high-speed boat chase in a lightning storm as their denouement."

"For which we are eternally grateful," Rita muttered, serving herself another pancake.

Morty flipped to another page in his notebook. "What remains unclear is the exact sequence of events on the night of the murder, and particularly Brock's motivation for willingly meeting with Fleur and potentially Meredith, given his known fear of water."

"Blackmail seems plausible," Daisy suggested. "Or perhaps he believed he was meeting someone else entirely."

"According to Captain Crustybutt's statement this morning—once he'd dried off and retained a lawyer—Brock specifically arranged for the captain to transport him and Fleur to Turtle Rock that night," Morty revealed. "Apparently, Brock told him it was for a 'private business discussion away from prying eyes.'"

"That suggests Brock trusted Fleur," Mae observed thoughtfully. "Or at least didn't view her as an immediate threat."

"Which aligns with the captain's claim that the mood seemed civil when they departed his boat," Morty confirmed. "He says he was instructed to return in one hour, and when he did, only Fleur was waiting. She told him Brock had 'changed his mind about their arrangement' and taken a water taxi back to shore."

"And the captain didn't find that suspicious?" Babs asked incredulously. "A man terrified of water suddenly deciding to take an alternate boat ride in the middle of the night?"

"He claims Fleur was very convincing," Morty replied dryly. "Though he admits he'd been paid generously to 'not ask questions.'"

"The oldest justification for looking the other way," Daisy remarked. "Second only to 'I was just following orders.'"

"Indeed," Morty agreed. "In any case, the captain's testimony places Fleur at the scene, with opportunity and means—the stun gun was apparently in her purse during the boat meeting."

"And the motive was financial," Rita concluded. "The loss of potential profits from the original resort plan."

"That's where things get interesting," Morty said, leaning forward slightly. "According to Harold Jenkins, who we interviewed at length this morning, Brock's change of heart wasn't just about the resort design. He was planning to restructure the entire ownership arrangement, removing certain silent partners who'd been involved from the beginning."

This revelation caused all four women to exchange significant looks.

"Silent partners like Meredith Moneypenny?" Daisy suggested.

"Among others," Morty confirmed. "Jenkins was reluctant to name names without documentation, but he indicated that several prominent citizens had 'unofficial equity stakes' in the original project—stakes that would have become worthless under Brock's new eco-resort plan."

"How very convenient that those records were presumably with Brock when he met his untimely end in the bay," Babs observed.

"Actually," Morty countered with the first genuine smile they'd seen from him that morning, "that's another interesting development. The documentation wasn't with Brock that night. He'd already filed everything with his attorney, the town clerk, and somewhat surprisingly, the Conch Key Marine Conservation Society."

"Gladys Pickle's organization?" Mae asked, surprised.

"The very same," Morty confirmed. "Apparently, Brock had secretly donated a substantial sum to their turtle preservation efforts the day before his death, along with copies of his new resort plans and ownership structure. As a 'gesture of good faith,' according to the cover letter."

"So the paper trail survived even if Brock didn't," Daisy mused. "No wonder Fleur was so desperate to escape. The evidence against her would have emerged whether we caught her in the act of threatening Candi or not."

"Speaking of Candi," Rita interjected, "what's her status this morning? She seemed rather traumatized when we last saw her."

"Currently enjoying the hospitality of our holding cells," Morty replied, helping himself to another pancake. "Though in considerably more comfortable conditions than Fleur. We're treating her as an accessory after the fact, based on her admission that she provided the stun gun initially, albeit allegedly for non-lethal purposes."

"Poor deluded sequin enthusiast," Babs sighed. "Imagine believing a resort nightclub called 'The Sugar Shack' would launch your career. The acoustics alone would have been abysmal in that architectural monstrosity Brock originally planned."

"Her fashion choices may be questionable, but she doesn't strike me as a cold-blooded killer," Mae offered charitably. "More a victim of manipulation by someone much more sophisticated."

"The courts will sort out degrees of culpability," Morty said. "Meanwhile, we're executing search warrants on Fleur's gallery, Meredith's home, and the captain's boat—what's left of it, anyway."

"And Meredith herself?" Daisy inquired casually. "I noticed her conspicuous departure from the docks last night, just as we were bringing Fleur ashore."

Morty's expression turned grimmer. "Currently unavailable for comment. Her house was empty when officers arrived to question her this morning, and her car is missing from its usual parking space at Town Hall."

"She's running," Rita stated flatly.

"It appears that way," Morty agreed. "Though she won't get far. We've issued alerts to all transportation hubs within a hundred-mile radius, and her face is currently being distributed to every law enforcement agency in the state."

"Don't underestimate a desperate politician with financial resources," Daisy cautioned. "Meredith strikes me as someone who would have contingency plans for contingency plans."

"Like her partner Fleur claimed," Babs recalled. "Something about 'international connections' and 'contingency plans.'"

"We're pursuing all angles," Morty assured them, though a flicker of concern crossed his features. "Including financial investigations into potential offshore accounts and properties held under alternate identities."

"Well," Daisy said briskly, "it seems you have matters well in hand, Chief. Was there anything specific you needed from us beyond clarification of our statements?"

Morty hesitated, closing his notebook with uncharacteristic uncertainty. "Actually, there was one other thing. More of a personal request than an official one."

"Do tell," Babs encouraged, leaning forward with undisguised curiosity. "Personal requests from law enforcement always make for the most interesting conversations."

Morty cleared his throat, suddenly finding the remaining crumbs on his plate fascinating. "The thing is... Mayor Huffington is organizing a press conference for this afternoon. About the murder, the arrests, and the future of the resort project. He's asked me to provide a statement about the investigation."

"As would be expected from the Chief of Police," Daisy noted, not seeing the issue.

"Yes, well..." Morty shifted uncomfortably. "Given the, ah, unusual nature of how certain evidence came to light, and the mayor's insistence on presenting a 'united community response' to these events..."

Understanding dawned on Rita's face first. "He wants us there," she concluded. "To present a heartwarming story about civic-minded seniors assisting local law enforcement."

Morty winced slightly. "His exact words were 'Conch Key's very own Golden Girls solve the case of the Bulldozer's demise.'" He looked profoundly pained. "There may have been mention of human interest angles and tourism potential."

"Absolutely not," Daisy declared firmly, setting down her coffee mug with enough force to slosh liquid over the rim. "I have no intention of being paraded before cameras as some kind of geriatric Nancy Drew."

"Hear, hear," Babs seconded. "Unless, of course, there's a speaking role. With appropriate lighting. And perhaps a musical interlude."

"Babs!" the other three exclaimed in unison.

"What?" she defended herself. "If we're going to be exploited for publicity, we might as well negotiate favorable terms. It's called showbusiness for a reason, darlings."

"There will be no exploitation," Daisy stated with the finality of someone accustomed to ending academic debates with a single well-placed comment. "We assisted with an investigation as private citizens. We have no interest in publicity, press conferences, or public appearances of any kind."

Morty looked simultaneously relieved and disappointed. "I'll convey your decision to the mayor," he promised, rising from his chair. "Though I should warn you, Bartholomew Huffington can be rather persistent when he gets an idea in his head. Particularly ideas involving potential tourist attractions."

"We'll take our chances," Daisy assured him dryly. "Now, was there anything else, Chief? Or may we continue our recovery from last night's aquatic adventures in peace?"

"Just one final question," Morty said, retrieving his hat from the counter. "Out of professional curiosity, you understand."

"Of course," Daisy replied magnanimously.

"Where exactly did you learn to hot-wire a yacht club rescue boat?" he asked, his gaze fixed on Rita. "Because our harbormaster seems to think that procedure requires specialized knowledge not typically possessed by retired restaurateurs."

Rita met his questioning look with serene composure. "YouTube tutorials," she replied without missing a beat. "Remarkable what one can learn online these days. I also make an excellent soufflé and can rewire a ceiling fan, should the need arise."

Morty stared at her for a long moment before apparently deciding that some questions were better left unexamined. "Right. Well, thank you for the pancakes and the clarifications. I'll be in touch if we need anything further."

"Our pleasure, Chief," Daisy assured him, walking him to the door. "Do keep us informed about Meredith's capture. I find myself rather invested in seeing this case properly concluded."

"I imagine you would be," Morty acknowledged. "Just... no more amateur detective work, please? My blood pressure can't take another night like the last one."

"We make no promises we can't absolutely keep," Daisy replied diplomatically. "But we do have a rather full social calendar this week. The Garden Club meeting has been rescheduled, and Mae's gentle yoga class at the senior center remains a standing commitment."

"The criminal element of Conch Key should find that immensely reassuring," Morty observed dryly. "Good day, ladies."

As the door closed behind him, the four friends exchanged glances that encompassed relief, triumph, and the particular satisfaction that comes from successfully navigating both a murder investigation and a subsequent official inquiry without revealing all of one's methods.

"He took that rather well," Mae commented, gathering empty plates with efficient movements. "Considering that we essentially conducted a parallel investigation right under his nose."

"Morty's a pragmatist," Daisy replied, returning to her seat at the table. "He cares more about results than procedure, though he'd never admit it officially."

"Speaking of results," Babs interjected, helping herself to the last cheese danish, "what do we think about this mysterious disappearance of Councilwoman Moneypenny? Seems rather convenient, doesn't it?"

"Entirely too convenient," Rita agreed, running water into the sink for dishes. "And rather telling. Innocent people rarely flee in the middle of the night."

"Unless they're being framed," Mae suggested thoughtfully. "Which doesn't seem to be the case here, given Fleur's detailed confession."

"I'm more interested in those 'silent partners' Jenkins mentioned," Daisy mused, tapping her fingers rhythmically on the tabletop. "If Meredith was involved financially, who else might have had a stake in the original resort plan? And more importantly, who stood to lose the most from Brock's sudden conversion to environmental conservation?"

"Questions for another day," Rita declared firmly, closing the dishwasher with a decisive click. "Right now, we have more pressing matters to address."

"Such as?" Babs inquired, licking danish crumbs from her fingers with unabashed enjoyment.

"Such as the fact that Mae's yoga class starts in exactly forty-seven minutes, we have a rescheduled Garden Club meeting at two o'clock, and none of us has fully recovered from pretending to be significantly younger than our birth certificates would suggest while chasing criminals in the middle of a thunderstorm."

"Valid concerns," Daisy acknowledged. "Though I feel compelled to point out that I, at least, was pretending to be older as the baroness. The accent alone aged me at least a decade."

"Your accent migrated from Moscow to Mississippi with a brief stopover in Mumbai," Babs informed her bluntly. "It was less 'Russian aristocrat' and more 'international woman of mystery suffering from geographic confusion.'"

"Nevertheless," Daisy sniffed, "the disguise proved effective. Unlike a certain cocktail waitress whose wig maintenance left something to be desired during maritime emergency situations."

"Ladies," Mae interrupted gently, "perhaps we could save the performance critiques for a less pressing moment? Rita's right—we have commitments to keep."

"And recuperation to complete," Rita added. "I don't know about the rest of you, but my shoulders are informing me in no uncertain terms that high-speed boat piloting is not an approved activity for women of our vintage."

"Speak for yourself," Babs retorted, though she winced slightly as she adjusted her position. "I found the entire experience invigorating. Nothing makes one feel more alive than the imminent threat of death by drowning, electrocution, or homicidal art dealer."

"Your definition of 'invigorating' continues to concern me," Daisy remarked. "But I take your point. There is something rather... stimulating about successfully resolving a murder investigation. Even if the methods were somewhat unorthodox."

"And damp," Mae added with uncharacteristic dryness. "Let's not forget damp."

This observation triggered a moment of shared laughter—the kind that comes from surviving something both dangerous and absurd, a release of tension that had been building since their waterlogged return to The Barnacle in the early hours of the morning.

As their mirth subsided, Daisy found herself studying her friends with a newfound appreciation. They were an unlikely quartet—the sharp-tongued former professor, the flamboyant ex-Broadway designer, the practical restaurateur, and the gentle former nurse—yet somehow they had formed a formidable investigative team, each contributing their unique skills and perspectives to solve a murder that might otherwise have gone undetected.

"I believe," she said slowly, "that we make a rather effective team. Despite our various complaints about the physical aftermath."

"Hear, hear," Babs agreed, raising her coffee mug in toast. "To the Seaside Sleuths of Conch Key—solving crimes between hot flashes and Garden Club meetings."

"That's awful," Rita groaned, though she too raised her mug. "We are not calling ourselves that."

"Too late," Babs declared triumphantly. "I've already ordered business cards."

"You've what?" Daisy demanded, nearly choking on her coffee.

"Joking, darling," Babs assured her. "Mostly. Though I did sketch a rather fetching logo design while we were waiting for the police to finish questioning us last night. A magnifying glass over a seashell. Very tasteful."

"Heaven help us," Daisy muttered. "Next thing you know, we'll be accepting cases and charging fees."

"Now there's an idea," Babs mused, her eyes lighting up with entrepreneurial enthusiasm. "Daisy Picklesworth and Associates, Seaside Investigators. For when your criminal problem requires a mature perspective."

"Absolutely not," Daisy stated firmly. "This was a one-time assistance to local law enforcement in extraordinary circumstances. We are not establishing a detective agency at our age."

"Of course not," Mae agreed soothingly. "Though if another situation were to arise naturally..."

"Not you too, Mae," Daisy groaned. "I expected this madness from Babs, but you're supposed to be the sensible one."

Mae smiled serenely. "Even sensible people can enjoy a bit of excitement now and then. Besides, we did good work. Important work. And it was, as Babs said, rather invigorating."

"The world has officially gone mad," Daisy declared to no one in particular. "Next thing you know, Rita will be suggesting we install a crime lab in the garden shed."

"Don't be ridiculous," Rita replied, hanging up her dish towel. "The shed has terrible ventilation. The garage would be much more suitable. All it needs is proper lighting and perhaps some basic equipment."

Daisy stared at her in disbelief, unable to determine if she was joking. Rita's poker face had been perfected over decades of managing restaurant staff and handling difficult customers—it was essentially impenetrable.

"You're all incorrigible," Daisy finally said, throwing up her hands in defeat. "And possibly suffering from post-traumatic stress or oxygen deprivation from last night's adventures. We are not, I repeat, NOT becoming professional investigators."

"Of course not, dear," Babs patted her hand consolingly. "Nothing professional about it. Strictly amateur sleuthing. Now, who's driving to Mae's yoga class? I believe it's my turn, but after last night's excitement, I'm not entirely confident in my ability to distinguish between the accelerator and the brake."

"I'll drive," Rita volunteered. "But we need to leave in twenty minutes if we're going to make it on time."

This announcement triggered a flurry of activity as all four women dispersed to complete their morning preparations. Daisy, left alone in the kitchen for a moment, found herself smiling despite her protestations. There was something undeniably satisfying about their impromptu investigation—not just the resolution of the crime, but the process itself. The gathering of clues, the formulation of theories, the ultimate revelation of truth.

Perhaps, she admitted to herself as she rinsed her coffee mug, there was something to Babs' ridiculous "Seaside Sleuths" concept after all. Not as a business venture, certainly, but as a natural extension of their collective curiosity and complementary skills. And if another mysterious situation should happen to present itself...

Well, they would cross that bridge when they came to it. Preferably not during a lightning storm while in disguise and pursued by murderous art dealers, but one couldn't have everything.

For now, there was yoga to attend, a Garden Club meeting to survive, and the everyday rhythms of life in Conch Key to resume. The murder was solved, the criminals apprehended (or at least identified), and justice was, if not fully served, at least in the process of being properly catered.

"Twenty minutes, Daisy!" Rita's voice called from upstairs. "And wear something appropriate for downward dog this time! The last thing we need is another incident like February's class."

"That was not my fault," Daisy called back automatically. "No one warned me about the transparency issues with those pants under specific lighting conditions."

The familiar bickering continued as The Barnacle's residents prepared for their day, the events of the previous night already transforming from harrowing experience to shared anecdote in that peculiar alchemy that turns danger, once safely past, into story.

And if Daisy happened to tuck Morty's business card into her purse before leaving, well—that was merely practical information storage, not an indication of any intention to pursue further investigative endeavors.

At least, that's what she told herself as she locked the door behind them, casting one final glance at the beach where Brock Hamfist's body had appeared just two days earlier, setting in motion an adventure none of them had anticipated but all had, in their own ways, rather enjoyed.

"Hurry up, Daisy!" Babs called from Rita's sedan, already ensconced in the front passenger seat. "Crime-solving is no excuse for missing yoga. My hot flashes and I need that meditation portion like plants need sunshine!"

"Coming, coming," Daisy muttered, hurrying down the steps with as much dignity as her still-protesting joints would allow. "Heaven forbid we deprive Barbara Zuckerkorn of her weekly opportunity to traumatize the instructor with inappropriate modifications to standard poses."

"It's called creative interpretation," Babs corrected as Daisy slid into the backseat beside Mae. "And Sven appreciates my artistic approach to yoga. He said so himself."

"Sven said, and I quote, 'Please stop doing that before you dislocate something essential,'" Rita reminded her, starting the car with practiced efficiency. "Which is yoga instructor code for 'you're giving me an anxiety disorder.'"

As the car pulled away from The Barnacle, their good-natured bickering continued—four friends whose bond had been tempered by shared danger and midnight boat chases, now returning to the comforting routines of their golden years in Conch Key. Years that, as they had discovered, could still contain unexpected adventures, startling revelations, and the particular satisfaction of justice served.

Even if that justice came with wet shoes, ruined wigs, and the occasional hot flash.

Chapter Seven
Hidden Connections

"As fascinating as this semantic debate undoubtedly is, we have approximately forty-five minutes before we need to leave for the Garden Club meeting. I suggest we focus on lunch and save the philosophical examination of our investigative identity for later."

"Always the pragmatist," Daisy acknowledged with a nod of approval. "Very well. Chicken salad it is, followed by botanical diplomacy and a careful avoidance of murder-related topics."

"At least until Morty updates us on the USB drive contents," Babs amended, following Rita toward the kitchen. "Then all bets are off."

"One crisis at a time," Rita advised, already retrieving ingredients from the refrigerator with practiced efficiency. "Murder in the morning, gardening in the afternoon, and electronic evidence in the evening. A perfectly balanced day for retired ladies of a certain age."

"When you put it that way," Mae remarked, collecting plates from the cabinet, "it doesn't sound nearly as outlandish as it probably should."

"That's what concerns me," Daisy admitted, settling onto a kitchen stool to observe Rita's culinary preparations. "The ease with which we've adapted to these extraordinary circumstances. One might almost believe we were predisposed to investigative endeavors."

"Or desperate for stimulation beyond the typical retirement activities," Babs suggested, arranging herself artfully against the counter. "Bingo and beach walks can only entertain for so long before one craves the adrenaline rush of high-stakes detective work."

Their philosophical musings were interrupted by the distinctive chirping of the doorbell, causing all four women to exchange startled glances.

"Were we expecting someone?" Mae asked, pausing with plates in hand.

"Not to my knowledge," Daisy replied, rising from her stool with the mild caution that had become second nature since their involvement in Brock Hamfist's murder investigation. "Perhaps it's Morty with an update."

"If it's that Peterson man from the community theater asking about rights to our 'dramatic life story' again, tell him I've already sold the movie option to Meryl Streep," Babs called after her as Daisy made her way to the front door.

The familiar silhouette visible through the decorative glass panels was neither Morty's stocky frame nor Peterson's theatrical slouch, but rather the tall, imposing figure of Harold Jenkins, Brock Hamfist's attorney. His usual impeccable appearance—which had earned him the nickname "Dapper Counselor" among Conch Key's legal community—was notably disheveled. His thinning gray hair stood in uncharacteristic disarray, his wire-rimmed glasses sat slightly askew, and his normally pristine suit bore evidence of a hasty dressing.

"Professor Picklesworth," he greeted Daisy, his voice carrying the strained politeness of someone under considerable duress. "I apologize for the unannounced visit, but I believe we have matters of mutual concern to discuss."

"Mr. Jenkins," Daisy replied, studying him with the practiced assessment she'd developed over decades of determining which students were genuinely ill versus those merely unprepared for exams. "This is unexpected. Please, come in."

She led him to the living room, noting the subtle tremor in his hands and the way his gaze darted nervously around the space as if expecting to discover someone hiding behind the furniture.

"Ladies," Daisy announced as Rita, Babs, and Mae appeared from the kitchen, drawn by curiosity about their unexpected visitor, "Mr. Jenkins has come to discuss 'matters of mutual concern.' Perhaps we should postpone lunch briefly?"

"Nonsense," Rita decided, ever the practical hostess. "Mr. Jenkins looks like he could use some nourishment. I've made plenty of chicken salad, and conversations are always more productive when everyone's blood sugar is adequately maintained."

Jenkins appeared momentarily nonplussed by this domestic solution to what he clearly considered an urgent situation, but the combination of Rita's no-nonsense tone and the sudden realization that he was, indeed, quite hungry after what had evidently been a stressful morning led him to accept the invitation with awkward gratitude.

"That's... very kind, though I don't wish to impose," he managed, allowing himself to be guided to the kitchen where Rita efficiently set a place for him at the table.

"Imposing would be interrupting our lunch with urgent legal matters and then refusing to participate in the meal," she informed him, placing a generously filled plate before him. "This way, we maintain our schedule while accommodating your unexpected arrival. Efficient for everyone."

"I... see," Jenkins replied, seemingly both bewildered and impressed by this practical approach. He tentatively sampled the chicken salad, his expression shifting from distracted concern to surprised appreciation. "This is exceptional, Ms. Calabaza."

"The secret is in the—" Rita began, before catching herself. "Well, never mind that. You didn't come to discuss culinary techniques. What brings you to The Barnacle with such evident urgency, Mr. Jenkins?"

The attorney glanced around the table, taking in the four expectant faces with a hesitation that suggested he was reconsidering his impulsive visit. After a moment, he set down his fork with deliberate precision.

"I understand that you ladies have been... involved in the investigation surrounding Brock Hamfist's death," he began carefully.

"'Involved' is such a non-committal term," Babs observed, spearing a cherry tomato with unnecessary drama. "Rather like calling the Titanic's encounter with that iceberg a 'maritime incident.'"

"What Barbara means," Daisy clarified, shooting her friend a warning look, "is that yes, we have provided some assistance to Chief Crabbitz in his investigation. In an entirely unofficial capacity, of course."

"Of course," Jenkins echoed, not sounding entirely convinced. "Well, it's precisely that 'unofficial capacity' that brings me here. There are aspects of this situation that... concern me. Aspects that I'm not certain the official investigation is adequately addressing."

"How fascinating," Daisy remarked, her academic interest immediately engaged. "Perhaps you could elaborate on these concerning aspects?"

Jenkins hesitated again, adjusting his askew glasses with a nervous gesture. "Before I continue, I need to establish certain parameters. This conversation must remain confidential. I am potentially compromising my professional ethics by being here, but I believe circumstances justify extreme measures."

"We understand the need for discretion," Mae assured him gently. "Patient confidentiality was the cornerstone of my nursing career."

"And theatrical confidentiality was the cornerstone of my Broadway career," Babs added. "You wouldn't believe the secrets I've kept about leading men and their... inadequacies."

"Hardly equivalent, Babs," Daisy murmured, before turning her attention back to their increasingly uncomfortable guest. "Mr. Jenkins, while we cannot make legally binding promises of confidentiality, we can assure you that we are not in the habit of unnecessarily broadcasting sensitive information. If you've come to us rather than the authorities, I assume you have reasons to believe we might be more receptive or effective in addressing your concerns."

Jenkins nodded slowly, seeming to arrive at a decision. "What I'm about to share involves not just Brock's murder, but a complex network of influence and corruption that extends far beyond what the current investigation has revealed. Fleur DuBois and Meredith Moneypenny are merely the visible elements of a much larger system."

"We had begun to suspect as much," Daisy acknowledged, exchanging significant glances with her friends. "Particularly given certain information that has recently come to light."

"You're referring to the USB drive," Jenkins stated rather than asked. "Yes, I'm aware it's now in police possession. Ziggy Hamfist contacted me this morning, somewhat panicked about having shared it with you." A faint smile briefly crossed his tense features. "He seemed surprised that I already knew about its existence."

"You knew about the drive?" Rita asked, her practical nature immediately focusing on this critical detail.

"I helped Brock create it," Jenkins confirmed, the admission visibly costing him some professional discomfort. "Or rather, I helped him organize and document the evidence he had been gathering for months. Evidence that ultimately led to his death."

"So you knew about his plans to transform the resort project," Mae suggested. "The environmental conversion wasn't as sudden as everyone believed?"

"The public environmental awakening was somewhat theatrical," Jenkins acknowledged. "But the underlying disillusionment with his partners and their methods had been developing for some time. Brock may have been called 'The Bulldozer,' but he had certain ethical boundaries he was unwilling to cross. Boundaries that others in the development consortium regularly ignored."

"Such as money laundering?" Daisy suggested delicately.

Jenkins' eyebrows rose slightly. "You're remarkably well-informed for civilians who have been involved for less than seventy-two hours."

"We're quick studies," Babs informed him with mild indignation. "And surprisingly effective interrogators, as Fleur DuBois can now attest from her comfortable accommodations at the Conch Key Police Department."

"Yes, well," Jenkins continued, seemingly torn between professional reserve and urgent communication, "the money laundering operation was merely one component of a much more comprehensive criminal enterprise. Property manipulation, environmental regulation circumvention, strategic bribery of officials—a sophisticated system that has operated in this region for decades." He paused, appearing to consider exactly how much to reveal. "A system that has recently been expanding its reach and ambitions."

"And Brock discovered this system," Daisy concluded, fitting pieces together with practiced academic precision. "Initially as a participant, but eventually as a reluctant witness growing increasingly concerned about the implications."

"Precisely," Jenkins confirmed. "His environmental 'conversion' was partially genuine—he did have a near-drowning experience during a fishing expedition that apparently triggered some existential reconsideration—but it was also a convenient public explanation for changes that were primarily motivated by his desire to extricate himself from criminal entanglements."

"Changes that certain parties found unacceptable," Rita observed. "Hence the murder."

"Hence the murder," Jenkins agreed grimly. "Though I suspect Fleur and Meredith were acting on instructions rather than personal initiative. They had the most immediate financial motives, certainly, but they were merely mid-level operators in a much larger organizational structure."

This revelation caused a momentary silence around the table as the four friends absorbed its implications. Daisy was the first to speak, her tone measured but intense.

"Mr. Jenkins, you've shared potentially dangerous information with us, at evident personal risk. May I ask why? Why come to us rather than directly to Chief Crabbitz with these concerns?"

Jenkins set down his water glass with precise movements, his expression shifting from nervous apprehension to somber resolution.

"Because I believe the influence of this organization extends into local law enforcement," he replied quietly. "Not Morty himself—he's aggressively honest to a fault—but other elements within the department. Information has been leaking. Evidence disappearing. Lines of inquiry subtly redirected."

"That's a serious accusation," Daisy noted, her academic skepticism automatically engaging. "Do you have evidence of this corruption?"

"Circumstantial at best," Jenkins admitted. "But compelling in aggregate. And recent events have accelerated my concerns." He leaned forward slightly, lowering his voice despite being in a private home. "Meredith Moneypenny's car was discovered abandoned this morning at Mangrove Key Marina, with what appears to be a suicide note."

"We're aware," Daisy confirmed. "Chief Crabbitz informed us earlier today."

"What you may not be aware of," Jenkins continued, "is that I received a text message from Meredith approximately thirty minutes after the car was discovered. A message sent from a number I've never seen before, containing information only she would know."

This revelation caused another round of significant glances between the four friends.

"She's alive, then," Babs concluded dramatically. "And apparently tech-savvy enough to establish untraceable communications."

"Alive and frightened," Jenkins corrected. "The message was brief but clear: 'They know everything. Not safe. Trust no one with a badge. J.A. is involved.'"

"J.A.?" Mae repeated, her brow furrowing in concentration. "Who might that be?"

A shadow crossed Jenkins' face as he replied. "Judge Anderson. Jonathan Anderson. The senior judicial authority in this jurisdiction, who coincidentally approved all the necessary legal variances for Brock's original resort project with remarkable speed and minimal scrutiny."

"Good heavens," Daisy murmured, the implications expanding exponentially. "If judicial authorities are compromised..."

"Then the entire legal mechanism for addressing these crimes is potentially corrupted," Jenkins completed her thought. "Which is precisely why I came to you. You've demonstrated both effectiveness and discretion in your investigation thus far, and—perhaps most importantly—you operate completely outside the established power structures of Conch Key."

"We're just four retired women sharing a beach house," Rita pointed out practically. "Hardly equipped to confront a sophisticated criminal organization with apparent tentacles throughout the regional power structure."

"And yet," Jenkins countered, "you managed to identify and apprehend two murderers that the official investigation had initially classified as a tragic drowning accident. You uncovered evidence that had eluded professional investigators. And you've demonstrated a remarkably effective approach to information gathering."

"We do have certain advantages," Daisy acknowledged thoughtfully. "People tend to underestimate women of our age and speak more freely in our presence. We have accumulated a lifetime of observational skills and professional expertise in our respective fields. And we have extensive connections throughout the community that transcend traditional social boundaries."

"Precisely," Jenkins nodded eagerly. "You are uniquely positioned to continue this investigation without triggering the defensive mechanisms that would immediately activate if, for instance, state or federal authorities became overtly involved."

"Mr. Jenkins," Mae said gently, her natural compassion evident in her tone, "while we appreciate your confidence in our abilities, I'm concerned about what exactly you're asking of us. This sounds potentially quite dangerous."

"More dangerous than confronting a murderer on a storm-swept dock during a lightning storm?" Jenkins countered with surprising specificity. At their startled expressions, he added, "Conch Key is a small town. Word travels, even when official reports are deliberately vague."

"The dock confrontation was... unplanned," Daisy clarified. "An immediate response to an urgent situation. What you seem to be suggesting is a deliberate investigation into an organized criminal enterprise with apparent influence throughout local governance. That's a different category of involvement altogether."

"I understand your reservations," Jenkins assured them. "I'm not suggesting you confront anyone directly or place yourselves in physical danger. Merely that you continue what you've already begun—gathering information, connecting seemingly unrelated events, identifying key players. But with awareness of the broader context."

"And what exactly is this broader context?" Rita asked, her no-nonsense approach cutting through the diplomatic circumlocution. "You've hinted at organized crime, corruption, and wide-ranging conspiracy, but without specific details, we're operating in a fog."

Jenkins hesitated only briefly before reaching into his jacket pocket and withdrawing a thumb drive similar in appearance to the one Ziggy had provided earlier.

"This contains a comprehensive overview of what Brock and I managed to document," he explained, placing it carefully on the table. "Financial transactions, property records, meeting notes, communication logs—all pointing to the existence of what appears to be a highly sophisticated operation focused on regional development and resource exploitation."

"And you're not taking this directly to state or federal authorities because...?" Babs prompted, eyeing the drive with undisguised curiosity.

"Because previous attempts to involve outside agencies have been mysteriously derailed," Jenkins replied grimly. "Investigations reassigned, evidence compromised, witnesses suddenly recanting or relocating. The organization's influence appears to extend beyond local boundaries."

"That seems almost implausibly comprehensive," Daisy observed, academic skepticism evident in her tone. "Few criminal enterprises achieve such perfect operational security."

"Not perfect," Jenkins corrected. "Just extremely effective. And they've had decades to establish their networks and protocols. This isn't a recent development—it's a long-standing operation that has gradually expanded its reach and ambition."

The four friends exchanged glances that communicated volumes without words—a silent conversation developed through years of friendship and recently honed by their unexpected foray into collaborative investigation.

"We need to discuss this privately," Daisy informed Jenkins, her tone gentle but firm. "I'm sure you understand that what you're suggesting requires careful consideration."

"Of course," Jenkins agreed, though his expression betrayed disappointment at their hesitation. "I should mention, however, that time may be a factor. With Brock's murder now officially classified as homicide and the USB evidence in police possession, the organization will be implementing containment protocols. Which likely includes addressing potential liabilities such as myself."

"Are you in immediate danger?" Mae asked with genuine concern.

"I've taken precautions," Jenkins assured her, though his nervous glances toward the windows suggested these precautions provided limited comfort. "But I would prefer not to leave this drive in my possession any longer than necessary."

"We understand," Daisy assured him. "And we appreciate both your trust and the risks you're taking in coming to us. If you'll excuse us briefly?"

Jenkins nodded, accepting this reasonable request with evident relief that they hadn't immediately dismissed his concerns. As the four women stepped into the adjacent living room for a hasty conference, he remained at the kitchen table, mechanically finishing his chicken salad with the distracted movements of someone whose mind was occupied with considerably weightier matters than lunch.

"Well," Babs said once they were reasonably private, keeping her voice low despite her natural tendency toward theatrical volume, "this certainly puts a different spin on our Garden Club plans for the afternoon."

"Indeed," Daisy agreed dryly. "Eugenia's succulent presentation suddenly seems less compelling when contrasted with allegations of region-wide criminal conspiracy."

"The question," Rita pointed out practically, "is whether we're seriously considering involving ourselves further. This goes well beyond finding a body on our beach and conducting a bit of amateur sleuthing. This is potentially dangerous territory."

"And yet," Mae said thoughtfully, "if Mr. Jenkins is correct about the extent of this organization's influence, who else can pursue this? If law enforcement and judicial authorities are compromised..."

"We're four retired women, not the FBI," Rita reminded her. "We don't have training, resources, or authority for this kind of investigation."

"We didn't have training for apprehending art dealers on storm-swept docks either," Babs pointed out. "Yet here we are, with Fleur DuBois enjoying the hospitality of the Conch Key holding cells largely thanks to our intervention."

"That was different," Rita insisted. "That was immediate and specific. This is vast and amorphous—a conspiracy that allegedly encompasses judges, developers, and who knows what other powerful entities."

"All the more reason they might underestimate us," Daisy mused, her academic mind already analyzing potential approaches. "No one expects four retirement-age women to pose any investigative threat. It's the perfect cover, in many ways."

"Now you sound like you're actually considering this," Rita observed with mild alarm.

"I'm considering all aspects," Daisy clarified. "Including the possibility that Jenkins is mistaken, delusional, or attempting to manipulate us for reasons we don't yet understand."

"He seemed genuinely concerned," Mae noted. "And his information aligns with what we've already discovered about Brock's murder and the financial crimes connected to the resort project."

"Alignment doesn't equate to accuracy," Daisy reminded her. "He could be building on known facts to construct a more elaborate narrative for purposes we haven't identified."

"Such as?" Babs challenged.

"Diversion, perhaps," Daisy suggested. "Drawing attention away from his own potential involvement. Or testing our receptiveness to conspiracy theories to determine whether we might pose a threat to whatever actual operations are underway."

"You think he's what—a criminal mastermind conducting counterintelligence on us?" Rita asked skeptically. "The man who once fainted during the Conch Key Amateur Theatre production of 'Witness for the Prosecution' because his bow tie was too tight?"

"People contain multitudes," Daisy replied, though she acknowledged the point with a small smile. "But no, I think it's more likely he's genuinely concerned and potentially correct, at least in broad strokes. The question remains whether we're the appropriate parties to address these concerns."

"If not us, then who?" Mae asked simply.

The question hung in the air between them, its straightforward logic challenging their natural inclination toward cautious disengagement. Before they could continue their deliberation, a sharp crack from the kitchen interrupted their whispered conference—the distinctive sound of breaking glass followed by a thud.

They rushed back to find Harold Jenkins slumped forward at the table, a small dart protruding from the back of his neck and blood spreading slowly from a neat hole in the window directly behind his chair.

"My God," Daisy gasped, professional composure momentarily abandoned in the face of such unexpected violence. "Call 911!"

Mae was already moving, her medical training overriding shock as she checked Jenkins for vital signs while Rita hurried to the phone. Babs, displaying surprising presence of mind, immediately dropped to a crouch below window level and pulled Daisy down alongside her.

"Sniper," she hissed, her theatrical whisper carrying surprising urgency. "Whoever fired might still be watching."

Daisy nodded her agreement, shocked but quickly recovering her analytical faculties. "The angle suggests the shot came from the dunes behind the house. Rita, stay low when making that call. Mae, status?"

"Pulse present but weak and irregular," Mae reported, her voice remarkably steady as she applied pressure to the wound with a kitchen towel. "Breathing shallow. The dart appears to be some kind of delivery system—probably a toxin or sedative based on his rapid deterioration."

"This is Rita Calabaza at The Barnacle," Rita was saying into the phone, her body hunched below the kitchen counter for protection. "We have a man down with what appears to be a projectile wound. Harold Jenkins, the attorney. Yes, immediate medical assistance. And police. Chief Crabbitz specifically, if possible."

Daisy's gaze fell on the thumb drive, still sitting on the table where Jenkins had placed it moments before. With careful movements, staying low and using the table for cover, she retrieved it and slipped it into her pocket. As she did so, she noticed a small folded paper that had apparently fallen from Jenkins' hand as he collapsed, now partially hidden beneath his slumped form.

"Mae," she whispered urgently. "There's a note under his left hand. Can you retrieve it without compromising his medical situation?"

Mae nodded, carefully extracting the paper while maintaining pressure on Jenkins' wound with her other hand. She passed the note to Daisy, who unfolded it with fingers that were surprisingly steady given the circumstances.

The message was brief, typed rather than handwritten, and chillingly direct:

"EVIDENCE SECURED. JENKINS COMPROMISED. PROCEED WITH CAUTION. CONTACT ONLY THROUGH ESTABLISHED CHANNELS. – M.M."

"Meredith Moneypenny," Babs breathed, reading over Daisy's shoulder. "She's monitoring the situation—probably anticipated Jenkins would come to us."

"And someone else was monitoring Jenkins," Rita observed grimly, rejoining them after completing her emergency call. "Someone with access to specialized weaponry and the skill to use it with precision."

"Ambulance is five minutes out," she reported. "Morty is responding personally. And I told them to approach with caution given the possibility of an active shooter."

"Good thinking," Daisy acknowledged, her mind racing through implications and possibilities. "This rather definitively answers our question about whether Jenkins was being truthful regarding the existence of a dangerous criminal organization."

"And whether we should involve ourselves further," Babs added, her naturally dramatic personality for once subdued by the gravity of actual violence. "I believe that decision has been rather forcefully made for us."

"How so?" Rita challenged, though her tone suggested she already anticipated the answer.

"Because," Daisy replied, holding up the note with grim determination, "we've just become active participants whether we intended to or not. Jenkins was shot mere minutes after entering our home. We now possess both his evidence drive and an apparent communication from Meredith Moneypenny. We are, by any reasonable assessment, directly involved in whatever conspiracy Jenkins was attempting to expose."

The wail of approaching sirens punctuated her statement, the familiar sound somehow transformed from reassuring to ominous by Jenkins' warning about compromised law enforcement. As they waited for help to arrive, maintaining what medical assistance they could for their unexpected and now grievously injured visitor, the four friends exchanged glances that communicated a complex mixture of fear, determination, and resolve.

Their brief adventure into amateur detection had just evolved into something far more serious—a dangerous conspiracy with potentially lethal consequences. The Garden Club meeting would definitely need to be rescheduled.

And somewhere in Conch Key, watching from a carefully selected vantage point, a figure with specialized equipment was reporting mission status through secure channels:

"Target neutralized. Evidence status unknown. Four witnesses present—elderly females, property owners. Awaiting instructions regarding containment protocols."

Chapter Eight
Under Siege

The next thirty minutes at The Barnacle unfolded with the surreal quality of a particularly implausible television drama—sirens wailing, emergency personnel rushing in with practiced urgency, and four stunned women attempting to process their abrupt transition from retirement to apparent targets in what Jenkins had described as a "sophisticated criminal enterprise."

"So let me make sure I've got this straight," Chief Crabbitz said, his perpetually sunburned complexion now approaching an alarming shade of crimson as he paced the living room. "Harold Jenkins shows up unannounced, tells you there's a massive criminal conspiracy operating throughout the region, hands over evidence on a thumb drive, and then gets shot with some kind of poisoned dart through your kitchen window. All before lunch."

"The timeline is accurate, though your tone suggests skepticism," Daisy replied from her position on the sofa, where she sat with perfect posture despite the chaos around them. "And technically, it was during lunch. Rita's chicken salad was involved."

"The chicken salad is irrelevant, Daisy," Rita murmured from beside her.

"On the contrary," Daisy countered. "It establishes that this was a casual social interaction that turned violent, not a prearranged meeting that might suggest our prior knowledge of or involvement in whatever conspiracy Jenkins was describing."

Morty pinched the bridge of his nose, a gesture they had come to recognize as his response to mounting frustration. "I'm not accusing you ladies of being criminal conspirators. I'm trying to understand how you've managed, yet again, to place yourselves at the epicenter of what's rapidly becoming the most complex case in Conch Key history."

"We didn't place ourselves anywhere," Babs objected, adjusting her position on the loveseat where she and Mae were huddled together. "Jenkins came to us. The dart came through our window. We're victims here, Morty! Victims with excellent investigative instincts, but victims nonetheless."

"Victims who somehow came into possession of potentially crucial evidence," Morty noted, his sharp gaze falling on the thumb drive that now rested in an evidence bag on the coffee table. "Evidence that might explain why someone tried to silence a respected attorney in broad daylight."

"We merely secured it during the chaos of the moment," Daisy explained primly. "It seemed the responsible action, given the circumstances."

"Uh-huh," Morty replied, his skepticism evident. "And the note from Meredith Moneypenny? The supposedly dead or fleeing councilwoman who's now apparently sending you cryptic warnings?"

"That was unexpected," Mae admitted softly. "Though it certainly suggests Mr. Jenkins was telling the truth about the extent of the conspiracy."

The chief's radio crackled with an update from the paramedics who had transported Jenkins to Conch Key Memorial Hospital. The prognosis was cautiously optimistic—the dart had contained a powerful sedative rather than a lethal toxin, and they had stabilized his condition sufficiently for transfer to the intensive care unit.

"Well, that's something at least," Morty muttered, tucking the radio back onto his belt. "Now, about the thumb drive..."

"We didn't access it," Daisy assured him quickly. "Unlike our previous collaborative investigation, we recognized this situation required immediate professional involvement."

"Collaborative investigation," Morty repeated with a pained expression. "That's one way to describe four civilians impersonating yacht club staff and engaging in a high-speed boat chase during a lightning storm."

"Semantics," Babs dismissed with a wave of her bejeweled hand. "The point is, we're being responsible this time. Turning over evidence, providing detailed statements, letting you handle the dangerous elements." She leaned forward conspiratorially. "Though if you need assistance with the more cerebral aspects of the investigation, our consulting services remain available."

"Your consulting—" Morty broke off, visibly counting to ten before continuing. "What I need is for you ladies to be extremely careful. If Jenkins is right about this criminal organization, and if they were willing to shoot him in your kitchen in broad daylight, then you may be in serious danger."

"A logical conclusion," Daisy agreed. "Though one wonders why they used a sedative rather than a more permanently silencing method."

"Perhaps they wanted to question him later?" Mae suggested, her normally gentle features creased with worry. "About what he might have told us?"

"Or they're sending a message," Rita proposed grimly. "Demonstrating their reach and capabilities without crossing the line into murder that would trigger a more intensive investigation."

"All plausible theories," Morty acknowledged. "Which is why I'm posting officers outside your house until we better understand what we're dealing with."

"Is that really necessary?" Daisy asked, though her tone suggested she already knew the answer.

"Someone shot a dart through your kitchen window less than an hour ago," Morty reminded her. "So yes, I'd say it's necessary."

"What about the Garden Club meeting?" Mae asked with such genuine concern that it momentarily halted the serious discussion. "Eugenia has been preparing her succulent presentation for weeks."

"I think Eugenia's succulents will have to soldier on without you today," Morty replied, his expression softening slightly at Mae's characteristic prioritization of social obligations even in the face of apparent danger. "I need you all to stay put while we process the scene and set up appropriate security."

"House arrest," Babs declared dramatically. "Imprisoned in our own home! Though I suppose there are worse places to be confined. At least we have Rita's cooking and Daisy's extensive library of mystery novels, which have suddenly become instructional rather than recreational reading."

"It's not house arrest," Morty corrected her with strained patience. "It's protective custody. And it's temporary—just until we assess the threat level and implement appropriate security measures."

"Which will take how long, exactly?" Rita inquired, practical as always.

"That depends on what we find on this thumb drive," Morty replied, carefully placing the evidence bag in his pocket. "And how it connects to the information we've already recovered from the USB drive Ziggy provided."

"Speaking of which," Daisy said, adopting the tone she had once used to guide doctoral candidates through particularly challenging theoretical concepts, "given Jenkins' concerns about compromised elements within local law enforcement, perhaps you should consider involving state or federal authorities in analyzing that evidence. As a precautionary measure, of course."

Morty's expression suggested he had already considered this possibility. "I've made some calls," he admitted. "Got an old academy buddy in the Florida Department of Law Enforcement. He's sending a digital forensics team that should be here by evening." He hesitated, then added with evident reluctance, "And I'd appreciate it if you didn't mention that to anyone. Including Officer Butterworth."

This revelation caused four pairs of eyebrows to rise in synchronized surprise.

"Not Peanut?" Mae gasped. "Surely he's not involved in anything nefarious?"

"I don't think so," Morty assured her. "But at this point, I'm operating on a need-to-know basis. And the fewer people who know about the state investigation, the better."

"Very cloak-and-dagger," Babs commented with undisguised relish. "I'm getting strong film noir vibes from this entire situation. All we need is some atmospheric lighting and a world-weary voiceover."

"This isn't one of your theatrical productions, Barbara," Morty reminded her with exasperation. "Real people are getting hurt. Jenkins is in intensive care, Meredith Moneypenny is either dead or on the run, and you four are potential targets of what appears to be a highly organized criminal enterprise."

"All the more reason to maintain our spirits through appropriate humor," Babs replied with surprising dignity. "Laughter in the face of danger is a time-honored coping mechanism. And frankly, after tackling a murderous art dealer off a dock during a lightning storm, my bar for alarming situations has been significantly raised."

Before Morty could formulate a suitably professional response to this declaration, Officer Butterworth appeared in the doorway, his youthful features set in lines of focused concentration that made him appear temporarily older than his twenty-eight years.

"Chief," he reported, "crime scene techs have finished processing the kitchen. They recovered the dart and are dusting the window frame for prints, though they're not optimistic given the professional nature of the attack."

"Professional?" Daisy inquired, latching onto the term with academic precision.

Butterworth nodded grimly. "The dart is military-grade, not something you can pick up at a sporting goods store. And the trajectory suggests the shooter was positioned in the dunes approximately seventy-five yards from the house—a difficult shot requiring specialized training and equipment."

"So we're dealing with professionals," Morty concluded, his expression darkening further. "All the more reason for you ladies to stay put and let us handle this."

"Of course," Daisy agreed, perhaps a bit too readily. "We have no intention of interfering with your investigation or placing ourselves in additional danger."

Morty's skeptical look suggested he found this sudden compliance somewhat suspect. "Uh-huh. And I suppose if I check back in an hour, I'll find all four of you sitting quietly in the living room, not planning any amateur detective work or unauthorized information gathering?"

"Define 'unauthorized,'" Babs requested innocently.

"Barbara," Morty sighed, "I'm trying to keep you alive. Could you please, for once, make that job slightly easier?"

"We understand your concerns, Chief," Mae assured him, her gentle voice carrying surprising authority. "And we appreciate the protection. We'll be careful and prudent."

"Thank you, Mae," Morty replied, seeming genuinely relieved that at least one resident of The Barnacle appeared to grasp the seriousness of the situation. "I'll have officers stationed at both exits and regular patrols checking the perimeter. Do not—and I cannot stress this enough—do not leave the house for any reason without police escort."

"What about bathroom breaks?" Babs asked with exaggerated concern. "Are we to be accompanied even in our most private moments?"

"I meant outside the house, Barbara," Morty clarified with heroic patience. "You're free to move about inside your home without tactical support."

"Well, that's something at least," Babs conceded. "Though if this confinement extends beyond twenty-four hours, I may require an emergency delivery of my special conditioner. This salt air plays absolute havoc with red hair, you know."

Morty visibly chose not to engage with this particular concern. "I'll have Officer Butterworth coordinate with you regarding any essential needs. In the meantime, please just... stay put. And maybe consider turning off the lights and staying away from windows after dark."

"Now that does sound ominously film noir," Babs observed. "Should we be developing secret knocks and password protocols as well?"

"If it keeps you from opening the door to potential assassins, then yes," Morty replied with unexpected seriousness. "Jenkins was targeted for a reason. Until we understand what that reason was and whether you ladies are also considered threats by whoever is behind this, extreme caution is warranted."

With that sobering assessment, he departed to oversee the ongoing crime scene processing and security arrangements, leaving the four friends to contemplate their unexpectedly dramatic afternoon.

"Well," Babs said once they were alone, "this certainly puts our Garden Club obligations in perspective. Poor Eugenia will be disappointed about her succulent presentation, but 'avoiding professional assassins' does seem like a reasonable excuse for absence."

"I'll call her," Mae volunteered, reaching for the phone. "Though I'm not entirely sure what to say. 'Sorry we missed the meeting, we're under police protection after an attorney was shot in our kitchen' sounds rather alarming."

"Perhaps something vaguer," Daisy suggested. "A household emergency requiring immediate attention."

"Technically accurate," Rita agreed, rising from the sofa with a practical air that suggested she was already adapting to their altered circumstances. "And speaking of household matters, we never did finish lunch. I don't know about the rest of you, but stress always increases my appetite."

"Food does seem advisable," Daisy acknowledged. "Though I admit my enthusiasm for eating in the kitchen has been somewhat diminished by recent events."

"We can set up in the dining room," Rita decided. "It's more defensible anyway—no direct sight lines from the dunes."

"Listen to you," Babs marveled. "Five minutes of police protection and you're already thinking like a tactical expert."

"I dated a Marine Corps sergeant for six months in my forties," Rita explained with a dismissive wave. "He was perpetually assessing defensive positions and escape routes. Exhausting in a relationship, but apparently useful knowledge for unexpected sieges."

As Rita busied herself with relocating their interrupted lunch to the more secure dining room, and Mae placed a carefully worded call to the Garden Club president explaining their absence, Daisy found herself drawn to the front window, where she could observe the police activity now surrounding The Barnacle.

Crime scene tape created a garish yellow boundary around their previously peaceful property. Officers in uniform established a perimeter, communicating via radio with professionally serious expressions. The crime scene technicians moved with practiced efficiency, photographing, measuring, and collecting evidence from the area where the shooter had presumably positioned themselves among the dunes.

It was, Daisy reflected, an extraordinary transformation of their peaceful retirement existence. Just days ago, their most pressing concerns had involved book club selections and the appropriate color scheme for the community garden plantings. Now they were potential targets in what Jenkins had described as a "sophisticated criminal enterprise" with apparent connections throughout regional governance.

"Penny for your thoughts," Babs said, joining her at the window despite Morty's warning about exposing themselves to potential observers. "Though given inflation, perhaps I should offer a dollar."

"I'm contemplating the remarkable speed with which the ordinary can become extraordinary," Daisy replied, her academic mind naturally inclined toward philosophical assessment even in crisis. "How quickly one transitions from mundane concerns to matters of life and death."

"A rather grim observation for someone who once spent an entire afternoon debating the merits of Oxford commas," Babs noted. "Though not inaccurate. One minute we're planning for succulent presentations, the next we're analyzing dart trajectories and contemplating criminal conspiracies."

"It's not entirely unexpected, though, is it?" Daisy mused. "Our involvement in Brock's murder investigation was bound to have repercussions. We disrupted something significant—more significant than we initially realized, apparently."

"The question," Babs said, uncharacteristically serious, "is what we do now. Morty clearly expects us to sit quietly and let the professionals handle the situation."

"And you find that prospect..."

"Boring," Babs declared without hesitation. "And frankly implausible. We've already demonstrated an aptitude for this type of investigation, and we possess contextual knowledge that might prove valuable. Not to mention the fact that we're directly involved now, whether we chose to be or not."

"A compelling analysis," Daisy acknowledged. "Though there is the small matter of professional assassins potentially targeting us, which does somewhat alter the risk-benefit calculation."

"Details," Babs dismissed with a theatrical wave. "Besides, what safer place to continue our investigation than right here, surrounded by Conch Key's finest? We have phones, internet access, and our collective intelligence. We can gather information without leaving our protective cocoon."

Before Daisy could formulate a suitable response to this surprisingly logical argument, the distinctive chime of the doorbell interrupted their conversation, causing both women to step instinctively away from the window.

"Are we expecting visitors?" Babs whispered, suddenly alert to potential threats despite her previous bravado.

"Unlikely," Daisy replied, moving cautiously toward the entryway where they could see a uniformed officer speaking with someone on the porch. "Given the police perimeter, it must be someone Morty has cleared."

The mystery was resolved moments later when Officer Butterworth ushered in a familiar figure—Ziggy Hamfist, looking even more disheveled than usual, his dreadlocks hastily secured in a messy bun and his hemp clothing bearing evidence of what appeared to be a hasty departure from somewhere.

"Ladies," Butterworth announced with formal politeness, "Mr. Hamfist insists he has information relevant to the current situation. The Chief said to use your discretion about speaking with him, but he's been searched and cleared."

"Searched?" Babs repeated, eyebrows rising. "My, we are taking this seriously."

"Standard protocol for visiting persons under protective custody," Butterworth explained with professional detachment. "I'll be right outside if you need anything." With a nod that somehow conveyed both respect and caution, he stepped back onto the porch, pulling the door closed behind him.

"Ziggy," Daisy greeted their unexpected visitor. "This is a surprise. I understood you were maintaining a low profile at the Conch Key Cabanas."

"I was," Ziggy confirmed, his usually laid-back demeanor replaced by visible agitation. "Until someone tried to break into my room about an hour ago. Fortunately, I was in the bathroom—heard them picking the lock and managed to slip out the window before they got in."

"How athletically resourceful of you," Babs commented, eyeing his lanky frame with newfound appreciation. "Though one wonders why you came here rather than directly to the police station."

"Because the people who were breaking in were wearing police uniforms," Ziggy replied grimly. "Or at least, what looked like police uniforms."

This revelation caused a momentary silence as Daisy and Babs exchanged significant glances.

"Perhaps you should join us in the dining room," Daisy suggested, gesturing toward the interior of the house. "Rita has prepared lunch, and it seems we have much to discuss."

Ziggy followed them with obvious relief, the tension in his shoulders visibly easing as he entered the relative security of The Barnacle's dining room, where Rita and Mae were setting the table with the practical efficiency of women accustomed to accommodating unexpected developments.

"Ziggy," Rita acknowledged with mild surprise. "I assume this isn't a social call."

"Not exactly," Ziggy confirmed, accepting the seat Mae pulled out for him with gentle hospitality. "Someone tried to grab me at the motel. And before that, I got a weird text from a number I didn't recognize."

"Let me guess," Daisy said, taking her own seat at the table. "From someone with the initials M.M., containing cryptic warnings about trust and safety?"

Ziggy's eyes widened in surprise. "How did you know?"

"Because we received a similar communication," Daisy informed him. "Right before Harold Jenkins was shot with a poisoned dart through our kitchen window."

"Holy shit," Ziggy breathed, forgetting himself momentarily. "Sorry, I mean—wait, Jenkins was shot? Is he...?"

"Alive," Mae assured him quickly. "Though in intensive care. The dart contained a powerful sedative rather than a lethal toxin, fortunately."

"And now we're under police protection," Babs added, gesturing vaguely toward the officers visible through the dining room windows. "Like witnesses in a mob movie, only with better real estate and significantly more stylish outfits."

"This is insane," Ziggy muttered, running a hand through his disheveled hair. "All because my dad suddenly decided to grow a conscience about some development project?"

"We believe the situation may be considerably more complex than that," Daisy explained carefully. "According to information Jenkins shared before his unfortunate sedation, your father had discovered evidence of a sophisticated criminal enterprise operating throughout the region, using development projects as vehicles for various illegal activities."

"Like money laundering," Ziggy suggested, revealing an unexpected familiarity with criminal terminology. "Yeah, that tracks with some of the weird stuff Dad was saying that night. About how he'd been 'blind to the real costs' and needed to 'make things right before it was too late.'"

"Did he elaborate on what making things right entailed?" Daisy inquired, her academic mind automatically seeking precise details.

"Not really," Ziggy admitted. "He was being all cryptic and dramatic. Said he'd been 'shown the truth' and couldn't continue 'participating in destruction for profit.' I figured it was just some midlife crisis thing, maybe triggered by that near-drowning experience he had."

"Near-drowning?" Mae echoed, her nursing instincts immediately engaged. "When did this occur?"

"About a month ago," Ziggy recalled. "He was out on some fishing charter—which was weird in itself since he hated water. Apparently fell overboard during rough weather. The captain pulled him out, but Dad said he was underwater long enough to... I don't know, see something that changed him."

"A transformative near-death experience," Daisy mused. "Fascinating from a psychological perspective, though perhaps not a complete explanation for his subsequent actions."

"Whatever caused it, he definitely changed," Ziggy insisted. "Started talking about legacy and responsibility. Even apologized for being hard on me about my environmental activism." He shook his head in lingering disbelief. "That's when I knew something serious was happening. Dad never apologized. For anything."

"And after this change of heart, he began gathering evidence about whatever criminal activities he had discovered," Rita concluded. "Which potentially made him a threat to whoever is running this enterprise."

"Which now apparently includes people in police uniforms breaking into motel rooms," Babs added. "Assuming Ziggy's identification was accurate and not influenced by recreational substances."

"I was stone-cold sober," Ziggy insisted with indignation. "Haven't touched anything stronger than chamomile tea since Dad died. Needed to keep my head clear, you know? And I know what I saw—two guys in Conch Key PD uniforms using professional lock-picking tools on my door."

"Disturbing if accurate," Daisy acknowledged. "And consistent with Jenkins' warning about compromised elements within local law enforcement."

"So what do we do now?" Ziggy asked, accepting the plate of chicken salad Rita placed before him with distracted gratitude. "I mean, if we can't even trust the police..."

"We can trust Morty," Mae stated with firm conviction. "He's as honest as they come."

"And he's bringing in state investigators," Daisy added. "Which suggests he shares our concerns about potential local corruption."

"In the meantime," Rita said practically, "we eat. Crisis management requires adequate nutrition."

They settled into an oddly normal lunch routine despite the extraordinary circumstances—passing serving dishes, refilling water glasses, and engaging in the familiar rhythms of shared meals that had defined their friendship long before murder investigations and criminal conspiracies had entered the picture.

It was during a momentary lull in conversation that Mae, who had been unusually quiet, suddenly spoke up with unexpected urgency.

"The fishing charter," she said, eyes widening with realization. "Ziggy, do you know which charter company your father used for that trip? The one where he had his near-drowning experience?"

Ziggy considered the question, chewing thoughtfully. "I think it was Captain Bob's outfit. You know, the crusty old guy with the ancient boat? Dad said something about it being a 'private expedition' that wasn't on the regular schedule."

"Captain 'Barnacle' Bob Crustybutt," Daisy identified immediately. "The same captain who transported Brock and Fleur to Turtle Rock on the night of the murder."

"And who coincidentally appeared in the path of Fleur's escape attempt during our dramatic yacht club confrontation," Babs added. "Rather a lot of nautical overlap for supposedly unrelated events."

"Do you think the captain is involved in this criminal enterprise?" Rita asked, her practical nature demanding clear connections.

"Or could he be another victim?" Mae suggested, her natural compassion seeking alternative explanations. "Perhaps being used or manipulated by those with greater influence?"

"Either way," Daisy concluded, "he appears to be a significant node in this network of connections. One worth exploring further."

"How exactly do you propose to 'explore' while under house arrest?" Babs inquired, gesturing toward the police officers visible through the dining room window. "Unless you're planning to tunnel out through the basement, which I feel compelled to remind you we don't actually have."

"We don't need to leave physically," Daisy replied, her academic mind already formulating a research strategy. "We have phones, internet access, and now an additional team member with direct familial connections to the victim." She nodded toward Ziggy, who appeared simultaneously alarmed and flattered by his apparent recruitment.

"Team member?" he repeated uncertainly. "I'm not sure I signed up for that."

"Consider it drafted rather than enlisted," Babs informed him cheerfully. "Welcome to the Seaside Sleuths, Environmental Division."

"We are not calling ourselves that," Daisy insisted automatically, though with noticeably less conviction than previous iterations of this recurring debate.

"Nomenclature aside," Rita interjected practically, "what exactly are you proposing, Daisy? A phone campaign? Internet research? Seance?"

"Nothing quite so dramatic," Daisy assured her. "Simply a coordinated information-gathering effort focused on Captain Crustybutt's connections, activities, and potential motivations. Ziggy can provide insights into his father's interactions with the captain. Mae can leverage her extensive network at the senior center, where the captain's ex-wife apparently attends weekly bingo. Rita knows the harbor community through her restaurant connections. And Babs..." She hesitated, searching for a specific investigative advantage.

"Can charm information out of anything with a pulse," Babs completed helpfully. "Plus, I dated his cousin briefly in the nineties. Terrible kisser but very talkative after a few rum punches."

"There we have it," Daisy concluded. "A perfectly reasonable approach to continuing our investigation without violating Morty's safety protocols."

"And you think Morty would approve of this 'perfectly reasonable approach'?" Rita asked skeptically.

"What Morty doesn't know won't increase his already concerning blood pressure," Babs replied with a dismissive wave. "Besides, we're just making phone calls and conducting internet searches. Hardly high-risk activities."

"Unless those calls alert the very people who tried to silence Jenkins and grab Ziggy," Rita pointed out. "We have no idea how extensive this network is or what resources they might have for monitoring communications."

This sobering observation created a momentary pause in their enthusiasm, the reality of their situation reasserting itself through Rita's practical assessment.

"A valid concern," Daisy acknowledged. "Perhaps we should discuss appropriate security measures before proceeding with any information gathering."

"Burner phones," Ziggy suggested immediately, earning surprised looks from around the table. "What? I've participated in enough environmental protests to know about avoiding surveillance. You get prepaid phones with cash, use them for specific communications only, then discard them."

"How very Jason Bourne," Babs remarked, visibly impressed. "I wouldn't have expected such cloak-and-dagger knowledge from someone whose fashion choices suggest a permanent Woodstock residence."

"Stereotyping isn't cool," Ziggy informed her with mild offense. "Besides, you'd be surprised how much overlap there is between environmental activism and security protocols. Corporate polluters have serious resources for tracking opposition."

"An illuminating perspective," Daisy acknowledged. "And a potentially useful skill set for our current circumstances. Though acquiring burner phones while under police protection presents certain logistical challenges."

"Not necessarily," Ziggy countered, reaching into his hemp messenger bag and extracting three identical prepaid phones still in their packaging. "I picked these up after I got the warning text. Figured better safe than sorry."

"Well," Babs said after a moment of surprised silence, "it appears our Environmental Division comes with unexpected tactical advantages. Perhaps we should reconsider our organizational hierarchy."

"Three phones," Rita noted practically. "That's one short for our expanded team."

"I can share with Ziggy," Mae offered. "Since I'll be primarily contacting seniors who are unlikely to be part of a sophisticated criminal conspiracy."

"A reasonable assumption," Daisy agreed. "Though we should establish clear communication protocols. No specific mentions of our investigation or objectives. No real names if possible. And regular check-ins to ensure everyone's safety."

"We need code names," Babs declared with theatrical enthusiasm. "I call 'Scarlet Shadow.'"

"We don't need code names," Daisy countered automatically. "This isn't a spy novel, Barbara."

"Says 'Professor Precision,'" Babs retorted. "See? I've already created yours. Rita can be 'Culinary Commando' and Mae is 'Gentle Justice.' Ziggy is obviously 'Environmental Avenger.'"

"I'm actually okay with that," Ziggy admitted with a small grin.

"Focus, please," Daisy requested, though her tone lacked real irritation. "Before we finalize our approach, we should consider what specific information we're seeking regarding Captain Crustybutt and how it connects to the broader investigation."

"His relationship with Brock beyond the obvious charter service," Rita suggested. "Financial connections, shared business interests, mutual acquaintances."

"The details of that near-drowning incident," Mae added. "If it truly was transformative for Brock, understanding exactly what happened might provide insights into his subsequent actions."

"And the captain's connections to other key players," Babs contributed. "Particularly Meredith Moneypenny and Fleur DuBois. Was he merely a convenient water taxi, or a more integral part of whatever operation they were running?"

"All excellent avenues of inquiry," Daisy approved. "Ziggy, since you have the most direct connection through your father, perhaps you could—"

Her strategic planning was interrupted by the sudden blaring of sirens and the distinctive sound of police radios crackling with urgent communications. Through the dining room windows, they could see officers moving with tactical purpose, weapons drawn and attention focused on something beyond their field of vision.

Officer Butterworth appeared at the dining room door, his youthful features set in lines of professional concern. "Ladies—and sir," he acknowledged Ziggy with a brief nod, "we have a situation developing. I need you to move to the central hallway, away from windows and exterior walls."

"What kind of situation?" Daisy inquired, already rising from her chair with the others.

"Potential hostile approach," Butterworth replied with careful understatement. "Unmarked vehicle breached the outer perimeter. Driver fled into the dunes. We're establishing a secure cordon and requesting backup."

"Another assassin?" Babs asked with inappropriate enthusiasm. "My, we're popular today."

"We don't know their intentions," Butterworth corrected firmly. "But until we do, standard protection protocols apply. Please, move to the designated safe area now."

As they hastily relocated to the central hallway—the most defensible position within The Barnacle's otherwise exposed Victorian architecture—the reality of their situation became increasingly apparent. The research project they had been casually planning over lunch now seemed almost quaint in the face of what appeared to be a coordinated effort to silence them.

"Still think this is just making phone calls and internet searches?" Rita murmured to Daisy as they huddled in the hallway, the sounds of police activity outside creating an ominous soundtrack to their unexpected confinement.

"Perhaps I understated the potential complications," Daisy acknowledged. "Though I maintain that information gathering remains our most valuable contribution to resolving this situation."

"Assuming we live long enough to share what we discover," Rita replied dryly.

"Such pessimism," Babs chided from her position near the bathroom door. "We've survived murderous art dealers, lightning storms, and high-speed boat chases. What's a simple siege situation compared to that?"

"I'm starting to think retirement was safer before I moved in with you three," Ziggy remarked, though his tone suggested more admiration than complaint.

"Retirement is what you make of it, young man," Daisy informed him with the authority of someone who had thoroughly reimagined the concept. "Some play shuffleboard. Others solve criminal conspiracies and occasionally evade professional assassins."

"I'd have settled for bingo and beach walks," Mae admitted softly. "Though I must say, I never expected to find this particular version of excitement in my golden years."

"Golden years, golden opportunities," Babs declared, striking a dramatic pose despite their cramped quarters. "Now, who's for establishing those communication protocols while we wait for the all-clear? I'm still advocating for code names, by the way. They add a certain dramatic flair to covert operations."

As Butterworth returned with updates on the security situation outside—the intruder remained at large but additional tactical support was en route—the residents of The Barnacle plus their unexpected environmental recruit settled into what appeared to be an extended lockdown. Their planned Garden Club attendance was now the least of their concerns, replaced by the more immediate challenge of surviving what had rapidly evolved from an amateur investigation into something considerably more dangerous.

Somewhere in the dunes surrounding their previously peaceful beach house, someone was watching, waiting, and potentially planning another attempt to silence them. The question that hung unspoken in the air as they huddled in their improvised safe room was whether their newfound investigative skills would be sufficient to identify the threat before it found a way through their police protection.

And whether Morty's blood pressure would survive the inevitable escalation of what he had initially dismissed as "amateur detective work" but now appeared to be a central element in exposing what might be the largest criminal conspiracy in Conch Key history.

Daisy, ever the academic, found herself contemplating the irony. They had worried about missing Eugenia's succulent presentation at the Garden Club. Now they were worrying about professional assassins with military-grade weaponry. Perspective, she reflected, was everything.

Unfortunately, their current perspective included being trapped in a hallway while unknown hostiles attempted to breach their perimeter. Not exactly the peaceful retirement she had envisioned when selecting The Barnacle for its "serene beachfront location and vibrant community opportunities."

The real estate listing had failed to mention "occasional sieges" among the property's features. An oversight that, under different circumstances, might have warranted a strongly worded letter to the agency. Under current circumstances, it merely warranted a burner phone and possibly—though she would never admit it to Babs—a code name.

Professor Precision did have a certain ring to it, after all.

Chapter Nine
Unexpected Allies

Night had fallen on The Barnacle, transforming its cheerful mint-green Victorian charm into something more ominous. Shadows stretched across walls, police radios crackled with coded communications, and the four friends plus their unexpected environmental recruit found themselves experiencing a very different version of their usual evening routine.

"I should be moisturizing right now," Babs lamented, peering cautiously through a crack in the living room curtains despite repeated warnings about exposing herself to potential snipers. "My nighttime skincare regimen is sacred. Fighting wrinkles is already an uphill battle without adding 'siege conditions' to the list of challenges."

"Your vanity in the face of potential assassination is almost admirable," Daisy remarked from her position on the sofa, where she had been methodically reviewing notes on her phone. "Though perhaps prioritizing survival over pore refinement might be advisable under current circumstances."

"One can do both," Babs insisted, finally abandoning her surveillance to rejoin the group. "Looking fabulous and staying alive aren't mutually exclusive goals. In fact, I've found that maintaining appearances often provides psychological fortitude during crises."

"There's actually scientific evidence supporting that perspective," Mae offered from her corner armchair, where she had been knitting with remarkable calm considering the tactical police unit deployed throughout their garden. "Studies show that maintaining familiar routines during high-stress situations can reduce anxiety and improve cognitive function."

"See?" Babs said triumphantly. "Science supports moisturizing during siege conditions. I knew I wasn't being frivolous."

"While this dermatological debate is fascinating," Rita interjected dryly, emerging from the kitchen with a tray of sandwiches and thermoses, "I thought we might need sustenance for what's shaping up to be a long night. Even Special Forces need to eat, so I've prepared provisions for our protective detail as well."

"Always the practical one," Daisy observed with approval. "Though I wonder if Officer Butterworth will allow food deliveries to the officers outside, given the security concerns."

"He's already cleared it," Rita assured her. "After thoroughly inspecting each sandwich for potential tampering. That young man takes his job very seriously."

"As he should," Ziggy contributed from his position near the hallway, where he had been uncharacteristically quiet for the past hour. "Whoever tried to get to me at the motel was wearing a police uniform, remember? Trust is a luxury we can't afford right now."

This sobering reminder temporarily halted the lighthearted banter that had been their natural response to tension throughout decades of friendship. The reality of their situation—confined to their home while unknown hostile forces potentially circled outside—was difficult to disguise with humor, no matter how well-honed their deflection skills.

"Any updates from Morty?" Mae asked, setting aside her knitting with careful precision.

"Nothing specific," Daisy replied. "Officer Butterworth reports they've secured the perimeter and are conducting systematic searches of the surrounding area, but so far they haven't located our mysterious visitor. The abandoned vehicle is being processed for evidence."

"And Jenkins?" Rita inquired, distributing sandwiches with practiced efficiency. "Any change in his condition?"

"Stable but unconscious," Daisy reported. "The hospital has him under guard, with strict instructions about approved visitors and medical personnel. Morty's taking no chances with potential follow-up attempts."

"This is wild," Ziggy muttered, accepting a sandwich with distracted gratitude. "Two days ago, I was just trying to process my dad's death. Now I'm hiding out from some kind of criminal organization with four senior citizens who apparently moonlight as amateur detectives."

"The term 'senior' is subjective and largely irrelevant," Daisy informed him with academic precision. "And our detective work is circumstantial rather than vocational, though I admit recent events have pushed us toward increasing professionalization."

"What she means," Babs translated, patting Ziggy's arm consolingly, "is that we're making this up as we go along, just with exceptional style and surprising effectiveness. It's less 'moonlighting' and more 'accidentally stumbling into criminal conspiracies and then handling them with unexpected competence.'"

"That's... not actually reassuring," Ziggy said, though a reluctant smile tugged at the corner of his mouth.

"It wasn't meant to be reassuring," Babs assured him cheerfully. "Just accurate. Reassurance implies certainty, and if there's one thing we've learned from recent events, it's that certainty is in short supply when dealing with murderous criminal conspiracies."

"Speaking of which," Daisy interjected, steering the conversation back to more productive channels, "perhaps we should use this enforced confinement to consolidate what we know and identify the most critical information gaps."

"A structured approach?" Rita suggested. "Like those murder boards they use in detective shows? With photographs and connecting strings?"

"While visually satisfying, I'm not sure we should create physical evidence of our investigation," Daisy cautioned. "Given the concerns about compromised law enforcement, anything we document could potentially be accessed by the wrong parties."

"We could use one of the burner phones," Ziggy proposed. "Keep notes in the memo app, delete as needed. No cloud backup, no trace."

"Excellent suggestion," Daisy approved, nodding appreciatively. "Your technical paranoia is proving quite valuable in our current circumstances."

"Years of evading corporate spies at environmental protests," Ziggy explained with a modest shrug. "You learn to think digital footprints."

As Ziggy retrieved one of the prepaid phones from his hemp messenger bag, a sudden commotion outside drew their attention. Raised voices, hurried footsteps on the porch, and the distinctive sound of Officer Butterworth's professional-but-stressed tone suggested a development in their siege situation.

"Stay back from the windows," Rita warned, automatically moving toward Mae in a protective gesture that spoke volumes about their friendship.

The front door opened after a series of authorization codes were exchanged, revealing Butterworth's tense expression as he ushered in an unexpected visitor—Eugene Finch, the harbormaster, looking considerably less composed than during his recent appearance as Baroness Volkov's yacht club escort.

"Eugene?" Daisy exclaimed, rising from the sofa in surprise. "What on earth are you doing here? And how did you get through the security perimeter?"

"Official harbor business," Eugene replied, holding up an identification badge that apparently carried sufficient authority to navigate police blockades. "And a rather urgent message for you ladies." He glanced at Ziggy, adding, "And gentleman."

"Mr. Finch has been cleared by the Chief," Butterworth explained, though his expression suggested the clearance had been granted with reservations. "He insisted it couldn't wait until morning."

"Thank you, Officer," Daisy acknowledged. "We'll take it from here."

As Butterworth retreated to resume his security duties, closing the door behind him, the five occupants of The Barnacle regarded their unexpected visitor with varying degrees of curiosity and suspicion.

"This must be important to risk navigating an active security zone after dark," Daisy observed, gesturing for Eugene to take a seat. "Please, enlighten us about this urgent harbor business."

Eugene's weather-beaten face creased with uncharacteristic concern as he settled awkwardly onto the edge of an armchair, his substantial frame perched like a great seabird contemplating immediate flight.

"It's about Captain Crustybutt," he began without preamble. "He's missing."

"Missing?" Mae echoed, her gentle features contracting with concern. "Since when?"

"Since approximately two hours after Harold Jenkins was shot," Eugene replied grimly. "He took his spare boat out—not the one damaged during the yacht club incident—claiming he was checking crab pots. Never returned. His primary vessel is still undergoing repairs, so he was using his smaller skiff. Coast Guard found it drifting empty near Pelican Point about an hour ago."

"That seems... significant," Daisy remarked carefully. "Particularly given recent events and the captain's connections to several key players in our ongoing situation."

"Significant doesn't begin to cover it," Eugene agreed. "Especially considering what was found in the boat." He reached into his jacket and withdrew a waterproof pouch, which he placed on the coffee table with the reverence normally reserved for religious artifacts. "This was sealed in a compartment under the center seat. Coast Guard almost missed it during their initial search."

"And you're sharing this with us rather than law enforcement because...?" Rita prompted, practical as always.

Eugene's expression turned guarded. "Because the pouch has your names on it," he revealed, turning the package to display the unmistakable block lettering: "FOR PICKLESWORTH, ZUCKERKORN, CALABAZA & NOODLEMAN - OPEN ONLY IN PRIVATE."

"How intriguing," Daisy murmured, leaning forward to examine the package without touching it. "And you're certain this was in Captain Crustybutt's vessel?"

"Sealed in a hidden compartment," Eugene confirmed. "One I helped him install last year, ostensibly for storing valuable fishing equipment securely." He hesitated, then added with evident discomfort, "I should mention that I was explicitly instructed—by the captain himself, about a month ago—to bring anything found in that compartment directly to you ladies if anything ever happened to him."

This revelation caused a momentary silence as the implications settled over the group.

"A contingency plan," Daisy concluded. "Established well before our involvement in this situation began. How very interesting."

"And somewhat alarming," Rita added. "Why would he prepare for something happening to him, and why designate us as recipients of whatever information he wanted preserved?"

"Questions I've been asking myself during the entire drive here," Eugene admitted. "Along with whether I'm potentially compromising an active investigation by following his instructions."

"Or participating in one," Babs suggested brightly. "Perhaps the captain recognized our natural investigative talents before we did ourselves."

"Unlikely," Daisy countered. "Given the timeline Eugene described, this contingency was established before Brock's murder and our subsequent involvement. There must be another connection we're not seeing."

"Maybe it's related to Dad's near-drowning experience," Ziggy proposed, all eyes turning to him with renewed interest. "The one he had about a month ago—on Captain Crustybutt's boat. The timing matches when Eugene says these instructions were given."

"A compelling hypothesis," Daisy acknowledged, her academic mind automatically seeking patterns and correlations. "If something significant occurred during that incident—something that potentially implicated the captain or others in whatever conspiracy we're dealing with—he might have created this fail-safe to ensure the information wasn't lost if he was silenced."

"But why us?" Mae wondered, her gentle features creased with puzzlement. "We had no connection to any of this a month ago."

"Perhaps because we had no connection," Rita suggested thoughtfully. "If the captain suspected corruption within local authorities or established power structures, designating complete outsiders as his information recipients would make strategic sense."

"Especially four retired women who would be presumed harmless by anyone monitoring conventional threats," Babs added with surprising insight. "We're practically invisible to systems designed to track traditional opposition."

"Until recently," Daisy amended dryly. "I believe our current siege conditions suggest our 'harmless' status has been significantly revised by whoever is behind this conspiracy."

Eugene, who had been following this rapid analytical exchange with increasingly bewildered expression, cleared his throat awkwardly. "So... do you want the package or not? Because I'd rather not be caught in possession of potential evidence if it's connected to the captain's disappearance."

"Of course we want it," Babs declared before anyone else could respond. "Mysterious packages from missing sea captains are exactly the sort of plot development that keeps an investigation interesting."

"What Barbara means," Daisy translated with practiced patience, "is that yes, we'll accept responsibility for this item, given the captain's explicit instructions. Though we'll need to consider carefully whether to share its contents with Chief Crabbitz, depending on what we discover."

"That's between you and your conscience," Eugene replied, visibly relieved to be transferring responsibility. "I'm just following specific instructions from a man who might well be..." He trailed off, apparently reluctant to voice the obvious conclusion.

"Dead?" Babs supplied helpfully. "Murdered by the same people who tried to silence Jenkins and grab Ziggy? Victim of the vast criminal conspiracy that has us trapped in our own home surrounded by tactical police units?"

"Babs, please," Mae admonished gently. "Eugene is clearly distressed about his friend's disappearance."

"Colleague," Eugene corrected automatically. "Bob and I weren't exactly friends. More like reluctant professional associates with occasional fishing overlap."

"Regardless of the relationship taxonomy," Daisy interjected, steering the conversation back to practical matters, "we appreciate you following his instructions and bringing this to us despite the potential complications. I assume the Coast Guard and police have been notified about the captain's disappearance?"

"Full alert," Eugene confirmed. "Search patterns established, aircraft with thermal imaging deploying at first light. Standard missing mariner protocols." He hesitated, then added with evident reluctance, "Though given recent events, expectations for a positive outcome are... limited."

"You believe he's been eliminated by the same people targeting us," Daisy stated rather than asked.

"The timing is suspicious," Eugene acknowledged. "And Bob wasn't the type to have boating accidents. Despite his crusty appearance and questionable maintenance habits, he was meticulous about safety protocols. Falling overboard from his own skiff during routine operations would be highly uncharacteristic."

"Unless he was assisted overboard," Babs suggested with unnecessary dramatic emphasis.

"Thank you for that clarification," Daisy said dryly. "Now, Eugene, is there anything else about the captain's disappearance or this package that we should know before you depart? Any context or background that might help us understand what we're dealing with?"

Eugene considered the question, his weathered features settling into thoughtful lines. "Only that Bob changed about a month ago—around the same time as that incident with Brock Hamfist. Became more cautious, started varying his routes and schedules, installed that hidden compartment. And he asked a lot of questions about underwater survey equipment and deep-water topography."

"Underwater survey equipment?" Daisy repeated, her academic curiosity immediately engaged. "What specifically?"

"Sonar mapping systems, primarily," Eugene replied. "High-resolution bottom contour technology, the kind used for detailed underwater archaeological work. Way beyond the gear typically used for fishing or recreational boating."

"And did he acquire such equipment?" Rita inquired.

"Not through official channels," Eugene said. "But he mentioned making arrangements with a private research outfit from Miami. Said he needed to 'document something before it disappeared.'" He shrugged. "I assumed he'd found a wreck or something that might have salvage value."

"Or something else entirely," Daisy mused. "Something potentially connected to whatever conspiracy has emerged around Brock's murder and subsequent events."

"That's above my pay grade," Eugene declared, rising from his chair with the air of a man who had completed an uncomfortable but necessary task. "I've delivered the package as instructed. What you do with it is your business."

"We appreciate your discretion," Daisy assured him. "And your willingness to navigate an active security situation to fulfill your commitment."

"Just doing what Bob asked," Eugene replied simply. "Though I'd appreciate it if you didn't mention my involvement to anyone outside this room. I've got a marina to run, and getting tangled in whatever this is doesn't help me maintain the channel markers."

"Your visit will remain confidential," Daisy promised. "Though I suspect Officer Butterworth has already documented your arrival in his security logs."

"Unavoidable," Eugene acknowledged. "But delivering a package from a missing colleague is considerably less suspicious than some alternatives. Speaking of which, I should go before my presence raises additional questions."

As he moved toward the door, Eugene paused, turning back with an expression of genuine concern. "Be careful with whatever's in that package," he advised. "Bob wasn't the paranoid type, generally speaking. If he went to these lengths to protect information, it's likely significant—and potentially dangerous to possess."

"We've already survived two murder attempts and are currently under police protection due to an active threat," Babs informed him cheerfully. "I think we've crossed the 'potentially dangerous' threshold and set up housekeeping on the other side."

"What Barbara means," Daisy translated, "is that we're aware of the risks and will exercise appropriate caution. Thank you for the warning."

With a final nod that somehow conveyed both professional completion and personal concern, Eugene departed, escorted by Officer Butterworth who had been hovering discreetly near the door throughout the exchange.

As soon as they were alone, all eyes turned to the waterproof pouch sitting innocuously on the coffee table—a mysterious communication from a missing sea captain, specifically designated for them, potentially containing information significant enough to justify elaborate contingency planning and possibly connected to whatever criminal conspiracy had transformed their peaceful retirement into an active security situation.

"Well," Babs declared into the expectant silence, "don't all leap to open it at once. It's only a mysterious package from a potentially murdered sea captain containing information someone might have killed to suppress. Hardly worth interrupting our evening routine."

"Caution seems advisable," Daisy replied, eyeing the package with academic suspicion. "Given recent events, we should consider the possibility that this could be some form of trap."

"A trap specifically targeting us, delivered through Eugene who followed instructions established a month ago, before we had any connection to this situation?" Rita challenged skeptically. "That would require remarkable prescience on the part of our theoretical conspirators."

"Or a more recent interception and substitution," Daisy countered. "We can't assume the package remained secure after the captain's disappearance. Eugene himself noted that the Coast Guard conducted an initial search before finding the hidden compartment."

"So we should just leave it sitting there while we debate potential security scenarios?" Babs asked with theatrical exasperation. "At this rate, whoever's besieging us will break through before we even look at the mysterious sea captain package. Some detectives we are."

"I could check it," Ziggy offered unexpectedly. "I've dealt with suspicious packages at environmental protests. Companies trying to infiltrate or disrupt activist groups sometimes send doctored 'evidence' or materials designed to discredit the movement."

This suggestion earned him surprised looks from around the room.

"What?" he defended. "Corporate environmental sabotage is serious business. We developed protocols for handling potentially compromised materials."

"And these protocols involve...?" Daisy prompted, genuinely curious.

"Visual inspection first," Ziggy explained, already moving toward the package with surprisingly professional focus. "Check for tampering evidence on seals and closures. Then careful opening in a controlled environment, preferably with protective gear. Document everything before touching, maintain chain of custody notes."

"My goodness," Mae remarked. "Environmental activism sounds considerably more structured than I had imagined."

"When you're taking on billion-dollar corporations, you learn to be methodical," Ziggy replied, circling the package with careful scrutiny. "They have teams of lawyers looking for any procedural mistake that could discredit your findings."

The others watched in fascinated silence as Ziggy conducted what appeared to be a remarkably professional examination of the waterproof pouch, even producing a pair of latex gloves from his messenger bag ("Always carry them for collecting water or soil samples") before carefully manipulating the package.

"Seals appear intact," he reported, slipping into what Daisy recognized as the impersonal documentation tone of scientific observation. "No evidence of tampering with the closure mechanism. Material is standard marine-grade waterproof canvas with double-sealed seams. Professional quality, consistent with high-end boating equipment."

"The captain did not skimp on his mysterious message delivery system," Babs observed. "One almost appreciates the attention to detail, even in potential death messages."

"Consistent with Eugene's description of the captain as 'meticulous about safety protocols,'" Daisy noted. "If he believed this information required protection, he would presumably apply the same thoroughness to its packaging."

"I'm going to open it now," Ziggy announced, positioning the package in the center of the coffee table where all could observe while maintaining a safe distance. "Everyone ready?"

"As we'll ever be," Rita replied practically. "Though I'm wondering if we should alert Officer Butterworth, just in case..."

"And explain how we're opening mysterious evidence from a missing person without official authorization?" Daisy countered. "I think we've established a certain operational independence that would be complicated by official involvement at this stage."

"Translation: let's see what's in the super-secret captain package before telling the cops," Babs interpreted helpfully.

"Precisely," Daisy acknowledged without apology. "Proceed, Ziggy."

With careful, methodical movements that belied his usual laid-back demeanor, Ziggy released the waterproof closure system and gently opened the pouch. The group collectively held their breath as he peered inside, expression shifting from concentrated focus to surprise.

"It's... a portable hard drive," he reported, carefully extracting a small black electronic device. "And a handwritten note." This second item emerged as a sealed envelope with the same block lettering as the exterior package: "READ FIRST."

"Well, that seems straightforward," Babs remarked. "Though I was rather hoping for treasure maps or ancient amulets. Hard drives lack a certain dramatic flair."

"Information is the most valuable treasure in our digital age, Barbara," Daisy informed her, academic instincts automatically engaging. "Particularly information someone might have killed to suppress."

"The note first, then?" Rita suggested, practical as always.

Ziggy nodded, carefully opening the sealed envelope with methodical precision and extracting several pages of handwritten text. He cleared his throat and began to read aloud:

"'To the ladies of The Barnacle: If you're reading this, I am likely dead or otherwise permanently unavailable. While we have limited personal acquaintance, circumstances have made you the most logical recipients of information I have uncovered. Information that others have gone to great lengths to conceal.'"

"How flattering," Babs interjected. "We've become the mysterious message recipients of choice for the cryptically imperiled."

"Shh," Rita hushed her. "Let him continue."

Ziggy resumed reading: "'Approximately one month ago, during a private fishing charter with Brock Hamfist, an incident occurred that has since been mischaracterized as a 'near-drowning experience.' The reality was considerably more complex and has led me to discover evidence of activities that threaten not only local environmental systems but potentially public safety throughout the region.'"

"Environmentally hazardous activities," Daisy noted, glancing at Ziggy. "Connecting directly to your area of expertise and your father's apparent change of heart."

Ziggy nodded grimly and continued reading: "'During what was intended as a routine fishing expedition in the deeper waters beyond Turtle Rock, Hamfist and I observed unusual underwater activity that prompted further investigation. Using specialized equipment borrowed from marine research contacts, I have documented extensive unauthorized underwater construction approximately three miles offshore, in an area officially designated as protected marine habitat.'"

"Underwater construction?" Mae echoed, brow furrowing in confusion. "What could they possibly be building in protected waters?"

"Let's find out," Daisy suggested, gesturing for Ziggy to continue.

"'The attached hard drive contains sonar imaging, underwater photography, and coordinate mapping of what appears to be a sophisticated underwater pipeline system, constructed without permits, environmental impact studies, or public disclosure. Based on structural analysis and consultation with engineering contacts who wish to remain anonymous, this system seems designed for large-scale waste disposal directly into the ocean floor, bypassing all regulatory oversight and environmental protections.'"

"Illegal waste dumping," Rita concluded grimly. "Hardly surprising, given the history of industrial malfeasance in vulnerable environments."

"But on this scale?" Ziggy questioned, looking up from the letter with genuine alarm. "A pipeline system three miles offshore would require massive investment and coordination. We're not talking about some small operation dumping barrels at night."

"Hence the 'sophisticated criminal enterprise' Jenkins described," Daisy observed. "Continue, please."

Ziggy returned to the letter: "'Hamfist's reaction to this discovery was unexpected. Despite his reputation as a developer with limited environmental concerns, he appeared genuinely disturbed by the implications. Our subsequent conversations revealed his growing awareness of being unwittingly involved in something far beyond normal development corner-cutting or regulatory evasion. He described it as 'environmental terrorism hidden behind luxury facades.'"

"Dad said something similar that night," Ziggy interrupted himself, looking up with dawning comprehension. "About being 'blind to the real costs' and needing to 'make things right.' I thought it was just dramatic talk, but he was being literal. He had discovered actual environmental crimes."

"And was murdered for his intention to expose them," Daisy added softly. "Please, continue with the captain's letter."

"'In the weeks following our discovery, Hamfist began gathering financial and legal documentation connecting the underwater construction to various development projects throughout the region, particularly the Conch Key resort. Meanwhile, I focused on documenting the physical evidence of the operation itself. We agreed to compile our findings separately, creating redundancy to ensure the information survived even if one of us was... neutralized.'"

"Prudent," Daisy remarked. "Though evidently insufficient, given subsequent events."

Ziggy nodded grimly and resumed reading: "'Hamfist intended to present his findings to federal environmental authorities, bypassing local officials whom he had come to believe were compromised. His 'eco-resort' conversion was partially genuine—a legitimate attempt to salvage something positive from his previous environmental ignorance—but also strategic cover for his information-gathering activities.'"

"The timing aligns perfectly with Dad's behavioral changes," Ziggy confirmed, looking up from the letter with a mixture of pride and sorrow. "He really was trying to make amends."

"A redemption story cut tragically short," Mae observed gently. "But perhaps not entirely thwarted, if the captain's information allows us to continue what your father started."

"There's more," Ziggy said, returning to the letter: "'I have reason to believe the organization behind this operation has extensive influence within local governance, law enforcement, and regulatory bodies. Their financial resources and willingness to eliminate obstacles have become increasingly apparent as Hamfist and I pursued our separate investigations. By the time you read this, they will have likely moved against me as they did against him.'"

"A chillingly accurate prediction," Daisy noted. "The captain understood precisely what he was facing."

"'I've designated you as recipients of this information for several specific reasons,'" Ziggy continued reading. "'First, you operate completely outside the local power structures that appear compromised. Second, your backgrounds suggest both integrity and analytical capability. Finally, your residence directly overlooks the primary offshore survey area, providing potential observational advantages for monitoring suspicious maritime activity.'"

"Our beachfront location was a strategic consideration," Rita marveled. "And here I thought we just had a nice view of the sunset."

"'The hard drive contains comprehensive documentation, including coordinates, timestamps, photographic evidence, and technical analysis of the underwater construction. I've also included a contact list of trusted individuals outside the local area who may provide additional resources or protection if needed. Some are former military or coast guard colleagues, others environmental specialists or independent journalists with relevant expertise.'"

"A network of potential allies," Daisy observed with approval. "The captain was remarkably thorough in his contingency planning."

"Final paragraph," Ziggy announced, turning to the last page: "'I recognize that I am placing you in potential danger by designating you as custodians of this information. For that, I apologize. But the environmental and public health implications of this operation are too significant to allow intimidation to ensure silence. Whatever motivations drive you—justice, environmental protection, or simple outrage at the corruption of our community—I trust you will use this information more effectively than I have managed to. Navigate carefully. —Captain Robert 'Barnacle' Crustybutt.'"

As Ziggy finished reading, a profound silence settled over the room, each occupant processing the implications of the captain's final communication. What had begun as an unexpected murder investigation had expanded into something far larger and more ominous—a sophisticated criminal conspiracy with environmental terrorism at its core, connections throughout local power structures, and apparent willingness to eliminate anyone who threatened to expose its operations.

"Well," Babs finally declared, breaking the weighted silence with characteristic dramatic timing, "this certainly puts our cancelled Garden Club attendance in perspective. Eugenia's succulents can wait when we're apparently the last line of defense against underwater environmental terrorism."

"The question," Rita said practically, "is what we do with this information now. Given the security concerns the captain outlined, simply turning it over to authorities seems potentially counterproductive if we can't determine who is compromised."

"Morty isn't compromised," Mae insisted with quiet certainty. "I would stake my life on his integrity."

"You might be doing exactly that if you're wrong," Daisy cautioned gently. "Though I share your assessment of his character. The question is more whether he has the resources and authority to address something of this magnitude, particularly if the corruption extends as broadly as suggested."

"We need to examine the hard drive contents before making any decisions," Ziggy proposed, eyeing the device with professional interest. "Assess exactly what evidence the captain gathered and its potential impact if properly deployed."

"Agreed," Daisy nodded. "Though we should exercise extreme caution in accessing that data. If it's as significant as the captain suggests, it represents a direct threat to whoever is behind this operation—a threat they've already demonstrated willingness to kill to suppress."

"So we add 'analyzing potentially lethal environmental crime evidence' to our evening plans," Babs summarized brightly. "Along with avoiding snipers, maintaining police perimeter security, and—in my case at least—addressing the critical moisturizing situation that this siege has so inconveniently interrupted."

"Priorities, Barbara," Rita sighed, though a small smile tugged at the corner of her mouth.

"Survival first, skincare second," Babs conceded. "Though it's a distressingly close competition at my age."

As the group prepared to examine the hard drive contents, setting up Ziggy's laptop with appropriate security precautions (including physically disconnecting its wireless capabilities to prevent potential remote monitoring), they were unaware of developments occurring just beyond their protective police perimeter.

In the deepening darkness of the dunes, a figure in tactical gear observed The Barnacle through specialized night vision equipment, noting the police positions with professional assessment. Into a secure communication device, the observer reported:

"Package delivery confirmed. Targets have recovered the captain's data. Awaiting instructions regarding containment protocol escalation."

The response, when it came, was chillingly brief: "Eliminate all copies. No witnesses."

As Officer Butterworth completed another perimeter check, his flashlight beam sweeping across the seemingly empty dunes where the tactical observer had melted into the darkness, the residents of The Barnacle remained focused on the hard drive contents—unaware that their siege situation was about to evolve from protective confinement to active targeting.

The evening's unfolding events would test not only their investigative skills but their survival instincts as well. And somewhere in the waters off Conch Key, whatever the captain and Brock Hamfist had discovered continued its clandestine operations, its secrets temporarily preserved but increasingly threatened by the unexpected resilience and resourcefulness of four retirement-age women and one environmental activist with a hemp messenger bag.

Environmental terrorism hidden behind luxury facades, indeed.

Chapter Ten
Digital Revelations

"Good Lord," Daisy murmured, leaning closer to Ziggy's laptop screen where a series of high-resolution sonar images slowly rotated in three-dimensional rendering. "The scale of this operation is... remarkable."

The five of them had gathered around the dining room table, which now resembled an impromptu command center. Ziggy's laptop occupied the central position, surrounded by notepads, coffee mugs, and Rita's emergency stress-baking results—a plate of chocolate chip cookies that had materialized with impressive speed once the contents of Captain Crustybutt's hard drive began revealing their disturbing scope.

"It's not just the scale," Ziggy replied, using keyboard commands to zoom in on a particular section of the underwater structure. "It's the sophistication. This isn't some makeshift disposal system. It's engineered for maximum dispersal with minimal surface indicators. Whoever designed this knew exactly what they were doing—and what regulations they were violating."

"Dispersal of what, exactly?" Mae asked, peering through her reading glasses with concerned focus. "The captain's letter mentioned waste disposal, but what kind of waste requires this level of concealment?"

"According to these files," Ziggy replied, navigating to another folder on the hard drive, "chemical byproducts from pharmaceutical manufacturing, industrial solvents, and—this is the really disturbing part—potentially radioactive materials from medical equipment processing."

"Radioactive waste?" Babs exclaimed, instinctively taking a step back from the laptop as if the digital images themselves might be contaminated. "In our lovely ocean? Where we swim and fish and occasionally engage in ill-advised post-retirement skinny dipping?"

"The radioactive component appears to be low-level," Ziggy clarified, though his expression remained grave. "Not weapons-grade or anything apocalyptic. But still absolutely prohibited from ocean disposal under about fifteen different environmental regulations and international treaties."

"And this is connected to the resort development how, exactly?" Rita asked, practical as always despite the increasingly alarming revelations.

"That's where it gets interesting," Ziggy said, opening yet another folder containing spreadsheets and financial documentation. "According to the captain's notes, the underground pipeline system connects to a supposed 'water treatment facility' that was part of the original resort infrastructure plan. The facility appears on all the official blueprints as an environmental feature—allegedly processing and recycling gray water for the resort's extensive landscaping needs."

"Clever," Daisy observed with reluctant admiration. "Hiding illegal waste disposal infrastructure within an ostensibly environmentally friendly water recycling system. The perfect cover story."

"And explaining why Brock's sudden conversion to eco-friendly design posed such a threat," Rita added. "If he eliminated the water treatment facility from the plans..."

"He'd be cutting off their primary disposal system," Ziggy confirmed grimly. "Dad's environmental 'awakening' wasn't just bad for their profits—it threatened to expose their entire illegal operation."

"No wonder they killed him," Babs remarked, biting into a cookie with surprising aggression. "Though murder seems rather an extreme response to permit problems. Couldn't they have just bribed more officials? That's the traditional approach to regulatory inconveniences, isn't it?"

"Not when the potential exposure involves international environmental crimes," Daisy countered. "This goes well beyond local zoning variances or building code violations. If verified, these activities could trigger federal investigations, international sanctions, and criminal prosecutions with substantial prison terms."

"Not to mention the civil liability," Mae added softly. "The health impacts on marine life, local fishing industries, and potentially human populations could be catastrophic—and financially ruinous for whoever is responsible."

"Speaking of responsibility," Rita said, leaning closer to examine a spreadsheet Ziggy had opened, "does the captain's evidence identify who's actually behind this operation? Beyond the obvious local connections like Meredith and Fleur?"

"That's where things get murky," Ziggy admitted, navigating to a folder labeled 'Organizational Structure.' "The captain managed to trace some financial connections, but the ownership layers are deliberately complex—multiple shell companies, offshore registrations, holding corporations nesting inside each other like Russian dolls."

"A classic obfuscation strategy," Daisy noted. "Designed specifically to prevent accountability and shield the actual decision-makers."

"But he did identify some interesting patterns," Ziggy continued, opening a document containing a hand-drawn organizational chart with extensive annotations. "Most of the shell companies funnel back to a parent corporation called Oceanic Ventures International, which has no public-facing operations or website but appears to control significant funding across multiple development projects in coastal communities throughout the southeastern United States."

"Oceanic Ventures," Daisy repeated thoughtfully. "The name suggests legitimate marine-based business activities—development, research, tourism. Another layer of misdirection."

"According to the captain's notes, it's registered in the Cayman Islands with satellite offices in Miami and Charleston," Ziggy elaborated. "The Miami office is particularly interesting because it shares an address with—" he paused dramatically, looking up from the screen, "—the law firm of Anderson, Pritchard & Weiss."

"Anderson," Mae gasped, immediately connecting the dots. "As in Judge Jonathan Anderson? The one Jenkins mentioned?"

"The very same," Ziggy confirmed. "The captain included notes from property records searches showing the judge is not just associated with the law firm—he's a founding partner who ostensibly 'retired' from active practice when he took the bench, but maintained his ownership stake and office space."

"A sitting judge with direct financial connections to the corporate entity apparently orchestrating environmental crimes," Daisy summarized, her academic mind automatically organizing the information into logical patterns. "That would certainly explain Jenkins' concern about the judiciary being compromised."

"And why previous attempts to involve outside regulatory agencies mysteriously stalled," Rita added. "If a respected local judge was making calls to colleagues or regulatory officials..."

"He could effectively smother investigations before they gained traction," Daisy completed the thought. "Particularly if supported by Meredith Moneypenny's political influence and whatever other officials they've compromised."

"So we're dealing with corrupt judges, vanishing sea captains, and radioactive waste pipelines," Babs summarized with theatrical dismay. "All while trapped in our own home under police protection that may or may not include infiltrators from the very conspiracy we're investigating. I must say, retirement has taken an unexpected turn."

"Indeed," Daisy agreed dryly. "Though I find myself more concerned with the immediate question of what we do with this information. Particularly given the captain's warnings about compromised local authorities."

"We need to get it to federal agencies," Ziggy stated firmly. "EPA, FBI, Coast Guard—groups with jurisdiction over environmental crimes and the authority to initiate investigations beyond local interference."

"Assuming we can contact them securely," Rita cautioned. "If this organization has the resources and connections the captain's evidence suggests, they may be monitoring conventional communications channels."

"Hence the burner phones," Babs reminded them, gesturing to the prepaid devices Ziggy had distributed earlier. "Though I'm not entirely convinced they provide adequate security against sophisticated surveillance. My third husband worked briefly in intelligence before his unfortunate incident with the embassy cocktail party and the ambassador's pet ferret, and he always said digital communications were fundamentally compromised."

"Your third husband sounds increasingly fictional with each new biographical detail, Barbara," Daisy remarked skeptically.

"Martin was many things, but fictional wasn't one of them," Babs retorted with dignity. "His restraining order from the State Department was very real, I assure you."

"Setting aside Babs' colorful marital history," Rita interjected, steering the conversation back to more immediate concerns, "we need a secure way to transmit this evidence to appropriate authorities while ensuring it can't be intercepted or dismissed."

"The captain anticipated this problem," Ziggy noted, navigating to yet another folder on the hard drive. "He included contact information for several individuals he identified as trustworthy—former military colleagues, environmental journalists, and retired federal agents. People positioned to help bypass local interference and connect directly to higher authorities."

"How reassuring that our mysteriously missing sea captain thought of everything," Babs commented. "Though one wonders why his impressive foresight didn't extend to preventing his own disappearance."

"Even the most careful planning can't anticipate every contingency," Daisy observed. "And the captain was clearly operating with limited resources against a well-funded adversary."

"Speaking of which," Mae interjected, her gentle voice carrying unexpected urgency, "did anyone else notice the light that just swept across the dunes?"

All heads turned toward the dining room window, where Mae was gazing with uncharacteristic intensity.

"What kind of light?" Daisy asked, immediately alert.

"A narrow beam, like a tactical flashlight, but only for a second," Mae replied. "It moved from east to west across the dune line, approximately seventy-five yards from the house—the same position Officer Butterworth identified as the probable sniper location."

"Could be the police searching the perimeter," Rita suggested reasonably.

"The police have been using continuous illumination patterns and moving in pairs," Mae countered, surprising everyone with her observational precision. "This was a single, brief flash, as if someone was checking a specific location and didn't want to be noticed."

"When did you become such an expert on police search patterns?" Babs asked with newfound respect.

"I've been watching them all evening," Mae explained simply. "It helps with the anxiety to understand the protective measures. And that light didn't match their established pattern."

Ziggy immediately moved to power down his laptop. "We should alert Officer Butterworth. If someone's penetrated the perimeter again..."

"Wait," Daisy cautioned, placing a restraining hand on his arm. "Before we potentially trigger a tactical response, we need to secure the evidence. The captain's hard drive and any digital copies we've created are literally irreplaceable if something goes wrong."

"I've been making periodic backups to a micro SD card," Ziggy informed them, extracting a tiny storage device from the laptop's port. "Standard practice when handling sensitive environmental data. Companies have been known to seize or 'accidentally' destroy equipment during raids."

"Your paranoid environmental activism continues to prove surprisingly valuable," Daisy acknowledged with approval. "Now we need to ensure that backup is secured somewhere separate from the original drive."

"I can help with that," Mae offered unexpectedly. She opened her knitting bag and extracted what appeared to be a half-finished baby blanket in soft pastel colors. With deft movements that belied her age, she unraveled several rows of careful stitches to reveal a small, hollow space inside the yarn's structured pattern. "Hidden compartment," she explained at their surprised expressions. "For keeping spare emergency medication secure during travel. Small items slide right in and the knitting pattern conceals it perfectly."

"Mae Noodleman," Babs declared with dramatic admiration, "you continue to be the dark horse of our little investigative quartet. First observational security analysis, now covert storage techniques? What other espionage skills are you hiding beneath those pastel cardigans?"

"Just practical solutions to common problems," Mae replied modestly, though a small smile suggested she appreciated the recognition. She carefully inserted the micro SD card into the hollowed section of her knitting and expertly re-worked the yarn to conceal it. "There. Unless someone specifically looks for it while unraveling my careful gauge work, it should remain undetected."

"Excellent," Daisy approved. "Now, Ziggy, you should alert Officer Butterworth about the unusual light Mae observed, while the rest of us continue examining the captain's evidence. We need to identify the most compelling components to prioritize for secure transmission."

As Ziggy moved toward the front of the house to locate their police guardian, the four women returned their attention to the hard drive contents displayed on the laptop screen. The captain's meticulous documentation had organized the evidence into categories: technical specifications of the underwater pipeline system, environmental impact analysis, corporate connection mapping, and potential legal violations.

"The environmental impact data is particularly damning," Rita observed, studying a series of water quality test results the captain had apparently collected secretly over several weeks. "These contamination levels exceed regulatory limits by factors of ten or more in some cases."

"And the corporate connection mapping provides the crucial links to identifiable individuals," Daisy added, examining the organizational charts. "Without that, authorities might address the immediate environmental violation but miss the broader conspiracy."

"Not to mention the potential health impacts," Mae noted with concern, reviewing a document where the captain had compiled research on the specific contaminants identified in his water samples. "Some of these compounds have been linked to reproductive disorders, neurological damage, and increased cancer risks. If they've been dumping for as long as the construction timeline suggests..."

"The potential liability would be astronomically ruinous," Daisy concluded. "No wonder they're willing to resort to murder and intimidation to protect this operation. The financial and criminal exposure could destroy everyone involved."

"A sobering thought," came a voice from the doorway—not Ziggy's as expected, but Officer Butterworth's, his youthful features set in uncharacteristically grim lines. "And one that makes what I'm about to do particularly unfortunate."

All four women turned to find the young officer standing in the dining room entrance, his service weapon drawn and pointed directly at them with unwavering precision.

"Officer Butterworth?" Mae gasped, her gentle features contracting with shock. "What are you doing?"

"Following orders," he replied, his voice flat and emotionless in a way that seemed foreign to his usually eager personality. "I'm going to need that hard drive and any copies you've made. Immediately and without discussion."

"You're part of this," Daisy realized, academic mind rapidly reassessing everything they had assumed about their police protection. "Jenkins warned about compromised law enforcement, but we never considered..."

"That the baby-faced officer assigned to protect you might be on someone else's payroll?" Butterworth completed her thought with a humorless smile. "That's why it works. No one suspects the eager rookie of having complicated loyalties."

"Where's Ziggy?" Rita demanded, maternal concern overriding her usual careful diplomacy.

"Taking an involuntary nap in the hallway," Butterworth informed them casually. "Nothing personal—just a precautionary measure. He'll wake up with a headache but otherwise unharmed. Unlike the potential alternatives if you four don't cooperate immediately."

"You won't get away with this," Babs declared with theatrical defiance that would have seemed comical in other circumstances. "Chief Crabbitz will realize what you've done."

"Chief Crabbitz is currently responding to a reported disturbance on the opposite side of town," Butterworth countered smoothly. "Coincidentally occupying the entire night shift with a wild goose chase that will prove frustratingly elusive. By the time anyone realizes what's happened here, the evidence will be gone, and any unfortunate incidents will be attributed to the mysterious assailants who've been targeting you anyway."

"You've thought this through," Daisy observed, stalling for time as her eyes darted around the room seeking potential options.

"Not me personally," Butterworth admitted with disturbing candor. "I just follow instructions. Planning happens at levels well above my pay grade. Now, the hard drive, please. And the backup Mr. Hamfist so cleverly created. Don't make this more difficult than necessary."

"And if we refuse?" Rita challenged, her practical nature apparently calculating the odds of four elderly women and one unconscious environmental activist against an armed police officer.

"Then instead of a simple evidence removal operation, this becomes a cleanup situation," Butterworth replied, his tone making the euphemism chillingly clear. "One that involves explaining multiple casualties instead of just securing some inconvenient data. I'd prefer to avoid that complexity, but I'm authorized to escalate if required."

"You're talking about murdering four unarmed senior citizens," Mae said softly, her gentle voice somehow making the statement more powerful. "Is that really who you've become, Officer Butterworth?"

A flicker of something—perhaps doubt, perhaps simple annoyance—crossed the young officer's features before his professional mask reasserted itself. "What I've become is irrelevant. What matters is completing this assignment efficiently. The hard drive and backup, now."

Daisy, recognition dawning that cooperation might be their only path to survival, moved toward the laptop with deliberate slowness. "Very well. The original drive is connected to the USB port on the left side of the computer. The backup..." she hesitated, glancing toward Mae with an almost imperceptible nod.

Mae, understanding the unspoken message, clutched her knitting bag closer. "I believe Ziggy had it in his pocket," she improvised with surprising conviction. "In that hemp messenger bag he carries."

Butterworth's eyes narrowed slightly, but he didn't challenge the claim. "I'll check his belongings after securing the primary evidence. Don't move," he instructed, approaching the laptop with his weapon still trained on the group.

With practiced one-handed efficiency that suggested this wasn't his first evidence-removal operation, he ejected the hard drive and slipped it into his uniform pocket, all while maintaining his aim on the women.

"Now, I'm going to need all of you to move into the living room where I can keep you contained while I complete my search," he directed, gesturing with his weapon toward the adjoining space. "Slowly and together."

As the four friends moved reluctantly toward the living room, Mae clutching her knitting bag with white-knuckled intensity, a sudden crash from the front of the house shattered the tense standoff. Glass breaking, a heavy thud, then urgent footsteps approaching rapidly.

Butterworth spun toward the new threat, weapon reorienting with professional speed—but not quite fast enough to prevent the blur of tie-dyed hemp fabric that launched itself from the hallway entrance in a surprisingly athletic tackle that sent both officer and assailant crashing into the dining room table.

"Ziggy!" Rita exclaimed, maternal instinct immediately identifying their unexpected savior despite his disheveled state and the rapidly developing bruise on his forehead.

What followed was a chaotic scramble that would later be described by each participant with wildly varying details. Babs would insist she executed a "perfect stage combat maneuver" to disarm

Butterworth, while Daisy would maintain it was simply an accidental collision as everyone moved at once. Rita would claim strategic deployment of a heavy serving platter, and Mae would modestly suggest that perhaps her strategically extended knitting needle had contributed to the officer's subsequent loss of balance.

What was indisputable was the end result: Officer Peanut Butterworth facedown on Rita's antique Persian rug, his service weapon secured by Ziggy's surprisingly competent handling, and four slightly breathless retirement-age women standing over him with expressions ranging from Daisy's calculated assessment to Babs' theatrical triumph.

"Well," Babs declared, adjusting her silk blouse which had become disheveled during the altercation, "I believe that's what they call 'citizen's arrest' in the detective novels. Though I don't recall the procedural details involving corrupt police officers who threaten elderly women with firearms."

"The more pressing concern," Daisy noted pragmatically, "is what we do now. Our protective custody has been compromised, the evidence is partially in enemy hands, and we have no way of knowing which, if any, of the remaining officers outside are trustworthy."

"I vote we tie him up with my emergency macramé supplies," Ziggy suggested, still holding Butterworth's weapon with the careful attention of someone acutely aware of its potential danger. "I've got hemp cord that'll hold him securely without causing circulation damage."

"Of course you do," Daisy remarked dryly. "Your environmental activism preparedness continues to prove surprisingly applicable to criminal investigation scenarios."

"Sustainable materials have multiple uses," Ziggy replied with the faintest hint of a grin despite the gravity of their situation. "That's kind of the point."

As they secured the still-dazed Butterworth with Ziggy's remarkably professional knot work ("Protest lockdown training includes restraint escape techniques, so I know the most effective counter-approaches"), the group conducted a hasty strategic assessment of their drastically altered circumstances.

"We need to contact Morty directly," Mae insisted, her normally gentle features set in uncharacteristically firm lines. "If Butterworth is compromised, others on the force might be as well. But I still trust the Chief implicitly."

"Assuming we can reach him," Rita pointed out practically. "If Butterworth was telling the truth about the diversionary operation across town..."

"We use the burner phones," Daisy decided. "And we don't just call Morty—we implement multiple parallel communication strategies. Mae attempts to reach the Chief directly. Ziggy contacts some of the environmental journalists on the captain's trusted list. Babs and Rita use their extensive social networks to create public awareness that can't be easily suppressed. And I'll attempt to reach Jenkins' law office for legal support."

"A diversified approach," Rita nodded approvingly. "Reducing the risk of complete communication failure."

"Meanwhile," Daisy continued, "we need to secure ourselves against potential follow-up attempts when Butterworth fails to report success. Ziggy, what are our defensive options given the current circumstances?"

"Limited but not hopeless," he assessed, surveying their surroundings with tactical consideration that seemed incongruous with his laid-back appearance. "The Barnacle's Victorian architecture isn't ideal for defense—too many windows and multiple entry points. But we can create choke points using furniture barricades, utilize the upper floor for surveillance advantage, and potentially exit through the beach side if necessary."

"You've given this considerable thought in a remarkably short time," Daisy observed with newfound respect.

"Environmental activists spend a lot of time in occupation scenarios," Ziggy explained with a shrug. "Defensive positioning becomes second nature when you've chained yourself to enough endangered trees."

"A skill set I never anticipated finding relevant to our retirement activities," Daisy admitted. "But one I'm currently quite grateful for."

As they began implementing their multi-faceted response plan—Mae making careful use of a burner phone to attempt contact with Chief Crabbitz, Ziggy and Rita securing potential entry points with strategically positioned furniture, and Babs cataloging the silverware for what she termed "improvisational defensive implements"—Daisy found herself contemplating the extraordinary transformation of their circumstances.

Just days ago, their primary concerns had been Garden Club politics and the appropriate seasonal rotation of porch furniture. Now they were barricading themselves against potential assault while attempting to expose a sophisticated environmental crime conspiracy with apparent tendrils throughout local governance. The contrast was so extreme it verged on the absurd, yet here they were, four retirement-age women and one environmental activist, standing as the last line of defense for critical evidence that might otherwise be permanently suppressed.

"You know," Babs observed, arranging serving utensils by potential effectiveness as improvised weapons, "when I suggested we needed more excitement in our golden years, this wasn't precisely what I had in mind. I was thinking more along the lines of salsa dancing lessons or perhaps a wine tasting club."

"Life rarely delivers excitement in the precise format we anticipate," Daisy replied philosophically. "Though I admit the current situation exceeds even my most dramatic imaginings of retirement adventures."

"At least we're experiencing it together," Mae noted softly, temporarily covering the mouthpiece of her burner phone while waiting for a connection. "I can't imagine facing something like this alone."

"Nor I," Rita agreed, returning from securing the kitchen door with a makeshift alarm system involving stacked cookie sheets and precariously balanced mixing bowls. "Though I might have preferred our collective adventure to involve Mediterranean cruises rather than environmental crime conspiracies and corrupted police officers."

"Details, details," Babs dismissed with a theatrical wave. "Adventure is adventure. Though I do wish this particular version involved more glamorous costuming opportunities and fewer threats of bodily harm."

Before Daisy could formulate a suitably dry response to this characteristic prioritization, Mae's expression suddenly transformed from patient waiting to focused intensity.

"Chief?" she said into the burner phone, her voice carrying unexpected authority. "It's Mae Noodleman. Yes, from The Barnacle. We have an emergency situation involving Officer Butterworth and evidence of criminal conspiracy. No, this is not a social call or confusion." Her gentle features hardened into something almost unrecognizable as she delivered the coup de grâce: "Your rookie officer just threatened us with a firearm while attempting to seize evidence of environmental crimes connected to Judge Anderson and Oceanic Ventures International. We have him restrained and require immediate trustworthy assistance."

The others fell silent, watching Mae's transformation from their sweetest, most accommodating member to what Babs would later describe as "a steel magnolia revealing the steel beneath the petals." Even Butterworth, securely restrained in a dining room chair, seemed taken aback by the authoritative precision in her normally gentle voice.

"Yes," Mae continued after listening for a moment. "We understand the sensitivity. No, we haven't contacted anyone else yet." She glanced at Daisy with the slightest raised eyebrow, seeking confirmation of this technical untruth.

Daisy nodded approval. In crisis situations, information control sometimes necessitated strategic omissions.

"We'll remain secured at The Barnacle," Mae concluded. "But please understand, Chief—we need absolute certainty about who you send. Our trust has been rather severely compromised." She listened again, then added, "The private channel verification system sounds appropriate. Thank you."

As she ended the call, the others looked at her expectantly.

"Morty is approximately twenty minutes away," she reported. "He was indeed handling a situation across town, but recognized it as potentially diversionary when he received our call. He's en route personally, with only two officers he vouches for absolutely. They'll use a specific identification protocol he's established for sensitive operations—a childhood memory verification system that wouldn't be in any official records."

"Clever," Daisy approved. "Though that still leaves us with approximately twenty minutes of vulnerability before trustworthy reinforcements arrive."

"During which we should continue our defensive preparations," Rita suggested practically. "And perhaps consolidate the remaining evidence for secure handoff."

"I'll need my micro SD card back," Ziggy told Mae. "We should create additional copies while we can, using the captain's redundancy strategy."

As Mae carefully extracted the tiny storage device from its hiding place in her knitting project, Babs positioned herself near the front window, peering cautiously through a narrow gap in the curtains.

"Not to alarm anyone unnecessarily," she announced with the dramatic timing she had perfected through decades of theatrical training, "but there appears to be movement in the dunes again. And our protective police perimeter seems to have... thinned somewhat."

"Define 'thinned,'" Daisy requested, immediately alert.

"As in 'no longer visible at established checkpoint positions,'" Babs clarified. "Either they've adopted remarkable camouflage techniques or our protective detail has been reassigned. Neither scenario seems particularly comforting given recent developments."

"They're pulling back," Butterworth spoke up unexpectedly from his restrained position. "Standard protocol when an operation shifts from containment to active intervention. Clearing the operational zone."

Five heads turned toward their captive, whose matter-of-fact delivery made the statement all the more chilling.

"Active intervention?" Rita repeated, her practical nature immediately grasping the implications. "You mean they're preparing to breach the house."

"I wasn't supposed to fail," Butterworth explained with disconcerting professional detachment. "My assignment was simple evidence retrieval, minimal complications. Since I've missed my check-in window, the contingency protocol will activate. Three-person tactical team, multiple entry points, no witnesses." He shrugged as much as his restraints would allow. "Nothing personal. Just operational security."

"How reassuring," Daisy remarked dryly, though her expression betrayed genuine concern. "Our imminent demise is merely procedural rather than personal. That changes everything."

"You said a three-person tactical team," Ziggy noted, focusing on the practical details. "Entry points? Timeline?"

Butterworth assessed him with newfound professional respect. "Standard triangulation approach. Front door, rear beach entrance, and likely the east side picture window where the tree provides coverage. Timeline..." he glanced at his watch, which they had not removed during the restraint process, "approximately twelve minutes now, assuming my missed check-in triggered immediate escalation."

"Which gives us eight minutes before Chief Crabbitz arrives with legitimate reinforcements," Daisy calculated. "Assuming no delays and that your operational timeline estimate is accurate."

"It's accurate," Butterworth assured her with uncomfortable confidence. "These aren't amateurs. They're ex-military contractors with specialized training. If I were you, I'd surrender the evidence and take my chances with a memory-loss story. Sometimes they show mercy with minimal witnesses."

"Sometimes?" Babs echoed incredulously. "That's hardly a compelling statistical argument for cooperation, young man."

"We're not surrendering anything," Daisy stated firmly. "Nor are we passively awaiting potential execution by private military contractors. If we have twelve minutes before they breach, we have twelve minutes to prepare our response."

"Seven minutes to prepare, five minutes operational execution gap," Ziggy corrected, already moving toward the staircase with tactical purpose. "I need to check sight lines from the upper floor and identify potential counter-approach options."

"I'll secure the remaining evidence copies," Rita declared, taking the micro SD card from Mae and heading toward the kitchen. "And perhaps prepare some additional defensive measures of a culinary nature."

"Do I want to know what that means?" Daisy asked, momentarily diverted by this cryptic statement.

"Let's just say that certain cooking oils reach surprisingly dangerous temperatures and my pressure cooker has alternative applications beyond pot roast," Rita replied with uncharacteristic grimness. "Necessity breeds creative repurposing."

"Apparently we're all discovering hidden tactical depths tonight," Daisy observed. "Babs, Mae—primary floor defensive positions. I'll coordinate with Ziggy on upper level surveillance."

As they dispersed to their assigned responsibilities, Butterworth watched with an expression that had evolved from professional detachment to something approaching reluctant admiration.

"You know you're not going to win against a tactical team, right?" he called after Daisy as she headed for the stairs. "They have training, equipment, and the element of surprise."

"Perhaps," Daisy acknowledged, pausing at the base of the staircase. "But we have something they likely haven't encountered in previous operations."

"Which is?"

Daisy's academic features arranged themselves into an expression that managed to be simultaneously prim and terrifying. "Four retirement-age women with absolutely nothing to lose and a lifetime of accumulated problem-solving experience. I wouldn't underestimate that combination if I were orchestrating your tactical assault."

As she ascended to join Ziggy in establishing their defensive positions, Butterworth found himself experiencing an unexpected emotion in the face of imminent operational execution—doubt. The mission parameters had described the targets as "elderly female civilians with minimal threat potential." Nothing in his briefing had prepared him for the methodical, almost predatory focus with which these supposedly harmless senior citizens were now preparing to defend themselves.

For the first time since accepting his specialized assignment within the Conch Key Police Department, Officer Peanut Butterworth wondered if perhaps he had aligned himself with the wrong side of this particular operation. A concerning realization, given that his current position—restrained in the dining room of potential targets awaiting tactical elimination—placed him squarely in the crossfire of whatever was about to unfold.

Outside in the darkness, three figures in tactical gear moved with practiced coordination toward The Barnacle, unaware that their expected extraction of simple evidence from unsuspecting elderly witnesses had evolved into something considerably more complex. Their operational parameters were about to encounter a variable they hadn't accounted for in their planning: the surprising resilience and resourcefulness of the Seaside Sleuths.

The next twelve minutes would determine whether Daisy's confidence was justified or merely the final defiant stand of witnesses who had stumbled into a conspiracy far beyond their capacity to counter. Either way, The Barnacle was about to become the site of a confrontation that would permanently alter the quiet retirement community of Conch Key—assuming anyone survived to tell the tale.

Chapter Eleven
The Siege of The Barnacle

"Remind me again why we're not simply hiding in the bathroom with the door locked until Chief Crabbitz arrives?" Babs whispered as she and Mae crouched behind an overturned sofa in the living room, clutching what could only be described as improvised weapons—a heavy silver candlestick in Babs' case and a particularly lethal-looking knitting needle in Mae's.

"Because tactical teams don't respect bathroom locks," Mae replied with surprising authority for someone whose previous combat experience had been limited to aggressive garden club plant placement disputes. "And we need to maintain distributed defensive positions to counter their multi-point entry strategy."

"When did you become an expert on counter-tactical operations?" Babs asked, genuinely impressed by this new facet of her normally gentle friend.

"I read a lot," Mae offered modestly. "And my late husband Harold was quite interested in military history. We spent our fortieth anniversary touring Civil War battlefields. The strategies are surprisingly applicable to home defense, though with considerably less artillery involvement."

"One hopes," Babs muttered, adjusting her grip on the candlestick. "Though I wouldn't put artillery past Rita at this point. Did you see what she was doing with that pressure cooker?"

Their whispered exchange was interrupted by Ziggy's voice through the walkie-talkie system he had improvised using the burner phones—another unexpected skill derived from his environmental activism experience.

"Movement at the perimeter," he reported from his observation position in Daisy's upstairs bedroom. "Three figures approaching using standard triangulation formation, just as Butterworth predicted. Primary target appears to be the east side, secondary front door, tertiary beach access."

"Confirmed," came Daisy's calm response from her position at the top of the stairs. "Rita, status on defensive preparations?"

"Kitchen east entrance secured with the pressure cooker surprise," Rita's practical voice replied through the communication system. "Front door has the oil deployment system ready. Beach access is bobby-trapped with my special baking sheet alarm."

"I still can't believe we're setting booby traps instead of calling 911," Mae whispered, though her hands remained steady on her knitting needle.

"We did call the equivalent of 911," Babs reminded her. "It turned out to be Officer Backstabber in the dining room, who is apparently part of the conspiracy we're fighting against. Hence our current MacGyver meets Golden Girls home defense situation."

"Point taken," Mae conceded. "Though I suspect this may require more extensive therapy to process than my usual Tuesday morning sessions with Dr. Liebowitz."

"Movement accelerating," Ziggy's urgent voice interrupted through the walkie-talkie. "East team approaching window. Estimate breach in thirty seconds."

"Positions," Daisy commanded, her academic tone somehow transformed into battlefield authority. "Remember, our objective is delay and disruption until Chief Crabbitz arrives with legitimate reinforcements. Do not engage directly if avoidable."

Mae and Babs exchanged a final glance that communicated decades of friendship and newly discovered solidarity in crisis. Their silent communication was clear: whoever had expected four retirement-age women to spend their Tuesday evening defending their beach house against paramilitary operators had severely underestimated the resilience, resourcefulness, and sheer stubborn determination of The Barnacle's residents.

"Ten seconds to breach," Ziggy reported, his voice tight with focused tension. "Nine... eight..."

The countdown was interrupted by a sound that could only be described as a whisper of movement at the east window—the subtle scrape of a glass cutter followed by the carefully controlled tap of gloved fingers removing the resulting circle from the windowpane. A soft thump indicated what was likely a specialized entry tool extending through the opening to unlock the window from inside.

"East breach in progress," Daisy whispered into the communication system. "Rita, prepare kitchen countermeasures."

"Ready," came Rita's terse reply.

The window slid open with minimal sound—a testament to the professional nature of their opposition. A black-gloved hand appeared at the edge, followed by the unmistakable silhouette of a tactical helmet equipped with night vision technology.

"East intruder entering," Ziggy reported unnecessarily, as they could all see the dark figure now easing through the window with practiced efficiency.

"Wait for full commitment," Daisy instructed. "Rita, on my mark."

The intruder paused halfway through the window, head turning in a methodical scan of the room's interior. Through the tactical helmet's faceplate, nothing of their features was visible—just the anonymous threat of professional violence entering their home with practiced precision.

"Now," Daisy commanded as the figure committed to the entry, body fully extended through the window opening.

Rita's response was immediate and devastatingly effective. From her concealed position in the kitchen doorway, she activated what she had described as her "pressure cooker surprise"—which turned out to be a modified kitchen appliance positioned on a serving cart directly in the intruder's entry path. With a calculated push, she sent the cart rolling toward the window just as the tactical operator dropped to the floor inside.

What happened next would later be described by Babs as "like something from an extremely violent cooking show." The pressure cooker, which Rita had apparently superheated before venting the safety valve, executed a spectacular release of scalding steam directly into the intruder's face. This was immediately followed by a cascade of cooking oil that Rita had rigged above the window to deploy upon a tripwire activation.

The combination of steam and oil produced an immediate and dramatic result. The tactical operator let out a distinctly unprofessional howl of pain and surprise, hands flying up to the night vision equipment that was now not only compromised by steam condensation but also apparently shorting out due to oil infiltration.

"East intruder neutralized," Rita reported with the calm satisfaction of someone who had just executed a perfectly timed soufflé. "Temporarily, at least."

"Front door team reacting," Ziggy called urgently. "Abandoning stealth approach for accelerated entry. Impact breach likely."

As if to confirm his assessment, a sudden crash reverberated through The Barnacle as the front door was hit with what was likely a portable battering ram. The Victorian craftsmanship, while aesthetically pleasing, was not designed to withstand modern tactical entry techniques. The door frame splintered on the second impact, sending the door itself crashing inward.

"Front breach complete," Daisy narrated unnecessarily. "Second intruder entering."

The tactical operator who charged through the shattered doorway was larger than the first, moving with aggressive purpose rather than stealth now that the element of surprise had been compromised. Unlike their east window colleague, this intruder held a weapon at the ready—a compact submachine gun that confirmed the decidedly non-police nature of their opposition.

"Protect your position," Daisy instructed Mae and Babs through the communication system. "Ziggy, status on beach team?"

"Still approaching," Ziggy replied tensely. "Approximately thirty seconds from tertiary breach."

The front door intruder advanced into the entryway with professional caution, weapon sweeping in practiced arcs to cover potential threat zones. What they failed to account for was Rita's "oil deployment system"—which turned out to be a series of cooking oil bottles suspended from the ceiling on Mae's crochet thread, positioned to create a catastrophic spill when triggered by the nearly invisible tripwire now being approached by tactical boots.

"Three... two... one..." Rita counted down softly, before the distinctive sound of breaking glass and splattering liquid announced the successful deployment of her culinary countermeasure.

The result was both immediate and unexpectedly comical. The intruder's carefully measured advance transformed instantly into an ungainly slip-and-slide routine as combat boots lost all traction on the oil-slicked hardwood floor. Arms windmilled dramatically in a futile attempt to maintain balance, the tactical weapon flying in one direction while its operator crashed in another.

"Front intruder down," Rita reported with evident satisfaction. "Though I'm afraid our entryway floor may never fully recover from the oil treatment."

"Acceptable collateral damage under the circumstances," Daisy assured her. "Beach team status?"

Her question was answered by the sudden crash of breaking glass from the rear of the house, followed by the distinctive metallic clatter of Rita's baking sheet alarm system announcing the third breach point had been compromised.

"Rear breach confirmed," Ziggy called. "Third intruder entering through the sunroom. Moving toward kitchen access point."

"That's my position," Rita replied, her voice suddenly tense. "And I'm out of immediate countermeasures."

"Fall back to secondary position," Daisy instructed firmly. "Do not engage directly."

"Too late," came Rita's terse response. "Contact imminent."

The third intruder moved with heightened caution, presumably having heard the misfortunes befalling their teammates. Unlike the others, this operator advanced in a half-crouch, weapon raised, using available cover with professional discipline. As they reached the kitchen doorway, they paused for a tactical assessment before proceeding—which was when Rita executed what could only be described as an act of culinary combat.

With a chef's precision timing, she launched what appeared to be a cast iron skillet from behind the kitchen island, catching the intruder squarely in the tactical helmet with a resounding clang that echoed through the house like a misguided dinner bell. The impact wasn't sufficient to neutralize the threat completely, but it certainly disrupted the professional composure of their opponent, who staggered briefly before regaining balance and advancing with renewed aggression.

"Kitchen engagement ongoing," Rita reported, her breathing slightly elevated but voice remaining remarkably steady. "Could use some assistance if available."

"Moving to support," Daisy responded immediately, already descending the stairs with surprising agility for someone her age. "Ziggy, maintain overwatch position."

"Copy that," Ziggy acknowledged. "Be advised, front and east intruders recovering. Multiple threat convergence likely in approximately forty-five seconds."

The third intruder, having survived Rita's skillet attack, advanced into the kitchen with weapon raised—only to encounter Rita herself wielding what appeared to be a professional-grade meat tenderizer with remarkable determination. The incongruous matchup—tactical operator with military-grade weaponry versus retirement-age restaurateur with cooking implement—might have seemed comical in other circumstances. In the current situation, it represented a desperate last line of defense against lethal force.

"Drop your weapon," the intruder commanded, voice distorted through the tactical helmet's communication system. "Evidence recovery only. No targets if compliance is immediate."

"Interesting negotiating position considering you've broken into our home with military weapons," Rita replied with remarkable composure, meat tenderizer still at the ready. "Perhaps you'd care to explain that to Chief Crabbitz when he arrives? I believe your timetable for unopposed operation is rapidly expiring."

The mention of Crabbitz caused a noticeable shift in the intruder's posture. "Chief involvement was not in the operational briefing," the distorted voice stated, with the first hint of uncertainty entering their professional demeanor.

"Operational parameters have changed," Daisy announced from the kitchen doorway, where she had appeared with impressively silent movement despite her age. "Your informant failed to account for our contingency planning. Law enforcement is en route with full knowledge of this situation—genuine law enforcement, not your compromised assets."

This declaration might have carried more authority had Daisy been holding anything more threatening than what appeared to be an antique letter opener, but her academic confidence somehow imbued the statement with commanding credibility.

The tactical standoff was interrupted by the distinctive sound of sirens in the distance—multiple vehicles approaching with urgent purpose.

"Perimeter breach, law enforcement approach," the intruder spoke, apparently communicating with teammates through an internal system. "Mission parameters compromised. Extraction protocol alpha."

"Translation: they're running away," Babs interpreted from her position at the living room doorway, still clutching her silver candlestick with theatrical determination. "How disappointingly unoriginal for supposedly elite operatives."

The third intruder began a disciplined tactical retreat, weapon still trained on Rita and Daisy as they withdrew toward the sunroom breach point. "Evidence only. Final opportunity for compliant resolution."

"I believe that opportunity expired when you breached our home with military weapons," Daisy replied coolly. "Though you might want to assist your colleagues before departing. The one by the window appears to be experiencing significant discomfort from Rita's pressure cooker innovation."

As if to confirm this assessment, the first intruder was still emitting pained noises while attempting to clear compromised night vision equipment, now thoroughly contaminated with cooking oil and steam residue.

"Status report," came an authoritative voice through the tactical team's communication system, loud enough to be heard by The Barnacle's defenders. "Mission success confirmation required."

The third intruder, clearly weighing operational objectives against the rapidly deteriorating tactical situation, made a decision. "Mission compromised. Evidence not secured. Law enforcement approaching. Extraction recommended."

"Negative," the communication system replied with cold precision. "Mission parameters absolute. No witnesses, no evidence. Execute containment protocol. Authorization Oceanic Zulu Niner."

The change in the intruder's posture was immediate and alarming. Where there had been professional discipline with targeted objectives, there was now a more ominous purpose—the shift from evidence retrieval to something considerably darker.

"New operational directive acknowledged," the intruder confirmed, weapon adjusting to more direct targeting position. "Containment protocol initiating."

"I believe," Daisy observed with remarkable calm given the circumstances, "that our temporary defensive success has resulted in a tactical escalation. They're transitioning from evidence retrieval to elimination of witnesses."

"That's a very academic way of saying they're going to kill us all," Babs translated with characteristic bluntness. "Which seems excessively dramatic even by my theatrical standards."

"Not if I have anything to say about it," came a new voice from the shattered front doorway—the distinctive growl of Chief Mortimer Crabbitz, who stood framed in the entrance with his service weapon drawn and an expression of barely contained fury darkening his perpetually sunburned features. "Conch Key Police Department. Drop your weapons immediately."

The tactical standoff froze in perfect tableau—three intruders in various states of compromised effectiveness facing five civilian defenders and one extremely angry police chief whose arrival timing could not have been more dramatically perfect.

"Chief," the third intruder acknowledged, tactical helmet turning toward the new threat. "This is a misunderstanding. Private security operation, authorized by—"

"Save it," Morty cut them off with zero patience. "I don't care what paperwork you think you have or who authorized this operation. You've got about three seconds to drop those weapons before I demonstrate exactly how seriously I take armed home invasions in my jurisdiction."

The tactical team, recognizing that their operational parameters had been catastrophically compromised, made individual assessments that resulted in varying responses. The oil-soaked front door intruder, already at a significant disadvantage, wisely placed their weapon on the floor with careful movements. The steam-and-oil-compromised east window operator was still too busy dealing with equipment malfunction to offer meaningful resistance.

The third intruder, however, made a different calculation. With professional speed, they swung their weapon toward the most significant new threat—Chief Crabbitz.

What happened next would later be described by Babs with uncharacteristic accuracy rather than theatrical embellishment: "Pure chaos with a side of unexpected heroism."

As the weapon began its arc toward Morty, several things happened simultaneously. Rita launched her meat tenderizer with remarkable accuracy, striking the intruder's tactical helmet. Daisy executed what could only be described as a surprising tackle for someone her age and professional background, colliding with the intruder's legs. And from his position at the top of the stairs, Ziggy demonstrated unexpected marksmanship by hitting the tactical helmet with an expertly thrown decorative paperweight from Daisy's collection.

The combined assault disrupted the intruder's aim just as Morty fired his service weapon. The chief's shot struck the tactical helmet's faceplate, which apparently contained sufficient ballistic protection to prevent lethal injury but not enough to prevent the impact from incapacitating its wearer. The intruder went down in an ungraceful heap atop Daisy, who emitted a distinctly undignified "Oof!" at the sudden weight.

"Daisy!" Mae exclaimed with genuine alarm, abandoning her defensive position to rush to her friend's aid. "Are you hurt?"

"Only my dignity," Daisy assured her, extracting herself from beneath the now-unconscious intruder with remarkable composure given the circumstances. "Though I may require Rita's therapeutic hot pad for my back later. Tactical takedowns are apparently not recommended activities for women of a certain age."

"Speak for yourself," Babs declared, emerging from the living room with her candlestick still at the ready. "I found the entire experience invigorating. Though I do wish I'd had the opportunity to employ my weapon of choice. I've been practicing my candlestick swing for hours."

"Thank God you didn't need to use it," Morty interrupted, holstering his weapon as uniformed officers—presumably the trustworthy ones he had mentioned—secured the subdued intruders. "Would someone like to explain exactly what happened here? And why my officer is tied up in the dining room with what appears to be... is that hemp cord?"

"Sustainable restraint materials," Ziggy confirmed, descending the stairs to join the group. "Environmentally friendly and surprisingly effective for tactical applications."

Morty pinched the bridge of his nose in a gesture they had come to recognize as his response to mounting cognitive dissonance. "Let me get this straight. My rookie officer turned out to be a compromised asset who attempted to seize evidence and potentially harm you. You restrained him using environmentally friendly materials, then proceeded to defend yourselves against a tactical team using..." he glanced around at the aftermath, "pressure cookers, cooking oil, and cast iron kitchenware?"

"Don't forget the baking sheet alarm system," Rita added helpfully. "Quite effective for early warning, though admittedly limited in stopping power."

"Right," Morty acknowledged with the expression of a man rapidly approaching his capacity for bizarre explanations. "And the evidence these people were attempting to secure? I assume it's related to whatever you found on Captain Crustybutt's mysterious hard drive?"

"Extensive documentation of illegal underwater waste disposal operations connected to the resort development," Daisy confirmed, straightening her disheveled clothing with dignified movements. "Including corporate connections to Judge Anderson and an entity called Oceanic Ventures International. Evidence suggesting widespread corruption within local governance and law enforcement—present company excluded, of course."

"Of course," Morty agreed dryly. "And you didn't think to simply call me directly with this information because...?"

"We did call you," Mae reminded him gently. "After discovering Officer Butterworth's true allegiance. Though admittedly, we had already begun implementing defensive countermeasures by then."

"Defensive countermeasures," Morty repeated, surveying the considerable damage to The Barnacle's interior. "Including what appears to be approximately five gallons of cooking oil distributed throughout your entryway."

"Seven gallons, actually," Rita corrected. "I believe in comprehensive coverage when designing tactical impediments."

Morty closed his eyes briefly, visibly counting to ten before continuing. "And where is this evidence now? Please tell me it hasn't been lost or destroyed during this... whatever this was."

"Multiple secure copies," Daisy assured him. "Including one particularly well-hidden version." She glanced meaningfully at Mae, who patted her knitting bag with gentle satisfaction.

"We employed the captain's redundancy strategy," Ziggy explained. "Distributed storage with varying security protocols. Even if they had successfully neutralized us, they wouldn't have secured all copies."

"'Neutralized,'" Morty repeated with grim understanding. "That's a remarkably clinical term for what I suspect they were planning once evidence retrieval failed."

"Indeed," Daisy agreed soberly. "The communication we overheard suggested a transition from evidence recovery to 'containment protocol'—which I doubt involved polite requests for our continued silence."

Morty's expression hardened as he turned to observe the tactical team members now being secured by his trusted officers. "That would explain the military-grade weapons. Not standard equipment for simple evidence retrieval." He shook his head in evident disgust. "Private military contractors operating in my jurisdiction, targeting civilians... this goes beyond corruption into something much darker."

"The captain's evidence suggests the waste disposal operation represents potential health and environmental catastrophe," Daisy informed him. "The financial and criminal liability would be ruinous for everyone involved—powerful motivation for extreme containment measures."

"And you four just happened to find yourselves at the center of it," Morty observed with a mixture of exasperation and reluctant admiration. "Again."

"Five," Ziggy corrected, holding up his hand. "Environmental Division, remember?"

"How could I forget," Morty sighed. "Well, I suppose we should get formal statements and secure whatever evidence you've managed to preserve. And figure out exactly how compromised my department might be." This last thought seemed to physically pain him, his professional pride visibly wounded by the betrayal from within his own ranks.

"If it helps," Daisy offered with uncharacteristic gentleness, "Butterworth implied that the corruption was highly compartmentalized. Specific officers recruited for specific purposes, not wholesale departmental compromise."

"That does help, marginally," Morty acknowledged. "Though it means I can't trust anyone until we've completed a thorough investigation.

Which is why I'm going to need to arrange protective custody for all of you—legitimate protective custody this time, not the compromised version you've been experiencing."

"I assume that means relocation?" Daisy inquired, glancing around at the considerable damage to their home. "Given that The Barnacle has been rather thoroughly compromised as a secure location."

"Temporarily," Morty confirmed. "Until we can assess the full extent of the threat and implement appropriate security measures. I have a safe house arranged—one that isn't in any official system that could be accessed by compromised personnel."

"A safe house?" Babs repeated with theatrical delight. "How marvelously cloak-and-dagger! Will there be code names and disguises? I still have the platinum wig from my cocktail waitress ensemble, though it's seen better days after the yacht club adventure."

"No code names, no disguises," Morty replied firmly. "Just secure relocation with trusted protection until we can sort out this mess. And yes, before you ask, it includes the environmentalist." He nodded toward Ziggy. "Since he's apparently become part of whatever this is."

"The Seaside Sleuths, Environmental Division," Babs supplied helpfully. "We're thinking of having cards printed."

"We absolutely are not," Daisy contradicted automatically, though with noticeably less conviction than previous iterations of this recurring debate.

As Morty coordinated the secure crime scene processing and relocation logistics, the five unexpected defenders of The Barnacle gathered in the least damaged corner of the living room, surveying the considerable aftermath of their improvised home defense operation.

"Well," Babs declared, smoothing her disheveled silk blouse with dignified movements, "I believe we can officially classify this evening as exceeding standard retirement activities. Though I maintain that the experience would have been improved with better costume options."

"Tactical home defense generally prioritizes effectiveness over aesthetics," Rita observed dryly. "Though I admit, watching you swing that candlestick while wearing your silk loungewear had a certain dramatic flair."

"I'm more concerned about the damage to The Barnacle," Mae said softly, surveying the broken windows, shattered door, and oil-soaked floors with genuine distress. "This was our home."

"Is our home," Daisy corrected firmly. "Temporary relocation notwithstanding. Once this situation is resolved, we'll restore everything. Victorian architecture is remarkably resilient, as are its occupants."

"I'm just impressed you all handled a tactical team without military training," Ziggy admitted, regarding the four women with newfound respect. "Most professional activists I know would have been completely overwhelmed by that level of opposition."

"Never underestimate retirement-age women with household implements and sufficient motivation," Daisy informed him with academic precision. "We've spent decades developing problem-solving skills in environments that consistently underestimated our capabilities. This was simply a more extreme application of that experience."

"Plus, Rita's pressure cooker surprise was genuinely inspired," Babs added admiringly. "I never knew kitchen appliances could be weaponized so effectively. It almost makes me want to learn to cook. Almost."

"Necessity inspires creative repurposing," Rita replied modestly. "Though I doubt 'tactical applications for pressure cookers' will feature in my next cookbook."

As they continued their assessment of the evening's unexpected adventures, Morty approached with the focused expression that indicated operational plans had been finalized.

"We're ready to move you to the safe house," he informed them. "Trusted officers have secured a perimeter, and we have an unmarked vehicle waiting at the neighbor's property to avoid obvious departure from this location. We'll need to move quickly and discreetly."

"What about personal items?" Mae asked practically. "Medications, clothing, essentials?"

"Limited essentials only," Morty instructed. "Anything that can be carried in a single small bag. We need to minimize both time on-site and obvious relocation indicators."

"Very Jason Bourne," Babs approved. "Though considerably less exciting without the amnesia and unexplained combat skills. Unless..." She glanced speculatively at Daisy. "That tackle was remarkably effective for a former English professor. Is there something about your past you haven't shared, Daisy dear?"

"I played field hockey at Vassar," Daisy replied with dignified restraint. "Some skills remain useful despite decades of disuse."

As they gathered their limited essentials for the temporary relocation, each processing the extraordinary transformation of their circumstances in their own way, Daisy found herself contemplating the remarkable journey from peaceful retirement to active participants in exposing what appeared to be significant environmental crimes protected by corruption and violence.

Just days ago, her primary concern had been whether Eugenia's succulent presentation would conflict with her book club schedule. Now she was packing for emergency relocation to a safe house after defending her home against paramilitary operators using tactics that would never appear in any academic publication she had contributed to throughout her distinguished career.

Life, Daisy reflected as she carefully selected which reading materials to include in her limited essentials, contained infinite capacity for unexpected developments—particularly when shared with friends whose resilience, resourcefulness, and willingness to weaponize household items continued to surprise even after decades of acquaintance.

As The Barnacle's defenders prepared for their secure departure, none of them noticed the small, unobtrusive device that had been placed near the baseboard in the dining room—a listening device that continued transmitting even as the tactical team was taken into custody. Nor did they realize that their conversation about evidence copies and secure relocation was being monitored by someone who had not been present during the failed operation but maintained significant interest in its objectives.

Somewhere in Conch Key, in an office designed to project legitimate authority and civic responsibility, that transmission was being carefully monitored. The listener made notes about evidence copies, knitting bags, and safe house relocation with the methodical precision of someone accustomed to detailed planning and contingency management.

"Parameters adjusted," the listener spoke into a secure communication device. "Primary team compromised. Implement secondary approach. Non-standard targets require non-standard containment."

The response was immediate and professionally detached: "Understood. Timeline?"

"Extended observation. Identify secure location. Comprehensive containment when established."

"Acknowledged. Oceanic Ventures protocols active."

As the communication ended, the listener returned to monitoring the transmission from The Barnacle with the focused attention of someone not accustomed to operational failure. The elderly women and their environmental activist companion had demonstrated unexpected effectiveness in countering standard tactical approaches. The next containment attempt would need to account for their surprising resilience and resourcefulness.

The unexpected defenders of The Barnacle had won the first engagement in what was developing into a more complex conflict than either side had anticipated. But the forces behind Oceanic Ventures International were not accustomed to ultimate defeat—merely to adjusting strategies when initial approaches proved insufficient.

The Seaside Sleuths had demonstrated remarkable defensive capabilities. Whether those capabilities would extend to countering more sophisticated containment methods remained to be determined—a question that would be answered sooner than they might expect, despite Morty's best efforts to ensure their security.

For beneath Conch Key's peaceful surface, powerful interests remained committed to ensuring that certain secrets stayed buried—both figuratively and, if necessary, literally.

Chapter Twelve
Safe House, Unsafe Minds

"When you said 'safe house,' I was expecting something a bit more... safehouse-y," Babs remarked, surveying their new accommodations with theatrical disappointment. "Where are the steel reinforced doors? The bulletproof windows? The panic room with emergency provisions and perhaps a small arsenal? This looks suspiciously like someone's grandmother's vacation cottage."

"That's because it is someone's grandmother's vacation cottage," Morty confirmed, setting down the last of their hastily packed bags in what could generously be described as a living room, if one's definition of living room included macramé wall hangings featuring seashells, at least seventeen dolphin-themed decorative objects, and furniture upholstered in a pattern that could only be described as "tropical flamingo explosion."

"Specifically, it's my grandmother's vacation cottage," he added, his perpetually sunburned complexion deepening with what might have been embarrassment. "Or was, before she passed. I inherited it but never got around to updating the décor."

"Updating would be a crime against historical preservation," Babs declared, running an appreciative hand over a lamp shaped like a pelican wearing sunglasses. "This is pure 1980s Florida kitsch. Museums would pay for this level of authentic period styling."

"I find it rather charming," Mae offered diplomatically, though her gaze lingered with mild alarm on a collection of ceramic clowns arranged on a wicker étagère. "Very... distinctive."

"The strategic advantage," Morty explained, ignoring their design critique, "is that this property isn't registered in my name. It's still listed under my grandmother's trust, with a management company handling the limited rental activity. No connection to law enforcement, no digital trail leading to any of you."

"Clever," Daisy approved, her academic mind automatically assessing the tactical considerations. "Though I assume you've enhanced the security beyond what your grandmother originally implemented?"

"Considerably," Morty confirmed. "Modern locks, reinforced entry points, connectivity for remote monitoring, and a direct alert system to my personal phone. Plus, Officer Martinez will be stationed outside in an unmarked vehicle, with Officer Dalton handling perimeter checks on a randomized schedule."

"Martinez and Dalton," Rita repeated thoughtfully. "They're the ones you trust implicitly?"

"With my life," Morty assured her. "Martinez has been with me since I took over as chief. Dalton's newer but comes from outside the department—lateral transfer from Miami PD with impeccable references. Neither has any connection to the local power structure or suspicious financial activity."

"Always reassuring when 'not suspicious' is the primary qualification for police protection," Babs remarked dryly. "Though given recent experiences with Officer Butterscotch—"

"Butterworth," Daisy corrected automatically.

"Whatever," Babs dismissed with a wave of her bejeweled hand. "My point is, our standards for trusted law enforcement have undergone dramatic recalibration over the past twenty-four hours."

"Speaking of Officer Betrayal," Ziggy interjected from his position by the window, where he had been systematically checking sight lines and potential security vulnerabilities, "what's his status? Still doing his hemp-cord-macramé impression in our dining room?"

"Currently enjoying the hospitality of a secure holding cell at the county facility," Morty reported grimly. "Along with the tactical team members we apprehended. All being held without communication privileges under federal environmental crimes statutes, thanks to some rapid intervention by contacts at the EPA."

"The Environmental Protection Agency has a rapid response team?" Mae asked, surprised.

"For cases involving potential radioactive waste disposal? You bet they do," Morty confirmed. "Once I mentioned the evidence you recovered and the attempted assault on civilians possessing said evidence, they mobilized with impressive efficiency. Their investigators are en route from Atlanta as we speak."

"And Judge Anderson?" Daisy inquired. "Given his apparent connections to Oceanic Ventures International, I assume he's being investigated as well?"

Morty's expression darkened. "That's more complicated. Sitting judges have significant procedural protections. We're gathering evidence to present to the judicial ethics committee, but moving against him directly requires federal involvement and substantial documentation."

"Which we have provided," Daisy pointed out.

"Which you have provided partial evidence suggesting his involvement," Morty corrected carefully. "The captain's documentation establishes financial connections but doesn't directly link Anderson to knowledge of the illegal operations. We need more before the FBI's public corruption unit can move against a sitting judge."

"So we've done all this—found evidence, survived multiple assassination attempts, defended our home against paramilitary intruders, and relocated to Flamingo Fantasy Island—and the primary villain is still sitting in his chambers making judicial decisions?" Rita summarized with practical frustration.

"For now," Morty acknowledged. "But his activities are being monitored, his communications are under surveillance with appropriate warrants, and his freedom of movement is significantly constrained even if he doesn't realize it yet."

"The wheels of justice turn slowly," Daisy observed philosophically, "particularly when well-greased by corrupting influences."

"That's... both accurate and excessively cynical," Morty replied, looking mildly disturbed by Daisy's metaphorical flourish.

"I prefer 'realistic' to 'cynical,'" Daisy countered. "Though the distinction admittedly blurs with age and accumulated observation of human institutions."

"Deep thoughts aside," Ziggy interrupted, still focused on their immediate security concerns, "what's the timeline here? How long are we supposed to hide out in Dolphin Dreamland while the bureaucratic mechanisms grind toward potential justice?"

"Until we've confirmed the full extent of the threat and neutralized key elements," Morty replied. "I can't give you a specific timeframe, but the EPA's involvement accelerates things considerably. Environmental crimes with potential public health implications get prioritized, especially when there's evidence of official corruption protecting the perpetrators."

"And The Barnacle?" Mae asked softly, her genuine concern for their home evident. "Will it be... restored?"

"Insurance adjusters are already assessing the damage," Morty assured her. "I've expedited everything through official channels, citing it as a crime scene requiring rapid remediation. You won't be financially responsible for repairs resulting from the tactical incursion."

"How refreshing to know our premiums include 'paramilitary home invasion coverage,'" Babs remarked. "Though I doubt it extends to my limited-edition silk loungewear, tragically oil-stained during our defensive operations."

"I'll make a note for the claims department," Morty replied with surprising patience. "Now, let me show you the security features and protocols before I head back to coordinate the ongoing investigation."

The next fifteen minutes were occupied with Morty's detailed explanation of the cottage's enhanced safety measures—communication procedures, emergency exits, lockdown protocols, and the operation of what turned out to be a surprisingly sophisticated surveillance system discreetly integrated into Grandma Crabbitz's eclectic decorating scheme.

"The ceramic flamingo on the front porch contains a motion-activated camera," he demonstrated, pulling up a crystal-clear security feed on his tablet. "As does the mailbox, the bird bath, and the particularly disturbing garden gnome holding the fishing pole."

"That gnome has seen things no decorative lawn ornament should witness," Babs agreed solemnly. "The thousand-yard stare of ceramic garden statuary that has gazed into the abyss."

"Is she always like this?" Morty asked Rita in a stage whisper, gesturing toward Babs who was now dramatically communing with the gnome figure on the security feed.

"This is actually her restrained mode," Rita informed him. "You should experience her during actual crisis situations. The yacht club confrontation included a full Shakespearean soliloquy addressed to her waterlogged wig."

"It was more blank verse than proper Shakespearean structure," Daisy corrected automatically, "though the emotional intensity was appropriately dramatic given the circumstances."

Morty closed his eyes briefly, visibly recalibrating his tolerance for their particular interactive dynamic. "Moving on," he continued with professional determination, "you have secure communication devices here." He indicated five identical smartphones on the coffee table. "Encrypted, untraceable, and pre-programmed with only essential contacts. Use these exclusively until further notice. Your personal phones have been secured as evidence and potential surveillance targets."

"More burner phones," Ziggy noted with approval. "Though considerably higher-tech than our prepaid models. Government budget versus environmental activist resources, I guess."

"These are actually FBI-issued secure communications devices," Morty admitted. "Called in a favor from a colleague in the Miami field office. They're normally reserved for witness protection scenarios."

"Which this essentially is," Daisy observed, examining one of the devices with academic interest. "Though I assume without the long-term identity reconstruction and relocation aspects traditional witness protection entails."

"Let's hope so," Rita said firmly. "I've invested too much effort in my current identity to start over as Rhonda Simpkins from Tucson with a fabricated background in dental hygiene."

"You've given this scenario considerable thought," Daisy noted with mild concern.

"I dated a U.S. Marshal briefly in my fifties," Rita explained with a dismissive wave. "He talked shop more than was strictly appropriate. I could probably design a credible witness protection program given adequate resources and administrative support."

"Your dating history continues to provide unexpectedly relevant skill transfers," Daisy observed. "Perhaps you should consider compiling a reference guide: 'Romantic Relationships as Professional Development: A Practical Approach to Acquiring Diverse Competencies.'"

"I'd read that," Babs declared enthusiastically. "Though my own contribution would be more along the lines of 'Men as Cautionary Tales: Learning What Not to Do Through Matrimonial Misadventure.'"

"If we could refocus on the security protocols," Morty interjected with admirable patience, "I need to ensure everyone understands the emergency procedures before I leave."

The remainder of his briefing covered evacuation routes, secure communication protocols, and the vitally important "absolutely do not leave the property under any circumstances without direct authorization from me personally, verified through established security questions" rule, which he repeated no fewer than four times with increasing emphasis.

"We understand, Morty," Daisy assured him after the fourth iteration. "Containment and security are paramount until the threat has been neutralized. We will maintain appropriate protocols and exercise due caution."

"Why don't I find that entirely reassuring?" he asked rhetorically, gathering his equipment with the resigned expression of someone who recognized the limits of his control over the situation.

"Because you have extensive experience with our investigative methods?" Mae suggested helpfully.

"Because the last time I left you with explicit security instructions, you ended up tackling murderous art dealers off a dock during a lightning storm?" Morty countered.

"In our defense," Babs pointed out reasonably, "we did solve the murder case, expose a money laundering operation, and apprehend the criminals. The lightning storm and dock tackling were merely theatrical flourishes adding production value to an already compelling narrative."

Morty pinched the bridge of his nose in what had become his signature gesture when interacting with The Barnacle's residents. "Just... stay inside. Monitor the security feeds. Use the secure communication devices if absolutely necessary. And for the love of all that's holy, don't start conducting independent investigation activities from inside the safe house."

"Define 'independent investigation activities,'" Daisy requested with academic precision.

"You know exactly what I mean," Morty replied, fixing her with a pointed look. "No unauthorized evidence analysis, no communication with potential witnesses, no elaborate conspiracy mapping using household objects and yarn connections."

"That last one seems oddly specific," Ziggy remarked.

"I've watched crime shows," Morty defended himself. "And based on recent experience, I wouldn't put it past you five to construct an entire criminal conspiracy evidence board using whatever materials are available."

"The dolphins would make excellent push pins for key suspects," Babs agreed, eyeing the extensive collection with professional assessment. "And I believe there's macramé cord in that basket by the television—perfect for establishing connection visualization."

"I'm leaving now," Morty announced firmly, "before I hear any more details about your potential violation of direct security protocols. Officers Martinez and Dalton have the perimeter. I'll check in every four hours through the secure communication system. Emergency protocol is triple-click the panic button on your devices if immediate assistance is required."

"Thank you, Morty," Mae said softly, her genuine appreciation momentarily cutting through the banter. "We understand you're taking significant professional risks to protect us, and we're truly grateful."

The chief's expression softened slightly at Mae's sincere gratitude. "Just doing my job, Ms. Noodleman. Though I'll admit this particular assignment has expanded my definition of 'routine police work' considerably." With a final nod that somehow conveyed both professional assurance and personal concern, he departed, leaving the five unexpected investigators alone in their flamingo-festooned safe house.

"Well," Babs declared into the momentary silence that followed Morty's exit, "who's ready to start constructing an elaborate conspiracy evidence board using household objects and yarn connections? I've already identified the optimal dolphin figurines for our primary suspects."

"Morty specifically instructed us not to do that," Mae reminded her gently.

"No, he instructed us not to conduct 'independent investigation activities,'" Babs corrected with theatrical precision. "If we investigate as an interdependent collective, we're technically complying with his directive."

"I believe that interpretation stretches the semantic boundaries beyond reasonable limits," Daisy observed, though her tone suggested more academic interest than genuine objection.

"Regardless of linguistic technicalities," Rita interjected practically, "we need to establish our immediate priorities. We've been forcibly relocated, separated from most of our belongings, and placed under protective isolation due to multiple attempts on our lives. Perhaps we should focus on adjusting to these circumstances before resuming active investigation."

"A reasonable suggestion," Daisy agreed. "Though I would argue that understanding the full scope of the conspiracy targeting us constitutes a form of self-defense. Knowledge is our most effective protection against threats we cannot anticipate through conventional security measures."

"So we're back to the evidence board," Babs concluded triumphantly. "I'll start gathering the dolphins."

"Before we transform Grandma Crabbitz's decorative menagerie into investigative tools," Ziggy suggested, "maybe we should review what we already know? Consolidate our understanding of the situation without physical evidence mapping?"

"A digital approach rather than analog visualization?" Daisy considered. "Not my preferred methodology for complex pattern recognition, but perhaps more aligned with Morty's explicit instructions against yarn-based connection mapping."

"Plus, it won't require dismantling the carefully curated dolphin tableau," Mae added, eyeing the collection with what appeared to be growing appreciation rather than her initial alarm. "I believe some of these are limited edition Lladró pieces. The craftsmanship is really quite remarkable once you adjust to the maritime theme."

"Fine," Babs conceded with theatrical disappointment. "Digital conspiracy mapping it is. Though I maintain that physical visualization with appropriately symbolic figurines would enhance our cognitive processing."

As they settled into the living room's flamingo-patterned seating arrangement—Rita and Mae taking the sofa, Daisy claiming the reading chair, Babs dramatically draping herself across a wicker chaise lounge, and Ziggy cross-legged on a surprisingly plush area rug—they began the process of systematically reviewing everything they had learned about the conspiracy that had transformed their retirement into a high-stakes criminal investigation.

"Let's start with the established facts," Daisy suggested, automatically adopting her academic organization approach. "Brock Hamfist discovered evidence of illegal underwater waste disposal connected to his resort development project. This discovery prompted his environmental conversion and subsequent murder."

"The waste disposal operation is connected to Oceanic Ventures International," Ziggy continued, "a shell corporation with links to Judge Anderson and potentially other local officials including Meredith Moneypenny."

"The physical infrastructure involves an underwater pipeline disguised as an environmental water treatment facility in the original resort plans," Rita added. "Designed to dispose of industrial and potentially radioactive waste directly into protected marine habitat."

"With projected environmental and health impacts severe enough to justify multiple murder attempts and the deployment of private military contractors against civilian witnesses," Mae completed the summary, her gentle voice contrasting sharply with the disturbing content.

"And here we are, fabulous retirees turned eco-warriors, hiding in Dolphin Disco Paradise while shadowy corporate interests presumably plan their next attempt to permanently silence us," Babs contributed with dramatic flair. "It's like 'Golden Girls' meets 'The Bourne Identity,' but with better accessories and more frequent bathroom breaks."

"Your summary lacks precision but captures the emotional essence," Daisy acknowledged. "The question remains: what is our optimal approach given current constraints? We have evidence secured and partially transmitted to authorities, but the full scope of the conspiracy remains undefined."

"And the primary orchestrators are still operationally active," Ziggy pointed out. "Judge Anderson maintains his position of authority, and we don't know who else might be involved in the power structure."

"Not to mention whatever 'secondary approach' the tactical team's controller mentioned," Rita reminded them. "After the primary team was compromised, they referenced implementing alternative containment strategies."

This sobering recall of imminent threat temporarily dampened even Babs' theatrical enthusiasm. The reality of their situation—targeted by powerful interests with demonstrated willingness to eliminate witnesses—had momentarily pierced the protective layer of humor and banter they had collectively developed.

"Perhaps," Mae suggested into the weighted silence, "we should focus on identifying potential vulnerabilities in our current security arrangements? If we anticipate likely approaches, we might better prepare countermeasures."

"Practical and prudent," Daisy approved, academic mind immediately engaging with the analytical challenge. "Let's conduct a systematic assessment. Physical perimeter security first, then digital/communication vulnerabilities, followed by potential infiltration vectors."

"I've already noted three suboptimal aspects of the physical layout," Ziggy volunteered. "The rear bathroom window has reinforced glass but the frame itself is original construction—potential weak point under determined assault. The side yard has limited visibility from existing camera positions, creating a surveillance gap approximately three meters wide. And the tree adjacent to the master bedroom could provide access to the roof for a sufficiently athletic intruder."

The four women stared at him with varying expressions of surprise at this detailed security analysis.

"What?" he defended. "Environmental activists develop site vulnerability assessment skills pretty quickly. You try chaining yourself to endangered trees for a living without learning to identify security weak points."

"Your alternative career background continues to provide unexpectedly relevant skill transfers," Daisy remarked, echoing her earlier observation about Rita's dating history. "Perhaps there's a pattern here worth examining—seemingly unrelated experiences providing crucial capabilities for our current circumstances."

"Like my theatrical training enabling convincing undercover personas," Babs suggested eagerly.

"And my nursing background providing both medical knowledge and heightened observational skills," Mae added thoughtfully.

"My restaurant management experience translating to tactical resource allocation and improvised weaponry development," Rita continued with surprising enthusiasm for this analytical framework.

"And my academic research methodology facilitating complex pattern recognition and hypothesis testing," Daisy completed the assessment. "Collectively, we represent a rather comprehensive skill set for investigative activities, despite lacking formal law enforcement training."

"The Seaside Sleuths," Babs declared triumphantly. "Bringing diverse life experiences to crime-solving since... last Tuesday, approximately."

"We are not adopting that name," Daisy insisted automatically, though with noticeably less conviction than her initial rejections of the designation.

"Yet you keep responding to it," Babs pointed out with the satisfied smile of someone winning a war of attrition. "Acceptance through repetition—basic psychological conditioning."

"Can we refocus on the security assessment?" Rita suggested, practical as always. "Ziggy's identified physical vulnerabilities. What about our communication security?"

"The devices Morty provided are likely secure against conventional interception," Daisy observed. "However, our verbal communications within this location remain potentially vulnerable. We should consider the possibility of preexisting surveillance devices."

Five pairs of eyes immediately began scanning the cottage interior with newfound suspicion.

"Are you suggesting Grandma Crabbitz's vacation home might be bugged?" Mae asked, her gentle features creased with concern.

"I'm suggesting we cannot eliminate any possibility given the demonstrated resources and determination of our opposition," Daisy clarified. "If this location was identified in advance as a potential safe house, it may have been compromised."

"That's... disturbingly logical," Ziggy acknowledged. "Though how would they have known to target this specific property? Morty said it wasn't registered in his name."

"Public records can be searched for family connections," Daisy pointed out. "A sufficiently motivated investigator could identify properties connected to Morty's grandmother through trusts or management companies."

"So we might be having this entire conversation under surveillance right now?" Babs asked, immediately striking a more photogenic pose on her chaise lounge. "I should have worn the blue caftan. It photographs better from all angles."

"If we are under surveillance, your clothing choice is the least of our concerns," Rita pointed out dryly.

"Speak for yourself," Babs retorted. "Just because we're targeted by corporate assassins doesn't mean we have to abandon aesthetic standards. Dignity in the face of danger, darling."

"Perhaps we should conduct a sweep for surveillance devices," Mae suggested practically, gracefully redirecting the conversation. "Ziggy, would your environmental activism background happen to include expertise in counter-surveillance techniques?"

"Some," he admitted. "Though without specialized equipment, we're limited to physical inspection and basic electronic interference detection. Most high-end listening devices are designed to be virtually undetectable without professional tools."

"We'll work with what we have," Daisy decided. "Systematic search protocols, starting with the most likely placement locations—ventilation points, light fixtures, electronic devices, and decorative objects that might conceal components."

"I volunteer to examine the dolphins," Babs declared immediately. "My theatrical training includes prop management and set dressing analysis. I'll know if they've been tampered with."

"I'm not entirely confident that Broadway prop management translates directly to counter-surveillance expertise," Daisy remarked skeptically.

"You'd be surprised," Babs assured her. "The backstage politics of 'Cats' involved more espionage and surveillance than most international conflicts. I once found three separate listening devices hidden in my headpiece after suggesting the choreographer's vision lacked dynamic tension."

As they divided the cottage into search zones and began their methodical examination of every potential surveillance point, the group maintained a running commentary of deliberately misleading conversation—Babs' suggestion that "we should verbally misdirect any listeners while we search" having been unanimously adopted as a reasonable precaution.

"I'm so looking forward to simply relaxing here and taking a complete break from our recent excitement," Mae announced with uncharacteristic projection while carefully examining the underside of a coffee table. "No more investigation activities for us!"

"Indeed," Daisy agreed, her tone carrying subtle theatrical emphasis as she inspected a ceiling vent. "Just peaceful retirement activities appropriate to our age and physical limitations."

"Perhaps some gentle crafting," Rita suggested, methodically checking behind wall hangings. "Or reminiscing about our numerous health concerns and prescription medications."

"I'm thinking of taking up extreme napping," Babs contributed while disassembling a particularly suspicious ceramic dolphin. "Competitive-level inactivity. Perhaps with occasional breaks for watching television at high volume due to our collective hearing impairment."

Ziggy, who had been systematically examining the electronic devices throughout the cottage, suddenly froze, his attention fixed on the vintage television cabinet in the corner of the living room. With careful movements, he gestured for the others to continue their misleading banter while he extracted a small toolkit from his hemp messenger bag.

As the women maintained their deliberately mundane conversation about potential recipes for dinner and whether the weather might affect their hypothetical gardening plans, Ziggy methodically disassembled the lower panel of the television cabinet with the practiced efficiency of someone familiar with covert operations.

His expression shifted from focused concentration to grim confirmation as he extracted a small electronic device attached to the cabinet's interior wiring—a professional-grade listening transmitter that had clearly not been installed by Grandma Crabbitz or Morty's security team.

Holding it up for the others to see without speaking, he pointed to a tiny logo etched into its surface: a stylized wave pattern that matched the Oceanic Ventures International symbol they had seen in the captain's documentation.

Five pairs of eyes widened in simultaneous realization. Their "safe house" had been compromised before they ever arrived—which meant their opposition had anticipated Morty's contingency plans and had resources sufficient to identify and prepare for their relocation.

In wordless communication developed through their recent adventures, they continued their misleading conversation while Ziggy carefully examined the device. After several tense minutes of inspection, he extracted a note from his pocket and wrote a brief message that he passed to Daisy:

"Active transmission. Military grade. Not just listening—tracking our location. Need to decide: disable or misinform?"

Daisy considered for a moment before writing back: "Can you redirect the signal? Make it appear we're still here while we relocate?"

Ziggy's expression shifted to thoughtful assessment as he evaluated this suggestion, eventually responding: "Possible with modifications. Need time and parts. Meanwhile, continue misinformation campaign."

With nods of understanding, the group maintained their carefully crafted facade of retired individuals discussing dinner plans and television preferences while Ziggy worked methodically on the surveillance device, periodically passing notes to update them on his progress.

"If properly modified, this can broadcast false presence indicators while masking our actual departure. Electronic signature suggests additional devices likely present. Comprehensive sweep required."

The impromptu counter-surveillance operation continued for nearly an hour, resulting in the discovery of three additional listening devices strategically placed throughout the cottage—in the kitchen clock, the master bedroom lamp, and perhaps most disturbingly, inside a ceramic clown figurine that Mae had found particularly unsettling upon their arrival.

"I knew that clown wasn't to be trusted," she whispered as Ziggy carefully extracted the device from its hollow interior. "Something about the eyes."

"Clowns are never to be trusted as a general principle," Babs agreed solemnly. "A lesson I learned during an unfortunate touring production of 'Pagliacci' in my early career. The tenor playing the lead had boundary issues and remarkable flexibility for a man of his proportions."

Once all four devices had been identified and carefully modified to Ziggy's specifications—"Environmental activism occasionally intersects with electronic civil disobedience," he explained with modest competence—they gathered in the bathroom with the shower running, which Ziggy assured them would provide sufficient acoustic masking for genuine private conversation.

"So our 'safe house' is essentially a surveillance trap," Rita summarized, practical as always despite the concerning circumstances. "Our supposedly secure location was identified and prepared for our arrival by the very people trying to eliminate us."

"Which means they have resources within or connected to law enforcement beyond Officer Butterworth," Daisy concluded grimly. "Someone with access to Morty's contingency planning or the ability to track our movement from The Barnacle."

"Do we think Morty's compromised?" Mae asked, genuine distress in her gentle voice at the possibility.

"Unlikely," Daisy assessed after careful consideration. "His response to the initial evidence and subsequent protection efforts appear genuine. More probable is surveillance of his activities by someone with sufficient resources and motivation to anticipate his movements."

"Like a judge with extensive connections throughout local governance and law enforcement," Ziggy suggested darkly.

"Precisely," Daisy agreed. "The question is what we do with this information. Alerting Morty risks compromising whatever operational security he currently maintains if his communications are under surveillance."

"And remaining here means our every movement and conversation is being monitored by people who have already tried to kill us multiple times," Babs pointed out with uncharacteristic gravity. "Neither option strikes me as particularly appealing."

"Ziggy," Daisy turned to their unexpected technical expert, "what is your assessment of the modifications you've made to the devices? Will they effectively mask our activities?"

"Temporarily," he replied with careful precision. "I've created a loop feedback system that should broadcast normal activity patterns and conversation fragments for approximately twelve hours before the pattern repetition would become detectable to sophisticated monitoring. But that assumes whoever planted these isn't physically observing the cottage as well."

"Which we must assume they are," Rita concluded grimly. "Professional operations don't rely on single surveillance vectors."

"Our options appear limited," Daisy observed, academic mind methodically assessing possibilities despite the bathroom's increasingly sauna-like conditions as the shower continued running. "Remain under surveillance in a compromised location, alert Morty and potentially expose him to additional risk, or attempt independent relocation without secure resources."

"There is another possibility," Mae suggested softly, her gentle features set in uncharacteristically firm lines. "We could deliberately feed false information through the modified devices while implementing a controlled exit strategy. Misdirection rather than simple evasion."

Four pairs of eyes turned to her with varying expressions of surprise at this strategic suggestion.

"Mae Noodleman," Babs declared with genuine admiration, "you continue to be the dark horse of our investigative quintet. From gentle retired nurse to tactical deception strategist in less than a week. I'm both impressed and mildly terrified."

"I read a lot of mystery novels," Mae explained modestly. "And I was very good at charades during hospital staff parties. Misdirection is simply a matter of convincing performance."

"A skill set we collectively possess in abundance," Daisy acknowledged, academic assessment shifting to practical application. "Ziggy, could you program the devices to broadcast specific misleading information of our choosing?"

"Within parameters," he confirmed. "The existing hardware limits sophistication, but I can establish basic conversational patterns and movement signatures that would suggest specific activities or intentions."

"Then I believe we have the outline of a plan," Daisy announced, her expression shifting to the focused determination that had emerged during their previous investigative challenges. "We create a deception operation suggesting specific intentions and activities through the compromised devices, while actually implementing an alternative approach they won't anticipate."

"And what alternative approach might that be?" Rita asked practically. "We're still faced with limited resources and multiple unknown threats."

Daisy's academic features arranged themselves into what Babs would later describe as "the expression of someone who has decided crime-fighting is actually her retirement calling rather than an inconvenient interruption to book club activities."

"We stop playing defense," she declared with quiet intensity. "If our opposition has the resources to compromise supposedly secure locations and anticipate conventional protection measures, continuing to hide simply postpones the inevitable. Instead, we take the initiative— identify the core of this conspiracy and expose it so comprehensively that even Judge Anderson's influence cannot suppress the evidence."

"That sounds suspiciously like what Morty specifically instructed us not to do," Mae pointed out gently.

"Morty's instructions were predicated on the assumption that this location was secure," Daisy countered logically. "That assumption has been proven false, which necessitates revised strategic considerations."

"So we're going rogue," Babs translated with theatrical delight. "From witnesses under protection to vigilante investigators bringing down the corrupt establishment through cleverness and sheer force of menopausal determination. I love this narrative evolution!"

"I wouldn't characterize it as 'going rogue' so much as 'implementing necessary security adaptations in response to compromised protective parameters,'" Daisy clarified with academic precision.

"Same thing, better vocabulary," Babs dismissed cheerfully. "The question is: what exactly does this proactive approach entail? Besides escaping from our dolphin-infested surveillance trap, of course."

"That," Daisy acknowledged, "requires further strategic development. But the first step is clear—we need to execute a controlled departure from this location without alerting our observers, while leaving behind convincing evidence of continued presence."

"A ghost operation," Ziggy nodded with professional understanding. "Classic counter-surveillance technique. The devices broadcast prepared content, physical indicators suggest occupancy, but the targets have actually relocated."

"Exactly," Daisy confirmed. "Ziggy, what would you need to enhance the device modifications for extended deception?"

As Ziggy outlined the technical requirements for their improvised counter-surveillance operation, the five unexpected investigators found themselves once again transforming from passive targets to active participants in what had become an increasingly complex conflict between environmental protection and corporate crime—their retirement activities now expanded to include electronic countermeasures and tactical deception operations in addition to the already unlikely skill set they had developed for murder investigation and home defense.

What none of them realized as they planned their strategic deception was that their bathroom strategy session was being observed—not through electronic surveillance, but via high-powered thermal imaging equipment positioned in the tree line behind the cottage. The figure monitoring their heat signatures made note of their extended presence in a single room with running water, a pattern inconsistent with normal residential behavior.

Into a secure communication device, the observer reported: "Targets demonstrating counter-surveillance awareness. Bathroom concentration with acoustic masking. Electronic measures likely compromised. Recommend accelerated containment timeline."

The response was immediate and chillingly concise: "Approved. Neutralize all targets. No witnesses. Authorization confirmed."

As the five inside continued developing their plan to seize the initiative, the timeline for their potential elimination was being dramatically compressed. Their deception operation would need to succeed not within the twelve-hour window Ziggy had estimated for the electronic modifications, but before the containment team already mobilizing could reach their supposedly secure location.

The Seaside Sleuths—a designation Daisy was increasingly unlikely to continue rejecting given their evolving operational status—were about to face their most significant challenge yet. And this time, Morty and his trusted officers were too far away to arrive in time, their protective perimeter already compromised by the sophisticated surveillance that had preceded their arrival.

Grandma Crabbitz's flamingo-festooned vacation cottage was about to become the site of either a remarkable escape or a tragic conclusion to their unexpected investigative career. The ceramic dolphins, silent witnesses to decades of peaceful family vacations, would soon observe a very different kind of activity—one involving desperate retirees, environmental activism techniques, and the kind of resourcefulness that only comes from decades of being consistently underestimated.

The bathroom strategy session concluded with a surprisingly comprehensive plan given the improvised nature of their circumstances and the limited resources available. Daisy, ever the methodical academic, had outlined a four-phase approach: deception establishment, controlled extraction, secure relocation, and proactive investigation.

"Ziggy will enhance the electronic countermeasures to create convincing occupancy patterns," she summarized as they prepared to disperse for their assigned tasks. "Rita and Mae will implement physical deception elements—lights on timers, strategic placement of clothing and personal items, and prepared food indicators suggesting ongoing presence."

"And I'll be creating our theatrical exit strategy," Babs added with undisguised enthusiasm. "Finally, my extensive costume design experience combines with my escape artist training from that magician I dated in the late eighties!"

"I thought he was a circus clown," Rita remarked, eyebrow raised skeptically.

"Darling, he contained multitudes," Babs replied with dignified reminiscence. "The clowning paid the bills, but the escape artistry was his true passion. Until that unfortunate incident with the water tank and the Portuguese acrobat twins, of course."

"While I hesitate to limit your theatrical scope," Daisy interjected diplomatically, "perhaps we should focus on practical disguise elements rather than elaborate performance aspects?"

"Spoilsport," Babs pouted. "But fine. Basic identity concealment it is. Though I maintain that a proper character backstory enhances the believability of any disguise. You can't just look different—you must become different."

"Let's aim for looking sufficiently different to avoid immediate recognition by hostile surveillance," Daisy suggested. "Full method acting transformations can wait for less time-sensitive circumstances."

With their roles established, they dispersed throughout the cottage to implement their respective phases of the plan, maintaining the casual conversation and movement patterns of retirees settling into temporary accommodations for anyone monitoring the compromised devices.

Ziggy worked with focused intensity on enhancing the surveillance device modifications, creating what he described as "interactive response loops" that would enable the systems to react to potential live questioning rather than simply broadcasting preset conversation fragments. The technical complexity was clearly stretching the limits of his self-taught skills, but the determined concentration with which he approached the challenge suggested a personal investment beyond their immediate tactical needs.

"You're taking this very personally," Daisy observed quietly as she assisted him by recording various conversation samples for the automated system. "Beyond the immediate danger to all of us."

Ziggy glanced up from the disassembled device, his expression momentarily vulnerable beneath the focused façade. "They killed my dad," he replied simply. "Maybe he wasn't perfect—definitely wasn't perfect—but he was trying to make things right at the end. Exposing what they're doing to the environment, the health risks they're creating for profit... I've been fighting these kinds of corporate criminals my whole adult life, usually with limited success. This time it's different. This time I have evidence, allies, and a direct connection."

"Justice and environmental protection as dual motivations," Daisy noted with academic assessment that didn't quite mask her underlying compassion. "Perfectly reasonable combined incentives for assuming personal risk."

"Plus," Ziggy added with a hint of his usual laid-back humor returning, "how many environmental activists get to team up with four retirement-age women who took down a tactical team using kitchen appliances? That's a coalition too unique to abandon."

"We do present an unconventional collective skill set," Daisy acknowledged with dignified understatement. "Though I maintain that Rita's pressure cooker deployment was improvisation rather than tactical planning."

"Effective either way," Ziggy grinned briefly before returning to his delicate electronic modifications. "Now, I need you to record several versions of the phrase 'I think I'll take a nap' with different intonations—casual, tired, slightly irritated, and what Babs calls your 'academic dismissal tone.'"

Meanwhile, in the kitchen, Rita had established what could only be described as a deception staging area, methodically preparing food items that would create the impression of ongoing occupancy: a casserole in the oven set to low heat, coffee cups with varying levels of consumption placed strategically around the living areas, and a detailed schedule of meal preparation activities that would align with normal eating patterns for the surveillance monitors.

"The coffee cup with the dolphin handle goes in the living room with exactly 1.2 centimeters of liquid remaining," she instructed Mae with the precision of a surgical team leader. "The half-eaten cookie beside it should have exactly three visible bite marks forming an asymmetrical pattern."

"You've developed a surprisingly detailed approach to deception staging," Mae observed as she carefully arranged the cookie according to Rita's specifications.

"Food presentation is psychological as well as aesthetic," Rita explained, adjusting the casserole temperature with mathematical precision. "Creating convincing consumption patterns requires understanding the subtle visual cues that register as authentic versus artificially constructed. It's no different from plating a gourmet meal—the difference between artistic arrangement and natural use indicators."

"I had no idea restaurant management involved such detailed observational psychology," Mae remarked with genuine admiration.

"You don't survive forty years in the culinary business without understanding how people interact with food environments," Rita replied practically. "The principles apply equally to creating a welcoming dining establishment or a convincing deception operation, apparently."

In the master bedroom, Babs had transformed the space into what appeared to be a theatrical costume department explosion. Clothing items from the limited supply they'd brought were being systematically modified, combined with elements borrowed from Grandma Crabbitz's remaining wardrobe items found in the back of the closet, and arranged into what Babs insisted were "character-appropriate ensembles for covert extraction."

"The key is creating visual distraction from our identifiable features," she explained to Daisy when she returned from her recording session with Ziggy. "For you, we need to minimize the distinctive silver bouffant that screams 'academic precision with Southern formal training.' I'm thinking this sun hat combined with the oversized sunglasses and perhaps a casual scarf arrangement."

"While I appreciate the theatrical approach," Daisy replied with measured skepticism, "I'm not certain that disguising ourselves as tourist stereotypes will significantly enhance our security during extraction."

"Darling, effective disguise isn't about complex prosthetics or elaborate costumes," Babs informed her with the authority of decades in theatrical production. "It's about altering the immediate visual profile and projecting a character essence that diverts attention from identifying features. No one looks closely at obvious tourists—they're visual white noise in a coastal community."

"A surprisingly insightful tactical assessment," Daisy acknowledged, regarding the assembled outfit with newfound consideration. "Though I maintain that the flamingo-patterned shirt is excessive even for a tourist characterization."

"That's why it's perfect," Babs insisted. "The eye focuses on the outrageous pattern, not the face above it. Disguise 101, darling—give them something more interesting to look at than your identifying features."

As the preparation continued throughout the cottage, Ziggy called them together for a critical security briefing, his expression uncharacteristically grave as he outlined an unexpected complication to their plan.

"We have a problem," he announced without preamble. "I've been monitoring the thermal imaging reflection patterns from the windows while setting up the electronic countermeasures, and there's definitely an observation position in the tree line beyond the rear property boundary. Based on the reflection consistency and positioning, they're using military-grade surveillance equipment—probably the same team that's been tracking us from the beginning."

"How does this affect our extraction plan?" Daisy asked immediately, academic mind shifting to tactical adaptation.

"It means they're not just relying on the planted devices," Ziggy explained grimly. "They have real-time human surveillance supplementing the electronic monitoring. Our device modifications will handle the audio and basic movement patterns, but actual visual confirmation of our presence requires a higher level of deception."

"We need body doubles," Babs declared dramatically. "Or at the very least, convincing silhouettes that register on thermal imaging as human occupants."

"Exactly," Ziggy confirmed, looking mildly surprised at her technical accuracy. "Thermal signatures are the key vulnerability in our deception operation. We need heat sources that mimic human thermal patterns located where observers would expect to find us."

"Could we use heating pads or electric blankets?" Mae suggested practically. "I noticed several in the linen closet, presumably for Grandma Crabbitz's visitors with arthritis or muscle complaints."

"Basic heat sources would help, but the thermal profile is too uniform," Ziggy explained. "Human bodies have distinctive heat distribution patterns—higher concentrations at the core and head, lower in the extremities. We need something that can create that variable pattern."

"Water bottles," Rita proposed immediately. "Different temperatures in specific arrangements. I use the technique for tempering chocolate when precision heat distribution is required. We could create human-shaped arrangements with varied water temperatures to simulate body heat patterns."

"That... might actually work," Ziggy acknowledged with newfound respect. "If we can create four or five distinct thermal shapes and program movement patterns between key locations in the cottage, it could be enough to convince distance observers that we're still inside."

"While we execute our actual extraction through a less observed approach vector," Daisy completed the tactical adjustment. "Which means we need to identify their surveillance blind spots."

"Already working on it," Ziggy assured her. "Based on the reflection patterns and optimal observation positioning, there's a significant blind spot on the east side where the neighbor's ornamental hedge creates both visual and thermal shadowing. If we time our movement correctly between their scan patterns, we should have a narrow extraction window."

"How narrow?" Rita asked practically.

"Approximately forty seconds every twelve minutes," Ziggy calculated. "Based on the systematic sweep pattern I've observed."

"Forty seconds to extract five people without triggering visual or thermal alerts," Daisy summarized with academic precision. "A challenging parameter but not impossible with proper coordination and preparation."

"Especially with appropriate distraction elements," Babs added thoughtfully. "We need to give them something specific to focus on at the critical moment—draw their attention to a particular window or activity while we utilize the extraction route."

"A diversionary tactical element," Daisy agreed, academic terminology adapting to their increasingly militarized circumstances. "Staged activity in the main living area while we exit through the east side blind spot."

"I can program a specific thermal surge in the kitchen area," Ziggy offered. "Timed to coincide with our extraction window. The oven turned to maximum temperature would create a heat bloom that might draw infrared attention momentarily."

"And I'll set up a corresponding movement pattern with the hot water bottles," Rita added, already mentally calculating the required temperature differentials. "A simulated gathering in the kitchen area that would appear natural for dinner preparation activities."

As they refined their extraction plan with increasingly technical precision, Mae—who had been quietly monitoring the security feeds Morty had established—suddenly raised her hand for attention, her gentle features arranged in uncharacteristic alarm.

"I hate to interrupt the planning," she said softly, "but I believe our timeline has been significantly compressed. There's a vehicle approaching from the south access road—unmarked black SUV with tinted windows, moving at what appears to be tactical speed rather than casual approach."

Ziggy immediately moved to the surveillance monitor, his expression shifting from focused planning to genuine concern. "That's not Martinez or Dalton," he confirmed grimly. "The vehicle profile is all wrong, and the approach vector suggests familiarity with surveillance blind spots. We have unwelcome visitors incoming."

"Timeline adjustment required," Daisy announced with remarkable calm given the circumstances. "Extraction initiation immediate rather than prepared. Ziggy, status of electronic countermeasures?"

"Eighty percent complete," he reported tersely. "Enough for basic deception but not the interactive response capabilities I was implementing. They'll cover our initial absence but won't withstand direct interaction testing."

"Rita, thermal body doubles?"

"Two completed, three partial," Rita replied with efficient assessment. "Sufficient for initial deception but not sustained observation."

"Babs, disguise elements?"

"Basic identity concealment ready, narrative development incomplete," Babs reported, shifting seamlessly from theatrical enthusiasm to professional focus. "Enough to avoid casual recognition but not sustained scrutiny."

"Acceptable given compressed parameters," Daisy decided. "Mae, extraction route security assessment?"

"East side blind spot appears continuous based on current surveillance positioning," Mae confirmed, studying the security feeds with surprisingly technical evaluation. "Visual confirmation of SUV approach indicates two visible occupants, tactical positioning suggests potential additional personnel."

"We move now," Daisy concluded. "Basic extraction protocol, minimal possessions, maintain communication discipline. Assemble at east exit point in ninety seconds."

The five unlikely tactical operators dispersed with remarkable efficiency given their varied backgrounds and the unexpected acceleration of their plan. Babs distributed the basic disguise elements—hats, sunglasses, and outer garments that altered their silhouettes—while Rita activated the thermal decoys and positioned them in primary observation locations. Ziggy completed the essential electronic countermeasure programming while Mae continued monitoring the approaching threat on the security feeds.

Daisy, with the authoritative precision that had defined her academic career and now transferred surprisingly effectively to their impromptu escape operation, conducted a final assessment as they gathered at the designated extraction point—a narrow bathroom window on the east side that opened onto the shadowed area created by the neighbor's ornamental hedge.

"Ninety-second status report," she requested with quiet intensity. "Surveillance countermeasures?"

"Active and stable," Ziggy confirmed. "Audio loops running, thermal decoys positioned, basic movement patterns established."

"Extraction security?"

"SUV has stopped approximately one hundred meters from the primary entrance," Mae reported. "Two individuals visible, tactical movement pattern consistent with approach preparation. Estimated time to perimeter breach approximately three minutes."

"Escape route?"

"Window opens onto blind spot with approximately twenty meters of hedge coverage before reaching adjacent property line," Ziggy outlined. "Secondary road access beyond requiring limited open ground traversal."

"Transportation options?"

"Limited," Rita acknowledged with practical concern. "Without access to vehicles, we're restricted to foot movement or public transportation, both with significant exposure risk."

"We need wheels," Babs translated bluntly. "Preferably something less conspicuous than a flamingo-colored convertible, though I maintain that would be thematically appropriate given our current accommodations."

The critical transportation problem hung in the air between them, a fundamental flaw in their hastily accelerated extraction plan. Without secured vehicles, their escape options were severely limited—a tactical vulnerability that could prove fatal given the approaching threat.

"I might have a solution," Mae said unexpectedly, her gentle voice carrying surprising confidence. "But it requires accepting some unconventional transportation methods and trusting me with something I haven't done in approximately thirty-five years."

Four pairs of eyes turned to her with expressions ranging from curiosity to mild alarm.

"Before I became a nurse," Mae explained with uncharacteristic haste, "I had a brief rebellion phase after high school. My boyfriend was part of a local motorcycle club—nothing criminal, just enthusiasts—and he taught me to ride. I was actually quite proficient before my parents discovered my extracurricular activities and insisted on a more appropriate pursuit for a young lady with college aspirations."

"You know how to ride motorcycles?" Babs clarified, her theatrical eyebrows reaching unprecedented heights of surprise.

"And," Mae continued, pointing through the window toward the adjacent property visible beyond the hedge, "if I'm not mistaken, that's a restored vintage Triumph Bonneville in the garage next door. I noticed it earlier while checking the property boundaries on the security feeds. The garage door is partially open, and the property appears unoccupied."

"You're suggesting we steal a motorcycle?" Rita asked with uncharacteristic alarm.

"Borrow," Mae corrected gently. "In extraordinary circumstances. With every intention of returning or compensating the owner once our situation is resolved."

"The ethical considerations, while valid, are superseded by immediate survival requirements," Daisy assessed with pragmatic precision. "The approaching threat appears to have lethal intent, creating moral justification for temporary property appropriation under duress."

"We're stealing a motorcycle because assassins are coming to kill us," Babs translated bluntly. "And apparently Mae 'Secretly Rebellious' Noodleman is our getaway driver. This retirement adventure continues to exceed all reasonable narrative expectations."

"The logistics remain challenging," Rita pointed out practically. "A single motorcycle cannot transport five people, regardless of Mae's rediscovered riding skills."

"It creates a critical distraction and initial extraction capability," Daisy countered. "Mae can transport one person immediately—logically Ziggy, given his technical expertise and relative youth—to establish secure secondary transportation for the rest of us."

"While we three maintain the deception operation as long as possible," Babs concluded with unexpected tactical insight. "Creating maximum confusion and divided pursuit resources. Devious and dramatically satisfying."

"The ethical compromise disturbs me," Mae admitted softly. "But I see no viable alternative given the imminent threat."

"Threat which has now deployed personnel approaching the front entrance," Ziggy reported tensely from his position monitoring the security feed on his phone. "Two visible operators with tactical gear partially concealed under civilian outerwear. Classic deniable operation profile."

"Decision point reached," Daisy announced with quiet authority. "Extraction proceeds as outlined. Mae and Ziggy execute primary motorcycle appropriation and secondary transportation acquisition. Remaining team maintains deception operation to maximum sustainable duration before secondary extraction."

"In English: Mae and Ziggy steal the bike and get a car, while we three keep the bad guys busy as long as possible before they rescue us," Babs translated cheerfully. "Risky, improvised, and potentially disastrous. I love it."

"Communication protocols established?" Daisy asked Ziggy, ignoring Babs' theatrical enthusiasm in favor of operational details.

"Burner phones on encrypted text only, no voice communication," he confirmed, distributing the devices. "Single-use code phrases for status updates and extraction coordination."

With remarkably efficient final preparations given their diverse backgrounds and the improvised nature of their operation, the unlikely tactical team prepared for separation. Mae and Ziggy would execute the immediate extraction through the east side window, while Daisy, Rita, and Babs would maintain the deception operation as long as possible before secondary extraction.

"Stay alive," Ziggy told them simply as he prepared to follow Mae through the narrow window opening. "We'll be back for you as soon as humanly possible."

"We've survived murderous art dealers, lightning storms, and tactical home invasions," Babs reminded him with determined cheerfulness. "A few more assassins seem like a relatively minor escalation at this point."

As Mae and Ziggy disappeared through the window into the shadowed protection of the ornamental hedge, Daisy turned to her remaining teammates with the focused intensity that had defined their unexpected transformation from peaceful retirees to active participants in what had become a life-or-death struggle against corporate environmental criminals.

"Phase one implementation," she instructed with quiet precision. "Maximum deception sustainability, optimal positioning for potential defensive countermeasures if deception fails. Remember, our objective is time extension, not confrontation engagement."

"We keep them guessing as long as possible without actually fighting assassins," Babs clarified. "Though I maintain my silver candlestick technique has shown promising results in previous encounters."

"Let's hope it doesn't come to improvisational weaponry," Rita remarked dryly as they moved to their assigned positions. "I left my pressure cooker at The Barnacle, and Grandma Crabbitz's kitchen implements are suboptimal for tactical applications."

As they dispersed throughout the cottage to implement their deception operation, the security feed showed the approaching figures reaching the front porch—professionally nondescript individuals who moved with the controlled precision of experienced operators rather than casual visitors. Their relaxed demeanor might have fooled casual observers, but to the increasingly experienced eyes of the Seaside Sleuths, the contained readiness in their movement patterns screamed "trained professionals with lethal intent."

The doorbell rang with deceptive normalcy, a mundane sound that carried ominous significance in their current circumstances. Phase one of their hastily modified escape plan was officially underway, with lives literally hanging in the balance of their improvisational capabilities.

Through the east side hedge, Mae Noodleman—retired nurse, gentle soul, and apparently former motorcycle enthusiast—was about to attempt grand theft auto for the first time in her seventy-one years of largely law-abiding existence. The fact that she was doing so to escape professional assassins targeting her for uncovering environmental crimes merely added another surreal layer to what had become the most unexpected retirement activity imaginable.

The doorbell rang again, more insistently this time. Inside the compromised safe house, three women who had expected their golden years to involve book clubs and beach walks prepared to match wits with trained killers, armed with nothing but household objects, hastily assembled electronic countermeasures, and the collective resourcefulness that had already proven surprisingly effective against previous lethal threats.

Just another Tuesday in the increasingly extraordinary lives of the Seaside Sleuths.

Chapter Thirteen
Grandma's Wild Ride

"I believe proper etiquette dictates we answer the door when someone rings the bell," Babs whispered from her position behind the living room sofa, clutching what appeared to be a ceramic dolphin with disturbing intensity. "Though I admit most etiquette guides don't cover appropriate protocols when the visitors are likely professional assassins."

"Maintaining established deception parameters requires simulated normal response patterns," Daisy replied in an equally hushed tone, her academic precision somehow intact despite their dire circumstances. "Rita, are you prepared for reception duties?"

Rita, who had donned a bathrobe over her clothes and arranged her hair into a convincingly disheveled approximation of someone recently awakened from a nap, gave a terse nod. "Remember, I'm hard of hearing, confused about visitors, and expecting a grocery delivery that's late. Maximum time extension through conversational obstruction."

"Your community theater performance as Aunt Eller in 'Oklahoma' suggests untapped dramatic potential," Babs assessed professionally. "Though perhaps dial back the murderous glare? Confused elderly residents rarely look like they're contemplating homicide techniques."

"I'm working on it," Rita assured her, consciously adjusting her expression to something more befuddled and less tactical. "How's this?"

"Much better," Babs approved. "The slight mouth-breathing adds a wonderful touch of cognitive disconnect."

The doorbell rang a third time, now accompanied by an authoritative knock that suggested rapidly diminishing patience. With a final confirming nod from Daisy, Rita shuffled toward the entrance, activating their hastily established deception operation while her friends concealed themselves in strategically selected positions throughout the cottage.

"Coming, coming," she called in a wavering voice that bore little resemblance to her usual practical tone. "No need to wake the dead with all that knocking. Some of us were enjoying our afternoon nap."

Through the security feed discretely positioned on her phone, Daisy observed the transformation of Rita Calabaza—respected restaurateur and improvisational home defense specialist—into a convincingly befuddled elderly woman annoyed at having her rest disturbed. The performance was surprisingly compelling, from her shuffling gait to the slightly vacant expression she adopted upon opening the door.

"Yes?" Rita inquired peevishly, squinting at the two professionally nondescript individuals on the porch. "If you're selling something, I already told the last fellow I don't need any vacuum cleaners. Got perfectly good brooms."

The lead figure—male, approximately forty, with the carefully cultivated forgettable features of someone professionally trained to avoid distinctive description—produced a badge that flashed too quickly for proper inspection. "Ma'am, we're with the Department of Environmental Protection. Routine inspection of coastal properties for compliance with new regulations. May we come in?"

"Environmental Protection?" Rita repeated with exaggerated confusion. "Don't recall anyone saying anything about inspections. My granddaughter handles all the paperwork for this place. She's not here right now. Gone to get groceries. Supposed to be back twenty minutes ago but that girl has no concept of time. Just like her mother."

The tactic—establishing a fictional absent property manager while suggesting imminent return—was intended to create hesitation and potential timeline reconsideration. Based on the subtle glance exchanged between the supposed inspectors, it had at least introduced a moment of uncertainty in their approach.

"This won't take long, ma'am," the second figure assured Rita with practiced courtesy that didn't quite mask the professional assessment happening behind her seemingly friendly smile. "Just a quick walkthrough to ensure compliance. All coastal properties in this zone are being checked this week."

"Well, I suppose it's alright," Rita reluctantly agreed, stepping back with the careful movements of someone concerned about balance. "Though I don't know what you expect to find. Place is exactly as it's been for forty years, except for that ridiculous dolphin collection my daughter-in-law keeps adding to. As if one porcelain fish wasn't enough."

As she ushered the "inspectors" into the living room, Rita maintained her cover story with remarkable commitment, launching into a rambling narrative about fictional family members and their questionable decorating choices. The intruders made a show of polite listening while their eyes conducted professional assessment of the cottage interior, likely noting potential exit points, occupancy indicators, and tactical positioning options.

From her concealment point behind the substantial living room curtains, Daisy observed the subtle hand signals exchanged between the operatives—confirmation gestures indicating the presence of the planted surveillance devices and acknowledgment of apparent occupancy patterns. Their confidence seemed to waver slightly at the unexpected presence of Rita, whose performance as a confused grandmother had apparently not featured in their operational briefing.

"My granddaughter should be back any minute with the groceries," Rita reminded them with the repetitive emphasis of someone whose conversational patterns included frequent restatement. "She said she was just going to the corner store. That was almost an hour ago now. Young people have no concept of time these days. Too busy with their cellular telephone devices."

"We'll be quick, ma'am," the lead operative assured her, clearly attempting to establish interior access without the complication of additional witnesses arriving. "If we could just see the main living areas and perhaps check the exterior drainage systems?"

"Drainage systems?" Rita repeated with convincing bewilderment. "Nobody said anything about drains. They worked fine when I took my shower this morning. Though the hot water does make that funny clanking noise. I've told Marjorie about that a dozen times but does she call a plumber? No, she does not. Says it's charming. Charming! As if pipes are supposed to sound like someone dropping silverware down a garbage disposal."

The improvisational expansion of their fictional family drama was buying precious seconds, but Daisy could see the operatives' professional patience wearing thin. Through the secure communication system Ziggy had established before his departure, she received a text update from the extraction team: "Transportation secured. Secondary approach in approximately 12 minutes. Status update?"

She typed a terse reply: "Intruders inside. Conducting apparent search operation disguised as environmental inspection. Maintaining deception protocols. Rita engaged in primary distraction. Estimated compromise timeline uncertain."

The response was immediate and concerning: "Accelerated approach. Be prepared for extraction in 8 minutes. Potential tactical situation. Defensive preparations advised."

Daisy's academic mind rapidly calculated the implications. Mae and Ziggy had secured transportation faster than anticipated, but believed the situation sufficiently urgent to risk an accelerated approach—potentially exposing themselves to the surveillance still likely monitoring the property. The suggestion of "defensive preparations" implied they anticipated direct confrontation rather than subtle extraction.

Things were about to get considerably more complicated.

Meanwhile, approximately two miles from the supposedly safe cottage, Mae Noodleman was experiencing what could only be described as a profound second adolescence. The vintage Triumph Bonneville motorcycle—"borrowed" from the neighboring property with a combination of technical assistance from Ziggy and mysteriously retained skills from her rebellious youth—responded to her guidance with thrilling precision as they navigated the coastal back roads at speeds suggesting Mae's concern for traffic regulations had been temporarily suspended alongside her usual gentle demeanor.

"You're really good at this!" Ziggy shouted over the engine's rumble, his arms wrapped perhaps more tightly than strictly necessary around Mae's waist as she executed another expert turn. "Where did you learn to ride like this?"

"Tommy Barton, 1969!" Mae called back, the exhilaration in her voice suggesting the revival of long-dormant memories. "He said I had natural talent! My parents said I had natural insanity! They were both probably right!"

The motorcycle's powerful engine carried them swiftly through the less populated areas of Conch Key, avoiding main thoroughfares where their unusual appearance—a seventy-something woman in a pastel cardigan piloting a vintage motorcycle with a dreadlocked environmental activist passenger—might attract unwanted attention. Mae's unexpected skill level had significantly compressed their timeline for securing secondary transportation, creating both advantages and complications for their hastily constructed extraction plan.

"There!" Ziggy pointed toward a small rental car lot nestled between a bait shop and a souvenir store. "Low security, older vehicles less likely to have integrated tracking systems, cash-based rental options for tourists!"

Mae nodded acknowledgment, executing a perfect deceleration as she guided the Triumph into an inconspicuous position behind the nearby public restroom building. The momentary cover would allow them to approach the rental office without immediately connecting them to the distinctive motorcycle.

"I haven't felt this alive since my hospital skydiving fundraiser in 1992," Mae confessed as she removed the borrowed helmet, her silver-gray bob emerging remarkably intact despite their high-speed journey. "Though I suspect my blood pressure is currently at levels my doctor would find concerning."

"Some things are worth elevated blood pressure," Ziggy assured her with a grin that suggested newfound appreciation for the gentle retired nurse's unexpected depth. "Now, let's acquire some family-friendly transportation for extraction purposes."

Their approach to vehicle acquisition proved considerably less dramatic than the motorcycle appropriation. Ziggy's environmental activism apparently included experience with cash-based anonymous transactions, and Mae's grandmotherly appearance inspired minimal suspicion as they negotiated the rental of a thoroughly unremarkable beige sedan with Florida plates and the faded remnants of a "My Child is an Honor Student" bumper sticker partially obscured by a more recent "I'd Rather Be Fishing" decal.

"Perfect anonymity through aggressive normality," Ziggy approved as they completed the paperwork under the aliases "Margaret Wilson" and "Michael Wilson," the fictional grandmother-grandson pairing apparently inspiring no curiosity from the disinterested rental agent. "Now for extraction phase implementation."

As they transferred from motorcycle to sedan—the Triumph regretfully abandoned but with an envelope containing adequate compensation and an apology note carefully secured to the seat—Ziggy received the concerning update from Daisy regarding the "environmental inspectors" now inside the cottage.

"Timeline compression required," he informed Mae as they settled into the anonymous vehicle. "Our friends have unexpected visitors conducting interior assessment under false pretenses."

"Accelerated approach with potential complications," Mae translated with surprising tactical precision for someone whose normal conversation centered around gentle encouragement and knitting patterns. "Direct extraction versus subtle removal?"

"I'm thinking something in between," Ziggy replied, his environmentalist problem-solving skills adapting to their unique circumstances. "A distraction significant enough to create extraction opportunity but not immediately identifiable as tactically motivated."

"Like what?" Mae inquired, her normally gentle features set in uncharacteristically determined lines as she navigated the sedan back toward their compromised safe house.

Ziggy's expression transformed into something that combined his usual laid-back demeanor with newly emergent strategic calculation. "How do you feel about creating a minor environmental incident as a tactical diversion?"

Back at the cottage, the deception operation was approaching critical sustainability limits. Despite Rita's impressively committed performance as a confused grandmother, the "environmental inspectors" had completed a thorough assessment of the main living areas and were now asking increasingly pointed questions about the other occupants referenced in the surveillance they had obviously been monitoring.

"And your other friends are where exactly?" the lead operative inquired with professional persistence thinly disguised as casual conversation.

"Oh, they're around somewhere," Rita replied vaguely, maintaining her befuddled character with remarkable consistency. "Daisy's probably reading. That woman goes through books like I go through baking powder. Barbara's likely doing her beauty regimen. Takes her hours. More creams and potions than a witch's kitchen. And Mae... well, Mae could be anywhere. Quiet as a mouse, that one. Sometimes I forget she's even here until she offers me tea."

The calculated references to their supposedly current but temporarily absent presence seemed to satisfy the operatives' immediate suspicions, but Daisy—still observing from concealment—could see their patience wearing thin as the thorough search revealed no direct visual confirmation of the additional occupants.

A subtle vibration from her secure phone indicated another message from the extraction team: "Approach initiated. Northeast exterior. Distraction imminent. Prepare for immediate departure on signal."

Before she could fully process the implications of this cryptic update, a commotion erupted outside—car horns, shouting, and what sounded distinctly like a small explosion. The "inspectors" immediately tensed, professional training overriding their casual façade as they moved toward the windows with tactical precision.

"What in heaven's name?" Rita exclaimed, maintaining her character despite the unexpected development. "Sounds like the Fourth of July out there!"

Through her concealed observation position, Daisy could see a rapidly developing situation in the street outside—smoke billowing from what appeared to be a series of small but enthusiastic homemade smoke bombs, strategically placed to create maximum visual disruption without actual danger. Neighbors were emerging from nearby houses, confusion evident in their body language as they attempted to identify the source of the disturbance.

Amidst the chaos, an unremarkable beige sedan had positioned itself at the edge of the property, driver's door slightly ajar in unmistakable extraction readiness. Ziggy's environmental activism apparently extended to tactical distraction techniques utilizing what Daisy strongly suspected were improvised smoke devices crafted from commonly available household chemicals—concerning from a strictly legal perspective but remarkably effective for their current purposes.

The "inspectors" were now fully distracted, professional assessment focused on the exterior disturbance which clearly hadn't featured in their operational briefing. The lead operative gave a terse instruction to his colleague: "Check the perimeter. This could be interference."

As the second operative moved toward the front door, Daisy recognized their critical opportunity. Using the secure communication system, she sent a single word to both her concealed teammates and the extraction vehicle: "NOW."

What followed could only be described as synchronized chaos—a testament to the surprising effectiveness of their improvised tactical coordination despite wildly diverse backgrounds and minimal preparation time.

Babs emerged from concealment with theatrical timing, projecting her voice to Broadway back-row specifications: "FIRE DRILL! EVERYONE OUT! THIS IS NOT A TEST!" Her performance as a panicked fire safety enthusiast was delivered with such committed intensity that even the professional operative momentarily faltered in surprise.

Rita, seamlessly abandoning her confused grandmother persona, executed what could only be described as a tactical stumble, positioning herself to block the lead operative's direct path to the rear of the cottage where Daisy was already moving toward their designated emergency exit.

"My medication!" Rita wailed with convincing distress. "I can't leave without my heart pills! Where did I put them? Young man, you have to help me find my pills or I'll have an episode right here!" Her flailing arms and seemingly uncoordinated movements effectively created a human obstacle that would require either assistance or physical force to circumvent—the latter option problematic for operatives attempting to maintain non-threatening cover identities.

Daisy, utilizing the momentary disruption, made her way swiftly to the side door where their escape route had been prepared. The years she had spent navigating crowded faculty events with strategic precision served her surprisingly well as she maneuvered through the cottage's limited space without drawing direct attention from the increasingly suspicious but temporarily distracted operatives.

Outside, the smoke bombs continued their enthusiastic performance, creating a visual screen that obscured clear sight lines from potential observation positions. The beige sedan had inched closer to their designated extraction point, Mae's face visible through the partly lowered window, her gentle features set in uncharacteristically intense focus.

The critical challenge remained coordinating the extraction of all three remaining team members without allowing the operatives to realize their true intentions. The "fire emergency" provided temporary cover, but professional tactical assessment would quickly identify the actual situation once the initial surprise faded.

As if recognizing this exact problem, Ziggy emerged from the passenger side of the sedan with what appeared to be yet another smoke device, this one considerably more substantial than those already deployed on the street. With practiced movements suggesting alarming familiarity with improvisational distraction techniques, he activated the device and hurled it with impressive accuracy onto the cottage's front porch.

The resulting smoke production was spectacular—billowing clouds of dense white vapor that within seconds had enveloped the entire front of the building and was rapidly penetrating through the open door. While not actually harmful, the visual impact was undeniably effective, creating both genuine confusion and perfect cover for their extraction movement.

"GO GO GO!" Babs stage-whispered with unnecessary theatrical intensity as she reached Daisy's position near the side exit. "Our chariot awaits!"

Rita, having successfully entangled the lead operative in her medication emergency performance, executed a surprisingly agile disengagement that suggested previously undisclosed physical capabilities. "Sorry about the pills, young man," she called over her shoulder as she abandoned the increasingly smoke-filled living room. "Just remembered I took them this morning!"

The operative, professional training now fully overriding his inspector cover, reached inside his jacket with ominous purpose—only to find himself completely engulfed in Ziggy's enthusiastic smoke production, visibility reduced to mere inches and coordination severely compromised by the unexpected environmental manipulation.

Outside, Mae had maneuvered the sedan to within steps of their exit point, rear doors already open in anticipation of rapid entry. "Hurry!" she urged with uncharacteristic intensity. "I think they're calling for backup!"

The three escaping women moved with remarkable coordination for individuals whose typical physical activities involved book clubs, cooking classes, and occasional gentle yoga rather than tactical extraction under hostile conditions. Within seconds, they had transferred from cottage to vehicle, Ziggy already in the passenger seat providing navigational guidance as Mae executed a driving maneuver that suggested her surprising motorcycle skills extended to four-wheeled transportation as well.

"Did we actually just escape from professional assassins using smoke bombs and a fake fire drill?" Rita asked incredulously as they accelerated away from the compromised safe house, the continuing chaos visible in the rearview mirror as confused neighbors, increasingly suspicious "environmental inspectors," and billowing smoke created a scene of perfect tactical confusion.

"With theatrical flourish and impeccable timing," Babs confirmed, her expression suggesting this ranked among her finest performances despite the absence of formal staging and appropriate costume elements. "Though I maintain we could have enhanced the dramatic impact with better lighting and perhaps a musical underscore."

"I believe our current priority is establishing secure distance rather than performance assessment," Daisy suggested, academic precision intact despite their adrenaline-infused circumstances. "Ziggy, status of pursuit potential?"

"Limited immediate follow capability due to environmental disruption," he reported with professional assessment that seemed increasingly natural as their unlikely partnership evolved. "However, they'll establish vehicular pursuit within minutes once they confirm our departure. We need to implement the secondary evasion protocol immediately."

"You mean the protocol we haven't actually established yet because we were too busy stealing motorcycles and creating smoke bombs?" Rita clarified with practical assessment.

"Improvised tactical adaptation has been our primary methodology thus far," Daisy pointed out reasonably. "Initial success suggests continuing the approach."

"So we're just making this up as we go along," Babs translated cheerfully. "Wonderful! I've always performed best when working without a script. The spontaneity creates a certain authentic energy that rehearsed performance often lacks."

"Perhaps we could focus that spontaneous energy on developing an actual plan?" Rita suggested as Mae navigated through increasingly busy streets, heading toward the commercial district where greater vehicle density would provide temporary visual cover. "Preferably one that doesn't involve further felonies or smoke-producing chemicals?"

"I have a suggestion," Mae offered unexpectedly, her gentle voice carrying surprising authority as she executed another expert driving maneuver. "But it requires accepting that our traditional approaches to law enforcement cooperation may need significant adjustment given current circumstances."

Four pairs of eyes turned to her with varying expressions of surprise and curiosity.

"Mae Noodleman," Babs declared with theatrical admiration, "you continue to be the dark horse of our merry band of fugitives. First motorcycle theft, now cryptic references to non-traditional law enforcement interactions. What other hidden depths lurk beneath those pastel cardigans?"

"Remember I mentioned my rebellious phase with the motorcycle boyfriend?" Mae asked, smoothly navigating around a slow-moving tourist vehicle with unexpected expertise. "Tommy wasn't just interested in motorcycles. His family had certain... connections... in the Miami area. Nothing serious!" she hastened to add, noting their expressions. "Just some import-export businesses with occasionally flexible approaches to customs regulations."

"Are you suggesting we seek assistance from organized crime connections you established in the late 1960s?" Daisy asked, her academic precision struggling to accommodate this unexpected historical revelation.

"Not organized crime," Mae corrected gently. "More... independent business operators with specialized logistics expertise and non-traditional approaches to authority structures."

"Smugglers," Rita translated bluntly. "Mae dated a smuggler in her youth, and now she's suggesting we involve his family connections in our current predicament."

"Tommy's nephew Victor runs a fishing charter business in the harbor," Mae explained with surprising matter-of-factness. "Officially, they take tourists to the prime fishing spots. Unofficially, they sometimes transport packages with minimal documentation requirements. They're very discreet, extremely protective of clients, and have exceptional knowledge of waterways not featured on standard navigational charts."

The sedan fell momentarily silent as this unexpected resource option percolated through their collective strategic assessment.

"The tactical advantages are significant," Daisy acknowledged, academic mind automatically evaluating the strategic implications. "Maritime escape routes offer distinctive advantages over land-based evasion when opposing forces have superior vehicular resources and potential aerial surveillance capabilities."

"Plus, Tommy's family always had certain ethical boundaries," Mae added earnestly. "They never transported drugs or weapons, just luxury items avoiding import taxes. They considered themselves entrepreneurs navigating excessive regulatory burdens rather than genuine criminals."

"A philosophical distinction that likely provides limited comfort if apprehended by actual authorities," Daisy observed dryly.

"Which is precisely why they've never been apprehended in sixty years of operations," Mae countered with unexpected firmness. "They're very good at what they do."

"I vote yes to Mae's smuggler acquaintances," Babs declared enthusiastically. "This retirement adventure continues to exceed all reasonable narrative expectations. From book clubs to criminal confederates in less than a week is remarkable character development by any standard."

"They're not criminals," Mae insisted with gentle reproach. "They're alternative maritime transportation specialists with flexible documentation approaches."

"Do these 'alternative maritime transportation specialists' have capabilities extending beyond Conch Key's immediate waters?" Daisy inquired, academic mind already calculating potential extraction parameters. "Our evidence regarding the environmental crimes would be most effectively delivered to federal authorities outside local jurisdictional interference."

"Tommy's family has operated throughout the Caribbean for generations," Mae confirmed. "Victor's uncle maintains certain commercial relationships in the Bahamas that could potentially serve as an intermediate destination before connecting with formal authorities."

"So our revised strategic approach involves utilizing unofficial maritime transportation provided by Mae's smuggler ex-boyfriend's family to escape local jurisdictional boundaries with our environmental crime evidence," Rita summarized with practical precision. "While evading both corrupt official pursuers and private tactical operators with demonstrated lethal intent."

"When you put it that way, it sounds almost reasonable," Babs remarked cheerfully. "Compared to our recent activities, traditional maritime smuggling seems almost quaint and nostalgic."

As Mae navigated their unremarkable beige sedan toward the harbor district, the five unlikely fugitives found themselves contemplating yet another extraordinary evolution in their unexpected investigative career. What had begun as a simple murder investigation had expanded into environmental crime exposure, tactical home defense, and now apparent maritime escape planning utilizing resources from Mae's surprisingly colorful past.

"I think we should call Victor directly rather than surprising him at the docks," Mae suggested practically. "This kind of arrangement benefits from advance preparation."

"You have his number?" Rita asked, eyebrow raised in surprise.

"We exchange Christmas cards," Mae explained with gentle dignity. "Just because Tommy and I ended our romantic relationship doesn't mean we abandoned basic social courtesy. Victor always sends a lovely note about his children's accomplishments."

As Mae used one of their secure phones to contact her apparent smuggler connections, the others exchanged glances that communicated both amazement at this continuing revelation of hidden depths and growing appreciation for the unexpected resourcefulness of their seemingly gentle friend.

What none of them realized, as they implemented their improvised maritime escape plan, was that the evidence they had worked so hard to preserve and transmit had already set in motion forces beyond their immediate awareness—forces that would converge at their intended destination with consequences none of them could anticipate.

For as they navigated toward the harbor and Mae's mysterious maritime connections, a call was being placed from an office in Miami to a secure line in the Bahamas: "Package incoming. Multiple witnesses with evidence material. Containment authorization confirmed. No survivors."

The Seaside Sleuths were sailing directly into deeper and more dangerous waters than even their increasingly effective improvisational tactics might be prepared to navigate.

Chapter Fourteen
Dangerous Tides

"You know, when I pictured my retirement," Rita remarked dryly, clutching the boat's railing as they bounced over another wave, "somehow 'fleeing the country on a smuggler's vessel in the middle of the night' never made my vision board."

The boat in question—colorfully named "The Salty Opportunist" according to its weathered stern—was cutting through the dark waters at a speed that suggested both impressive mechanical maintenance and a captain with limited concern for standard maritime safety protocols. Their unlikely escape vessel was officially registered as a sport fishing charter but, as Mae's contact Victor had explained with professional discretion, was "equally adept at transporting certain specialty clients with privacy requirements."

"Don't think of it as fleeing," Babs suggested cheerfully, her theatrical voice carrying over the engine's rumble. "Think of it as an impromptu international cruise with exclusive accommodations and complementary adrenaline surges."

"The accommodations being a fishing boat that smells strongly of yesterday's catch, and the complementary adrenaline coming from the very real possibility of being intercepted by either corrupt officials or professional assassins," Daisy clarified with academic precision. "Though I admit the narrative reframing has imaginative merit."

Victor Barton—a stocky, weathered man in his early fifties whose facial features suggested both his familial connection to Mae's former paramour and decades of sun exposure—navigated the powerful vessel with the practiced confidence of someone intimately familiar with both the official shipping channels and the considerably less documented passages between them.

"Aunt Mae's friends worry too much," he called from the wheelhouse, his voice carrying the distinctive accent of a Florida native whose linguistic patterns had been shaped by maritime professions and minimal formal education. "We've been running these waters since my grandfather's day. Coast Guard knows better than to look too close at our operations, and the corporate security types don't have our local knowledge. You ladies just relax and enjoy the moonlight tour."

"See? Our maritime transportation specialist exudes confidence," Babs translated helpfully. "Though I maintain we could enhance the experience with appropriate cocktails. Every proper escape at sea should include tropical beverages with little umbrellas."

"I believe traditional maritime smuggling operations prioritize operational security over cocktail service," Daisy observed, though her tone suggested she wasn't entirely opposed to the concept.

Mae, who had been quietly conversing with Ziggy near the stern, rejoined the group with the serene expression of someone whose unexpected life choices had been thoroughly validated by current circumstances. "Victor says we'll reach international waters in approximately twenty minutes, and the rendezvous point in just over an hour. Everything is proceeding according to the established plan."

"Wonderful," Rita remarked with qualified enthusiasm. "Now perhaps someone could clarify exactly what this established plan entails? Beyond 'get on boat, go to Bahamas' which seems insufficiently detailed given our current circumstances."

"The essential framework involves maritime transportation to neutral territory beyond local jurisdictional influence," Daisy explained, academic mind automatically organizing the strategic elements. "Followed by secure evidence transmission to federal environmental authorities through Mae's surprisingly extensive connection network."

"Tommy's family has maintained certain relationships with individuals who prioritize environmental protection over corporate interests," Mae elaborated with delicate phrasing. "Some of these connections include retired federal agents who maintain active communication channels with their former colleagues."

"So we're using smuggler networks to contact ex-federal agents to expose corporate environmental crimes," Rita summarized with practical precision. "While evading both corrupt officials and private assassins. I just want to be clear on our current operational parameters."

"When you phrase it that way, it sounds almost reasonable compared to our previous activities," Babs noted cheerfully. "At least this phase doesn't involve pressure cookers as tactical weapons or disguising ourselves as yacht club staff during lightning storms."

Their conversational assessment of their extraordinary circumstances was interrupted by Victor's sudden alert: "We've got company. Fast mover approaching from the northwest, running dark."

The group moved quickly to the wheelhouse, where the boat's radar display showed an unmistakable contact moving at high speed on an intercept course with their position. Victor's previously relaxed demeanor had shifted to focused professional assessment, his weathered features arranged in the calculating expression of someone evaluating tactical maritime options.

"Coast Guard?" Daisy inquired, though her tone suggested she already anticipated a less official explanation.

"Not their operational pattern," Victor replied tersely, making minute adjustments to their course. "They announce approach on standard channels and run with identification lights. This is someone trying not to be seen while moving fast. Private pursuit, most likely."

"The 'environmental inspectors' must have established our escape vector and mobilized maritime assets," Daisy concluded, academic assessment shifting seamlessly to tactical calculation. "Impressive response time, suggesting pre-positioned resources."

"These folks came prepared for contingencies," Victor acknowledged with professional respect. "Lucky for us, so did I." He reached for the radio handset, keying a specific channel. "Pelican to Mockingbird, Pelican to Mockingbird. We've got dance partners. Initiate scatter pattern alpha. Repeat, scatter pattern alpha."

Within moments, the radar display showed multiple new contacts emerging from what had appeared to be routine fishing vessel positions scattered across the nearby waters. Each began moving in different directions at accelerated speeds, creating a confusing pattern of potential targets for any pursuing vessel.

"Mutual assistance network," Victor explained with a hint of smuggler pride. "Standard protocol when unauthorized interests take too much notice of our operations. Creates confusion about which vessel to pursue."

"A maritime shell game," Babs translated with theatrical appreciation. "Misdirection on a grand scale. I heartily approve of both the tactical effectiveness and the dramatic presentation."

"It buys us time but won't stop determined pursuit," Victor cautioned, his eyes fixed on the radar display where the fast-moving contact was now showing signs of hesitation, its course adjusting as it attempted to determine which of the suddenly active vessels was its actual target. "We need to implement secondary evasion protocols."

"Which are?" Rita prompted when Victor's explanation paused for what she clearly considered an unnecessarily dramatic interval.

"Going dark and going deep," he replied, already moving to the control panel where he systematically began shutting down non-essential systems. "We kill all electronics except minimal navigation aids, extinguish running lights, and head for shallower waters where larger vessels can't follow."

"That sounds both tactically sound and potentially catastrophic," Daisy observed, academic precision intact despite the increasingly tense circumstances. "I assume 'shallower waters' still provide adequate clearance for this vessel while somehow impeding pursuers with presumably similar draft requirements?"

"The Salty Opportunist has certain modifications," Victor explained with professional smuggler discretion. "Reinforced hull, adjustable ballast system, shallow-water propulsion adaptations. We can navigate passages that standard vessels wouldn't attempt, especially in darkness."

"Your family's commitment to specialized maritime engineering is both impressive and concerning from a regulatory perspective," Daisy remarked. "Though currently advantageous to our specific situation."

As Victor implemented their "dark and deep" evasion protocol, the vessel transformed from standard fishing charter to something considerably more specialized. External lights extinguished, engine noise dampened by what appeared to be custom sound suppression systems, and their course shifting toward a section of coastline that appeared featureless to casual observation but apparently contained navigable passages known only to certain maritime specialists with generational knowledge.

"Everyone below deck," Victor instructed tersely. "Less visible profile. And secure any loose items—this ride's about to get interesting."

"Interesting being a euphemism for terrifying, I presume," Babs translated as they made their way to the cabin area. "Though I must say, clandestine maritime evasion adds an unexpected dimension to our retirement adventures. The memoirs practically write themselves at this point."

The cabin area—designed to accommodate sport fishing clients for overnight expeditions—had been hastily converted to their current needs, with evidence materials secured in waterproof containers and emergency supplies arranged with the methodical precision that suggested Victor's "specialty transportation" business was considerably more organized than his casual demeanor might suggest.

"Pursue course Kingfish," came Victor's voice through the cabin's communication system. "Secure positions for dynamic maneuvering."

"That doesn't sound promising," Rita observed, already positioning herself on one of the built-in benches with practiced efficiency. "I recommend securing handholds immediately."

Her advice proved prescient as the vessel suddenly executed what could only be described as a tactical turn, banking at an angle that suggested maritime physics were being challenged by Victor's aggressive piloting. The cabin contents shifted alarmingly despite their secured status, and the five passengers found themselves bracing against the unexpected G-forces with varying degrees of success.

"I believe we're implementing evasive maneuvers," Daisy remarked with academic understatement as another sudden course change sent an inadequately secured coffee mug sliding across the cabin to shatter against the opposite wall. "Victor's maritime operational capabilities appear surprisingly robust."

"Translation: our smuggler captain drives boats like a maniac," Babs clarified unnecessarily as she clung to her seat with white-knuckled determination. "Though I appreciate his enthusiasm for our continued freedom and survival."

The vessel continued its erratic course, a series of sudden turns, accelerations, and decelerations that suggested both impressive mechanical capabilities and a captain with intimate knowledge of the coastal geography they were navigating. Through the cabin's small windows, they caught occasional glimpses of shoreline features appearing at alarming proximity before disappearing again as Victor guided them through what must have been extremely narrow passages between islands or shoals.

"Is this normal maritime smuggling procedure or special VIP treatment?" Rita inquired with remarkable composure given the circumstances, her practical nature apparently extending to high-speed boat evasion scenarios.

"Tommy's family always prided themselves on customer service excellence," Mae replied with unexpected matter-of-factness. "Victor mentioned this is their standard 'premium evasion package' usually reserved for clients with significant legal complications."

"How reassuring to know we qualify for premium service in the smuggling hierarchy," Daisy remarked dryly. "One hopes it includes successful arrival at our destination rather than merely prolonged pursuit entertainment."

Their conversation was interrupted by another announcement from the wheelhouse: "Contact has committed to pursuit of alternative target. Repeat, pursuit diverted to secondary vessel. Resuming standard operational parameters in three minutes."

"We escaped?" Ziggy asked, breaking his uncharacteristic silence during the maritime evasion sequence. "Just like that?"

"The scatter protocol combined with our specialized evasion capabilities creates significant targeting confusion," Victor's voice explained through the communication system. "Our mutual assistance network includes designated distraction vessels specifically equipped to draw pursuit away from high-value transports."

"Designated distraction vessels," Daisy repeated thoughtfully. "You maintain specialized maritime assets specifically designed to attract and divert pursuit from primary operational transport. That suggests a level of organizational sophistication well beyond casual smuggling operations."

"Aunt Mae's boyfriend always said our family business was three generations ahead of law enforcement understanding," Victor replied with undisguised pride. "We're not criminals—we're logistics specialists who recognize certain regulatory frameworks as optional rather than mandatory."

"A philosophical distinction that would likely provide limited comfort if apprehended," Daisy observed, unconsciously echoing her earlier assessment of their maritime escape option.

"Apprehended?" Victor's laugh carried genuine amusement. "The Barton family has operated in these waters since Prohibition. We've outrun Coast Guard, DEA, FBI, and corporate security operations for longer than most of their agents have been alive. This little corporate pursuit is amateur hour compared to some of the situations we've navigated."

The cabin lights brightened as Victor restored standard operational systems, the vessel's movement settling into a more conventional cruising pattern that suggested they had successfully transitioned from urgent evasion to standard transport mode. A moment later, the captain himself appeared in the cabin doorway, his weathered features arranged in the satisfied expression of someone who had just successfully practiced their professional specialty.

"Ladies and gentleman, welcome to international waters," he announced with the practiced delivery of a cruise ship captain, though with decidedly different contextual implications. "We've cleared local jurisdiction and established secure distance from pursuit assets. Estimated arrival at our Bahamian rendezvous point in approximately forty minutes, weather and further pursuit complications permitting."

"Complications like the Coast Guard vessels now visible on our starboard side?" Ziggy asked tensely, peering through one of the small windows where the unmistakable profile of official patrol boats could be seen maintaining parallel course at some distance.

Victor's expression showed mild professional concern rather than alarm as he moved to assess the situation. "Standard monitoring pattern rather than active interdiction positioning," he concluded after a moment's observation. "They've noted our presence but aren't committing to inspection protocols. Likely just maintaining visible presence to discourage any obvious contraband transfers."

"And if they do decide to implement inspection protocols?" Rita inquired practically.

"We have approximately fifteen contingency options depending on specific approach vectors and interdiction methodologies," Victor replied with surprising specificity. "But the most likely scenario involves implementing our legitimate business cover—you fine folks are simply enjoying a premium night fishing expedition with optional sunrise Bahamian excursion, all properly documented with the appropriate, if somewhat creatively interpreted, permits and licenses."

"You maintain fraudulent documentation as standard operational procedure," Daisy noted, her tone suggesting academic observation rather than moral judgment.

"I prefer 'alternative compliance demonstration materials,'" Victor corrected with professional smuggler linguistic precision. "Technically accurate in content while strategically flexible in interpretation."

"The bureaucratic equivalent of Babs' theatrical costume collection," Rita translated practically. "Designed to present a specific appearance for contextual purposes without necessarily reflecting complete underlying reality."

"I resent that characterization of my costume collection," Babs protested with theatrical dignity. "My ensembles are artistic interpretations rather than misrepresentations. Though I admit a certain spiritual kinship with creative documentation approaches."

Their maritime legal philosophy discussion was interrupted by an urgent communication from the wheelhouse, where Victor's first mate—a taciturn individual introduced only as "Pelican" whose actual name remained undisclosed—had been monitoring their navigation systems.

"Cap, we've got a situation developing at the rendezvous coordinates," came the terse report through the cabin speaker. "Satellite communication from Mockingbird reports unauthorized vessels maintaining position at our scheduled transfer point. Pattern suggests anticipatory interdiction positioning rather than routine patrol activity."

Victor's expression shifted from professional confidence to focused tactical assessment, his weathered features arranging themselves into the calculating look of someone rapidly evaluating contingency options. "Description of vessels?"

"Three contacts, non-standard configuration, running with minimized profile. Mockingbird confirms not affiliated with known official assets or registered commercial operations."

"They're waiting for us," Ziggy translated unnecessarily, his environmental activist experience apparently extending to tactical situation assessment. "Someone anticipated our destination and pre-positioned interception resources."

"Which means our operational security has been compromised at some level," Victor confirmed grimly. "Either communication channels, rendezvous protocols, or direct pursuit tracking despite our evasion measures."

"The latter seems unlikely given your demonstrated maritime capabilities," Daisy observed, academic mind automatically analyzing the tactical possibilities. "Communication interception or informant compromise appear more probable."

"Agreed," Victor nodded, professional respect evident in his acknowledgment of her assessment. "Which means we need to implement contingency destination protocols. Pelican, signal Mockingbird to activate secondary rendezvous coordinates. Authorization Kingfish Alpha Niner."

"Executed," came the prompt response. "Mockingbird acknowledges. Secondary coordinates confirmed secure as of last verification. Adjusting course now."

"I assume this represents a significant deviation from our original destination?" Daisy inquired as Victor moved to return to the wheelhouse.

"Standard operational security measure," he confirmed. "We maintain multiple potential transfer points with encrypted designation protocols. If primary coordinates are compromised, we simply shift to secondary or tertiary options while maintaining ultimate destination objectives."

"Your family's smuggling operations are impressively organized," Daisy remarked with academic appreciation. "The systematic contingency planning and communication security suggest multiple generations of refined methodology."

"Three generations of staying one step ahead of people who'd prefer we didn't operate," Victor acknowledged with professional pride. "You don't survive in this business without comprehensive planning for potential complications."

As he returned to navigational duties, the five unlikely maritime fugitives found themselves contemplating yet another extraordinary evolution in their unexpected adventure. What had begun as a simple murder investigation had now expanded to include international maritime escape aboard a professional smuggler's vessel, evading both official interdiction and private pursuit while navigating to clandestine rendezvous points through waters apparently contested by multiple interested parties.

"I find myself wondering," Rita mused as they adjusted to their vessel's new course heading, "at what precise point our retirement activities transitioned from book clubs and beach walks to international maritime escape from professional assassins. The escalation timeline seems remarkably compressed."

"I believe it occurred approximately when Brock Hamfist's body washed up on our beach," Daisy replied with academic precision. "Though one could argue the substantive transition happened when we discovered the environmental crime evidence, as that elevated our status from witnesses to active threats against significant financial interests."

"The narrative progression has been rather extraordinary by any standard," Babs agreed with theatrical assessment. "Though I maintain we've demonstrated remarkable adaptability for individuals whose previous crisis management primarily involved Garden Club scheduling conflicts and occasional plumbing emergencies."

Their collective self-assessment was interrupted by another urgent communication from the wheelhouse: "All passengers secure positions immediately. We have multiple fast movers approaching from southeastern quadrant. Pattern indicates coordinated intercept methodology."

Through the cabin windows, they could see what had prompted this alert—the dark shapes of vessels moving at high speed on converging courses with their position, running without navigation lights in a manner that suggested neither standard maritime operations nor official patrol activities.

"Those aren't Coast Guard," Ziggy observed tersely, his environmental activism apparently having included sufficient maritime protest activities to recognize the distinction. "Profile suggests private security vessels—probably the same operators who've been pursuing us from the beginning."

"How would they have established our position in international waters?" Mae wondered, her gentle features creased with genuine concern. "Victor's evasion measures seemed quite effective."

"Unless they weren't tracking our vessel specifically," Daisy suggested, academic mind rapidly calculating possibilities. "If they had advance knowledge of our destination coordinates and simply established a patrol perimeter, they wouldn't need to maintain continuous pursuit."

"They knew where we were going before we did," Rita translated with practical alarm. "Which means—"

"Comprehensive operational compromise," Victor's grim voice completed her thought as he appeared briefly in the cabin doorway.

"They've anticipated both primary and secondary rendezvous coordinates. Standard contingency protocols are insufficient for current pursuit parameters."

"What does that mean for our immediate situation?" Daisy inquired, academic precision focusing on tactical implications rather than the concerning security breach.

"It means we implement Hail Mary protocols," Victor replied with the determined expression of someone accessing rarely required contingency options. "Pelican, signal the network. Authorization Kingfish Omega. All assets converge on our position, maximum confusion pattern."

"Kingfish Omega acknowledged," came the terse response. "Network assets responding. Estimated convergence time twelve minutes."

"We may not have twelve minutes," Victor acknowledged grimly, gesturing toward the radar display visible through the wheelhouse door, where multiple contacts were now converging on their position with alarming speed. "Ladies and gentleman, I need to execute some rather extreme navigational maneuvers. Secure yourselves as thoroughly as possible and prepare for significant gravitational variations."

"Translation: hold onto something sturdy because we're about to experience maritime tactics that probably violate several laws of physics," Babs interpreted unnecessarily as she secured herself to the cabin's built-in seating with remarkable efficiency for someone whose previous boating experience had primarily involved cocktail cruises.

What followed could only be described as tactical maritime maneuvering that suggested Victor's professional capabilities extended well beyond standard smuggling operations into something approaching specialized military training. The vessel executed a series of high-speed turns, course reversals, and sudden accelerations that tested both its mechanical capabilities and the vestibular tolerance of its passengers.

"I believe we're experiencing what naval operations would classify as 'combat evasion patterns,'" Daisy observed with remarkable composure given the G-forces currently affecting her academic dignity. "Victor's piloting skills suggest specialized training beyond civilian maritime certification."

"Tommy mentioned his brother served in some special operations branch," Mae explained between particularly dramatic course changes.

"Apparently the family business benefited from certain tactical knowledge transfers."

"How reassuring to know our smuggler captain has military-grade evasion training," Rita remarked dryly, her practical nature somehow extending to maintaining conversational composure during extreme maritime maneuvers. "Though I question whether even specialized tactics can overcome the numerical advantage currently converging on our position."

Her concern appeared well-founded as the radar display visible through the wheelhouse door showed the pursuing vessels adjusting to their evasive patterns with professional coordination that suggested equally specialized training. Despite Victor's impressive piloting, the pursuers were maintaining intercept courses through what appeared to be coordinated pincer movements designed to eliminate potential escape vectors.

"They're herding us," Ziggy observed grimly, his environmental activism apparently having included sufficient pursuit scenarios to recognize the tactical approach. "Coordinated vessel positioning to eliminate maneuvering options and force us into a contained operational area."

"Standard maritime interdiction methodology," Victor confirmed through the communication system, his voice tight with focused concentration as he continued executing increasingly extreme evasion maneuvers. "They're implementing professional pursuit protocols with multiple assets. Even with Kingfish Omega support, our extraction options are becoming limited."

"Are we actually going to be caught?" Babs asked with uncharacteristic directness, theatrical flourishes momentarily abandoned in favor of tactical clarity. "Because while I imagine 'captured by corporate assassins at sea' would make a fascinating chapter in my memoirs, I'd prefer it remain hypothetical rather than experiential."

"The Barton family has never lost a client in three generations of operations," Victor replied with professional determination. "We're not starting today. Pelican, prepare Phantom Protocol. Authorization Kingfish Ultimate."

"Kingfish Ultimate acknowledged," came the unnervingly calm response. "Phantom systems active. Deployment on your command."

"Phantom Protocol?" Daisy inquired, academic curiosity apparently undiminished by their increasingly dire circumstances.

"Final contingency option," Victor explained tersely. "Specialized countermeasure system for extreme pursuit scenarios. Experimental technology with limited operational history but significant theoretical effectiveness."

"Is this the maritime equivalent of Ziggy's smoke bombs, but more sophisticated?" Babs inquired with remarkable intuitive accuracy.

"Similar conceptual approach with substantially enhanced technological implementation," Victor confirmed. "Prepare for potential sensory disruption and unusual physical phenomena. Protective eyewear under your seats, apply immediately."

As they hastily donned what appeared to be specialized goggles stored in compartments beneath their seating, the vessel suddenly decelerated with stomach-churning rapidity before executing an impossibly tight turn that suggested hull design modifications well beyond standard maritime engineering parameters.

"Deployment in three, two, one—" Victor's countdown concluded with a series of mechanical activations audible throughout the vessel, followed by what could only be described as a localized atmospheric event surrounding their immediate position.

Through the cabin windows—now tinted by their protective eyewear—they could see a rapidly expanding cloud of what appeared to be luminescent particles enveloping their vessel and the surrounding waters, creating a visual disruption effect that seemed to distort spatial perception and electromagnetic properties in ways that defied conventional understanding.

"What on earth is that?" Rita exclaimed with uncharacteristic alarm as the phenomenon intensified, the luminescent cloud now pulsating with patterns that created disorienting visual effects even through their specialized eyewear.

"Proprietary countermeasure system combining aerosol dispersion technology with specialized electromagnetic frequency generators," Victor explained with the clipped precision of someone executing complex operational protocols. "Creates multi-spectrum disruption affecting visual, radar, sonar, and electromagnetic tracking systems."

"You've deployed what appears to be military-grade electronic countermeasure technology from a fishing boat," Daisy observed with academic understatement. "I believe that significantly exceeds standard smuggling operational parameters."

"The Barton family business has always maintained technological advantages," Victor replied with evident pride despite the tense circumstances. "Particularly when certain government contracts provide opportunities for mutually beneficial equipment transfers."

"You have government contracts?" Rita asked incredulously as the luminescent cloud surrounding their vessel continued its disorienting pulsation patterns. "While simultaneously operating a smuggling business that presumably violates multiple federal regulations?"

"The relationship is complex," Victor acknowledged cryptically. "Let's just say certain agencies appreciate specialized maritime capabilities for occasional operational requirements that benefit from limited documentation processes."

"You're government contractors AND smugglers?" Babs translated with delighted theatrical appreciation. "The narrative complexity is absolutely magnificent. This retirement adventure continues to exceed all reasonable expectations for plot development."

Their discussion of Victor's apparently multifaceted business model was interrupted by an urgent update from the wheelhouse: "Phantom deployment effective on primary pursuit vessels. Tracking systems disrupted, coordinated interception pattern broken. Convergence of friendly assets in approximately three minutes."

Through the disorienting luminescent cloud still surrounding their vessel, they could see the pursuing boats now moving in erratic patterns, their coordinated approach shattered by whatever electromagnetic disruption Victor's "Phantom Protocol" had created. Navigation systems, communication capabilities, and sensor arrays had apparently been compromised by the specialized countermeasure technology, reducing the formerly professional pursuit to disorganized individual vessels attempting to maintain basic operational control.

"The technological implications are fascinating," Daisy observed with academic interest despite their still-precarious situation. "Targeted electromagnetic disruption with apparent selective effect parameters, allowing our systems to function while compromising pursuit capabilities."

"Proprietary algorithmic tuning," Victor explained with smuggler pride. "Our systems are calibrated to specific frequency protection patterns while broadcasting disruptive sequences across alternative bands."

"You've essentially created an electronic smokescreen with selective penetration capabilities," Ziggy translated, his environmental activism apparently including sufficient technical knowledge to grasp the underlying principles. "Impressive for what appears to be a family-owned maritime transportation business."

"The Barton family has always been innovation-oriented," Victor replied modestly as he guided their vessel through the confusion created by his countermeasure deployment. "We prefer maintaining technological advantages rather than relying solely on traditional evasion methodologies."

As the pursuing vessels struggled to reestablish operational coordination, their vessel continued its now-straightened course toward what Victor identified as their tertiary rendezvous coordinates. The luminescent cloud gradually dissipated, leaving behind what appeared to be normal maritime conditions except for the disorganized pattern of pursuit craft now visible at increasing distance behind them.

"Friendly assets converging from multiple vectors," came Pelican's update from the wheelhouse. "Mockingbird confirms tertiary rendezvous coordinates secure. Estimated arrival seventeen minutes with current course and speed."

"We actually escaped?" Mae asked with gentle wonder, her typically serene features showing genuine amazement at their apparent survival of what had seemed an impossible tactical situation.

"The Barton family guarantee," Victor confirmed with professional satisfaction as he rejoined them briefly in the cabin. "Though I must admit, this particular extraction operation has involved more contingency implementations than our standard client transport scenarios. Your friends in the corporate security sector are remarkably persistent."

"They're protecting financial interests valued in the billions," Daisy explained with academic precision. "The environmental crimes we've documented represent potential liability sufficient to bankrupt even major corporations, not to mention criminal prosecution of executives and officials involved in the conspiracy."

"Which explains the resource commitment to your elimination," Victor acknowledged with professional assessment. "Though it creates certain operational complications for our remaining transport requirements. We'll need to implement additional security protocols for the final phase of your journey."

"Final phase?" Rita inquired with practical concern. "I thought we were heading directly to meet your contacts who would connect us with federal environmental authorities."

"The operational compromise of both primary and secondary rendezvous coordinates suggests our original approach vectors have been comprehensively monitored," Victor explained with the patient tone of someone accustomed to explaining tactical adjustments to civilian clients. "We need to implement more complex transfer protocols to ensure your evidence reaches appropriate authorities without interception."

"Meaning?" Daisy prompted when his explanation paused for what she clearly considered an unnecessarily dramatic interval.

"Meaning we'll be transferring you to a secondary vessel at the tertiary rendezvous point," Victor clarified. "Which will then implement an entirely separate approach methodology to connect with our federal contacts. Multiple transfer points, varying transport assets, compartmentalized destination awareness—standard advanced security protocols for high-value transports."

"We're being handed off like a particularly troublesome package through a series of smuggler relay points," Babs translated cheerfully. "How wonderfully cloak-and-dagger! Though I do hope the subsequent vessels maintain reasonable comfort standards. My tolerance for maritime adventure has certain aesthetic limitations."

As they continued toward their revised destination, the five unlikely fugitives found themselves contemplating the extraordinary circumstances that had transformed their peaceful retirement into something resembling an international espionage operation. The evidence of environmental crimes they had fought so hard to protect was securely stored in waterproof containers, ready for transfer to federal authorities who might actually have the jurisdiction and integrity to address the conspiracy they had uncovered.

What none of them realized, as their vessel cut through the dark waters toward what they believed was secure sanctuary, was that their journey had been compromised at a level even Victor's sophisticated security protocols couldn't detect. For while the Barton family smuggling network had indeed maintained impressive operational security for generations, they had never before encountered the specific resources now mobilized against their current clients.

In a secure facility far from the maritime chess game playing out across the waters, a conversation was taking place that would dramatically alter whatever remaining illusion of security they might have maintained:

"Asset Seven confirms tracking transmitter successfully integrated with evidence materials during cottage surveillance operation. Signal remains active despite countermeasure deployments."

"Excellent. Maintain passive monitoring only. Do not attempt further interdiction until final destination confirmation. The objective is the complete evidence package and all witnesses."

"Understood. Containment team standing by for coordinates."

"Authorization confirmed. No survivors."

The Seaside Sleuths, having survived professional assassins, tactical home invasions, and maritime pursuit operations, were sailing directly toward what they believed was safety but what had already been compromised by the very evidence they had worked so hard to protect. The final act of their extraordinary adventure was about to begin, with stakes higher than even their increasingly effective improvisational capabilities might be prepared to address.

Chapter Fifteen
The Final Confrontation

"You know what I miss most about normal retirement?" Rita asked as their third vessel in eighteen hours cut through the predawn waters toward what they had been assured was their final destination. "Predictable bathroom facilities. Maritime plumbing leaves much to be desired in both stability and privacy."

"I miss my extensive moisturizing routine," Babs contributed mournfully, patting her wind-ravaged complexion with genuine distress. "Salt air combined with high-speed boat chases creates dermatological challenges that no amount of emergency hydration can fully address. I'm developing texture, darlings. Actual texture."

"I find myself longing for my personal library," Daisy admitted with uncharacteristic wistfulness. "Particularly my first-edition collection of British mystery novels, which seems increasingly relevant to our current circumstances."

They had been transferred from Victor's vessel to a sleek speedboat operated by a taciturn individual introduced only as "Heron," who had piloted them through a complex series of island passages before rendezvous with their current transportation—an unremarkable fishing trawler whose weathered appearance disguised surprisingly powerful engines and what appeared to be military-grade navigation systems.

"Final approach," announced their current captain, a surprisingly youthful woman who had introduced herself simply as "Frigate" and whose precise, economical movements suggested specialized training well beyond standard maritime operations. "Secure personal items and prepare for transfer protocols. Estimated arrival at primary contact point in twelve minutes."

Through the trawler's salt-streaked windows, they could see the gradually lightening horizon revealing the outline of a small island—little more than a sandy outcropping crowned with a modest collection of structures that appeared to be a typical isolated fishing community.

"That's our federal contact point?" Ziggy asked skeptically, environmental activist experience apparently including sufficient covert operation knowledge to question the unimpressive rendezvous location. "Looks more like a forgotten fishing village than a secure government facility."

"Operational security through contextual camouflage," Frigate explained with the patient tone of someone accustomed to educating civilians on covert methodology. "Conventional surveillance expects government operations to utilize obvious security infrastructure—isolated compounds, communication arrays, visible protective measures. True covert facilities maintain contextually appropriate environmental integration to minimize detection signatures."

"They hide government operations in places that look exactly like they're supposed to look," Babs translated helpfully. "Like setting a spy headquarters in an actual laundromat that does actual laundry. Brilliant theatrical principle—the best disguise is one that serves a genuine function."

"I'm more concerned with what happens after we make contact," Daisy remarked, academic mind focused on operational outcomes rather than methodology. "Our evidence materials are secure, but will these federal contacts actually have the authority and incentive to act on environmental crimes of this magnitude? Particularly given the apparent influence of those involved in the conspiracy?"

"The individuals you're meeting operate outside standard jurisdictional limitations," Frigate informed them, her expression suggesting this was as much detail as she intended to provide. "Their operational parameters specifically address situations where conventional enforcement frameworks have been compromised by influence operations."

"Secret environmental crime fighters," Ziggy translated with unexpected enthusiasm. "Like a specialized EPA black ops team."

"I wouldn't use that specific terminology in their presence," Frigate advised with the faintest hint of a smile. "They prefer 'specialized accountability enforcement' as their operational designation."

As the trawler approached the island's modest dock, the five unlikely maritime fugitives gathered their limited personal possessions and the securely packaged evidence materials that represented the culmination of their extraordinary investigative journey. What had begun with a body on their beach had expanded into environmental crimes, corrupt officials, corporate conspiracy, and now apparently clandestine government operations on remote islands.

"I sincerely hope this represents the final phase of our unexpected adventure," Rita remarked as they prepared to disembark. "While I've developed a surprising tolerance for improvised tactical operations, I find myself increasingly nostalgic for mundane activities like grocery shopping and book club meetings that don't involve evading professional assassins."

"Though one must acknowledge a certain exhilarating quality to our recent experiences," Daisy admitted with academic precision. "The application of our collective problem-solving capabilities to genuinely consequential situations provides a specific type of satisfaction rarely found in conventional retirement activities."

"We've discovered hidden depths and unexpected skills," Mae agreed softly, her gentle features arranged in thoughtful assessment. "Though I confess I'm looking forward to resuming my Tuesday yoga classes without the complication of paramilitary pursuit operations."

Their philosophical reflection on their extraordinary circumstances was interrupted by Frigate's terse announcement: "Contact representatives approaching dock. Standard verification protocols in effect. Maintain positioned grouping and allow procedural confirmation before engaging."

Through the gradually lifting morning mist, they could see two figures walking toward the dock—a tall, angular man with the weathered features of someone who spent considerable time outdoors, and a compact woman whose precise movements and alert positioning suggested specialized training despite her casual attire. Both wore what appeared to be standard fishing village clothing, though with subtle quality differences that suggested functional durability rather than economic necessity.

"Confirmation phrase?" called the woman as the trawler eased against the dock's wooden pilings.

"Pelicans soar where eagles rest," Frigate responded with the careful enunciation of someone delivering a memorized code sequence.

"While mockingbirds sing of secrets kept," the woman completed what was evidently a predetermined authentication exchange. "Secure delivery confirmed. Transfer authorization approved."

As Frigate secured the vessel to the dock, the five passengers found themselves exchanging glances that communicated their collective assessment: after days of escalating danger and increasingly complex evasion operations, they had finally reached what appeared to be genuine security. The evidence they had fought so hard to protect would soon be in the hands of authorities with both the capability and authorization to address the environmental crimes they had uncovered.

"Welcome to Station Heron," the angular man greeted them as they disembarked onto the worn wooden planking. "I'm Carter. This is Shaw. We understand you've had an eventful journey."

"That's one way to describe fleeing professional assassins across multiple jurisdictions while experiencing various maritime pursuit operations," Babs replied with theatrical understatement. "Though 'eventful' does have a certain elegant simplicity as a summary term."

"Your extraction operation has been monitored with considerable interest," Shaw informed them, her professional demeanor suggesting limited patience for Babs' dramatic flourishes. "The evidence you've secured represents potentially significant actionable intelligence regarding ongoing environmental criminal activities."

"We have comprehensive documentation," Daisy confirmed, indicating the waterproof cases containing both Captain Crustybutt's original materials and their subsequent additions. "Including operational specifics of the underwater disposal system, corporate connection mapping, and jurisdictional compromise indicators."

"Excellent," Carter nodded with professional appreciation. "We'll conduct preliminary assessment immediately. Meanwhile, you'll be provided secure accommodation and debriefing facilities. Your safety remains a priority concern until containment operations can be implemented against identified hostile elements."

"Containment operations?" Rita inquired with practical interest. "I assume that means addressing both the corporate entities responsible for the environmental crimes and the individuals who have been attempting to eliminate us as witnesses?"

"Precisely," Shaw confirmed. "Multiple federal agencies are currently preparing coordinated enforcement activities. Your evidence materials provide essential probable cause documentation for warrant implementations that have been pending verification requirements."

"You've been investigating these operations already," Daisy concluded with academic assessment. "Our evidence simply provides the final documentation elements required for formal enforcement actions."

"Your assessment is accurate," Carter acknowledged. "Certain economic indicators and environmental monitoring anomalies had triggered preliminary investigative protocols approximately fourteen months ago. However, substantive evidence collection was complicated by the jurisdictional compromise issues you encountered."

"They knew something fishy was happening but couldn't prove it until we stumbled into the middle of everything," Babs translated unnecessarily. "Though I maintain our investigative methodology demonstrated remarkable effectiveness despite our lack of formal training or institutional resources."

"Your unconventional approach produced results that conventional operatives were unable to secure," Shaw acknowledged with professional respect that seemed slightly forced. "Now if you'll follow us, we'll proceed to the secure facility for evidence transfer and personal debriefing operations."

As they followed their official escorts along a weathered wooden walkway toward the modest collection of buildings comprising the fishing village, the five unlikely investigators found themselves experiencing an unexpected emotional confluence—relief at having apparently reached genuine safety, satisfaction at having successfully preserved critical evidence despite extraordinary obstacles, and a certain wistfulness that their remarkable adventure appeared to be reaching its conclusion.

"I'm almost going to miss the excitement," Babs confided in a stage whisper as they walked. "Though not the constant threat of violent elimination, of course. But the strategic improvisation, the unexpected skill application, the dramatic tension of our escape sequences—one doesn't experience that level of theatrical intensity in normal retirement activities."

"Perhaps we could find less life-threatening avenues for exercising our newly discovered capabilities," Daisy suggested with academic reasonableness. "Community service opportunities with investigative elements, for instance."

"The Seaside Sleuths, Environmental Division, accepting cases of moderate danger with limited assassination potential," Babs declared with enthusiastic approval. "I'll design business cards immediately upon our return to civilization."

"We are not calling ourselves that," Daisy insisted automatically, though her objection now seemed more ritual than genuine opposition. "And I believe our immediate priority should be successful evidence transfer rather than future business planning."

Their escorts led them to what appeared to be a modestly appointed fishing supply store, complete with weathered signage and window displays of tackle, bait options, and maritime equipment. Once inside, however, Carter activated a concealed mechanism that revealed the building's true function as the access point to a surprisingly sophisticated facility hidden beneath the unassuming structure.

"Welcome to Station Heron's operational center," Shaw announced as they descended a staircase into a space that contrasted dramatically with the rustic appearance of the surface buildings. "Secure evidence processing will be conducted here, followed by comprehensive debriefing procedures."

The underground facility featured advanced technology that would have seemed more appropriate in a military installation than a remote island outpost—computer systems, communication arrays, and what appeared to be specialized forensic equipment arranged in efficient workstations. Personnel in casual attire that nevertheless suggested functional uniformity moved with the purposeful efficiency of professionals in a well-established operational environment.

"This is considerably more sophisticated than anticipated," Daisy observed as they were guided through the facility toward what appeared to be a conference area. "The contextual camouflage is impressively comprehensive."

"Station Heron maintains specialized capability parameters while preserving operational security through environmental integration," Carter explained with the careful phrasing of someone accustomed to describing classified operations in appropriately vague terminology. "Now, if you'll place your evidence materials on the processing station, we can begin formal transfer procedures."

As Ziggy carefully positioned their waterproof containers on the designated surface, a team of technicians immediately began implementing what appeared to be standardized evidence handling protocols—documentation photography, container integrity verification, and chain of custody processing that suggested legitimate official methodology.

"Your personal debriefing will be conducted individually to ensure comprehensive information collection," Shaw informed them, gesturing toward a series of smaller rooms adjoining the main space. "Standard procedure for multi-witness scenarios to prevent cross-contamination of observational details."

"Seems reasonable," Daisy acknowledged, though her academic assessment instincts noted a subtle shift in the facility's atmosphere—personnel movements becoming more precisely coordinated, security positions adjusting in a pattern that suggested increasing rather than decreasing alert status. "Though perhaps we might begin with a collective overview of events to establish basic timeline parameters?"

"Individual processing is protocol for this type of operation," Carter replied with professional firmness that bordered on insistence. "Ms. Picklesworth, if you'll accompany me to the first debriefing room, we can initiate the documentation process."

As Daisy prepared to follow Carter toward the indicated room, a seemingly minor technical detail caught her attention—one of the evidence technicians was scanning their containers with a specialized device that appeared to be detecting something other than the expected security verification protocols. The technician's expression shifted from focused concentration to satisfied confirmation as the device emitted a soft tone near one of the waterproof cases.

"Transmitter located," the technician announced quietly, though not quite quietly enough to escape Daisy's attentive hearing. "Signal active since initial acquisition. Tracking confirmation verified."

The implications registered immediately in Daisy's academic mind—their evidence had been compromised by some form of tracking technology, apparently planted during one of their various locations or transitions. Which meant their entire journey, including their supposedly secure arrival at this facility, had potentially been monitored by the very forces they had been attempting to evade.

With the rapid assessment capabilities developed through decades of academic analysis and recently honed by survival necessities, Daisy cataloged a series of concerning indicators that had been subtly present since their arrival: the too-convenient validation exchange between Frigate and their contacts, the excessive security consciousness for a supposedly secure facility, and the insistence on separating them for "debriefing" despite the obvious advantages of collective information gathering.

They hadn't reached safety. They had sailed directly into an elaborate trap.

"I believe I've left my medication in the vessel," Daisy announced with careful casualness. "Age-related memory lapses, I'm afraid. Might I retrieve it before we proceed with the debriefing process? Certain cardiovascular regularity requirements, you understand."

"I can have someone retrieve it for you," Carter offered with professional courtesy that didn't quite mask a hint of impatience. "Which bag contains your medication?"

"The blue travel case beside my seat," Daisy replied with the precise detail of someone genuinely concerned about medication access. "Though I'm quite particular about handling my prescriptions. Perhaps I could simply accompany whoever you send? It would be most efficient."

The slight hesitation before Carter's response confirmed her suspicions. "That won't be necessary. We'll have your medications brought immediately. Meanwhile, we should proceed with the debriefing to maintain operational timelines."

As they engaged in this seemingly mundane exchange, Daisy managed to catch Rita's eye, subtly shaking her head in a warning gesture they had established during previous tense situations. Rita's almost imperceptible nod indicated both comprehension and readiness to communicate the alert to the others through their own subtle signaling system.

"Of course," Daisy agreed amiably, allowing herself to be guided toward the debriefing room while observing her friends' positions throughout the facility. "Though I do hope the process won't be excessively time-consuming. We've had rather an exhausting few days, as you might imagine."

"The debriefing will be as efficient as possible," Carter assured her with professional courtesy that seemed increasingly performative rather than genuine. "Your cooperation is appreciated."

As Daisy entered the small room—noting with academic precision both its institutional blandness and the concerning absence of windows or obvious secondary exits—she maintained her carefully cultivated appearance of elderly confusion coupled with cooperative goodwill. Meanwhile, her mind was racing through potential scenarios, escape options, and communication strategies that might alert her friends to the danger without triggering immediate containment responses from their increasingly suspicious "federal contacts."

What she couldn't possibly know was that her warning had already catalyzed a remarkable sequence of responses from her fellow Seaside Sleuths. Rita, having received Daisy's danger signal, had immediately implemented their emergency communication protocol—a series of seemingly innocuous gestures and phrases that conveyed specific threat assessments to their teammates.

Babs, with the situational awareness developed through decades of theatrical performance, had already positioned herself to observe key security personnel while maintaining the appearance of befuddled elderly confusion. Mae, her gentle demeanor providing perfect cover for tactical observation, was quietly noting potential exit routes and security vulnerabilities throughout the facility. And Ziggy, environmental activist experience translating seamlessly to current circumstances, was assessing potential improvised resources with the practiced eye of someone accustomed to creating operational advantages from limited materials.

Inside the debriefing room, Carter gestured toward a simple chair positioned before a small table equipped with recording devices. "Please, make yourself comfortable. We'll begin with basic background information before proceeding to specific observational details."

"Of course," Daisy agreed pleasantly, taking the indicated seat while continuing her strategic assessment. "Though I should warn you, at my age the chronological precision of memories can sometimes be affected by stress and excitement. You may find my friends' recollections more temporally reliable."

"We'll manage," Carter assured her with the tone of someone who didn't actually require accurate information—a concerning indicator given the supposed evidence-gathering purpose of their debriefing. "Now, please state your full name and residence for the record."

"Daisy Eleanor Picklesworth," she replied with academic precision. "Current residence at The Barnacle, 421 Seashell Lane, Conch Key, Florida. Though given recent events, I'm uncertain whether that property remains habitable or secure for future occupation."

"That won't be a concern," Carter remarked with troubling ambiguity. "Now, regarding the evidence materials you've provided—when did you first become aware of the environmental operations documented in Captain Crustybutt's records?"

"An interesting opening question," Daisy observed, her academic analysis automatically engaging. "Most standard investigative protocols would begin with establishing witness baseline through personal history and direct observational questioning rather than jumping immediately to evidence provenance details."

Carter's expression shifted subtly, professional courtesy giving way to more focused assessment. "We have limited time for procedural formalities, Ms. Picklesworth. The evidence timeline is critical for establishing enforcement parameters."

"Of course," Daisy acknowledged with elderly agreeability that disguised her tactical assessment. "Though I've always found that proper procedural adherence produces more reliable investigative outcomes. My late husband was quite insistent on methodological precision in his law enforcement career."

The fabricated law enforcement connection was a calculated gambit—introducing uncertainty about potential professional knowledge that might make their captors reconsider immediate action. Carter's momentary hesitation suggested at least partial success in creating doubt about her background and connections.

"Your husband was in law enforcement?" he inquired with carefully neutral interest.

"Thirty-seven years with federal investigative services," Daisy improvised smoothly, drawing on details from numerous crime novels for convincing specificity. "He always emphasized the importance of proper witness handling protocols. 'Daisy,' he would say, 'the difference between admissible testimony and procedural dismissal often comes down to initial interview documentation standards.'"

The strategic fabrication had its intended effect—introducing sufficient uncertainty to delay whatever "debriefing" process had been planned while Carter reassessed potential complications. As he reached for a communication device, presumably to consult with colleagues about this unexpected development, Daisy noted a subtle vibration from the secure phone Ziggy had provided during their escape preparations—the team's emergency signal indicating coordinated action was imminent.

Outside in the main facility, that coordinated action was already unfolding with remarkable effectiveness given their limited planning time and resources. Babs had launched into what could only be described as a theatrical medical emergency—clutching her chest with dramatic intensity while delivering a performance worthy of her Broadway background.

"Oh! The pressure! The pain!" she exclaimed with perfect projection that commanded attention throughout the facility. "I knew I should have taken my heart medication this morning! Agnes, where's my nitroglycerin? Is this what a cardiac event feels like? The literature was quite specific about radiating arm pain!"

The sudden medical drama created precisely the distraction they needed—security personnel momentarily diverted their attention, operational flow disrupted by the unexpected crisis. Rita immediately moved to Babs' side, implementing both supportive assistance and tactical positioning that placed them near one of the facility's equipment stations.

"Deep breaths, Barbara," she instructed loudly while using the coverage to whisper actual tactical directives. "Ziggy has identified the security control panel. Mae is positioned near the evidence. Execute Phase Two on my signal."

Meanwhile, Mae had utilized her unassuming appearance to drift closer to their evidence containers, gentle demeanor and elderly appearance allowing movement that would have triggered immediate security response in someone presenting as a more obvious threat. Ziggy, environmental activism experience translating to current tactical requirements, had positioned himself near what appeared to be the facility's power distribution panel, conveniently exposed during routine maintenance operations.

Inside the debriefing room, Daisy observed Carter's increasing agitation as reports of the developing situation outside reached him through his communication device. "Stay here," he instructed tersely. "I need to address a situation. We'll continue the debriefing shortly."

As he moved toward the door, Daisy implemented her part of their emergency protocol—tipping over the small table in a seemingly accidental movement that created both additional distraction and a momentary obstacle between herself and her captor. "Oh! How clumsy of me! Age and coordination issues, I'm afraid. Let me help straighten this mess."

The manufactured accident provided critical seconds of advantage as Carter instinctively moved to address the fallen furniture, his attention momentarily diverted from both Daisy's position and the developing situation in the main facility. It was all the opening the Seaside Sleuths required to implement their coordinated response to the trap they had identified.

In the main room, Rita gave the signal—a seemingly innocuous comment about Babs needing "fresh air treatment immediately" that triggered their prepared emergency actions. Ziggy immediately activated the improvised device he had assembled from materials in his ever-present hemp messenger bag, creating an electromagnetic pulse that temporarily disrupted the facility's power systems. Mae, with surprising dexterity for someone her age, secured their evidence containers while security personnel were momentarily disoriented by the sudden darkness.

Babs, abandoning her cardiac distress performance with theatrical efficiency, executed what could only be described as an impressively athletic roll behind a nearby console, emerging with a fire extinguisher that she immediately deployed to create both visual obscuration and confusion as the emergency lighting systems activated.

"Exit protocol initiated!" Rita announced with the authoritative tone of someone accustomed to managing restaurant kitchen crises—a skill that translated remarkably well to coordinating tactical extraction operations. "Daisy, southeastern corner, maintenance access point!"

Having escaped the debriefing room during the power disruption, Daisy rejoined her teammates with academic efficiency, automatically assessing their tactical situation while moving toward the indicated escape route. "Status of evidence materials?"

"Secured," Mae confirmed, indicating the container now firmly in Ziggy's possession. "Original documentation plus backup data sources."

"Extraction pathway?" Daisy inquired as they moved as a coordinated unit toward the maintenance access Rita had identified during her earlier assessment.

"Utility corridor connected to secondary dock facilities," Rita reported with practical precision. "Standard emergency evacuation route in marine installations—separate from primary access points for precisely this type of contingency."

"You've developed remarkably specific knowledge of clandestine facility design parameters," Daisy observed as they navigated the indicated pathway, their progress covered by the continuing confusion of darkness, fire suppression systems, and the facility personnel's disorganized response to their unexpected resistance.

"I dated a naval architect briefly in my forties," Rita explained with matter-of-fact efficiency. "He was quite detailed about emergency egress requirements in marine-adjacent structures. I found it tedious at the time, but apparently the information remained accessible."

"Your romantic history continues to provide unexpectedly relevant tactical advantages," Daisy acknowledged as they reached the maintenance access point—a reinforced door with an emergency release mechanism that Ziggy activated with environmental activist efficiency.

Beyond the door lay exactly what Rita had predicted—a utility corridor that sloped upward toward what appeared to be a secondary surface access point different from their original entry location. The functional lighting, separate power system, and clear directional markings confirmed her assessment of standard emergency evacuation design for marine installations.

"We have approximately three minutes before they implement full facility lockdown protocols," Ziggy estimated as they moved rapidly along the corridor. "Standard response timeline for security containment following unauthorized access to restricted egress pathways."

"Your detailed knowledge of security response parameters continues to suggest an interestingly specialized background for environmental activism," Daisy noted as they maintained their disciplined movement toward the increasingly visible exit point.

"Let's just say certain corporate research facilities have similar design implementations," Ziggy replied with environmental activist discretion. "Useful knowledge transfers across various direct action scenarios."

As they approached the exit—a reinforced hatch with both mechanical and electronic securing systems—they could hear the sounds of organized pursuit behind them, indicating the facility's security forces had recovered from their initial disorientation and implemented proper response protocols.

"Authentication required," Ziggy announced as they reached the hatch, indicating the electronic access panel that controlled the locking mechanism. "Standard dual-factor security implementation. Mechanical override unlikely within available timeframe."

"Allow me," Mae said softly, stepping forward with unexpected confidence. From her modest cardigan pocket, she produced what appeared to be a small electronic device approximately the size and shape of a makeup compact. "Tommy's family always emphasized the importance of maintaining certain specialized access capabilities."

"Mae Noodleman," Babs declared with theatrical admiration as the gentle nurse activated her unexpected electronic countermeasure, "you continue to be the dark horse of our investigative quintet. First motorcycle theft, then smuggler connections, and now apparently advanced electronic security bypassing capabilities?"

"Just a simple authentication emulator," Mae explained modestly as the device interfaced with the access panel, its small display cycling through potential code combinations with remarkable speed. "It replicates authorized credential signatures through iterative pattern analysis. Tommy's nephew Victor insisted I carry it during our maritime operations in case of emergency contingencies."

Within seconds, the panel emitted a confirmation tone and the hatch's securing mechanism disengaged with a solid mechanical thunk. Beyond lay a short passage leading to what appeared to be a concealed dock facility separate from the public fishing village infrastructure they had observed during their arrival.

"Secondary extraction transport options?" Daisy inquired as they emerged onto the hidden dock, academic assessment immediately cataloging potential escape vessels.

"There," Rita indicated with practical efficiency, pointing toward a sleek vessel secured at the furthest berth. "Emergency response craft. Dual engines, shallow draft design, ideal for rapid evacuation requirements. Likely maintained fueled and operational as standard contingency protocol."

"Your naval architect boyfriend was quite informative about facility design specifications," Daisy observed as they moved toward the indicated vessel.

"He was exceptionally dull at dinner parties but apparently retained certain valuable information transmission capabilities," Rita acknowledged as they reached the craft—indeed exactly as she had described, a purpose-designed rapid response vessel maintained in obvious operational readiness.

"Anyone with practical maritime operation experience?" Daisy asked as they boarded with the efficient coordination developed through their recent adventures. "Our previous transportation has always included designated pilots."

"Basic navigational capability," Ziggy volunteered, moving immediately to the control console with environmental activist confidence. "Protest flotilla operations occasionally require improvisational vessel management."

"Of course they do," Daisy acknowledged with academic resignation. "Our collective backgrounds continue to provide surprisingly specific skill transfers for current operational requirements."

As Ziggy initiated the vessel's startup sequence—revealing yet another unexpected area of competence in his remarkably diverse activist skill set—they could hear the security team emerging from the facility behind them, tactical movement patterns suggesting both professional training and considerable motivation.

"Departure timeline?" Daisy inquired with academic precision as the engines rumbled to life beneath them.

"Approximately thirty seconds to full operational capability," Ziggy reported from the control console. "Assuming standard safety protocols can be selectively bypassed for emergency implementation."

"Given the armed personnel currently approaching our position with apparent tactical intent," Babs observed as security forces emerged onto the dock with weapons visible, "I believe safety protocol adjustment is entirely warranted under current circumstances."

With environmental activist efficiency that suggested previous experience in unauthorized vessel appropriation, Ziggy implemented what could only be described as an emergency departure procedure—bypassing standard operational sequences in favor of immediate power application that sent their commandeered craft surging away from the dock with stomach-lurching acceleration.

"Pursuit likelihood assessment?" Daisy asked as they rapidly gained distance from the facility, academic mind automatically calculating tactical parameters despite the dramatic nature of their escape.

"High probability of immediate response," Ziggy confirmed, expertly guiding their vessel into deeper waters while monitoring the facility behind them. "Standard security protocols would include designated pursuit craft with superior performance specifications."

"So we've escaped an elaborate trap only to face additional maritime pursuit operations," Rita summarized with practical assessment. "Our retirement activities continue to exceed reasonable expectations for excitement and mortal peril."

"The narrative complexity is simply magnificent," Babs declared with theatrical appreciation despite their dire circumstances. "Though I would appreciate slightly less potentially lethal consequences in our continuing adventure."

"I believe our immediate priorities should include establishing secure communication with legitimate authorities," Daisy suggested as they continued their rapid progress away from the island. "Assuming such contacts can be reliably identified given our recent experiences with deceptive official representations."

"I might have a solution," Mae offered unexpectedly, once again reaching into her seemingly magical cardigan pocket to produce another electronic device—this one resembling a slightly outdated satellite phone. "Tommy's family maintains certain emergency communication capabilities for situations requiring direct access to specific government representatives."

"Your ex-boyfriend's smuggler family has a direct line to actual legitimate government officials?" Rita asked with practical skepticism.

"Certain operational arrangements involve mutual benefit parameters," Mae explained with delicate phrasing that suggested both discretion and surprisingly detailed knowledge of questionable maritime business models. "The Barton family has occasionally assisted with what Tommy called 'specialized import monitoring operations' in exchange for certain jurisdictional accommodations regarding their primary business activities."

"They're informants," Daisy translated with academic precision. "Providing intelligence on competing smuggling operations in exchange for operational tolerance of their own activities. A classic law enforcement compromise methodology for addressing criminal enterprises too entrenched for conventional elimination."

"Tommy preferred the term 'specialized information consultants,'" Mae corrected gently. "But yes, essentially that arrangement. This communication device connects directly to their federal handler—someone with both the authority and incentive to address our current situation."

As Mae activated the specialized communication device, implementing authentication protocols that suggested surprisingly detailed familiarity with covert operational procedures, the others maintained vigilant observation of both their escape progress and potential pursuit indicators from the island behind them.

"Confirmed pursuit craft launching," Ziggy reported from the control console, indicating the radar display where multiple contacts were now visible departing from the facility they had escaped. "Three vessels, high-performance specification indicators, coordinated deployment pattern suggesting professional tactical methodology."

"Our operational timeline appears increasingly compressed," Daisy observed with academic understatement. "Mae, status of communication establishment?"

"Authentication protocols completed," Mae replied with unexpected technical precision. "Secure connection established with designated federal contact. Transmission of situation assessment in progress."

As they continued their desperate flight across increasingly open waters, pursued by what appeared to be professionally equipped and trained hostile forces, Mae conducted what could only be described as a remarkably efficient emergency briefing with whoever had answered her specialized communication device. Her gentle voice somehow transformed into something carrying surprising authority as she detailed their situation, evidence materials, and immediate tactical circumstances with the precision of someone surprisingly familiar with official operational parameters.

"Assistance confirmation received," she announced after several minutes of concentrated communication. "Legitimate federal assets being mobilized from multiple locations. Rendezvous coordinates established at designated neutral territory. Extraction timeline approximately twenty-eight minutes assuming we can maintain current operational positioning."

"Twenty-eight minutes represents an optimization challenge given our pursuit situation," Daisy noted with academic assessment, indicating the radar display where the hostile vessels were now clearly gaining on their position despite Ziggy's impressive navigational efforts. "Their craft appear to possess superior performance specifications."

"Perhaps another distraction implementation?" Babs suggested hopefully. "Ziggy's environmental activism background has previously included surprisingly effective diversionary technologies."

"Limited resources for additional countermeasure deployment," Ziggy reported with environmental activist frustration. "Most effective options already utilized during facility extraction. Remaining capabilities insufficient for effective pursuit disruption."

As their situation appeared increasingly dire—hostile forces steadily closing distance behind them, limited defensive options available, and a significant time gap before legitimate assistance could arrive—Rita moved to the vessel's storage compartments with practical determination.

"Maritime emergency protocols include standard equipment requirements," she announced as she systematically examined the secured containers. "Flares, communication devices, medical supplies, and—" she paused as she opened a specific compartment, expression shifting to tactical satisfaction, "—emergency contingency packages."

From the compartment, she extracted what appeared to be a specialized equipment case marked with both official designations and warning symbols suggesting potentially hazardous contents. "Standard security vessel countermeasure systems," she explained as she expertly opened the sealed container to reveal sophisticated-looking devices nestled in protective foam.

"Your naval architect boyfriend's information sharing continues to demonstrate unexpected depth and applicability," Daisy observed as Rita removed what appeared to be deployment-ready packages labeled with technical designations and operational warnings.

"He was excessively detailed about maritime security implementations," Rita acknowledged as she efficiently assessed the available options. "Particularly after several cocktails, when professional discretion barriers tended to relax considerably."

With the practiced movements of someone implementing remembered instructions rather than improvising, Rita prepared what she identified as "maritime pursuit disruption systems"—specialized devices that combined visual obscuration elements with electronic countermeasures designed to confuse pursuit vessel navigation and targeting systems.

"Deployment requires specific timing coordination with navigational adjustments," she explained as she completed preparation sequences. "Ziggy, on my mark, implement a thirty-degree course change to create maximum pattern disruption during countermeasure activation."

The coordinated maneuver—expertly timed navigation adjustment combined with Rita's deployment of the specialized countermeasures—created a remarkable effect behind their fleeing vessel. A combination of dense visual obscuration (similar to but significantly more sophisticated than Ziggy's earlier smoke bombs) and what appeared to be electronic disruption patterns expanded rapidly across their wake, creating both physical and technical barriers between themselves and their pursuers.

"Impressive implementation," Daisy acknowledged as they observed the pursuing vessels encountering the countermeasure field, their coordinated formation immediately disrupted by the combined visual and electronic interference. "Though I question whether conventional security vessels typically maintain such specialized interdiction prevention systems as standard equipment."

"They don't," Mae confirmed softly, her gentle features arranged in an uncharacteristically knowing expression. "Tommy's family ensures certain specialized modifications to security vessels operating in their traditional transit areas. Professional courtesy arrangements with sympathetic maintenance personnel."

"Your ex-boyfriend's smuggler family sabotages law enforcement boats?" Rita asked with practical directness.

"Not sabotage," Mae corrected with gentle precision. "Selective enhancement with adaptable operational parameters. The systems function perfectly for legitimate security operations while maintaining certain conditional vulnerability options accessible to specialized activation sequences."

"Mae Noodleman," Babs declared with theatrical admiration, "you continue to reveal depths that dramatically exceed initial character assessment parameters. From gentle retired nurse to intimate familiarity with sophisticated criminal enterprise methodologies in less than a week."

"Tommy's family prefers 'alternative maritime logistics specialists' to 'criminal enterprise,'" Mae reminded them with gentle dignity. "And certain life experiences can be surprisingly educational regardless of one's primary career path."

As they continued their flight toward the designated rendezvous coordinates, their pursuers temporarily disoriented by Rita's expertly deployed countermeasures, Mae maintained communication with their apparent legitimate federal contact through her specialized device. The increasingly specific tactical exchanges suggested both authenticity in the communication and escalating official response to their situation.

"Aerial assets deployed," Mae reported from her ongoing communication with their apparent legitimate contact. "Helicopter support approaching from southeastern vector. Estimated arrival in eleven minutes."

"Aerial intervention represents a significant tactical advantage shift," Daisy observed with academic assessment, glancing toward the temporarily disrupted pursuit vessels still visible through the gradually dissipating countermeasure field. "Though our immediate situation remains precarious given the closing distance of hostile forces."

Indeed, despite Rita's impressive countermeasure deployment, the pursuing vessels were beginning to reestablish coordinated formation as they navigated through the disruption field. Their superior speed capabilities meant the tactical advantage created by the temporary confusion would soon be exhausted.

"We need additional diversionary implementation," Ziggy announced from the control console, his environmental activist experience apparently including detailed pursuit evasion assessment capabilities. "Their electronic systems are reestablishing targeting parameters. Estimated interception timeline approximately seven minutes."

"With aerial support still eleven minutes away," Rita calculated practically, "we have a four-minute survival gap requiring tactical solution implementation."

"Perhaps another maritime countermeasure deployment?" Babs suggested hopefully, gesturing toward the security equipment case Rita had discovered. "A dramatic sequel to our previous special effects extravaganza?"

"Limited to one-time deployment capability," Rita reported after checking the remaining contents. "Standard security protocol to prevent excessive unauthorized utilization. We've already implemented the primary system."

As they contemplated their increasingly dire tactical disadvantage, Mae looked up from her specialized communication device with unexpected determination. "Tommy's contact has authorized emergency protocol implementation," she announced with gentle authority that somehow carried surprising command presence. "Designation Kingfish Omega."

"The same protocol Victor authorized during our previous maritime evasion operation," Daisy recalled with academic precision. "Suggesting systematic emergency response methodology rather than improvisational tactics."

"The Barton family maintains consistent operational protocols across their network," Mae confirmed, already moving toward the vessel's communication system with surprisingly technical confidence. "Standardized emergency response designations trigger specific assistance patterns from affiliated assets."

With the practiced movements of someone implementing remembered instructions rather than improvising, Mae accessed the vessel's communication array and entered a specific frequency sequence that suggested specialized knowledge well beyond her apparent gentle nurse background. Into the system, she transmitted a precise message: "Mockingbird to Network. Kingfish Omega authorized. Authentication sequence Delta Seven Niner Echo. Coordinates follow."

Almost immediately, their radar display registered an extraordinary response—multiple new contacts appearing from various positions throughout the surrounding waters, each changing course to converge on their location with coordinated purpose that suggested professional operational methodology rather than coincidental presence.

"The mutual assistance network," Daisy identified with academic assessment. "Similar to the distributed response pattern Victor implemented during our previous maritime pursuit situation."

"Tommy's family maintains comprehensive cooperative arrangements throughout regional waters," Mae confirmed with modest pride that seemed incongruous given the criminal enterprise implications of such a network. "Mutual support protocols for emergency extraction requirements."

Within minutes, the tactical situation had transformed dramatically—their formerly isolated vessel now at the center of a converging pattern of diverse watercraft, each approaching with the purposeful coordination of assets responding to established operational protocols. The pursuing security vessels, observing this unexpected development, showed visible hesitation in their approach pattern, tactical advantage shifting from aggressive pursuit to cautious assessment.

"They're implementing containment evaluation," Ziggy observed from their vessel's monitoring systems. "Standard security response when encountering unexpected force multiplication during pursuit operations."

Indeed, the previously determined pursuit vessels had slowed their approach, maintaining observational distance while apparently reassessing tactical options given the dramatically altered situation. The mutual assistance network had effectively created a defensive perimeter around their position, transforming their vulnerable isolated status into a surrounded asset with significant protective resources.

"Aerial support ETA revised to seven minutes," Mae reported from her ongoing communication. "Tommy's contact has coordinated approach vectors with network assets to ensure integrated operational security during extraction procedures."

"Your ex-boyfriend's smuggler family appears to maintain remarkably professional coordination with legitimate federal authorities," Rita observed with practical assessment. "Suggesting a relationship considerably more complex than typical informant arrangements."

"Certain maritime operational specialties provide unique intelligence access valuable to appropriate government agencies," Mae explained with delicate phrasing that suggested both significant knowledge and practiced discretion. "Creating mutual benefit parameters that transcend conventional enforcement frameworks."

"They're government contractors AND smugglers," Babs translated with theatrical appreciation. "The narrative complexity continues to exceed reasonable developmental expectations. Though I would have appreciated this plot twist before experiencing multiple near-death maritime pursuit operations."

As the mutual assistance network established protective positioning around their vessel, the approaching federal helicopter became visible on the horizon—a sleek, unmarked craft whose approach pattern suggested professional operational methodology rather than standard transportation function. The pursuing security vessels, now clearly outnumbered and outpositioned by the combined network assets and incoming aerial support, began a tactical withdrawal that indicated mission abort parameters rather than temporary repositioning.

"They're retreating," Ziggy confirmed from the monitoring systems. "Standard security protocol when operational advantage shifts beyond acceptable risk parameters. They'll maintain observational positioning but discontinue direct interdiction attempts."

"A remarkably professional response for supposedly rogue operators," Daisy observed with academic assessment. "Suggesting organized methodology rather than improvised hostility."

"Certain corporate security operations maintain quasi-military operational protocols," Mae explained with surprising knowledge detail. "Tommy's contact indicates these particular assets likely represent private contractor elements rather than corrupted official resources—specialized deniable intervention capabilities maintained by corporate entities with sufficient financial resources."

The approaching helicopter executed a textbook extraction approach pattern, maintaining precise position above their vessel while deploying what appeared to be professionally trained operational personnel via rapid descent lines. The tactical team—four individuals in unmarked but clearly specialized equipment—secured the deck with practiced efficiency that suggested extensive experience in maritime intervention scenarios.

"Federal recovery team," announced the apparent team leader as they established perimeter positioning around the five unlikely maritime fugitives. "Authentication sequence Kingfish Verification. Status assessment and evidence security primary objectives."

"Authentication confirmed," Mae responded with the calm authority of someone familiar with such protocols. "Evidence materials secured. Hostile pursuit neutralized through network intervention. Medical assessment recommended for civilian assets due to extended operational stress exposure."

The team leader nodded professional acknowledgment as his colleagues implemented what appeared to be standard extraction methodology—securing their vessel to the helicopter via specialized attachment systems while maintaining tactical observation of surrounding waters. Within minutes, they had established a remarkably stable lift configuration that would allow both personnel and evidence materials to be extracted directly from the boat to the hovering aircraft.

"Priority evacuation sequence initiated," the team leader announced, indicating the harness systems being deployed from the helicopter. "Evidence materials first, followed by civilian personnel according to medical priority assessment."

"We prefer to remain together during extraction procedures," Daisy informed him with academic authority that somehow conveyed non-negotiable parameters despite her civilian status. "Our collective security has been maintained through cooperative methodology throughout this operation."

The team leader assessed her with professional evaluation before nodding acceptance. "Acknowledged. Group extraction implementation approved. Secure harness systems being deployed for simultaneous personnel elevation."

As they prepared for the remarkable culmination of their extraordinary adventure—direct aerial extraction from a boat in open waters surrounded by a smuggler mutual assistance network while pursued by corporate security assets—the five unlikely investigators found themselves experiencing a strange mixture of emotions: relief at apparent legitimate rescue, pride in their successful preservation of critical evidence, and a certain wistful acknowledgment that their remarkable adventure was approaching its conclusion.

"I'm almost going to miss the improvisational tactical operations," Babs confided as they secured themselves into the extraction harnesses being fitted by the professional team. "Though perhaps future applications could involve slightly less mortal peril and maritime pursuit scenarios."

"I believe our collective capabilities could be directed toward more controlled investigative environments," Daisy agreed as they prepared for elevation to the hovering helicopter. "Community service with analytical components rather than international fugitive operations with professional assassin pursuit elements."

"The Seaside Sleuths," Babs declared with theatrical satisfaction as the extraction team signaled readiness. "With prestigious underwater evidence preservation consultant Ziggy Hamfist providing specialized environmental expertise."

"We are not calling ourselves that," Daisy insisted automatically, though her objection now seemed purely ritualistic rather than genuine opposition.

As the extraction system activated—lifting them with surprising smoothness from the boat toward the hovering helicopter—they had a momentary panoramic view of the extraordinary scenario they had created: their commandeered vessel at the center of a protective formation of diverse watercraft from the smuggler mutual assistance network, retreating corporate security assets maintaining observational distance at the perimeter, and legitimate federal resources implementing professional extraction operations from above.

"This would make a magnificent final act curtain tableau," Babs observed with theatrical assessment as they ascended toward the helicopter. "Though I maintain the lighting could be improved with perhaps a sunset backdrop rather than morning marine conditions."

"I believe our immediate priorities should focus on successful extraction completion rather than theatrical presentation assessment," Daisy suggested as they approached the helicopter's open side door where additional operational personnel waited to secure their arrival.

"The evidence materials remain our primary security concern," she continued with academic precision. "Ensuring proper authentication of these extraction personnel and verification of their legitimate authority status before complete operational control transfer."

"Already implemented," Mae assured her softly as they reached the helicopter and were efficiently assisted inside by the waiting team. "Tommy's contact provided specialized verification protocols during our communication exchange. These are legitimate federal personnel with appropriate operational authority."

Indeed, the operational methodology within the helicopter suggested professional legitimacy rather than deceptive presentation—systematic evidence securing procedures, medical assessment protocols implemented by qualified personnel, and communication exchanges with apparent command authorities that included proper authentication sequences and operational terminology.

"Extraction complete," announced the team leader as the helicopter banked away from the maritime scene below, accelerating toward what they were informed was a secure processing facility on the mainland. "Evidence materials secured. All personnel accounted for. Mission parameters achieved. Well done, everyone."

"You're referring to us?" Rita inquired with practical surprise at being included in the operational assessment. "We're civilians who stumbled into this situation through completely unintentional investigative activities."

"Civilians who successfully preserved critical evidence of significant environmental crimes despite multiple professional elimination attempts," the team leader corrected with unexpected respect.

"Evaded corrupt local authorities, neutralized tactical home invasion, escaped sophisticated deception operations, and maintained operational security during complex maritime evasion scenarios. That represents impressive capability application regardless of formal training status."

"We did demonstrate certain unconventional problem-solving methodologies," Daisy acknowledged with academic precision. "Though our success relied heavily on coincidental skill set combinations rather than systematic tactical training."

"Sometimes the most effective operational assets are those without conventional predictability patterns," the team leader observed with professional assessment that suggested extensive field experience. "Your improvised response capability created advantages that traditional methodology would have eliminated."

As the helicopter continued its journey toward the mainland facility, they received a comprehensive briefing on what awaited them—formal debriefing with legitimate authorities, proper evidence processing protocols, and the implementation of what was described as "specialized witness security measures" given the demonstrated threat level they had experienced.

"You mean witness protection?" Babs asked with theatrical concern. "Because while I'm certainly adaptable to character transformation requirements, I have substantial reservations about permanent identity modification protocols. My personal brand has been carefully cultivated over decades of development."

"Nothing so dramatic," assured the federal agent conducting their briefing—a surprisingly young woman whose professional demeanor suggested significant authority despite her age. "Temporary security measures while enforcement operations are implemented against the identified criminal enterprise elements. Once the primary threat actors have been neutralized, you can return to normal activities with appropriate protective monitoring."

"And the evidence we've preserved?" Daisy inquired, academic concern focused on the substantive outcomes rather than their personal circumstances. "Will it actually result in meaningful enforcement against the environmental crimes we've documented?"

"The materials you've secured represent the critical evidentiary elements required for comprehensive enforcement actions," the agent confirmed with professional satisfaction. "Multiple federal agencies are already implementing coordinated response operations against both the physical infrastructure and the corporate entities responsible. Judge Anderson was taken into custody approximately thirty minutes ago, along with several other officials identified in your evidence documentation."

"What about Meredith Moneypenny?" Rita asked practically. "Last we knew, she had apparently staged her own disappearance while transferring operational blame to Fleur DuBois."

"Apprehended at a private airfield three hours ago," the agent reported with evident satisfaction. "Attempting to depart the country via chartered aircraft using falsified identification documents. Her offshore financial accounts have been frozen pending criminal proceeds investigation."

"And the underwater disposal system?" Ziggy inquired, environmental activist priorities focusing on the ecological impact rather than individual accountability. "Is it being secured to prevent further contamination while enforcement actions proceed?"

"Specialized environmental containment teams deployed immediately following evidence verification," the agent assured him. "The system has been shutdown with comprehensive monitoring protocols established to assess existing contamination parameters and implement appropriate remediation strategies."

As the helicopter approached what appeared to be a secure government facility—a substantial compound with multiple buildings, professional security infrastructure, and the unmistakable indicators of legitimate federal operations—the five unlikely environmental crime investigators found themselves experiencing an unexpected emotion beyond the anticipated relief and satisfaction of successful mission completion.

"I believe I'm experiencing a certain anticlimactic sentiment," Daisy observed with academic precision as they prepared for landing. "Despite the obvious advantages of safety, security, and proper evidence processing, there's a peculiar sense of... conclusion that seems somehow insufficient given the extraordinary nature of our recent experiences."

"The adrenaline withdrawal phenomenon," the federal agent identified with knowing assessment. "Common psychological response following extended high-stress operational conditions. The sudden transition to security and professional handling creates neurochemical adjustment requirements that can manifest as emotional dissonance."

"Or perhaps we've simply grown accustomed to solving problems through our own improvisational methodologies rather than relying on conventional authority structures," Rita suggested practically. "Given our recent experiences with supposedly legitimate officials who turned out to be corrupt or compromised."

"A reasonable adaptive response to your operational circumstances," the agent acknowledged with professional respect. "Though I can assure you that this facility and its personnel represent legitimate federal authority with appropriate jurisdictional oversight."

As the helicopter touched down on a designated landing pad and they were escorted into the facility with professional courtesy that suggested respected witnesses rather than suspicious detainees, the five unlikely investigators found themselves gradually accepting the remarkable transition from desperate fugitives to securely protected evidence providers.

The following hours unfolded with surprising efficiency—proper debriefing protocols conducted by obviously legitimate authorities, comprehensive evidence processing that respected both chain of custody requirements and their personal involvement in its preservation, and the implementation of witness security measures that balanced protection requirements with reasonable autonomy considerations.

"Your contribution to this enforcement operation cannot be overstated," the senior federal official informed them during a concluding briefing session after their individual statements had been properly documented. "The evidence you preserved and transported despite extraordinary obstacles has enabled us to implement one of the most significant environmental crime enforcement actions in recent history."

"Will there be public acknowledgment of the corporate criminal activities?" Daisy inquired, academic concern focused on systematic accountability rather than individual recognition. "Or will the enforcement be handled through confidential settlement processes that minimize disclosure requirements?"

"Full public prosecution with comprehensive evidence presentation," the official assured her with evident satisfaction. "The scale and nature of these violations demand transparent accountability. Multiple corporate executives have already been taken into custody, with additional enforcement actions proceeding against both organizational entities and complicit regulatory officials."

"And our personal security going forward?" Rita asked with practical assessment. "Given the demonstrated resources and determination of those who attempted to eliminate us as witnesses, what ongoing protection parameters should we anticipate?"

"Comprehensive security monitoring for approximately sixty days while primary enforcement operations are completed," the official outlined with professional precision. "Followed by gradually reduced protective measures as threat assessment indicators decline. Your residence will receive appropriate security enhancements, and certain communication protocols will be established for emergency response requirements."

"You mean we can actually return to The Barnacle?" Mae asked with gentle hope, her expression suggesting genuine attachment to their shared home despite its recent association with extraordinary danger. "Even after the tactical team invasion and resulting damage?"

"Full restoration already in progress," the official confirmed with the satisfied expression of someone delivering unexpectedly positive information. "Special response team deployed yesterday to implement comprehensive repairs, security enhancements, and evidence removal cleanup. The property should be ready for reoccupation within approximately seventy-two hours."

"With appropriate stylistic considerations for the decor restoration, I hope," Babs interjected with theatrical concern. "Certain aesthetic elements require specialized attention beyond mere structural repair implementation."

"Your personal property requirements have been noted in the restoration parameters," the official assured her with remarkable patience for what might seem a trivial concern given the circumstances. "Though priority was naturally given to security enhancement integration and structural integrity restoration."

"And Ziggy?" Daisy inquired, academic concern extending to their unexpected environmental activist ally who had become an integral part of their extraordinary adventure. "What security provisions apply to his circumstances?"

"Mr. Hamfist has been offered similar protective monitoring protocols," the official replied with a glance toward Ziggy, who had remained uncharacteristically quiet during the briefing. "Though his residential circumstances create certain implementation challenges given the transient nature of his current accommodations."

"I've been offered temporary housing at a secured government facility during the initial enforcement phase," Ziggy explained with environmental activist flexibility that suggested adaptability to changing circumstances. "Followed by potential witness consultant position with the EPA's special investigation division once the immediate security concerns are resolved."

"A professional application of your environmental activism experience," Daisy noted with academic approval. "Translating improvisational skills to systematic enforcement methodology."

"Apparently exposing massive corporate environmental crimes while evading professional assassins constitutes an impressive job application," Ziggy acknowledged with a hint of his usual laid-back humor returning after the intensity of their recent experiences. "Though I've been assured that future investigative operations will include significantly more procedural oversight and considerably fewer maritime pursuit scenarios."

As the briefing concluded and they prepared for temporary accommodation at the secure facility while their home was restored, the five unlikely environmental crime investigators found themselves gradually transitioning from the intense operational focus of the past several days to a more reflective assessment of their extraordinary adventure and its implications for their future activities.

"I believe we've discovered certain capabilities and cooperative methodologies that exceed traditional retirement activity parameters," Daisy observed as they settled into the surprisingly comfortable government accommodations provided for their temporary residence. "Perhaps suggesting potential application opportunities beyond our originally anticipated golden years experiences."

"The Seaside Sleuths," Babs declared with theatrical enthusiasm for perhaps the dozenth time since their initial investigative activities. "Environmental Crime Division, with special consultant Ziggy Hamfist providing technical expertise and youthful demographic appeal for potential media adaptation opportunities."

"We are not calling ourselves that," Daisy insisted automatically, though her objection now seemed purely perfunctory rather than genuine opposition. "And any future investigative activities would necessarily involve significantly reduced danger parameters and more systematic methodology than our recent improvisational operations."

"Yet you acknowledge potential future investigative activities," Rita noted with practical assessment. "Rather than returning exclusively to book clubs, beach walks, and Garden Club politics as originally anticipated."

"Perhaps certain moderate mystery resolution opportunities within our local community," Daisy conceded with academic precision. "Applying our demonstrated analytical capabilities to appropriate civilian investigation scenarios without the international fugitive elements or tactical home defense requirements."

"I've quite enjoyed discovering unexpected application opportunities for my varied life experiences," Mae admitted softly, her gentle features reflecting thoughtful consideration rather than her usual placid acceptance. "Though I would prefer future adventures include fewer armed pursuers and more convenient bathroom access than maritime escape vessels typically provide."

As they continued their reflective assessment of their extraordinary transformation from peaceful retirees to successful environmental crime investigators, federal agents arrived to provide their final briefing before evening accommodations—comprehensive updates on enforcement operations already underway, security protocols established for their protection, and the arrangements for their eventual return to The Barnacle once restoration operations were completed.

"The corporate network behind the environmental crimes is being systematically dismantled through coordinated federal action," the senior agent reported with professional satisfaction. "Judge Anderson is cooperating with investigators in exchange for sentencing considerations, providing extensive documentation of corruption networks throughout regional governance structures."

"And the actual environmental damage?" Ziggy inquired, environmental activist priorities focused on ecological impact rather than individual accountability. "What remediation procedures are being implemented for existing contamination?"

"Specialized environmental response teams have established comprehensive monitoring and containment operations throughout the affected areas," the agent assured him. "Preliminary assessment indicates the damage, while significant, can be effectively addressed through sustained restoration efforts funded by asset seizures from the responsible corporate entities."

"So justice is actually being served," Babs remarked with theatrical wonder. "How delightfully unexpected given our initially pessimistic assessment of systemic corruption barriers. Perhaps there's hope for institutional integrity after all, despite our recent experiences with compromised authority figures."

"Certain enforcement mechanisms maintain operational effectiveness despite corruption challenges," the agent acknowledged. "Particularly when provided with comprehensively documented evidence of the type you successfully preserved despite extraordinary obstacles."

"Speaking of extraordinary obstacles," Rita interjected practically, "what exactly happened to the personnel at the deceptive facility we escaped? The ones pretending to be federal agents while actually attempting to secure our elimination?"

"Specialized response team deployed immediately following your extraction," the agent reported with professional discretion suggesting limited disclosure parameters. "The facility has been secured with all personnel detained for appropriate processing. Preliminary investigation indicates a sophisticated private contractor operation with international connections rather than corrupted official resources."

"Mercenaries rather than compromised agents," Daisy translated with academic precision. "Suggesting a criminal enterprise with significant financial resources beyond local corruption networks."

"The investigation continues to expand as new evidence emerges," the agent confirmed without specific confirmation of her assessment. "Multiple jurisdictional authorities now involved in what appears to be a substantially larger criminal operation than initially identified."

"And Captain Crustybutt?" Mae inquired gently, her concern for the missing maritime operator who had initiated their evidence preservation journey evident in her expression. "Has there been any... resolution regarding his disappearance?"

The agent's expression shifted to professional regret. "Recovery operation implemented yesterday in the southern harbor region. I'm sorry to report that human remains were located that appear consistent with the captain's physical parameters. Formal identification pending but preliminary assessment suggests foul play rather than accidental circumstances."

"He died protecting environmental evidence and attempting to expose corporate crimes," Ziggy observed with environmental activist respect. "Despite his unconventional business operations and questionable regulatory compliance history."

"A complex individual with apparently contradictory ethical parameters," Daisy acknowledged with academic assessment. "Suggesting greater dimensional complexity than conventional categorical assessment would indicate."

"He was Tommy's favorite uncle," Mae said softly, genuine emotion evident beneath her gentle demeanor. "Despite certain operational irregularities in his professional activities."

As the agents departed, leaving them to settle into their temporary accommodations for the evening, the five unlikely investigators found themselves experiencing the emotional and physical aftermath of their extraordinary adventure—the accumulated fatigue of days spent in high-stress survival conditions finally manifesting now that immediate danger had been removed.

"I believe I'm experiencing what medical professionals would classify as delayed stress response," Daisy observed as she settled into one of the surprisingly comfortable chairs provided in their common area. "The neurochemical transition from sustained emergency response conditions to security parameters creating significant energy depletion indicators."

"You're exhausted," Rita translated practically, already arranging blankets and comfort items with the efficient hospitality developed through decades of restaurant management. "We all are. Adrenaline has remarkable short-term performance enhancement capabilities but creates substantial recovery requirements once safety is established."

"I haven't been this tired since the final performance week of 'Cats' during the Philadelphia summer season with non-functional air conditioning and that unfortunate norovirus incident among the supporting cast," Babs declared dramatically, collapsing onto a sofa with theatrical exhaustion that nevertheless contained genuine fatigue elements. "Though at least this exhaustion stems from heroic environmental crime-fighting rather than questionable seafood choices at the cast party."

As evening settled over the secure government facility providing their temporary shelter, the five unlikely environmental crime investigators found themselves gradually surrendering to much-needed recovery sleep after their extraordinary adventures. Security personnel maintained professional monitoring protocols outside their accommodations, legitimate federal authorities continued implementing enforcement operations against the criminal conspiracy they had exposed, and the restoration of their beloved beach house proceeded under specialized supervision.

Their remarkable journey had transformed them from peaceful retirees enjoying book clubs and beach walks to successful investigators who had preserved critical evidence despite professional elimination attempts, exposed massive environmental crimes despite systemic corruption barriers, and discovered unexpected capabilities within themselves despite conventional assumptions about retirement activities.

What none of them realized as they finally surrendered to well-earned rest was that their extraordinary adventure had not only changed them but had attracted attention well beyond the immediate criminal conspiracy they had exposed. Their unprecedented success against sophisticated opposition had identified them as uniquely effective investigators whose unconventional methodology created advantages that traditional approaches couldn't match.

In a secure government office far from their temporary accommodations, a conversation was taking place that would eventually transform their anticipated return to peaceful retirement into something considerably more interesting:

"The operational assessment confirms unusual effectiveness parameters despite civilian status and limited formal training," noted one senior official reviewing their case file with professional interest. "Their collective skill set combination creates unique investigative advantages in certain specialized scenarios."

"Are you suggesting what I think you're suggesting?" asked a colleague with skeptical assessment. "They're retirement-age civilians with no formal qualification for operational deployment."

"Who successfully preserved critical evidence despite multiple professional elimination attempts, exposed massive environmental crimes despite systemic corruption barriers, and demonstrated remarkable adaptive capability throughout extended high-stress operational conditions," the first official countered. "That represents potential resource application opportunities for certain specialized investigation requirements."

"The Conch Key situation has demonstrated concerning vulnerability indicators," acknowledged the skeptical colleague with reluctant recognition. "Traditional enforcement methodology has proven ineffective against certain localized corruption patterns. Unconventional approaches may indeed offer alternative effectiveness parameters."

"Precisely," confirmed the first official with satisfied conclusion. "I believe we've identified exactly the specialized investigative resource we've been seeking for the Henderson situation. Civilian status, unconventional methodology, and demonstrated effectiveness against sophisticated opposition—the perfect combination for our requirements."

"Authorized to proceed with recruitment assessment," confirmed the senior authority after careful consideration. "Conditional approval for specialized consultant designation pending operational readiness evaluation. The Seaside Sleuths may have additional adventure opportunities sooner than anticipated."

And so, as the five unlikely environmental crime investigators slept peacefully in their secure accommodations, the seeds of their next extraordinary adventure were already being planted—ensuring that their remarkable transformation from peaceful retirees to effective investigators would continue in ways none of them could possibly anticipate.

Epilogue
Six Months Later

The morning sun painted The Barnacle in cheerful hues of gold and amber, its restored Victorian charm showing no evidence of the dramatic events that had unfolded there half a year earlier. From her favorite reading chair on the newly reinforced porch, Daisy Picklesworth surveyed the peaceful beach where it had all begun—where Brock Hamfist's body had washed ashore and inadvertently launched four retirement-age women and one environmental activist into an extraordinary adventure that none of them could have anticipated.

"Coffee's ready," called Rita from the kitchen, her practical efficiency having long since restored normalcy to their daily routines. "And I've made those blueberry scones Mae's been craving all week."

"Bless you," Mae responded from her position at the porch railing, where she had been quietly knitting what appeared to be an impressively complex afghan. "Though I maintain my interest in your baking has nothing to do with emotional compensation for our recent adventures."

"Of course not," Rita agreed with practical skepticism as she emerged onto the porch with a tray of coffee and freshly baked goods. "Just as Babs' sudden interest in community theater directing rather than performing has nothing to do with her newfound appreciation for behind-the-scenes tactical coordination."

"I heard that!" came Babs' voice from inside the house, followed by her dramatic appearance through the French doors. She wore what could only be described as a director's outfit—beret, clipboard, and an unnecessary megaphone hanging from a cord around her neck. "My transition to directorial authority represents artistic evolution, not tactical application transference. Though I will admit certain skills seem surprisingly complementary."

Daisy accepted her coffee with dignified appreciation, the familiar banter of her friends creating a comforting backdrop to her morning contemplation. "Six months," she remarked, her academic precision finding satisfaction in the neat chronological marker. "Rather remarkable how quickly one can adjust to both extraordinary adventure and its subsequent absence."

Indeed, the past half-year had unfolded with surprising tranquility following their return to The Barnacle. The government restoration team had repaired the damage from the tactical incursion with impressive efficiency, even managing to preserve the architectural details Babs had insisted were "essential to our domestic aesthetic integrity." The promised security enhancements had been integrated with such professional discretion that only careful observation would reveal their presence—subtle reinforcements to doors and windows, advanced monitoring systems disguised as ordinary fixtures, and a direct communication link to federal authorities concealed within what appeared to be a vintage intercom system.

The criminal conspiracy they had exposed had been systematically dismantled through coordinated federal enforcement operations, resulting in numerous arrests, corporate dissolutions, and environmental remediation programs that continued to this day. Judge Anderson had indeed provided substantial cooperation in exchange for sentencing considerations, his testimony exposing corruption networks that extended far beyond their initial discoveries. Meredith Moneypenny was serving a considerably less comfortable version of retirement in federal prison, along with several corporate executives whose environmental crimes had finally caught up with them.

Even Fleur DuBois, the murderous art dealer whose attempt to eliminate Brock Hamfist had initiated their adventures, had received appropriate justice—her criminal trial had concluded just last month with a conviction that ensured she would be creating jailhouse art rather than gallery exhibitions for the foreseeable future.

"Has anyone heard from Ziggy recently?" Mae inquired, setting aside her knitting to accept a scone from Rita's tray. "His last postcard was rather vague about his new position with the EPA."

"Deliberately so, I imagine," Daisy replied. "His 'environmental compliance specialist' role appears to involve certain operational security parameters that preclude specific disclosure."

"He's hunting down corporate polluters with government authority instead of protest signs," Babs translated unnecessarily. "Quite the career advancement for someone who was living in a motel and making hemp jewelry six months ago."

"I believe he's found appropriate application for his rather specific skill set," Daisy observed with academic approval. "Much as we have readjusted to our more traditional retirement activities, albeit with occasional moments of... nostalgia for certain aspects of our adventure."

This last admission was perhaps the most significant shift in The Barnacle's atmosphere over the past six months. Despite their grateful return to safety and security, despite the considerable relief of no longer being pursued by professional assassins, despite the undeniable comfort of sleeping in their own beds without immediate evacuation contingency plans—there remained a certain wistfulness among them for the extraordinary experiences they had shared.

"I miss the adrenaline sometimes," Babs confessed, dropping her theatrical persona momentarily in favor of genuine reflection. "Not the mortal peril, obviously, but the exhilaration of discovering capabilities I never knew I possessed. The immediacy of existence when every decision carried significant consequences."

"The focused application of our collective problem-solving skills," Rita added with practical assessment. "The satisfaction of addressing genuinely consequential challenges rather than minor everyday concerns."

"The sense of purpose beyond conventional expectations," Mae contributed softly. "Though I certainly don't miss maritime plumbing facilities or sleeping in smuggler vessels."

Daisy nodded thoughtful agreement. "A rather unexpected outcome of our adventure—discovering that standard retirement activities, while pleasant and comfortable, lack a certain... consequential engagement that we experienced during our investigative endeavors."

What none of them voiced directly, though all understood implicitly, was the subtle sense of anticipation that had gradually emerged in their shared household—a collective readiness for something more than book club discussions and Garden Club politics, a preparedness for challenges beyond choosing seasonal dinner menus or selecting appropriate beach attire.

Not that they sought danger or courted disaster. But their extraordinary experiences had revealed capabilities that now seemed wasted on purely recreational activities. They had discovered strengths, adaptabilities, and cooperative methodologies that apparently lay dormant, waiting for appropriate application opportunities.

"Perhaps we could investigate something simple," Babs suggested, not for the first time in recent weeks. "A minor local mystery with limited criminal implications. The case of the missing Garden Club funds, perhaps, or the mysterious rearrangement of the library's mystery section."

"I believe we agreed that any future investigative activities would require formal authorization from appropriate authorities," Daisy reminded her, academic precision maintaining their established boundaries. "Rather than self-initiated amateur detection."

This reference to "formal authorization" represented another significant development in their post-adventure circumstances. Approximately two months after their return to The Barnacle, they had received an unexpected visitor—a representative from a specialized federal agency that none of them had previously encountered, bearing an unusual proposal that had initially seemed almost comical.

"Your unique investigative capabilities have been noted at certain governmental levels," the representative had explained with professional courtesy that nevertheless contained unmistakable recruitment indicators. "Creating potential consultant opportunities for specialized investigative scenarios where conventional methodology might prove ineffective."

"You want to hire four retirement-age women as government investigators?" Rita had summarized with practical skepticism.

"Five, actually," the representative had corrected, including Ziggy in their assessment. "Your collective effectiveness against sophisticated opposition suggests unique operational advantages in certain specialized scenarios. Particularly those involving environmental crimes with localized corruption complications—precisely the parameters where traditional enforcement has proven vulnerable."

After considerable discussion, careful contract negotiation (with Daisy's academic precision proving remarkably effective in securing favorable terms), and thoughtful assessment of potential implications, they had ultimately accepted the unusual arrangement—becoming official consultants with specialized designation for appropriate investigative scenarios, complete with credentials, training protocols, and modest stipends that Rita described as "inadequate compensation for potential mortal peril but better than volunteer status."

And yet, despite this formal authorization, despite the training modules they had dutifully completed, despite the communication protocols established for potential activation, no actual investigative opportunities had materialized in the months since their agreement. Their official consultant status remained theoretical rather than practical, creating a peculiar anticipation that occasionally manifested in suggestions like Babs' proposal to investigate minor local mysteries.

"I maintain that our Garden Club treasurer's accounting discrepancies represent potential fraud indicators warranting professional assessment," Babs insisted, returning to her favorite example of accessible investigative opportunities. "Three consecutive months of unexplained expenditure variations suggests systematic manipulation rather than computational error."

"Eugenia is seventy-eight years old and consistently transposes numbers when recording transactions," Mae reminded her gently. "Malice requires both intent and competence, neither of which apply to her accounting methodology."

Their good-natured debate about appropriate investigation targets was interrupted by the distinctive sound of the newly installed security gate opening at the front of the property. Moments later, a government-issue sedan with deliberately forgettable appearance pulled into their shell-lined driveway, driven by an equally forgettable-looking man in a nondescript suit that nevertheless suggested federal authority.

"It appears we have official visitors," Daisy observed, academic detachment masking the immediate interest that surged through their collective awareness. "Perhaps our consultant designation has progressed from theoretical to practical application."

The man who approached their porch moved with the careful efficiency of someone professionally trained in situational assessment, his unremarkable features arranged in the pleasant but reserved expression of a government representative with specific operational objectives. He carried a slim briefcase whose contents, they all immediately understood, might represent exactly the engagement opportunity they had been unconsciously anticipating.

"Ladies," he greeted them with professional courtesy. "I hope I'm not interrupting your morning activities."

"Not at all, Agent Johnson," Daisy replied, recognizing their liaison from the specialized federal agency that had established their consultant arrangement. "Coffee? Rita's scones are particularly excellent this morning."

"Thank you, but I'm afraid this isn't a social call," he declined with polite regret. "A situation has developed that appears to match the specialized parameters of your consultant designation. If you're available, I've been authorized to provide operational briefing materials for your assessment."

The four women exchanged glances that communicated volumes without words—interest, anticipation, a certain vindication of their continued preparedness, and perhaps a hint of concern about what might be required of them.

"We're available," Daisy confirmed with academic precision. "Though I believe our agreement specified certain risk limitation parameters for any potential assignments."

"The situation involves minimal direct security concerns," Agent Johnson assured them, opening his briefcase to extract several folders bearing subdued but official-looking security classifications. "What we require is primarily analytical capability rather than field operational engagement. Your unique perspective on certain behavioral indicators and community dynamics appears particularly relevant to the scenario."

As they moved inside to the dining room, which had become their default briefing location during their training modules, Agent Johnson efficiently arranged materials across the table—photographs, documents, and what appeared to be surveillance transcripts organized with professional methodology.

"Approximately three weeks ago, environmental monitoring systems detected anomalous chemical signatures in the waterways surrounding Pelican Bay," he began, indicating a coastal community approximately sixty miles south of their location. "Initial assessment suggested industrial contaminants inconsistent with known regional manufacturing operations."

"Another illegal disposal operation?" Rita inquired with practical assessment, immediately focusing on the core issue rather than peripheral details.

"That was our initial theory," Johnson confirmed. "Standard investigative protocols were implemented—water sample analysis, source tracking methodology, regulatory compliance verification of known industrial entities in the area. However, the investigation encountered... unusual complications."

"Define 'unusual complications,'" Daisy requested, academic precision automatically engaging with the analytical challenge.

"The chemical signatures appear inconsistent with traditional industrial waste products," Johnson explained, indicating a series of technical analysis reports. "Suggesting specialized synthetic compounds rather than standard manufacturing byproducts. Additionally, local officials have demonstrated concerning response patterns to federal inquiry attempts."

"Obstructionism disguised as cooperative engagement," Babs translated with theatrical insight. "Providing technically accurate but substantively useless information while creating procedural delays to prevent effective investigation."

"Precisely," Johnson acknowledged with professional respect for her assessment. "Creating suspicion of localized corruption similar to the patterns you encountered in your previous experience. However, unlike your Conch Key situation, we've been unable to establish clear connection patterns between local officials and potential responsible entities."

"Because you don't know what you're actually looking for," Daisy observed with academic assessment. "The unusual chemical composition creates identification challenges for both the substances themselves and their potential sources."

"Correct," Johnson confirmed. "Conventional investigation methodology relies on established parameters—known contaminants with documented industrial sources, predictable corruption patterns connecting officials to identifiable corporate entities. This situation lacks those referential frameworks, creating standard procedure effectiveness limitations."

"Which is where we come in," Rita concluded practically. "Unconventional methodology for anomalous parameters where traditional approaches prove ineffective."

"Exactly," Johnson agreed. "Your demonstrated capability for identifying nonstandard connection patterns and implementing improvised investigative approaches in corruption-compromised environments suggests potential effectiveness where our conventional operations have stalled."

"What specifically would this assignment entail?" Daisy inquired, her academic precision focusing on operational details rather than conceptual framework.

"Initial community integration for observational assessment," Johnson outlined. "Utilizing your civilian status and age demographic as non-threatening presence parameters to gather information about local dynamics, potential unusual activities, and behavioral indicators that might suggest involvement patterns. Essentially, you would visit Pelican Bay as tourists while maintaining specialized observational protocols."

"Tourist cover with investigative undertones," Babs summarized with theatrical appreciation. "I'll need to prepare appropriate resort wear with concealed observation enhancement accessories. Perhaps those oversize sunglasses with the reflective coating that allows peripheral surveillance without direct eye contact indicators."

"I believe standard vacation attire without specialized surveillance modifications would be more appropriate," Daisy suggested diplomatically. "Our effectiveness relies precisely on authentic presentation rather than theatrical espionage elements."

Johnson nodded agreement. "Your normal appearance and behavior patterns represent your primary operational advantage. Pelican Bay has a substantial retirement community, making your presence as visitors entirely contextually appropriate. You would simply be four friends enjoying a beach vacation while maintaining heightened observational awareness."

"And if we do identify potential connection patterns or contamination sources?" Rita asked practically. "What intervention protocols would apply?"

"Absolutely no direct confrontation or independent intervention," Johnson emphasized with professional firmness. "Your role would be strictly observational and analytical. Any actionable intelligence would trigger specialized team deployment for appropriate enforcement operations."

"So we look, we listen, we analyze, but we don't engage directly with potential hostiles," Daisy summarized with academic precision. "Minimizing personal security risk while maximizing information-gathering effectiveness."

"Precisely," Johnson confirmed. "Your previous experience involved unnecessary danger parameters precisely because you lacked proper operational support. This assignment includes comprehensive backup resources, emergency extraction protocols if required, and strict limitation of your personal involvement to intelligence gathering rather than enforcement action."

As they reviewed the detailed briefing materials—environmental reports, community maps, background profiles of key local officials, and technical analysis of the mysterious contaminants—the four women found themselves experiencing an unexpected but not unwelcome sense of purpose. The analytical challenge engaged their collective problem-solving capabilities, while the carefully structured operational parameters addressed their reasonable concerns about personal safety.

"The chemical composition appears deliberately designed for rapid dispersal and degradation," Daisy noted, her academic background allowing surprising insight into the technical reports. "Suggesting intentional concealment methodology rather than careless disposal practices."

"Which indicates sophisticated operations rather than opportunistic dumping," Rita added with practical assessment. "Someone knows exactly what they're doing and how to minimize detection likelihood."

"The local marina expansion project timing correlates with initial contamination detection," Mae observed softly, her gentle demeanor disguising remarkable analytical perception as she compared timeline documents. "Creating potential connection variables worth exploring."

"And the harbormaster's brother-in-law serves on the town council's environmental committee," Babs contributed, theatrical flair momentarily replaced by focused investigation as she traced relationship patterns through the background profiles. "Establishing possible influence pathways for regulatory oversight manipulation."

Johnson observed their rapid integration of disparate information elements with professional appreciation. "This is precisely why your consultant designation was created," he acknowledged. "Your collective analytical methodology creates connection identification capabilities that conventional investigators might overlook."

"When do we depart?" Daisy inquired, academic precision automatically shifting toward operational planning now that the analytical framework had been established.

"Accommodations have been arranged at the Pelican Bay Resort beginning tomorrow," Johnson replied, extracting reservation confirmations from his briefcase. "Your cover parameters include a week-long vacation with standard tourist activities—beach access, restaurant dining, community exploration, social engagement with other visitors and locals. All expenses covered through operational accounts, naturally."

"With appropriate clothing stipend consideration, I assume," Babs interjected with theatrical budgetary awareness. "Proper resort wear for extended undercover operations requires substantial wardrobe investment."

"Reasonable expenses have been authorized," Johnson acknowledged with diplomatic vagueness. "Though I would emphasize that authentic presentation rather than excessive new acquisitions would better serve operational effectiveness."

"My existing resort wear collection is both extensive and appropriately authentic," Babs assured him with dignified response to his implied moderation suggestion. "Though certain specialized accessories may prove necessary for optimal intelligence gathering implementation."

As Agent Johnson concluded the briefing with communication protocols, emergency procedures, and specific observational priorities, the four women found themselves experiencing a remarkable transformation—from peaceful retirees enjoying their morning coffee to activated government consultants preparing for specialized investigative operations.

"Transportation will be provided tomorrow morning at nine," Johnson informed them as he gathered his materials. "Standard civilian vehicle rather than official transportation, maintaining appropriate cover parameters. Your liaison contact in Pelican Bay will be established through seemingly casual encounter on your second day, providing secure communication channel for information transfer."

"Do we have authorization to include Ziggy in our operational team?" Daisy inquired, academic thoroughness ensuring all potential resources were considered. "His environmental expertise might prove valuable for technical assessment of the contamination parameters."

"Mr. Hamfist is currently engaged in a separate assignment," Johnson replied with professional discretion suggesting limited disclosure authorization. "Though arrangements could be made for technical consultation if specific expertise requirements emerge during your investigation."

After Johnson's departure, the four women remained at the dining room table, the breakfast dishes now pushed aside to accommodate the files he had left for their review. The morning sunshine streamed through the windows, creating an almost comical contrast between the cheerful domestic setting and the serious investigative materials spread before them.

"Well," Babs declared with theatrical assessment, "it appears the Seaside Sleuths have received their first official assignment. Complete with government authorization, expense accounts, and actual badges." She held up the consultant credentials Johnson had provided, admiring the official emblem with undisguised satisfaction.

"We are not calling ourselves that," Daisy insisted automatically, though her objection now seemed purely ritual rather than genuine opposition. "And I believe our immediate priority should be thorough review of these briefing materials before beginning preparation for tomorrow's departure."

"I'll handle the packing logistics," Rita volunteered with practical efficiency. "Appropriate attire for various environmental conditions, necessary personal items, and adequate supply of any required medications."

"I should notify my doctor about my temporary absence," Mae noted with characteristic thoughtfulness. "And perhaps prepare some of those specialized communication cards we developed during our training modules."

As they divided responsibilities and began methodical preparation for their unexpected assignment, a subtle but unmistakable energy permeated The Barnacle—the engaged purposefulness of individuals applying their specific capabilities to meaningful challenges, the collective satisfaction of cooperative problem-solving with consequential objectives.

"Rather remarkable how quickly one transitions from peaceful retirement to government investigative operations," Daisy observed as she organized the briefing materials into logical analytical categories. "Though I maintain that our primary advantage lies precisely in maintaining authentic presentation rather than adopting theatrical espionage behaviors." This last comment was directed pointedly at Babs, who was already sketching what appeared to be elaborate disguise concepts in her ever-present notebook.

"Authentic presentation with appropriate stylistic enhancements," Babs amended without conceding the core principle. "The effectiveness of observational positioning can be significantly improved through strategic accessorization. Statement jewelry creates conversational access points while oversized hats provide both sun protection and convenient visual concealment for surveillance activities."

Their good-natured methodological debate continued throughout the day as they prepared for their mysterious assignment in Pelican Bay. Rita developed efficient packing protocols with the precision of someone accustomed to restaurant inventory management. Mae quietly assembled a surprisingly comprehensive first aid kit that suggested both medical foresight and certain security contingency considerations. Daisy created detailed analytical frameworks for organizing their initial observational priorities based on the briefing materials. And Babs, despite ongoing negotiations regarding "appropriate stylistic enhancements," produced remarkably practical communication and documentation systems disguised as ordinary tourist accessories.

By evening, The Barnacle had transformed from peaceful retirement dwelling to efficient preparation center for specialized investigative operations—albeit one that maintained the comfortable domestic atmosphere that defined their home. As they gathered for dinner on the porch, watching the sunset paint the Gulf waters in spectacular oranges and purples, their conversation shifted from operational details to more philosophical assessment of their extraordinary circumstances.

"Six months ago, we were fleeing professional assassins through international waters on a smuggler's vessel," Rita noted with practical wonder. "Now we're official government consultants preparing for authorized investigative operations with proper procedural protocols. Life contains remarkable adaptational requirements."

"The narrative progression continues to exceed reasonable developmental expectations," Babs agreed with theatrical assessment. "Though I maintain that our current assignment lacks certain dramatic elements that made our previous adventure so cinematically compelling."

"I believe reduced mortal peril parameters represent positive procedural improvements rather than dramatic deficiencies," Daisy observed dryly. "The objective is effective investigation, not theatrical presentation quality."

"Though one must acknowledge a certain anticipatory excitement regarding our assignment," Mae admitted with gentle honesty. "Not for danger or disruption, but for the meaningful application of our capabilities to consequential challenges."

As darkness settled over their beach and the first stars appeared in the evening sky, the four women continued their thoughtful conversation—balancing practical preparation with philosophical consideration, professional assessment with personal reflection. Tomorrow they would depart for Pelican Bay as officially designated government consultants with specific investigative objectives. Tonight, they remained friends sharing dinner on their porch, appreciating both the remarkable journey that had brought them to this unexpected juncture and the extraordinary bond that had developed through their shared experiences.

"Whatever awaits us in Pelican Bay," Daisy remarked as they prepared to retire for the evening, "I find considerable reassurance in our collective capabilities. We have, after all, demonstrated remarkable effectiveness against far more challenging circumstances than a mysterious chemical contamination investigation."

"With considerably fewer resources and absolutely no official authorization," Rita added practically. "Now we have proper credentials, operational support, and emergency extraction protocols if required."

"Plus expense accounts for appropriate resort wear acquisition," Babs noted with theatrical budgetary appreciation. "Though I maintain that certain specialized accessories remain inadequately covered under standard operational allowances."

As they completed their evening preparations—reviewing briefing materials one final time, confirming packing details, establishing morning departure procedures—none of them could have anticipated the extraordinary circumstances awaiting them in Pelican Bay. For the mysterious chemical contamination they had been assigned to investigate represented merely the surface indication of something far more complex, dangerous, and consequential than even their specialized federal handlers had realized.

Beneath the picturesque coastal community's charming exterior lay secrets that would test even their proven investigative capabilities—connections that extended far beyond local corruption, technologies that defied conventional understanding, and adversaries with resources that made their previous opponents seem amateur by comparison.

The Seaside Sleuths' first official assignment was about to become considerably more complicated than anticipated.

The Pelican Bay Resort epitomized upscale coastal accommodations—pristine white buildings with terracotta tile roofs, lush tropical landscaping surrounding multiple swimming pools, and privileged access to a private beach featuring meticulously groomed white sand. Their two-bedroom suite offered spectacular ocean views, spacious living areas, and the kind of tasteful luxury that suggested significant operational expense authorization.

"This represents a substantial improvement over our previous investigative accommodations," Babs observed as she arranged her extensive resort wear collection in the bedroom she would share with Mae. "Particularly compared to Grandma Crabbitz's flamingo-infested safe house or the various maritime vessels we experienced during our escape operations."

"The operational framework does seem considerably more civilized," Rita agreed as she efficiently organized their kitchen area with practical assessment of available resources. "Though I maintain that comfortable accommodations shouldn't distract from our investigative objectives."

Their first day unfolded according to Johnson's briefing parameters—establishing normal tourist behavioral patterns through standard resort activities, casual exploration of public areas, and initial community familiarization. They spent the morning at the beach, the afternoon exploring the resort's extensive grounds, and the evening dining at the property's signature restaurant, presenting the perfectly unremarkable appearance of four retirement-age friends enjoying a well-deserved vacation.

Yet beneath this ordinary exterior, their collective observational capabilities remained actively engaged—noting staff interaction patterns, assessing guest demographics, identifying community connections, and establishing environmental baseline impressions that would inform their subsequent investigation.

"The marina development project is clearly visible from the eastern beach area," Daisy reported during their evening debriefing, which they conducted on their suite's private balcony under the guise of enjoying after-dinner drinks. "Significant construction activity despite supposed permitting delays mentioned in our briefing materials."

"The restaurant staff demonstrated interesting reaction patterns when I inquired about local seafood sourcing," Rita added, her practical conversation with their server having yielded unexpectedly valuable intelligence. "Specific mention of certain fishing areas being temporarily restricted due to 'water quality testing' created visible discomfort indicators among senior staff members."

"Several guests at the pool mentioned unusual water discoloration in the northern cove about two weeks ago," Mae contributed softly, her gentle demeanor having elicited remarkable information sharing from fellow swimmers. "Apparently the area was quickly restricted by local authorities citing 'seasonal ecological protection measures' despite no previous history of such restrictions during this time period."

"And the bartender confirmed unusual activity patterns at the marina during early morning hours," Babs completed their initial intelligence gathering summary. "Specifically, vehicles with non-local registration accessing restricted areas between approximately 2 AM and 4 AM several times weekly."

Their combined observations, while seemingly disparate, began creating preliminary connection patterns that aligned with the anomalous parameters Johnson had outlined in their briefing. Something unusual was indeed occurring in Pelican Bay, with apparent coordination between local authorities, marina operations, and potentially external entities utilizing the facility during non-standard hours.

"Tomorrow we implement community integration phase," Daisy outlined, academic precision naturally establishing their investigative progression. "Expanding our observational parameters beyond resort boundaries to include marina proximity assessment, local business engagement, and preliminary official contact through appropriate tourist inquiry scenarios."

Their second day proceeded with the methodical effectiveness that had defined their previous investigative success, each team member utilizing their specific capabilities for maximum intelligence gathering potential. Rita engaged local restaurant owners with professional courtesy that created natural information sharing about community operations. Mae visited a nearby senior center where her gentle demeanor elicited remarkable candor from long-term residents about historical development patterns. Babs utilized theatrical shopping enthusiasm to establish conversational access with retail operators regarding local economic conditions and business relationship networks.

And Daisy, academic background providing perfect cover, visited the local historical society with scholarly interest that granted access to development records, community archives, and crucially, environmental monitoring documentation dating back several decades.

"The historical water quality data reveals anomalous pattern variances beginning approximately fourteen months ago," she reported during their evening debriefing. "Subtle chemical signature alterations that wouldn't trigger standard regulatory thresholds but demonstrate cumulative modification inconsistent with natural environmental fluctuation."

"The harbormaster's recent construction projects have required specialized permitting variances from standard environmental protection protocols," Rita added, information gathered through seemingly casual conversation with a marina restaurant owner. "Facilitated through expedited review procedures by the environmental committee chaired by his previously identified brother-in-law."

"Several senior residents mentioned unusual illness patterns among long-term swimmers in the northern cove area," Mae contributed with gentle concern. "Specifically, skin irritation and respiratory complications inconsistent with standard marine exposure reactions."

"And three separate business owners confirmed unusual delivery patterns at the marina's new storage facility," Babs completed their intelligence summary. "Specialized containment vehicles with hazard classifications arriving during non-business hours, apparently operating under some form of special authorization that bypasses standard commercial access protocols."

Their third day brought the promised "casual encounter" with their local liaison—a remarkably forgettable man who struck up conversation at a beachfront coffee shop, commenting on the pleasant weather before subtly establishing authentication parameters through specific phrase patterns they had been briefed to recognize.

"Your preliminary observations have created significant interest at analytical levels," he informed them quietly during their seemingly ordinary conversation about local attractions. "Particularly the historical water quality data variance patterns and specialized delivery vehicles. Targeted surveillance has been implemented based on your initial intelligence."

"Has technical analysis revealed additional information about the contaminant composition?" Daisy inquired, academic interest providing perfect cover for the operational question.

"Preliminary assessment suggests sophisticated synthetic compounds with potential pharmaceutical applications," the liaison replied with careful discretion. "Creating concerning implications regarding possible development objectives beyond simple waste disposal operations."

This new information dramatically altered their investigative parameters. What had initially appeared to be another environmental crime scenario—illegal waste disposal through corrupted local officials—now suggested something potentially more complex: deliberate compound testing or development utilizing the marine environment as experimental medium.

Their fourth day implemented adjusted observational protocols focused on potential pharmaceutical connection elements. Rita investigated local medical facilities through the perfectly plausible cover of addressing a minor skin irritation supposedly developed during beach activities. Mae expanded her senior center connections to include specific health condition discussions with residents. Babs utilized theatrical beauty treatment interest to engage spa operators regarding local health trends. And Daisy, academic precision providing ideal methodology, researched regional pharmaceutical research operations through publicly available business registries.

"There's no officially documented pharmaceutical research facility within fifty miles," she reported during their increasingly detailed evening briefing session. "However, historical property records indicate a specialized research installation approximately three miles offshore on what was originally designated a natural marine preserve."

"A local clinic nurse mentioned unusual non-disclosure agreement requirements implemented approximately eighteen months ago," Rita added, information gleaned during her minor medical inquiry. "Specifically regarding certain symptomatic presentation patterns among patients with regular marine exposure history."

"Several senior residents described a restricted island facility visible from certain fishing locations," Mae contributed softly. "Referred to locally as 'the research station' but absent from official maritime navigation charts or tourist information materials."

"And I overheard a fascinating conversation between two marina employees regarding specialized transportation requirements for 'the island delivery,'" Babs completed their intelligence update. "Specifically mentioning hazardous material handling protocols and restricted personnel clearance levels."

Their combined intelligence gathering was creating an increasingly concerning picture: an undocumented offshore research facility apparently conducting pharmaceutical compound testing through controlled marine environment exposure, utilizing corrupted local officials to maintain operational secrecy while monitoring community health impacts as potential experimental data points.

"This significantly exceeds our briefed investigation parameters," Daisy observed with academic precision. "Suggesting coordinated experimental operations rather than simple environmental compliance violations."

"We should implement immediate information transfer protocols," Rita suggested practically. "This situation potentially requires specialized intervention resources beyond our investigative authorization."

Their liaison contact, when briefed through secure communication channels, confirmed their assessment with professional concern that validated their investigative effectiveness. "This intelligence represents significant escalation from initial contamination assessment," he acknowledged. "Specialized response team being assembled for appropriate intervention operations. Continue observation protocols but implement heightened security awareness until extraction procedures can be established."

Their fifth day at Pelican Bay unfolded with this adjusted operational framework—maintaining tourist cover activities while implementing more cautious information gathering methodologies and increased personal security awareness. They visited different areas of the community in pairs rather than individually, established more frequent check-in protocols, and limited their investigative inquiries to lower-risk information sources.

Yet despite these enhanced security measures, their effectiveness had apparently not gone unnoticed by whatever entities were operating the mysterious offshore facility. During dinner at a local seafood restaurant, Daisy observed a concerning pattern—two individuals at different tables demonstrating coordinated observation behaviors focused specifically on their group, with tactical positioning suggesting professional surveillance methodology rather than casual interest.

"We appear to have attracted attention," she noted quietly between courses, academic observation disguised as ordinary dinner conversation. "Northwestern corner, blue shirt, and eastern wall, beige jacket. Coordinated positioning with optimal visual coverage of our table and all potential exit routes."

"Operational security compromise," Rita assessed practically, maintaining casual dining behaviors despite the concerning development. "Suggesting our investigative activities have been identified despite cover methodology."

"Perhaps they're simply admiring my resort wear ensemble," Babs suggested with theatrical optimism that didn't quite mask her tactical awareness of their situation. "Though their attention patterns suggest professional assessment rather than fashion appreciation."

"Should we implement emergency protocols?" Mae inquired gently, her concerned expression perfectly aligned with their cover as tourists experiencing minor dining dissatisfaction rather than government consultants discovering hostile surveillance.

"Not yet," Daisy decided after careful consideration. "Premature extraction could compromise ongoing intelligence gathering operations. We should maintain normal behavioral patterns while implementing heightened security procedures and accelerated communication timelines with our liaison contact."

They completed their meal with remarkable composure given the circumstances, departing the restaurant with the unhurried movements of satisfied diners rather than concerned investigators. Yet their return route to the resort incorporated subtle counter-surveillance techniques they had learned during their training modules—varied pacing, multiple direction changes, and brief separations that would reveal direct pursuit patterns if implemented by their observers.

"Confirmed surveillance," Rita reported quietly as they regrouped in a well-lit shopping area near the resort. "Two additional personnel established forward positioning along our most direct return route. Suggesting coordinated interception capability rather than simple observation objectives."

"Time to call for extraction," Daisy decided, academic assessment shifting to tactical implementation as the situation parameters changed.

"Mae, please contact our liaison through the secure communication protocol. We'll proceed to the resort through the beach access route while maintaining group integrity and public visibility positioning."

As Mae implemented the emergency communication procedure they had established with their liaison, the other three maintained casual shopping behaviors while assessing potential approach vectors and security vulnerabilities in their immediate environment. Their previous experience with professional threat situations, while unfortunate in its occurrence, had created valuable adaptive capabilities for their current circumstances.

"No response from established contact protocols," Mae reported with gentle concern that disguised genuine alarm. "Both primary and secondary communication channels appear non-functional."

"Communication disruption suggests sophisticated operational capability," Daisy analyzed with academic precision that remained steady despite the increasingly concerning situation. "Potential signal jamming technology affecting our specific communication frequencies."

"Which means our observers have access to classified technical specifications regarding our operational equipment," Rita concluded practically. "Suggesting significant resource parameters and potential internal information access."

"In theatrical terms, the villains appear to have inside information about the heroes," Babs translated unnecessarily. "Creating dramatic third-act complications requiring improvised resolution methodologies."

"We need to implement independent extraction procedures," Daisy decided after rapid assessment of their options. "Utilizing public transportation infrastructure to maintain civilian protection parameters while establishing distance from current surveillance positioning."

With remarkable coordination developed through their previous adventures, they implemented an improvised exit strategy—boarding a public shuttle bus that serviced the coastal communities with perfect tourist behavioral presentation, transferring to commercial transportation at the regional transit center, and establishing temporary secure positioning at a carefully selected chain hotel approximately thirty miles from Pelican Bay.

"We should attempt emergency communication protocols from this new location," Daisy suggested once they had secured their impromptu accommodations—but before she could finish the sentence, Mae stepped out of the bathroom, visibly pale, holding a crumpled piece of hotel stationery in her hand.

"This was slid under our door while we were checking in," she said softly, her voice tight with unease. "I found it just now."

Rita took it with a furrowed brow and unfolded the note, the handwriting bold and unmistakably deliberate:

You've stirred waters better left still. Pelican Bay is just the beginning. If you don't want to lose what you've just found—go home. While you still can.

The room fell into stunned silence.

Babs was the first to recover, narrowing her eyes and slowly lowering her sunglasses—not for effect this time, but because they were no longer necessary.

"Oh, please," she said, her voice low and sharp. "If they think a cryptic threat is going to scare us off, they clearly didn't do their research."

But Daisy's face had gone still, her academic focus sharpening into something far more calculating. "No signature. No identifiers. Which means whoever sent this had close enough access to bypass our surveillance detection but distant enough to avoid direct confrontation."

"They knew our location almost immediately," Rita added grimly. "They were waiting for us to run."

"And now they're warning us to stop," Mae said, voice barely a whisper.

Daisy looked toward the hotel window where the coastal lights glittered in the far distance—Pelican Bay just a shadow on the horizon now.

"They've underestimated us," she said, her tone like a quiet bell before a storm. "Again."

From somewhere outside, a siren wailed briefly—distant but rising.

And then the hotel room phone rang.
One sharp, sudden ring. Just once.
Then silence.
They stared at it, unmoving.
Then it rang again.
Slow. Deliberate.

Babs stepped forward, her hand hovering over the receiver, a glint of excitement sparking behind her calm.

"Ladies," she said, eyes locked on the phone, "I believe Act Two has just begun."

She picked up the receiver.

And everything changed.

Hot Flashes & Homocide

1. Daisy's Gardenia Porch Muffins (Blueberry Streusel Muffins)

(Inspired by Rita serving blueberry muffins at the Barnacle)

Ingredients:

- 2 cups all-purpose flour
- 1 cup sugar
- 2 tsp baking powder
- 1/2 tsp baking soda
- 1/2 tsp salt
- 1/2 cup unsalted butter, melted
- 1 cup sour cream
- 2 large eggs
- 1 tsp vanilla extract
- 1 1/2 cups fresh blueberries

For the Streusel Topping:

- 1/3 cup sugar
- 1/4 cup flour
- 3 tbsp butter, melted
- 1/2 tsp cinnamon

Instructions:

Preheat oven to 375°F. Line a muffin tin.
Mix dry ingredients together. Whisk butter, sour cream, eggs, and vanilla separately. Combine wet and dry. Gently fold in blueberries.
Mix streusel ingredients and sprinkle over each muffin.
Bake 18–20 minutes until golden.

2. Rita's Key Lime Morning Pie
(Inspired by Rita's award-winning key lime pie that Brock insulted)

Ingredients:

- 1 1/2 cups graham cracker crumbs
- 1/3 cup sugar
- 6 tbsp butter, melted

Filling:

- 4 egg yolks
- 1 can (14 oz) sweetened condensed milk
- 1/2 cup fresh key lime juice (or bottled if needed)
- 1 tbsp key lime zest

Instructions:
Preheat oven to 350°F.
Mix crust ingredients, press into pie pan, bake for 8 minutes.
Whisk egg yolks, add condensed milk, lime juice, and zest.
Pour into crust and bake 12–15 minutes. Chill 3 hours.
Serve with whipped cream and a dusting of extra lime zest.

3. The Barnacle Frittata Supreme
(Inspired by Rita's frittata getting cold during the beach body discovery)

Ingredients:

- 8 large eggs
- 1/4 cup heavy cream
- 1/2 cup shredded sharp cheddar

- 1/2 cup diced ham or bacon
- 1/2 cup diced bell peppers (red and green)
- 1/4 cup diced onion
- 2 tbsp butter
- Salt and pepper to taste

Instructions:
Preheat oven to 400°F.
Sauté ham, onions, and peppers in butter until soft.
Whisk eggs, cream, salt, and pepper. Stir in cheese.
Pour egg mixture into skillet over fillings.
Bake 10–12 minutes until puffed and set.

4. Babs' "It's Five O'Clock Somewhere" Mimosas
(Inspired by Babs justifying champagne for breakfast)

Ingredients:

- 1 bottle chilled prosecco or champagne
- 2 cups chilled orange juice
- Optional: splash of cranberry juice for a "sunrise" effect

Instructions:
Fill a flute halfway with prosecco.
Top with orange juice.
Optional: a splash of cranberry for color. Garnish with an orange twist.

5. Mae's Gentle Yoga Sweet Tea
(Inspired by Mae's nurturing nature and Southern hospitality)

Ingredients:

- 6 black tea bags
- 1 cup sugar
- 8 cups water
- 1/2 lemon, sliced
- Fresh mint sprigs for garnish

Instructions:
Boil 4 cups of water. Remove from heat, add tea bags, steep 10 minutes. Remove tea bags, stir in sugar until dissolved. Add remaining water. Chill and serve over ice with lemon slices and mint.

6. Candi Bubbleshine's "Turtle Beach" Trifle
(Inspired by the seaside setting and Candi's over-the-top personality)

Ingredients:

- 1 box vanilla cake mix, baked and cubed
- 2 cups vanilla pudding
- 1 1/2 cups whipped cream
- 1/2 cup crushed graham crackers
- 1/4 cup mini chocolate chips
- Gummy turtles (optional garnish)

Instructions:
Layer cake cubes, pudding, whipped cream, and graham cracker crumbs. Repeat layers. Top with mini chocolate chips and gummy turtles. Chill until ready to serve.

7. Conch Key Crab Cakes

(Inspired by the crab cake contest drama with Brock Hamfist and Gladys Pickle)

Ingredients:

- 1 lb lump crab meat, picked over for shells
- 1/2 cup breadcrumbs (preferably panko)
- 1/4 cup mayonnaise
- 1 egg, lightly beaten
- 1 tbsp Dijon mustard
- 1 tbsp Worcestershire sauce
- 1 tbsp fresh lemon juice
- 1 tbsp chopped parsley
- 1 tsp Old Bay seasoning
- 2 tbsp butter for frying

Instructions:

Gently mix crab meat with breadcrumbs, mayo, egg, mustard, Worcestershire, lemon juice, parsley, and Old Bay until just combined.
Form into patties and refrigerate for 30 minutes.
Melt butter in a skillet over medium heat. Fry crab cakes 3–4 minutes per side until golden brown.
Serve with lemon wedges and tartar sauce.

(Optional bonus: Add a sprinkle of microgreens on top to make them "Garden Club Approved.")

8. Salty Mermaid's Famous Chowder

(Inspired by Lou's Fishy Business chowder argument and Rita's pride in her cooking)

Ingredients:

- 4 slices thick-cut bacon, diced
- 1 small onion, diced
- 2 cloves garlic, minced
- 2 medium Yukon Gold potatoes, peeled and diced
- 3 cups seafood stock or clam juice
- 1 cup heavy cream
- 1 cup milk
- 2 cans clams, drained (reserve liquid)
- 1 cup fresh or frozen corn kernels
- 1 bay leaf
- Salt, pepper, and a dash of hot sauce

Instructions:

Cook bacon until crisp in a large pot. Remove and set aside, leaving drippings.
Sauté onion and garlic in the bacon drippings until translucent.
Add potatoes, bay leaf, seafood stock, and clam juice. Simmer until potatoes are tender.
Stir in cream, milk, clams, and corn. Heat gently, but do not boil.
Season with salt, pepper, and hot sauce to taste.
Top with crumbled bacon before serving.

9. Daisy's "Dead Man's Float" Cocktail
(Dark humor cocktail for book club parties or launch events!)

Ingredients:

- 2 oz dark rum
- 2 oz coconut cream
- 4 oz pineapple juice
- 1 scoop vanilla ice cream
- Crushed ice
- Maraschino cherry for garnish

Instructions:

Blend rum, coconut cream, pineapple juice, and a scoop of ice cream until frothy.
Pour into a tall glass over crushed ice.
Float a maraschino cherry on top.
Serve with a playful straw — preferably shaped like a flamingo or a skull!

(It's creamy, tropical, and a little "sinful" — just like Daisy would approve.)

10. Officer Peanut Butterworth's Peanut Butter Pie
(In honor of the adorably clumsy young officer who's always hungry for Rita's muffins)

Ingredients:

- 1 pre-made graham cracker crust
- 1 cup creamy peanut butter
- 8 oz cream cheese, softened

- 1 cup powdered sugar
- 1 tub (8 oz) whipped topping, thawed
- Mini peanut butter cups for garnish (optional)

Instructions:
Beat peanut butter, cream cheese, and powdered sugar together until smooth.
Fold in whipped topping until fully combined.
Spread mixture into crust. Chill 2–3 hours.
Top with chopped mini peanut butter cups before serving if desired.

11. Candi Bubbleshine's Sugar Shack Champagne Cupcakes
(Because Candi would never say no to champagne AND sparkles)

Ingredients:

- 1 box white cake mix
- 1 cup champagne or prosecco
- 1/3 cup vegetable oil
- 3 egg whites
- 1 tsp vanilla extract

Champagne Buttercream Frosting:

- 1 cup unsalted butter, softened
- 3 cups powdered sugar
- 3–4 tbsp champagne
- 1 tsp vanilla extract
- Edible glitter or sugar pearls for garnish

Instructions:
Preheat oven to 350°F. Line cupcake tins.
Mix cake mix, champagne, oil, egg whites, and vanilla until smooth.
Bake 18–20 minutes. Cool completely.
For frosting, whip butter until fluffy, gradually add powdered sugar, champagne, and vanilla. Frost cupcakes and sprinkle with edible glitter.

(They sparkle as much as Candi's outfits.)

12. Murder at the Garden Club Lemon Bars
(Perfect for Garden Club gossip... and solving murders over dessert)

Ingredients:

- 1 cup unsalted butter, softened
- 2 cups all-purpose flour
- 1/2 cup powdered sugar

For the Filling:

- 4 large eggs
- 1 1/2 cups granulated sugar
- 1/4 cup all-purpose flour
- 2/3 cup fresh lemon juice
- Zest of 1 lemon

Instructions:
Preheat oven to 350°F.
Mix butter, flour, and powdered sugar until crumbly. Press into a greased 9x13-inch pan.
Bake crust for 18–20 minutes until lightly golden.
Whisk filling ingredients together. Pour over hot crust.

Bake another 20–25 minutes until set. Cool completely.
Dust with powdered sugar and slice into "evidence squares."

(Optional garnish: a sprig of edible flowers to make it even more "garden club.")

13. Suspicious Seaweed Dip

(Inspired by all the jokes about seaweed-covered corpses... this one's edible!)

Ingredients:

- 1 package (10 oz) frozen chopped spinach, thawed and drained
- 1 cup sour cream
- 1 cup mayonnaise
- 1 package (1 oz) ranch dressing seasoning mix
- 1 can (8 oz) water chestnuts, drained and chopped
- 1/2 cup chopped green onions

Instructions:

Mix spinach, sour cream, mayo, ranch seasoning, water chestnuts, and green onions.
Chill at least 1 hour before serving.
Serve with tortilla chips, crackers, or bread cubes.

(Optional presentation: Serve it in a shallow dish and sprinkle thin strips of nori (seaweed) over the top for a fun beachside "suspicious seaweed" look.)

14. Dead Man Walking Key Lime Cocktails
(A tart, punchy drink to honor poor Brock Hamfist... may he rest in tartness)

Ingredients:

- 2 oz key lime rum (or plain white rum with fresh lime juice)
- 1 oz triple sec
- 1 oz fresh key lime juice (or regular lime juice)
- 1 oz simple syrup
- Crushed ice
- Graham cracker crumbs for the rim
- Lime wheel for garnish

Instructions:
Rim a glass with lime juice and dip in graham cracker crumbs.
Fill the glass with crushed ice.
Shake rum, triple sec, lime juice, and simple syrup in a cocktail shaker with ice.
Strain over crushed ice. Garnish with a lime wheel.

(It's a little dangerous... just like finding bodies on your beach.)

15. Conch Key Crime Scene Sundaes
(Because no investigation is complete without ice cream and suspicious toppings!)

Ingredients:

- Vanilla ice cream
- Chocolate syrup ("crime scene blood")

- Crushed graham crackers ("sandy evidence")
- Gummy sharks or jellyfish ("marine life witnesses")
- Mini handcuff toppers (optional novelty decoration)

Instructions:
Scoop vanilla ice cream into a bowl.
Drizzle with chocolate syrup to create "bloody" swirls.
Sprinkle crushed graham crackers over the top.
Add gummy sharks or jellyfish for extra flair.
Optional: stick a tiny handcuff or crime scene tape pick into the sundae for humor.

(The perfect "last meal" for any murder-solving team.)

Patti Petrone Miller

Meet Patti, the creative force behind "Where the Magic Happens." More than just an author, Patti brings stories to life as the Executive Producer of an animated TV series based on her heartwarming tale "ELLIOT FINDS A HOME"—the story of a special dog with thumbs and his silent friend who prove that sometimes, actions speak louder than words.

Patti's writing journey has been nothing short of remarkable. A cherished author at Polygon Entertainment, she's danced her way onto the USA TODAY bestseller list and claimed Amazon's #1 spot multiple times. With 7 dozen books spanning from Urban Fantasy to Horror, Patti weaves tales that transport readers to worlds limited only by imagination.

Her life reads like an adventure novel filled with fascinating chapters:

At just 4 years old, she charmed audiences on "Romper Room" She shared memorable moments with Captain Kangaroo and Mr. Green Jeans She once enjoyed a train ride and sandwich with Sidney Poitier She high-fived President Nixon during a circus visit She attended school alongside magician David Copperfield She roller-skated with John Travolta before his rise to fame She warmed her hands and heart sharing cocoa with Abe Vigoda

When she's not crafting bestsellers, Patti embraces life as a teacher, grandmother, and devoted pet parent. Known affectionately as the "Queen of Halloween," this Wiccan High Priestess infuses her spooky stories with authentic magic that keeps readers spellbound.

Patti's books fly off shelves as quickly as they're stocked, so follow her social media to stay connected with this one-of-a-kind storyteller whose magical worlds welcome all who dare to dream.

www.ingramcontent.com/pod-product-compliance
Lightning Source LLC
LaVergne TN
LVHW041656060526
838201LV00043B/451